*To my father, who never stopped seeking new frontiers
and always marked the trail so I could find my way.*

CHAPTER ONE

October 1867, Unorganized Territory, Western U.S.

NO BURDEN PROVES MORE TERRIBLE TO A LONER THAN THE holding of a life in his hands. Jake Paynter held two hundred while staring down the barrel of his captain's revolver.

"Lieutenant," growled Captain Sherrod, "you will obey my order or receive a bullet."

Jake flicked his eyes aside to find the buffalo soldiers of K-Troop and the lone Shoshone scout watching the unfolding tragedy with frozen alarm in the broken hills above the Green River basin. The light snow that had been falling for an hour obscured the distance, creating a bubble of horses and men crowned with a dusting of white atop hats, blue coats, and manes. He met the riveting gaze of Sergeant Gus Rivers, who'd fought alongside him since '62 after escaping the cotton fields of Alabama. Gus slowly shook his head while sliding a hand toward the trigger of his carbine. Jake returned his attention to the captain.

"No, sir. I will *not* lead the men into that draw."

Sherrod's scowl deepened as he thumbed back the hammer. "Damn you, Paynter. This is your last chance."

Seconds passed in the silence of the deadening snowfall, marred only by the stamping and huffing of impatient horses. The gun's barrel began to quiver, and the captain lowered his weapon. "You contemptible coward. You shame a nation." He whipped his head aside. "First Sergeant!"

"Sir!" A chiseled man with a peppered moustache and manic eyes stepped toward them.

"Shoot this man."

"With pleasure."

A rifle butt met the side of Jake's skull, dumping him to his knees in the snow-covered sage. He looked up to find the sergeant looming over him. Ambrose Blackburn had seemed like the second coming of God Almighty when Paynter had first laid eyes on him as a seventeen-year-old looking to join the fight in Texas. He had quickly learned otherwise. When Jake had finally fled Blackburn's command, he'd never imagined encountering the man again. But when the Plains Army began accepting former Confederate officers to fill noncommissioned officer roles, Blackburn had joined up. The mocking hand of fate had placed him under Jake's command, where Blackburn had resumed his mission of corruption and violence. In service to those twin devils, his former commander pressed the barrel into Jake's throbbing temple and leaned over the stock toward his ear.

"Been waitin' five years for this, Paynter," he whispered. "Shoulda never turned coat."

A vision of violence erupted from Jake's memory. Of Blackburn reveling in the blood and frenzy of wanton death, framed by a wall of fire consuming innocent souls. Jake's anger surged, and he ripped the carbine away from Blackburn's grasping hands even as a shot roaring past his head robbed sound from his left ear. He rolled to his feet just in time to catch his would-be executioner in the chin with the rifle butt. Blackburn crumpled into a heap. Another shot whistled past Jake, raising a burning line alongside his neck. He flipped the rifle in his hands and put a bullet between Sherrod's eyes before the captain could arrange a second shot. His commanding officer rocked back from the blow and stared in disbelief while a line of blood leaked down his forehead to the bridge of his nose. He toppled to the ground, spreading a red halo in the snow around his head, a dark angel of war gone still. Jake ejected the spent cartridge while stumbling to his feet and swung the rifle

DEAD MAN'S HAND

DAVID NIX

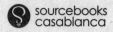

sourcebooks
casablanca

Published by Sourcebooks Casablanca, an imprint of Sourcebooks
P.O. Box 4410, Naperville, Illinois 60567–4410
(630) 961-3900
sourcebooks.com

Printed and bound in Canada.
MBP 10 9 8 7 6 5 4 3 2 1

toward the man nearest him, ready for a fight. Corporal Stubbs raised his eyebrows while holding his carbine loosely in one hand. He stretched out an open palm.

"I don't never poke my nose into the quarrels of white officers. Like to get a man killed."

Jake spun in a half circle to find similar restraint from the rest of the troop. He lowered the rifle and put a hand to his stinging neck while Sergeant Rivers pushed through the startled ranks.

"Lemme look." Gus probed the wound until Jake winced. His old fighting mate grunted. "Missed the artery. Luckier'n a goose the day after Christmas."

Jake's eyes drifted to his dead captain and the bleeding first sergeant. "Not for long."

Gus nodded and pointed to Jake's unattended horse. "You know you gotta run now, right?"

"Where?"

"Anywhere." Gus gripped Jake's shoulder and steered him toward his mount. "Penalty for killing a superior officer is death. Don't matter the reason."

"Go north." Jake looked aside to find the Shoshone scout, Darwin Follows the Wind, addressing him. "North to the Wind River country. Find Beah Nooki, my grandfather. He will give shelter."

"Beah Nooki," Jake mumbled. He paused to spare the unconscious Blackburn a parting glance and entertained the whispering urge to put a lead ball in the man's brain. He was already in neck-deep, and nobody deserved it more than Blackburn. The whispers passed, and he rocked back into motion without satisfying his bloodlust. He was a killer, not a murderer. He turned over the first sergeant's rifle to Gus and mounted his horse. Corporal Stubbs handed up a cloth sack.

"Hard tack and jerky. For the journey."

Jake let the offer hang before reluctantly taking another man's ration. "Many thanks."

"G'luck, sir."

Jake surveyed his troop a final time. Good men. Strong men. Determined men who served the Tenth Cavalry, one of two all-black mounted regiments in the U.S. Plains Army. The plains tribes had taken to calling them buffalo soldiers, a designation of respect. Jake felt the same. He nodded before addressing Gus. "You're in charge. Lead the troop back to the fort. The white officers will look to place blame on you for not tryin' to stop me. Tell 'em whatever you must to spare yourself and the men."

"I will tell the truth."

"Please, Gus. You know what'll happen."

"Right." Gus cast a gaze into the draw. "Way I see it, you fled into the basin and we lost you in the snowfall."

Jake dipped his chin. "See ya, Gus."

"Only if the devil don't see ya first."

Jake wheeled his mount and rode north through the parting soldiers. Across the treeless expanse of rolling hills lay the Wind River country and the coming teeth of winter. He hoped the Shoshone would show him more mercy than Sherrod and Blackburn had, but lamented the fact that he deserved none for all the terrible things he'd done.

CHAPTER TWO

Seven Months Later, St. Joseph, Missouri

"Seems a good day to die."

Jake tore his gaze from the crystal-clear sky beyond his cell window to find Corporal McQuaid grinning through the bars, clearly pleased with his observation. Jake locked an unwavering gaze on the young soldier until the smile became a memory.

"Ain't no such animal, kid. Death has the gall to ruin even the best of days."

McQuaid launched a study of his beaten cavalry boots. "I reckon so. Hadn't given it much thought."

"Youth never does."

McQuaid lifted narrowed eyes at him. "But you ain't more'n, what, twenty-five?"

"Twenty-four."

The soldier rocked his head back and forth in apparent consideration. "Don't matter anyhow. We've come to take you."

Jake nodded. He'd waited three days for this moment. Oddly, the end of waiting brought him relief, an extra expanse of lung that seemed to have closed before. "They gonna give me a trial before they hang me?"

McQuaid's boyish smile returned. "You ain't heard? They ain't said nothin'?"

"No." He drew the word out slowly to mask his annoyance. "But if you are so inclined, might you share with me what I've not heard?"

"Telegraph arrived from Fort Bridger not one hour ago. Seems they want you shipped back to the territories for trial and hanging. General's considering it now. Although I wouldn't get yer hopes up. He seems itchy for a public spectacle."

The corporal's advice proved pointless. Jake had long ago decided that hope was for the delusional and children. Everyone else should know better. "Let's go, then."

The corporal motioned to the jailer, and within a minute, Jake found his wrists and ankles clapped in irons. As he shuffled from the cell block, a pair of soldiers clad in cavalry blue fell in behind him. His rank-and-file escorts seemed less enthused than he was. McQuaid motioned to the men.

"Privates Evans and Muñoz, in case you were wonderin.'"

"I wasn't."

Once outside, he scouted the area with a grimace. Still a hell-hole. Peeling-paint buildings crowded a street turned marsh from three days of rain. He turned aside to find a familiar face waiting for him, now clad in civilian clothing rather than cavalry blue.

"Gus. You still here?"

"Clearly." Sergeant Rivers offered an apologetic grin. Paynter recalled the first time he'd met him, just before the skirmish at Island Mound in '62. The man's relentless optimism had rallied the men against the enemy and earned him a promotion. That, and his angular frame turned steel in the cotton fields of Alabama before his escape to freedom. Too bad he'd gotten caught up in Jake's quagmire.

"Thought you'd be long gone by now."

Gus shook his head and flashed his recurring wry smile, like he knew about a really good surprise and was just waiting for everyone else to catch up. "Nope. Army cut me loose and told me to bring you back. I don't get back pay lest I do. Now that I'm mustered out, I need the coin. Sorry I was the one to track you down. It was either me or someone who'd just as soon put a lead plum in ya."

"You did what you had to. I'm just glad if someone's making a dollar on this fiasco, it's you."

"Here, I brought somethin' for ya. You left it at Fort Bridger with all your stuff." Gus extended a familiar slouch hat, faded from six years of wear during war and peace. The emblazoned "1" of First Kansas Colored stood in the center of the crown, uneven from blood, sweat, and sun. He recalled the day the regimental tailor had stitched the emblem into the crown after the battle at Honey Springs to cover a near-miss bullet hole, and how that simple kindness had transformed the hat into more than just headwear. Jake accepted the hat and placed it on his head, where it settled comfortably in a joyful reunion with his skull. He rubbed his fingers along the brim to meet at the tassels.

"Thanks, Gus. Thought this was tossed on the rubbish heap long ago."

McQuaid stepped between them. "Got to move on, Paynter."

Gus fell in behind the soldiers as the procession moved along. The run of boardwalk ended, forcing the parade onto the road. Paynter's manacled slide-step passage along the rutted street would have raised a cloud of dust if not for six inches of mud and manure. By the time they arrived at the office of the military liaison, his boots had disappeared beneath a sheath of Missouri crud.

"Wait here," said McQuaid before he stepped inside. Jake decided to pass the time by memorizing the smell of biscuits wafting from the restaurant across the street. He'd miss biscuits. And sausage gravy.

The door flinging open recaptured his attention. General Bartlett, the Butcher of Blacksburg, strode toward him before halting the distance of a dead body away. Why did all generals walk like that? As if each step eternally possessed the soil beneath it. Was the attitude a product of the rank? Or was the rank a result of the attitude?

"You're a lucky dog, Paynter." The general's upper lip curled left as if drawn by a fisherman's hook. "As much as I'd like to stretch your neck myself, the War Office wants you returned to the scene of your disgrace as a lesson to the soldiers. Don't want those boys in the Tenth contemplating the prospect of killing an officer without dire consequences. You know what they're like."

Jake returned the general's disdain with an unflinching gaze. "I do know what they're like. You, on the other hand, seem to know nothin' but how to return men to their families in pieces."

The general's palm lashed Jake's cheekbone, rocking his head to one side. He returned his glare to the man, tasting blood. Red feelers crawled into the general's cheeks to rise above his well-manicured beard.

"Rot in hell, Paynter." He spun on his heel and strode away. "Take him to Blue."

Jake was in motion again as a nervous McQuaid prodded him along the road.

"Why'd you do that?" The corporal seemed distraught at the display of disrespect to a commanding officer. Jake smiled for the first time in weeks.

"It's what I do. Or so I'm told."

He plodded along, accruing more mud than he thought possible, while pondering what "Blue" meant. Was it a grim moniker for the gallows or some other torture device? He almost hoped so. Dying in Missouri seemed preferable to an eight-hundred-mile journey for the purpose of hanging at a remote outpost. He groaned when they approached a line of prairie schooners stretched along the border of town, outlined against the setting sun. No such luck. He continued shuffling until McQuaid halted before a man whose face seemed constructed of discarded saddle leather. A spectacular moustache covered all but the point of his chin, and blue eyes pierced Jake like a dagger in a tavern brawl.

"You the killer?"

Jake winced at the question. "More than you know, Mr..."

"Blue. Cornelius Blue. Wagon master for this train. We depart before first light for Fort Bridger and the Idaho Territory beyond. You do as I say, and I'll let you live long enough to hang in the hinterlands. I am highly proficient at the digging of shallow graves, just so you know."

The hard set of Jake's lips softened. Honesty. Now that his days in the flesh were drawing to a close, he prized that above nearly all things. "Understood."

The man nodded. "Good." He jerked his head sharply to one side and pointed. "You there! What the hell'd I say about over-tightening the straps? Contrary to popular belief, one *can* break an ox!"

He was gone in an instant to rectify the strap situation, with Jake an afterthought. Jake watched him go before eyeing McQuaid. "Why are we traveling with civilians? Seems out of sorts."

"Because the army is tighter'n a minister's girdle at a potluck supper."

"Oh?"

"Yeah." He pointed to the other soldiers. "We're already assigned to guard this train, courtesy of Senator Ashley. They decided to send you along for no extra charge."

Jake frowned. A military escort for a band of settlers? He'd never heard of such. Before he could press McQuaid further, a sharply dressed stranger blithely stepped into his face with the force of entitlement.

"So you're the murderous baggage foisted upon us by the War Office." The man was tall, blond, and so full of piss that Jake immediately wanted to plant a fist in his face. The stranger pushed back his pristine bowler hat and swept judging eyes over Jake before his nose wrinkled. "You look as criminal as I'd feared."

Gus's grip on the back of Jake's shirt reminded him to breathe. That breath gave him a moment to meet the man's gaze, eye to eye. "The worst criminals I've known wore hundred-dollar suits." Jake plucked a piece of lint from the man's impeccable coat and flicked it away. "Just how much did that suit set you back?"

The stranger's face flared red until Jake was certain he'd be struck for a second time in an hour. However, a hand stayed the man's rising arm. Jake followed the hand to its owner and blinked. She was as finely dressed as the man, but wore the ensemble with grace, not arrogance. Her striking brown eyes met his, and she dipped her forehead before addressing the man.

"Lucien. As this situation is irreversible, and as we are to share passage with this man for the next two months, might I suggest a modicum of civility?"

The man, Lucien it seemed, glanced at the woman. The clench of his jaw softened, and he straightened his lapels. "Very well." He returned his gaze to Jake and melted back a step. His eyes narrowed, like fading hope. "Mr. Paynter, I am Lucien Ashley. This is my sister, Miss Rosalyn Ashley. My father is a senator for the great state of Missouri, and this is my expedition. If you endanger so much as a single hair on anyone's head, I will see to your necessary demise along the way."

He snatched his sister's hand and casually strolled away, confident that the sun would rise and set on his proclamation. Jake wondered briefly what kind of general he might make.

"Gosh all Friday, Paynter." He found McQuaid again wide-eyed. "Do you *try* makin' enemies, or is it just a natural gift?"

"Both," said Gus with a laugh. "Breeding that much immediate hostility in strangers takes practice *and* talent."

Jake knew Gus was right. His first reaction to any new acquaintance was to convince them to stay away. It worked, mostly, but Gus had stymied him thus far.

"What now?" he said, ignoring the conversation. "Or do we just stand here all night?"

Gus grinned. "You ain't gonna appreciate this."

McQuaid led Jake toward the wagon at the tail end of the line.

A trio of curious faces peeked at him from behind the bonnet before a woman stomped up and stuffed them inside the flap with commands of "Innen! Schnell!" She peered at Jake with warning before rejoining her husband inside a small tent adjacent to the wagon. McQuaid led Jake to a rear wheel and pointed to the ground.

"Kneel."

Jake squinted. "You're kiddin.'"

"Nope."

He kneeled. The soldier unlocked his wrist irons, made Jake thread his arms around either side of a spoke, and relocked the irons before removing the leg manacles. Private Muñoz produced a blanket and tossed it at Jake's chest.

"In case you get cold."

Jake sighed. At least he was under the wagon bed. He'd slept in far worse conditions. "Thanks."

McQuaid slapped his comrades on their shoulders. "C'mon, Evans, Muñoz. Let's drink as much whiskey as possible before we leave the confines of civilization." He pointed at Jake. "Stay put, Paynter."

The three soldiers strolled away laughing, already relishing an evening of heavy drinking. Jake lifted his eyes to Gus. "And you?"

"Sounds like a good plan to me."

"You know they won't serve you there."

"I got my places. Cheaper liquor, friendlier company. Bring you a shot if I can."

"Do that."

Jake watched with mild envy as Gus sauntered away. He inhaled a deep breath, curled next to the wagon wheel, and tried to forget he was a dead man, if only for a little while.

CHAPTER THREE

JAKE WASN'T SURE WHICH WOKE HIM—THE WHISPERS OF children or distant overtones of approaching hostility. His eyes blinked open to find three small outlines huddling in the darkness behind the opposite wagon wheel, whispering furiously and too loudly. When he lifted his head, they froze. One expelled a nervous giggle. With children identified, he rose to his knees in search of the hostility. He needed only half a second. In the near distance, torches bobbed in the darkness on a direct line for the wagon train. His first suspicion was a hanging mob, but he quickly discarded it. Nobody in St. Joseph cared enough to execute him. Regardless, the malice underlying the unresolved conversation was as clear as spring water. A horrifying vision seized Jake, of small children on the killing end of a Smith carbine pleading for their lives, and then the repeated flash of a muzzle. He clawed out of the morass of memory.

"Kids," he whispered harshly. "Get under the wagon and stay behind me. Don't make a sound. Schnell!"

Three small bodies scrambled under the bed and huddled into a tight knot as if a flood could sweep them away—which it might. Jake crouched against the wheel and tested the range of his shackled reach. Two feet at most, with around a foot of link between his hands. As the voices of perhaps eight men drew nearer, the snatches of conversation began to resolve, and with them, a name. Lucien Ashley.

"He must have it here somewhere," said the leader of the mob. "Let's start at the end and work forward."

As the leader stepped to the wagon and reached for the flap, Jake lunged to scissor the man's legs with his and twisted him violently to the ground beside the wheel's rim. He stabbed his arms through the spokes to encircle the man's neck with the manacle and pulled hard. His opponent struggled against the irons before lifting a revolver over one shoulder for a blind shot. Jake stripped the weapon from his hand and pressed it to the stranger's temple while keeping his free hand clamped around the man's shoulder. His adversary froze.

"There's children present, for God's sake," Jake spat in the man's ear. "Have you no decency?"

The man's rigid body slackened. "I…I didn't know."

"Well, now you do. So, what's your play?"

He called to his associates. "Step back. Steer clear of yer triggers."

Jake watched the others comply. "A good start."

"We want no trouble with you, mister," said his prisoner. "We come for Lucien Ashley. He cheated us, and now he's lightin' out for the territories with our money. We want it back."

"And you all expected to stroll in here and just take it with no consequences?"

"We hoped eight guns would help him find a little remorse."

Jake grunted. "He doesn't seem like a man overly fond of remorse. Or empathy. I think you're just compounding trouble with calamity."

The man turned his head to eye Jake sidelong. The flickering torchlight revealed his morbid interest. "What do ya mean?"

Jake ran the barrel of the revolver across his prisoner's temple. "Let me ask you somethin'. Do you have a house? A family? A livelihood?"

"I…I do."

"And your friends?"

"Yes."

"Care for some advice?"

"I reckon."

Jake tightened his grip on the man's shoulder. "If you tangle with a senator's son, you'll lose those things too. Men with power love nothin' more than wielding it. Right now, your little band looks like somethin' resembling a target."

The shoulder beneath his hand flexed. "But we want what's ours."

Jake laughed darkly. "You should just go while you have the chance."

"Damn right!" A stranger's voice sounded from beside the wagon bed. A woman's voice. He glanced to his right to find pantalooned legs and a torso pressed against the side of the wagon in a shooter's stance. "I got me a scattergun, and if any of you so much as twitch, I'm gonna show you the color of yer guts."

"We don't want no trouble, missy," said one of the others.

She edged a step nearer. "Call me 'missy' again and I'll aim for your head."

Silence fell for the space of a few ragged breaths before Jake broke it. "I think she means it. Go home to your families. Forget Ashley. Your only comfort will be the day word arrives that his misdeeds finally caught up with him. And don't worry. They always do."

The fight seemed to leak from the man in an instant as his body went slack. Jake let go of his shoulder, flipped the revolver around, and offered it to him. His former prisoner accepted the gun gingerly and rose. He glanced at the woman, then at Jake once more, before turning away with slumping shoulders. "C'mon, fellas. We're done here."

As the torches began receding toward town, the children's mother emerged from the shadows beside the wagon, dragged the astonished younglings from beneath the bed in the manner of an angry bear, and sent them packing to the interior with epithets that included *dumme gänse and böse kinder*. Jake was left with the distinct feeling that she'd be handy in a fight.

"You the killer?"

Jake pulled his head around to find his unexpected ally crouched on the other side of the wheel, outlined by moonlight, long-barreled shotgun dangling from the crook of an elbow.

"O' course you're the killer," she said in response to her own question. She pushed her infantry-style forage cap higher on her forehead, but the darkness left her face a cipher. "Who else'd be strapped to a spoke with not so much as a peashooter to defend himself? I ain't seen many killers up close. You don't look much like a killer. So, how'd ya do it? How'd you kill your captain?"

"Go away, little sister."

"No, really. How'd ya do it? Knife? Gun? Did you beat him with your hands?"

"Go away."

"I can pester you all night."

Jake expelled a huff of pent-up breath. "I bored him to death."

"C'mon, mister."

"Go away."

The woman shuffled closer, her spurs clinking as she did so. "Then tell me *why* you did it. Why'd you kill your commander?"

Jake growled. "He asked too many questions."

She threw back her head and laughed. "You're funny, mister. And a little *awump*."

"I ain't crazy."

She froze and cocked her head. "You speak Shoshone?"

"A little."

"Where'd ya learn it?"

He inhaled a deep breath, profoundly uncomfortable sharing such information with a stranger. "I wintered with them. They fed me. I helped them hunt for game."

"Well, if that don't beat all," she said with wonder. "My mama was Shoshone. We're practically cousins!" She stabbed a hand toward his. "Stacy Blue."

"Wagon master's wife?"

She belted another laugh. "No! His daughter. Mama died of the pox when I was six, and I been taggin' along with Pa ever since. I'm his right-hand man now."

Jake eyed her extended hand, which held steady. He figured she wouldn't leave until he shook it, so he did. "Folks call me Paynter."

"And you let 'em?"

Her joke nearly made him smile, but approaching footsteps saved him the trouble.

"Heard the commotion and witnessed the retreat, tails tucked and all." Jake spied Gus as he walked up on the wagon. "Anybody hurt?"

"No," said Stacy. "We sent 'em packin', Paynter and me."

Gus laughed. "So, now y'all are friends? You botherin' Paynter, Miss Blue?"

"He ain't busy," she said with affront. "And I done told you yesterday, don't call me Miss Blue."

"All right, ma'am."

"And don't call me ma'am!"

Gus squatted beside Paynter and waved a hand at Stacy. "Run along, kid. Let the men have a conversation."

"As if there were any *men* here." She popped to her feet with a grunt of contention and huffed away.

Gus laughed slowly. "She's a firecracker, that one."

"And you seem to enjoy lightin' her fuse."

He cocked an eyebrow. "I do not know of which you speak, sir."

They lapsed into silence as Jake felt for his blanket. Gus didn't move. "Why Missouri? Why not continue west where nobody'd know ya?"

Jake found the blanket and pulled it over his shoulders, debating the answer to the question. "I needed to catch a train."

"A train? To where?"

"Chicago."

"Why Chicago?"

"I have my reasons. Had 'em, anyway." He let Gus stew on the response before changing the subject. "You should've let someone else come after me. Someone more willing to shoot me."

"Oh, come now." Gus put a hand on Jake's shoulder. "As long as yer breathin', you have a chance at justice."

Jake shook his head. "There ain't no justice."

Gus rose slowly to his feet and extended a finger at Jake. "Don't thump your pulpit at me about justice. If one of those fine folk with the torches had put a bullet in you, even though you're a condemned man, they woulda been tried for murder. But if they'd put a bullet in me? They woulda just discussed it calmly, decided I had it comin', and called it a day. *You* don't get to tell *me* about justice, amigo."

The castigation shamed Jake. "Sorry, Gus."

"Damn right you should be." Gus exhaled a pair of forced breaths. "You got a chance at justice because o' who you are. Don't go throwin' away a gift like that."

When Jake nodded, Gus withdrew his accusatory finger. "G'night, Paynter."

"G'night, Gus."

In the man's absence, Jake considered what he'd said. His life didn't seem much like a gift, and hadn't since his mother passed from fever when he was a kid. Buried in his dark musings, he failed to notice the other man until a hunk of bread and a cup of water appeared on the ground before him. He looked up to find another stranger.

"I am Emshoff. This is for protecting my children." His accent marked him as the father of the invasive younglings. German. Austrian, perhaps. Without another word, the man returned to his tent. Jake picked up the bread and held it beneath his nose. Rye. He inhaled the earthy scent for a solid half minute before wolfing it down as if he'd never eaten before. For a shining moment, he felt almost free.

CHAPTER FOUR

"G'MORNING, TENDERFEET! IT'S A BEAUTIFUL DAY AT THE gates of hell."

Gus's far too loud and much too enthusiastic wake-up call yanked Jake from fitful sleep. He squinted to the east to find no hint of dawn.

"Get me off this wheel," he growled. "Or bury me here. I don't care."

Corporal McQuaid opted for the former. A half hour later in twilight, Jake found himself mounted on a sleek mare who accepted his presence with quiet hostility. Yep, they would get along just fine. The mare was tethered to the rear of the German family's wagon by eight feet of leather strap, so Jake's manacled and reins-free hands lay uselessly against the base of her shaggy mane. The still-unenthused privates, Evans and Muñoz, took up guard duty behind him. While Jake was scowling at the situation, Gus circled by on his buckskin with a smile.

"Don't look so much like a beaten dog, Paynter. Gonna be a good day."

"I doubt it."

Up ahead, Lucien was giving a stump speech that apparently rallied those who could hear him. From Jake's vantage, his voice just sounded like sporadic cannon fire. Shortly after, the train of eighteen rigs lurched forward ahead of the sun, which had yet to make an appearance but was considering the possibility. His escorts, who appeared to be nursing disastrous hangovers, groaned and grunted in his wake. After covering exactly fifty feet, the Emshoff wagon stopped again as the first pair of rigs in the train crawled onto the massive flat-bottom boat that would ferry them across a thousand feet of the Missouri River into Kansas. Jake sighed and bided his time. By the time he crossed three hours later, the soldiers had recovered sufficiently to exchange insults with one another. Jake pulled his bandana over his nose and peered back at them until they fell quiet.

"You may want to cover up."

Muñoz cocked his head. "Why?"

"We're at the tail end of this parade. Every speck of dust kicked up by a hundred oxen and horses'll find its way back here before we've covered the first mile. Just a suggestion, though."

He faced forward without waiting to see if they heeded his advice. Three little faces peeked back at him through the wagon bonnet. The littlest one, a flaxen-haired girl of maybe five, raised her hand in greeting until he looked away. He exhaled a grunt. It was going to be a long trip.

Another three hours on, Jake hadn't changed his opinion as to the grinding nature of the upcoming journey. Six hours down, maybe fifteen hundred to go. The train stretched some three hundred yards into the distance, chewing up the Kansas grass like a herd of bison. A cloud of choking dust obscured the sky in every forward direction, rendering the leading Conestoga virtually invisible. With nothing of interest to view, Jake had pinned his attention to the tail of the Emshoff wagon. Despite the tedium, his mind had been far from idle. Since leaving St. Joseph, he had already worked out at least a half-baked plan of escape that he could refine over time. Though the Platte near Grand Island was a mile wide and an inch deep, the column would spend much of a day wading through its muddy bottom. If he bolted at the right moment, he could be halfway across before anyone gave pursuit. Then, it was only a matter of finding a blacksmith who might take his manacles in trade for removing them. His only concern was Gus. The man could shoot the left eye out of a gnat at two hundred yards. Jake didn't think his old war mate would put a round in his back, but he couldn't be certain, not when money was on the line.

As if thoughts of Gus had somehow summoned him like a resurrected spirit, he emerged around the end of the train with Stacy jawing in his ear. She rode a magnificent calico, tribal stock most likely. Gus laughed on catching sight of Jake.

"You boys are eatin' dust by the bushel back here." He pulled his mount alongside Jake and slapped his shoulder, a maneuver that liberated a cloud of accumulated soil. "We'll spread 'em out in a few miles when we hit the Big Flat."

Jake offered no reply. Stacy brought her horse up on his left, opposite Gus. The light of day revealed something of her Shoshone ancestry in the form of large brown eyes and black hair pulled into a thick braid, topped by the tall forage cap of the style worn by Union and Confederate infantry. She grinned. "Paynter don't seem to wanna talk."

"That's his natural state," said Gus. "There was a time, early in the war, when I'd consider myself lucky to hear him speak ten words in a day."

Jake coughed. "I had no need to speak, what with you using up *all* the words on behalf of the entire company."

Stacy laughed and pointed at Gus. "Didn't I tell ya? You got the vocabulary of a Sunday preacher and the endurance of a blowhard politician."

"I'm playin' both sides, just in case, Miss Blue. You should consider adopting my strategy."

"I don't need no strategy. And don't call me Miss Blue."

"Yes, ma'am." When she leveled a glare at him that could kill at ten paces, he held up both hands. "Sorry. But tell me. What is Stacy short for?"

"I ain't tellin.'"

"You won't tell me?"

"No."

Gus chuckled. "We'll see about that."

Jake rubbed his neck, hoping they'd take their conversation elsewhere. He looked up when they fell abruptly silent. He followed Stacy's gaze to the three men riding by in the same direction as the train. One of them, a man clad mostly in black and with a shiny revolver strapped to his hip, tipped his hat as he passed. "Where ya headed?"

"Fort Bridger and beyond," Stacy replied. "You?"

"More or less the same."

As the men moved on, Jake's brow creased. Something about the trio raised his hackles. He stewed on it for half an hour as Gus and Stacy continued lobbing mortar shells at each other over his deeply entrenched position. It was only when a second pair of riders passed, this time farther off the track, that he realized what was bothering him.

"Gus."

His friend looked at him with mild surprise, as if having forgotten he was still there. "Paynter?"

"Those men who passed us."

"What about 'em?"

"How many days' provisions d'ya think they were carrying?"

Gus frowned in consideration. "With no pack horse? Can't be more'n three or four."

"That's what I thought." He turned to Stacy. "You been along this route before?"

"Eight times. Nine countin' this trip."

"Then let me ask you somethin'. If you wanted to ambush, say, a column of wagons, within three to four days' ride of here, where would you do it?"

Stacy's eyes narrowed. "That's a far-fetched question."

"Answer the question, Miss Blue." Gus's expression had become deadly serious. She shrugged.

"Probably at the Big Nemaha Join, maybe fifty miles ahead. The branches of the river have cut the banks steep. Lots of places to lay in wait as wagons cross ahead of the join." Her eyes went abruptly wide. "Do you think those men…"

"I do." He turned to Gus. "Those weren't cattle pokes, or settlers, or soldiers. They were men on a job. And I think waylaying this wagon train *is* the job."

"Why?" said Gus. "Why waylay a bunch of settlers, especially this close to civilization?"

Jake shook his head. Good question. He looked over his shoulder at his escorts, who seemed abruptly concerned about what they'd overheard. "Take me to Mr. Ashley," he told them.

They required no convincing, and Gus had already begun detaching the tether from the tailgate. Jake studied the train as he passed each wagon. Nearly all appeared to be converted farm wagons, none more than ten feet long and stuffed to the rim with possessions and supplies, pulled by teams of four or six oxen. Some had in tow a riding horse, a draft horse, a milk cow, a spare ox, or some combination thereof. With no room inside the bed and the discomfort of the rough ride, nearly everyone short of small children elected to walk alongside their teams, encouraging the animals with long switches. The Ashleys' rig at the front of the column proved the outlier—an actual Conestoga nearly twice the size of the smaller wagons, its ends bowed up and out like the prow and stern of a sailing vessel, lugged along by ten oxen.

Mounted on his horse, Lucien twisted his lips with disdain when Jake and his attendants reached his wagon at the front of the train. Rosalyn, however, smiled and dipped her chin as she walked alongside the trailing pair of oxen. "What brings you to see us, Mr. Paynter?"

Lucien held up a hand. "Quiet, Rosalyn." He glared at Jake. "What do you want?"

Jake straightened in his saddle, suddenly unnerved. When it came to leading expeditions, Lucien was clearly an amateur. Amateurs were dangerous when left in charge.

"Mr. Ashley, is there any reason someone might wish to ambush this wagon train?"

Even as Lucien gathered a denial, Jake could see that he'd hit paydirt. The slight widening of the eyes. The flex of the jaw. The tightening of his grip on the reins.

"I can think of nothing." However, Rosalyn's glare at her brother's back told a different story. "Why do you ask?"

"Because I think those men who passed us mean to do just that."

Lucien rocked in his saddle, repositioning his boots as his jaw set firmer still. "Corporal, escort Mr. Paynter back to his place and make sure he stays put."

"Yes, sir."

Without another word, Jake was unceremoniously returned to his position as human caboose.

"Idiot," he mumbled. He spent the next several hours moving up his timetable for escape. He had troubles enough without getting caught in someone else's death wish.

———

Though under Muñoz's watchful eye, Jake was minding his own business after the train had halted for the night when Rosalyn presumed to scatter his gathered isolation. Before sundown, Cornelius had ridden ahead to mark out the precise circle the wagons now occupied. The circle created a makeshift corral for horses while the bulky oxen were picketed outside the ring, as they were less interested in bolting. Small tents dotted the ground beside the wagons while some families chose to sleep beneath the wagon beds. The Emshoffs had pitched their tent only ten feet away from Jake, while the children slept on blankets laid across the jumble of possessions inside the wagon bed. Confined children were less likely to wander away in the night to become lost or crushed beneath livestock hooves. Due to the nature of the circle, the Ashleys' Conestoga met up with the Emshoff's trailing wagon. As a result, Rosalyn's journey to interrupt him consisted of twenty steps.

"I brought you some cornbread." He looked up to find her standing with the setting sun against her back, highlighting wispy locks of brown hair that had escaped her bonnet. "We had a piece left over."

He eyed her suspiciously before accepting it with manacled hands. "Thanks."

He waited for her to go away, but she failed to cooperate. "Can I help you, Miss Ashley?"

She exhaled audibly. "Did you mean what you told my brother?"

"Every word."

She frowned and blinked several times. "I was afraid of that. Thank you for trying to help."

"Look," he said with weariness, "I don't really care. And you shouldn't show kindness to a man like me."

"But I try to show kindness to everyone."

"You should stop. Kindness where you're going is as likely to get you killed as anything else."

Her eyes flashed before the hurt settled in. "I see."

As she turned away, a new vision came to Jake. Of what would happen when the gunmen hit the train, with her perched in the first wagon in line. Remorse stabbed his gut. "Miss Ashley."

She halted but didn't turn around. "What?"

"Convince your brother to hear me out. If not to me, then at least listen to Gus."

She swayed in place briefly. "I will."

He watched her walk away, wishing he'd handled the conversation with more aplomb. However, he and aplomb had never been particularly well acquainted. Only a few minutes passed before Lucien stomped toward him.

"Well done, Paynter. You have gone and given my sister cause for concern. So now it has become my concern." He squatted beside Jake. "Let's hear it, then."

Jake nodded and explained his belief about the why and where of an ambush. The fine lines at the corners of Lucien's mouth deepened as he listened. He was definitely hiding something.

"At least send Gus to scout ahead and then slow down the wagons before we blunder into a fight," Jake finished. "If I'm right, you'll need to turn back or find another route before it's too late."

Lucien leveled a narrowed gaze at Jake for half a minute in silence. "Very well. He'll go at first light." He leaned nearer and lowered his voice. "But I'm watching you. If this is a thinly disguised plot to escape, I'll put a bullet in your brain myself."

"It's not a plot, and you wouldn't be the first to promise me that."

"And stay away from my sister or I'll put *two* slugs in your head."

Jake grunted. "Fine, but tell *her* that. I already warned her about me."

Without another word, Lucien stood and strode away. In his absence, Jake found three little pairs of eyes studying him from the flap above. He shook his head and mused over his sorry state. The more he wanted to be left alone, the more these people insisted on bothering him.

CHAPTER FIVE

AFTER TWELVE HOURS OF HARD RIDING, GUS'S BACKSIDE HAD become as raw as his unsettled nerves. Barreling into an ambush with naught but a Spencer carbine and a Colt forty-four was a sure way to render a man coyote fodder, and right quick. Stacy had predicted an ambush at the Big Nemaha Join—where the two Big Nemaha Rivers joined forces to become the actual and honest-to-God Big Nemaha. Gus wondered why there would be two Big Nemahas, but figured the mapmakers had run out of either names or interest by the time they had found themselves lost in Kansas. Regardless, he was betting his life on the intuition of an overgrown girl with more sass than sense.

Maybe ten miles out from the confluence of the rivers, he waded his horse across to the north side. He figured the gunslingers were too bristling with bravado to exercise any finesse and would simply wait on the dry side of the river for the wagons to show. They wouldn't expect an approach of a lone rider from the north. Besides, the dry southern wind akin to the breath of Satan would put him squarely upwind from jumpy horses. His strategy paid off when he spotted dust and men in the distance as the sun tumbled toward the flat Kansas earth. He expelled a relieved breath.

"Miss Blue, you clever girl." He reminded himself not to let her know how impressed he was. She'd never let him hear the end of it. He pulled up his horse behind a gentle roll of the prairie perhaps a mile out and staked the animal to the dirt. The buckskin gave him a baleful eye but complained only gently. There, he waited for the sun to finish setting proper while cleaning and reloading his weapons. As he blew blast residue from the chambers, he smiled from a wash of memory. Just before his first skirmish in '62, a smooth-faced boy called Sergeant Paynter had drilled the regiment in the rapid cleaning and loading of weapons whether in daylight or dark, showing little mercy even to those who had never held a weapon before in their lives. However, when the light failed during the skirmish, his troop had blazed away in darkness at the rattled adversary until forcing a retreat. Gus had never thanked Paynter. At the time, he had considered him a white son-of-a-bitch, just another taskmaster shouting commands at men twice his age in a southern country drawl. That first impression had passed in time. Mostly. Paynter could still be a son-of-a-bitch.

With the coming of night, Gus hobbled the buckskin and crept closer to the band of gunmen. He could almost smell their hubris on the wind, thick with arrogance and incautious manhood. They had begun drinking, and the liquor had dulled their senses. In their spirit-fueled haze of impending murder, they stoked the campfire until it bloomed in the night like a beacon of violence, certain that gods and beasts alike would cower from their awful presence. Their words, though many, remained indistinct, snatched away by the cathedral of the never-ending prairie sky. He shuffled closer on all fours, foot by silent foot, until the boasting became discernible.

"She'll do what I say," one man slurred, "once I show 'er this." He gripped his groin to a roar of approval from his mates.

A large, thickly bearded man belched. "Miss Ashley's too fine fer you, Burt. She'll shrivel you right up. Just leave 'er to me. After I cut her brother's throat, o' course."

They went on that way for a time, offering ever more vivid descriptions of what they'd do to the women after killing or subduing the men. And what they'd do to the women when they were done with them. And how they'd spend their share of the reward for completing the job of taking Lucien's cargo. Gus inched nearer. The lie he told himself was that he hoped for more details. The truth was that rage pulled him forward. The notion of bursting into the campsite and putting a bullet in each startled face drew him close enough for the heat of the bonfire to raise moisture on his brow. As he mopped away the sweat, one gunman lurched away from the fire directly toward him. Gus's knife was in his hand in the blink of a mosquito's eye, poised for a killing stroke. However, the man stopped five feet from Gus and began relieving himself while swaying with the warm wind. As the acrid smell drifted into Gus's nostrils, he contemplated whether he could slit the man's wind-pipe without drawing attention. He fingered the knife, testing the razor-fine edge. Fine enough to gut a hog, certainly sufficient to open a tender throat.

"Ketchum!" called the bearded man.

"Dammit, Sally. Don't talk to me 'til I finish." Gus instantly became one with the night, still as a stone and twice as innocuous as a pair of other men began hurling taunts at Ketchum. The drunk complained bitterly, but managed to finish his business in a series of fits and starts. He struggled to pull up his britches, which had drifted around his knees in the process. He nearly fell sideways onto Gus, which would have resulted in a one-way trip to the after-life for both of them, but caught his impaired balance. The glinting spur of the man's boot kissed Gus's cheek.

"I'm gonna kill you," said Ketchum. Gus tensed for a fight but the drunk stumbled away, still wrestling with his britches. "I'm gonna kill you, Burt, if'n you don't shut yer trap."

Gus slowly bled the tension from his muscles while willing his heartbeat to settle. After another few minutes of impersonating a stone, he began shuffling backward as deliberately as he had come. The bravado faded once again into the night before Gus stood to cover the remaining distance to his horse. As he rode away, he considered what he'd heard. These men intended to kill many or all of the travelers, perhaps just for sport. Gus had seen such men before and during the war, on both sides of the fight. Men who lusted for blood as they would for a woman. Men of violence for whom abusive power was not enough. Men who would drive the lash long after the victim had fallen insensible or died. Men who would cut off a child's hand to teach them compliance. Men who would slaughter innocents when they exhausted the guilty. Yes, he'd seen such men, and knew the boasting gunmen were cut from that same corrupt cloth. The only way to stop their kind was to meet brutality with brutality, force with force. The only way to silence them was to leave their lifeless husks for the vultures to argue over.

In the throes of such thoughts, Gus risked himself and his horse by riding deep into the night back the way he'd come, hoping the prairie dogs in the area weren't overly industrious. The affair wasn't going to end well for some folks. His swift return could determine just which folks were which. He only hoped his buckskin was up to the task.

CHAPTER SIX

THE HARD HAUNT OF GUS'S EYES AS HE APPROACHED ACROSS a sea of rippling prairie grass told Jake what was coming. His old regiment mate rode down from the northwest directly to the Emshoff wagon, clearly wanting to speak to Jake before reporting to Lucien. Privates Evans and Muñoz both raised gloves in greeting, but their grins faded when they saw in Gus's expression what Jake had seen. Stacy, however, seemed oblivious while riding up just as Gus arrived. She let out a whoop.

"Well, if it ain't the prodigal himself. I was afraid you'd met someone and eloped."

When Gus narrowed his eyes at Stacy, her wry grin melted into bafflement. She had clearly never faced the prospect of killing men before, to have misread his expression so badly. When he failed to speak, her eyebrows rose slowly and she swallowed. "Oh. That bad?"

"That bad, Miss Blue."

Gus fell in beside Jake while Stacy again provided the bookend along his left. Evans and Muñoz crowded closer until Jake gave them his back-the-hell-off stare. They did. Then he leaned toward the three little pairs of eyes peeking from the wagon eight feet in front of him. He lurched toward them.

"Boo! Scat!"

The faces disappeared. An affronted Mrs. Emshoff immediately climbed inside and closed the flap as she lectured her children in rapid-fire German that would surely raise welts. Jake leaned toward Gus. "Tell me about it."

"Found 'em at the Big Nemaha Join, just as Miss Blue predicted."

Jake nodded at Stacy. He half-expected her to crow, but Gus's mood had seemingly infected her with a good dose of gravity. She simply nodded back.

"Seven in all," Gus continued. "Well-armed and waitin'. Professionals for sure."

"What kinda professionals?"

Gus again answered the question through the power of his gaze alone. However, he did not leave the words unsaid. "You told me about when you rode with Blackburn before switching sides. About the men you rode with and some of what you did."

Jake inhaled a deep breath to will away encroaching apocalyptic visions. Now was not the time. "Some, yes."

"Them what's waitin' for us are the same. They mean to rape and kill, and take whatever Ashley's hidin'."

In Gus's terse reply, Jake heard an epic poem of hellfire rising up to consume and destroy, to satiate depraved desires that could only hail from the realm of men, too loathsome even for the vile beasts that prowled the shadowy places of the world. He and Gus continued the unspoken conversation for another ten seconds before he looked back over a shoulder.

"Private Muñoz."

"Sir?"

"I need to speak to Mr. Ashley again."

Muñoz said nothing as he unhitched the tether of Jake's mare from the Emshoff wagon. His eyes held fear, though he fought valiantly to appear nonchalant. Muñoz had clearly been in a fight before and knew they were sailing into a storm of mammoth proportions. As a unit, Jake, Gus, Stacy, Muñoz, and Evans rode toward the front of the train. Corporal McQuaid and Cornelius Blue intercepted the column halfway. The wagon master blocked their advance with his horse.

"Stacy! What in the name of Homer's Odyssey are you doing leadin' the prisoner to Ashley again? You know the extent of his ill feelings toward Mr. Paynter." Then he turned on Gus. "And why'd you not come to Ashley right directly? Now he's in a wretched mood."

Gus gave Cornelius the same unspoken stare he'd first shown to Jake. The wagon master emitted a hum of understanding, spun his mount, and led the way to the front of the line. Lucien and Rosalyn were walking alongside their oxen, prodding them lightly with switches. When Lucien turned his head to find Gus, his eyes lit before he noticed Jake. He lifted a finger.

"Why is that man not tethered to the butt end of this train as is befitting of his character? Did I not make myself clear?"

"Speak *to* me, not about me," Jake said. "Do I make *myself* clear?"

Lucien stopped in his tracks as the unconcerned oxen continued to slip by. He seemed ready to erupt before Rosalyn seized the sleeve of his shirt. He frowned at her before resuming walking. "What did you see, Rivers?"

Gus matched Lucien's pace with his buckskin and relayed the events of his scouting mission up to the point of finding the men and slipping near enough to overhear their conversation.

"And what did you learn of their intentions?" asked Lucien.

Gus eyed Rosalyn, then Lucien. "Perhaps now is not the time."

Before Lucien could reply, his sister stepped next to Gus's ambling horse. "Mr. Rivers, you need not withhold details to spare my sensibilities. I knew what lay before me when I agreed to accompany my brother to the Idaho Territory. I am not afraid."

Gus shook his head. "You should be, Miss Ashley. You should be."

Her defiant expression lost its edges, like a candle just beginning to melt from a new flame. Jake decided to intervene on her behalf.

"Just say it, Gus. Can't spare anyone from the truth. Not out here."

"Suit yourself."

Gus described the overheard conversations, in morbid detail. As he spoke, Rosalyn's face grew slacker still. Jake shook his head. No degree of imagination could prepare a person for the reality of unwitnessed horrors. The only thing that could was having survived other horrors. Unfortunately for Rosalyn, she had led a genteel life. Jake envied her innocence, but pitied its inevitable loss in the days and weeks to come. When Gus finished, Jake rubbed his face.

"Did you say one was called Ketchum?"

"Yep."

"And Sally."

"Yep."

"Big man with a beard like a sprung bale of cotton?"

Gus's eyes narrowed. "Yeah. You know him?"

"I do." He failed to contain the darkness of his reply. The wagon train was in deep trouble.

"What if we fight them?" said Lucien. He seemed unbothered by what Gus had described. "After all, we have nearly thirty men—four of them soldiers. We carry plenty of rifles and ammunition."

"No," said Jake. Lucien shot him a withering glare, which Jake deflected as if waving off a wayward horsefly. "It's not that simple."

"I did not ask your opinion, Paynter."

"Let 'im speak," said Gus. "He has particular expertise with this sort of thing."

Lucien narrowed his eyes. "You've fought these kind of men before?"

"I've *been* these kind of men before." He glanced at Rosalyn apologetically. Her expression had become a cipher, unreadable.

"Explain, then," said an agitated Lucien.

Jake swept an arm toward the trailing wagons. "These men are no match for what's coming. They're farmers. Sodbusters. Men of the soil. They know plants and animals and seasons. Floods, droughts, pestilence—these are the enemies they have learned to fight. These are the adversaries they can defeat, as their fathers and grandfathers did before them." He paused to expel an exasperated breath. "The men that stalk us are stone killers. Men who fell in love with war and were disappointed that it ended. They live for blood and plunder and have grown restless. A bunch of farmers is just target practice for them. And the farmers' wives and daughters? Just spoils of war to be used and discarded, of no more value than an empty whiskey bottle."

Lucien's slack jaw tightened. "Surely you overestimate these bandits."

The haughty man's confidence flagged as Gus, the soldiers, and Cornelius grimly shook their heads. He stared ahead for a half minute in silence, still striding alongside the team of oxen pulling his wagon. He spoke again without turning his head.

"Right, then. We will not turn back, if that's what you expect."

"I do not," said Jake.

Lucien pinned the wagon master with a steel gaze. "Is there an alternate route that skirts this…?"

"Big Nemaha Join."

"Yes, that."

Cornelius nodded slowly. "Best option is to turn north immediately and cross ahead of the Join. We could be three days on before they figured what happened."

"And then? Will they give up?"

Cornelius raised his palms and shrugged. Lucien looked at Jake, apparently annoyed by having to ask him for anything. "Well? You're a killer. What'll they do?"

Jake clenched his fists, gripping the mare's mane tightly as he suppressed an urge for violence. He glared at Lucien until the man's eyes flickered and broke contact.

"They will not give up, Mr. Ashley. They brought little food along. They will go hungry if they turn back. This train is their best option for supplies."

"Is that all?"

"No." He continued to glare at Lucien. "Any reason that brings armed killers several days into the wilderness is reason enough for them to finish the job and leave no witnesses. I only wonder, what might that reason be?"

Lucien turned away again and slashed his switch across the lead oxen's withers. "Change the course, then, Mr. Blue. And McQuaid."

"Yes, sir?"

He pointed at Jake without looking at him. "If I see this man's face again during the next week, I will have you court-martialed when we arrive at Fort Bridger."

McQuaid frowned and seemed to bite back a retort. "Yes, sir."

He snatched the tether of Jake's horse from Muñoz, wheeled about, and led him back to the Emshoff wagon. Gus and Stacy chose not to join them. After Muñoz and Evans reestablished his honor guard, Jake engaged Corporal McQuaid's eyes.

"You know how this all ends, don't ya?"

McQuaid winced. "Just lay low, Paynter. Else a bullet in the head'll be your end, courtesy of his high-and-mighty up there."

McQuaid wheeled away. Jake's eyes fell into a study of his manacled hands and he soon tipped into the well of regretful memory, reliving the dark days of '61 when he'd been the hunter, the raider, the tormentor, riding alongside Sally in the service of Blackburn's maniacal mission so twisted that even the Confederate generals had disowned him. He soon became mired in a specific recollection and struggled to escape.

"Come with me, Paynter. Let's play a game."

Still seeking accolades from Blackburn's raiders, seventeen-year-old Jake followed Sally from the cookfire to the line of eight prisoners roped together beside the road, one of them a girl of twelve. The forlorn townspeople huddled in the ditch with devastation in their eyes. None wore uniforms. But because they hailed from a community that had deigned to defy Blackburn, they were to be taught a lesson in loyalty. Jake hadn't been told the nature of the lesson, but was about to learn. Sally nodded at him.

"Got a quarter in yer pocket?"

Jake fumbled around and produced a coin. "A half dime."

"That'll do." He stepped to the first prisoner, an elderly woman, and put the barrel of his hulking Colt Dragoon to her temple. "Heads or tails, lady."

The woman's eyes filled with shock as she understood the game. After a few seconds, she straightened her spine and glared at Sally. "Heads."

"Flip your coin, kid," said Sally.

Jake blinked three times as the coin nearly slipped from his hand. "What?"

"Toss the coin. Do it!"

Jake spun the coin into the air, caught it, and slapped it against his arm. "Tails."

He jerked at the gunshot and watched the defiant old woman crumple to the muck of the ditch. The man next to her began to rise. Sally belted him back down and pressed the revolver's barrel to his temple. "Heads or tails."

The man choked out a word. "Heads?"

"Toss the coin, kid."

Jake swept his eyes along the line of horrified prisoners to land on the small figure anchoring the chain. "But the girl. Surely not her."

"She's got a fifty-fifty chance, just like everybody else. Toss the coin."

"But…"

Sally swung his revolver toward Jake's forehead. "I can shoot you and then finish the game. Or you can toss the coin."

Jake fumbled the coin before tossing it from his shaking hand and catching it. He peeked at the result and lied. "Heads."

Sally bellowed a laugh at the cowering man. "Lucky guess."

He moved to the next person in line and resumed the game. The next five escaped execution as Jake continued to fabricate when necessary about the actual fall of the coin. With each spared life, Sally grew surlier. Upon arriving at the last prisoner, he peered at Jake through narrowed eyes while addressing the young girl at his feet.

"What's your call?"

The girl trembled forth a choice. "Tails?"

"Toss the coin, kid."

Jake complied and gritted his teeth when the half dime fell heads. "Tails."

Sally took a single step toward him. "Show me."

Jake snatched up the coin from the back of his arm before Sally could see it. "It was tails."

Sally grinned, casually extended the barrel of his revolver toward the girl's head, and pulled the trigger. Jake blinked several times before finding her slumped in the ditch. He leaped toward Sally until their chests collided. "It was tails! I said it was tails!"

Sally belted him to the dirt with the blow of a massive fist. He leaned over Jake, his features twisted with angry darkness. "You wanna join her now?"

Jake failed to answer, so Sally straightened. "Thought so. Next time, I toss and you pull."

When they finally rode away from what they had done, Jake left the half dime with the dead girl and a piece of his soul in that ditch.

"Chin up, Herr Paynter."

Mr. Emshoff's voice extracted Jake from the wastelands of desolate memory. "Pardon?"

The German handed him up another slice of rye. Paynter took it carefully and stuffed it into his shirt for later. Emshoff motioned to the wagons ahead. "They say you are a killer. My family believes you are a saint."

"And what do you think?"

"Somewhere in between, as with all men."

"Not all men."

Emshoff grunted and walked alongside the mare in silence for a minute. Then he looked up at Jake again. "I am happy you are here. If trouble comes, we will look to you."

Without another word, the man strode away to prod along his oxen. Jake stared ahead at the empty wagon flap, wondering what would become of the children in a fight. He knew what Blackburn would have ordered him to do, in another life. What he and Sally had done, in another life. What he might've done again had he not escaped Blackburn's web of horror. His eyes lifted briefly to the horizon on his right and the path to freedom. Conflicting desires tore at him, rending his soul stitch by stitch as the dust of the train threatened to bury him beneath a layer of numbing indecision.

CHAPTER SEVEN

THE WORST WAY TO DIE IS BY DEGREES, ONE WASTED BREATH at a time. By the time the line of wagons slipped over the Nebraska border, crossed the Big Nemaha River short of the Join, and struck a northwesterly course, Jake had decided he'd rather face the Reaper with at least enough gumption to spit in his sightless eye. When the procession next stopped for the night and McQuaid shackled him to the wheel, Jake grabbed the soldier's wrist. McQuaid leveled a puzzled stare at him.

"You gonna just let this happen without a scuffle?" said Jake.

McQuaid held his gaze, the line of his lips straight and thin. The carefree corporal from the jailhouse seemed to have stayed behind in St. Joseph, while a sullen soldier had taken his place. "You're talkin' about Mr. Ashley's plan to ignore the gunmen and hope for the best?"

"Yep."

McQuaid turned the key, stood, and stuffed it into his coat pocket. He glanced over a shoulder toward Ashley's rig before reengaging Jake. "Don't know what I can do about it. He's a by-God senator's son, and I'm just an errand boy sent by a man with lots more stripes to watch over Ashley's pampered hide. He won't listen to me."

Jake liked the corporal. He possessed a frankness that Jake found refreshing. He'd hate to see him die. "We don't need any man's leave to protect ourselves."

McQuaid squatted again, his eyes alive with interest. "What ya got in mind?"

"Get Gus and the soldiers, quiet-like. Bring 'em here."

The corporal stood and walked away. In his absence, Jake

debated again the sanity of involving so many in his bucking of authority. Presently, a pair of boots appeared beneath his nose, and upon closer inspection revealed the owner as Mr. Emshoff. The German handed him another slice of rye, and this time Jake accepted without guilt or hesitation.

"I overheard your conversation," he said. "I want to help."

"It'll be dangerous."

Emshoff laughed softly. "I left behind despot kings and iron authority when I brought my family here. I refuse to fall under such sway again."

"You'll likely be killed."

"I'm dead anyway if not free." He lifted his eyes to the stars. "If I cannot give my children a better life than mine, then what manner of father am I?"

Jake grunted approval. If only his father had been cut from similar cloth. "Right, then. You own a gun?"

"A Lorenz rifled musket. But I can reload it in under thirty seconds."

"You killed a man before?"

He sighed and studied his indicting hands. "I was conscripted to fight the Danes a few years ago. When I finally returned home, the Prussians invaded Bavaria. They stripped my farm before leaving behind two men to finish the job. When one decided he wanted my wife as well, I split his head with an axe. I used his musket to kill the other one. The same musket I carry now. The next day, we gathered what we could and set out for America. We have been traveling westward ever since."

Jake cocked his head in wonder. How could a man with so much blood on his hands appear so at peace? A burst of laughter from the children above him perhaps provided an answer. What a man fights for spells the difference between honor and dishonor, duty and disgrace, valor and simple violence. The sound of several pairs of approaching feet cut short his musings. Gus and the soldiers arrived and squatted around him.

"McQuaid said you called…"

"Jumpin' Joan! Wait for me." Stacy stomped into the middle of the circle, plopped cross-legged before Jake, and put her chin in her hands. "You may commence to explainin' now."

Jake knew better than to send her away. She'd find a way to get killed in this mess with or without his blessing. He glanced at Lucien's wagon and pushed his palms down, indicating secrecy. Everyone gathered near him in the closing darkness.

"Here's the way I see it," he said quietly. "You heard what I said about the riders ahead, right?"

Private Evans chuckled. "Everyone's heard. That's all the settlers been talkin' about for the last day and a half. Mr. Ashley tries to shut 'em up, but they don't listen. They just keep askin' us what we're gonna do about it, as if we knew."

"I figured as much," said Jake.

Before he could say another word, a pair of middle-aged farmers penetrated the circle as if to put the finest of points on Evans's claim. One with a mop of red hair stuck a hand toward Jake's manacles.

"Jed Roberson."

With little room to maneuver, he accepted the hand and shook it once before indicating the need for discretion with a finger to his lips. Another hand appeared and he shook it as well. "Philip Savoy. Me 'n Jed come out of Ohio together with our wives and half-growed young'uns. We heard from Emshoff here how you sent those Missouri boys packin' before we left. Then we heard about them gunmen anglin' to give us trouble. We're here to help."

Jake shook his head, thankful for the allies but already weary of the burden. He didn't want anyone relying on him. It was too risky for all parties involved.

"Your choice," he said. "We're headed for a nasty dustup and have few options. So, here's what we need to do."

Though the darkness obscured their features, the expectant

lean of every individual spoke of desperate interest in what Jake had to say. He hoped not to disappoint them, but feared inaction more than failing outright.

"Those men at the Join are bushwhackers of every breed. Ketchum rode with the Red Legs for the Union and burned his way up and down the Missouri River. Sally rode with Blackburn and Quantrill and gunned down more than his share of unarmed boys during the Lawrence raid of '63. Now that the war is over, all the scum of every despicable outfit has washed into the same cesspool. They've discovered more in common with their former enemies than with decent folk."

Jake shifted his position as his left foot fell asleep. He stretched it out while remembering his two tenures with Sally. One when they rode side-by-side, the other when they unleashed lead at each other while wearing opposing uniforms. Sally was death on the hoof, no two ways about it.

"The big man, Sally. He's got three dozen killers at his beck and call. They've been up to no good for a while now. Stealing, raping, pillaging, burning. Government's got two entire companies scouring the countryside for 'em. An undersized line of wagons guarded by a handful of blue coats is mere child's play to them. They won't leave such a ripe plum alone. And when they come, they'll be spittin' angry that we showed the unmitigated gall to slip their trap."

His small audience sat in lip-curled silence, as if viewing the dead body of someone who'd cheated them at cards and got their comeuppance. Gus broke the stalemate.

"So, they gonna come at us, guns blazin', and start killing until everyone lays down in the dirt and begs for mercy."

"That's how I see it."

Stacy hopped to her feet, agitated. Her whisper grew harsh. "We can't let 'em do that. Come in here like that and do as they wish."

Jake surprised himself with a short chuckle. "Glad you see

my point so clearly. Now, sit back down before you frighten the children."

She huffed and resumed her cross-legged position, but began fidgeting with the knife that had been sheathed on her belt. Jake looked at Gus. "You remember Island Mound?"

"Can't forget it, even if I tried. They outnumbered us double."

"That's right. So how'd we win?"

Gus's white teeth appeared in the dusk. "We took the fight to them, then stood our ground when they turned on us."

"That's the way I recollect it." Jake opened his palms to the others. "We gotta take the fight to these men and give 'em no chance to set the terms. We stand our ground until they die or run. And we start now by setting outriders to the south and east to watch for them coming. They won't jump us directly. They'll match our pace awhile and then attack at dusk."

"I'll do it," said Stacy. Gus shook his head at her.

"Now, Miss Blue…"

"Stop callin' me 'Miss Blue,' and stop telling me what I can and can't do. I been ridin' this trail since I was seven years old. I got a name for every creek and tree and rock between here and the Great Divide. If anyone can stay out of sight, it's me. And I can ride faster'n any two of you, I'll tell you that."

Gus belted a laugh, but cut it short to avoid drawing attention. "Fine, Miss Blue. You watch our tail, I'll watch the side. Starting in the morning."

"What about the rest of us?" McQuaid seemed eager to take action instead of waiting to be shot.

"Keep your weapons loaded and no more'n two feet from your hand. When they come, we ride at 'em like a spring flood."

Everyone grunted assent, apparently pleased with the plan. When they rose to leave, a confident spring imbued their steps. Jake knew the truth, though, and suspected Gus did as well. It wasn't so much a plan as a desperate charge that would likely kill most of them on the slim chance that some of the settlers would live to complete their journey. The prospect of dying didn't particularly annoy Jake. However, he detested the burden of leading others to a similar inglorious fate. As he rolled over to sleep, the phantoms of dead allies and enemies marched incessantly upon the dusty parade ground of his memory, beating their snares with whispers of "what about us?"

CHAPTER EIGHT

"He's a plague upon this expedition. A blight upon our party. Whispering plots with the others right under our noses."

Lucien's bitter epithet of Paynter as they trudged alongside their oxen in golden knee-high grass raised Rosalyn's pique. She understood his distrust of a man wanted for murder. She accepted his disdain for having to include him in their traveling party. However, she did not appreciate Lucien's curious level of antipathy that led him to curse and otherwise disparage Paynter every hour or two. His latest barrage drove her past simple nods of acknowledgment directly into disagreement.

"What about this man so offends you that you must invoke his name frequently and without provocation simply to malign him yet again?"

Lucien stared at her, seemingly surprised by her sudden fit of gumption. "What are you saying?"

"You heard me well. The world lies before you, a future for the taking, and all you can do is vilify a man in chains who has done nothing but try to protect you and this train since he arrived, even though such actions are of no benefit to his cause. Why such vitriol?"

Lucien's stare intensified and he flared his nostrils like a bull preparing to charge. "You want to know? Truly?"

"I do. Truly."

He peered ahead and scowled. "That castoff from the dung heap of humanity presumes to have your regard."

Rosalyn blinked with confusion. "My regard? What are you saying?"

Lucien lifted a finger toward her. "I saw how he looked at you.

As if you and he could be equals. As if you could conduct a civil conversation of like minds. I have beaten down much better men than Paynter who presumed the same. His presumption should offend you beyond the pale."

Rosalyn bristled at her brother's claim. Such eloquent outbursts had earned him the awe and admiration of folks who confused bluster for charisma. She was not so easily duped.

"You are correct," she said. "I am offended beyond the pale. Not by Mr. Paynter, but by you for pretending to know the soul of a man after spending five minutes with him. People are not political pamphlets that might be understood over the course of a luncheon. They are complex creatures who reveal their secrets over the span of a lifetime."

Lucien's face grew red with anger. He began to speak several times before biting back his words. "Stay away from him," he said finally.

"Or what? You will send me back to Missouri? Give me a loaf of bread and a skin of water and set me to walking east?"

"Come now, Rosalyn…"

"I will not." She clenched her fists. "In fact, I will speak with Mr. Paynter now. Excuse me."

She left behind his muffled curses and strode toward the tail of the column, only six wagons deep as the train had spread out on the flat ground between the boggy creeks that fed the Big Nemaha. Jake glanced at her, sleepy-eyed, when she swung around the end of the trailing wagon, seemingly awakening from a stupor. His lips grew tighter as she approached him.

"Mr. Paynter."

He lifted his manacled wrists to touch his hat brim but said nothing. He seemed a man of two ages, young by his looks but with the haunted eyes of a person twice his years. She waited for his horse to catch her and then walked alongside.

"You know my brother despises you."

He grunted as if amused. "I hadn't noticed."

She smiled at the sarcasm of his tone. Not hard and bitter, but reflecting the remnants of whimsy. "In fact, I think he blames you for our current predicament with the gunmen."

"Fine by me. I'm used to taking blame whether rightfully or not. What's one more accusation?" He looked down, meeting her eyes. "Why would he suffer you talking to me, then?"

She lifted her spine. "Mr. Ashley is not my lord and master. I do as I please."

"And this pleases you? Talkin' to a condemned man while choking on dust in the middle of the Nebraska prairie on your way to the armpit of civilization?"

She snorted a laugh. "Yes."

He shook his head and frowned. "You're as odd as loaded dice, Miss Ashley."

"Odd? How so?"

He shrugged and looked away. "Women like you don't generally leave behind the comforts of home for the rigors of the frontier."

"Women like me?" She bowed her neck. "Do you mean lazy women? Frivolous women? Fragile women?"

His chin dropped. "You ain't none of those. My apologies, ma'am."

She lifted the corners of her mouth ever so slightly. "I forgive you."

The silence stretched between them, like an unbridgeable chasm neither could cross. After a minute, he cleared his throat. "Perhaps you should listen to your brother. I'm not a good man. I've done terrible things."

"Like killing your captain?"

"Not that. Probably the *best* thing I've ever done."

"And you call *me* odd."

Her comment raised a smile from him that hung on his lips

like a wisp of cotton before the breeze seemed to sweep it away. His eyes hardened. "Stay away from me, Miss Ashley, if you know what's good for you."

The insistence of his advice brought her more disappointment than it should have. He was right, after all. However, there was a quality to him she could not dismiss. A glimmer of deeper character. A nobility, languishing beneath years of tarnish but nobility nonetheless.

"As you wish," she said. She increased her pace to leave him behind, when he called out.

"Miss Ashley."

"Mr. Paynter?"

"When they come, you fight 'em as if your life depends on it. Because it will. And if I'm not there to help you, then I am already dead."

The matter-of-fact desolation of his advice raised a shudder in her soul. She stared ahead at the falling darkness, wondering where all this was leading.

CHAPTER NINE

WITH EVERY PASSING HOUR, STACY RANGED FARTHER AFIELD from the wagons, a wayward planet on an eccentric orbit. When the column had become just a plume of dust on the horizon, she spun her horse and bolted south toward the Join. Her father, Paynter, and that irksome Gus would have strapped her to an ox if they'd guessed her true intentions. She took solace in the presence of her sheathed shotgun, an ancient but reliable Lefaucheux twelve-gauge that she'd bartered from an old fur trapper on the banks of the Snake River in the Idaho Territory. She'd brought down a thousand birds with it to feed hungry wagon trains. With uneasy thoughts about human targets, she swung a wide, hours-long arc across rolls of grassy plain embraced by shallow winding creek beds but shunned by trees, to approach from the east. As expected, she found no bandits in residence at the confluence of the rivers. However, they'd made no attempt to cover their sloppy tracks nor mask their design. Their muddy trail followed deep cuts in the Nebraska sod that led westward toward the source of the Big Nemaha.

"Cocksure bastards," she mumbled. She slipped up to the slight rise that gave the river its course and spurred her calico ahead, anxious, exhilarated, and wary. Just before the fall of dusk, she spied them in the far distance, dismounted and apparently settling in for the night. She snorted at their bravado, so certain of a field day that they would pitch camp rather than riding into the teeth of night. She angled north by northwest on a perimeter that would put her between the gunmen and her father's train. Satisfied, she set up in pitch darkness a camp consisting solely of a bedroll and dined on hard biscuits softened by water from her precious canteen.

The western prairie was a whimsical creature, fickle and capricious. It could bury a woman in eight feet of drifting snow, wash her away with a surprise flood, blow sand into her eyes until they caked shut. But it could also bestow gifts, such as the grandeur of pure silence, the stretch of a horizon two days' ride distant, lightning that forked across the sky between two corners of the map. On this night, it brought her voices. Though the bandits' camp lay two miles distant, the soft breeze carried indistinct snatches of conversation, laughter, and belligerence to Stacy's attentive ears, as if they convened just a hundred yards downwind. She lay on her blanket and gazed at the heavens, counting shooting stars until reaching perhaps seven before she drifted into sleep.

A distant shout awoke her as pink filaments of dawn bled into the purple night. She packed quickly, unstaked her horse, and led it carefully up the covering roll of earth between her campsite and those intent on malice. They moved lazily about, barking at one another. One man pushed another into the remains of the campfire, and he jumped out with a howl as his abuser threw back his head and laughed. Her frown grew deep. These were not men. They were beasts of the woods, shod with boots and sporting grand hats and prancing about on two legs as if something resembling humans.

For the next hour, Stacy continued her perimeter watch, paralleling the gang's course until she became convinced of their design. It seemed Paynter's prediction was accurate. They were casually angling away from the river on a slow intercept with their intended prey. She eyed the sun and figured they'd hit the wagons at dusk. Jaw gritted with conviction, she galloped her horse away from the gunmen on a more circuitous route toward the train. She patted her horse's neck in apology.

"I'm gonna need some wings from you for a while. We gotta eat up some ground."

The calico tossed his head and increased his gallop. Horse and rider powered intently across the vacant prairie for several miles before Stacy slowed him to a trot. He complained briefly before accepting the slower pace despite his heaving breaths and the spray of saliva coating his muzzle like errant flames. Three hours on, as the sun reached zenith, she spied the smudge just beyond sight that indicated the column of wagons. She adjusted her course and urged her horse again into a gallop toward a rise harboring a creek on the far side. On topping the hillock, she reined her mount to a dead stop.

"What in heaven's name?"

Below her, just across the pitiful creek, a giant stood beside a dismembered prairie schooner, and he was wielding a large hammer with both hands. He seemed as surprised as she was.

"Did they come back?"

The voice of a woman drifted from behind the ruined wagon, a flash of skirt and bonnet. The man cupped a hand over his eyes to cast away the glare of the sun. He shook his shaggy head.

"No. A stranger."

A baby began to cry. Stacy lifted her eyes into the distance toward her urgent destination, telling herself to keep moving and leave well enough alone. Instead, she prodded her horse down the gradual slope to ford the creek. The big man watched her with predator eyes while the woman tried to shush the baby. Stacy dismounted thirty feet away.

"I got some biscuits. They ain't no good, but with enough water, they'll fill your belly."

The man's grip slackened and he lowered his hammer. "You're a woman."

Stacy suppressed a laugh. If she had a dollar for every time she'd heard that, she'd live in a grand house in San Francisco. However, no one had ever said it with a Scottish brogue before. "Was when I woke up," she said, "but it's been a long day already."

The giant cocked his head. "What's a wee scrap of a lass like yourself doin' out here alone?"

"Call me a wee lass again and I'll have you eatin' that hammer instead of biscuits."

Her threat produced a smile. He spoke over his shoulder. "Come out, Maddie. The lady means us no harm."

The woman, Maddie it seemed, emerged from cover with the baby, whose wail had settled into a drone of mild complaint. "About those biscuits, miss."

Stacy dug them from her pouch and unwrapped the cloth as she approached the wary family. They converged next to a pair of spoked wheels with a small platform perched above the axle, all apparently scavenged from the dead wagon. She handed the man the biscuits and her waterskin. He broke a biscuit into pieces and gave it to Maddie. It took only one piece in the baby's stubby fingers to still its crying.

"Thank you," the man said. Stacy extended her hand to him.

"Stacy Blue."

He shook it with an iron grip. "Glen Dunbar. My wife, Maddie, and our little girl, Lily."

"A pleasure." She eyed the unhappy baby, mostly swaddled beneath a dirty blanket. "May I see?"

Maddie shifted the encompassing blanket to reveal a tiny face, red with dismay but consoled by the biscuit. No more than a year, Stacy thought. One corner of her mouth lifted. Maddie locked eyes with her.

"Would you like to hold her?"

Stacy began to reach for the child but stayed her hand. Babies had a way of dying on you the moment you became attached to them. She'd lost too many attachments without going out of her way to find new ones. She deliberately ignored the offer and engaged Glen. "What in the name o' Lord Harry happened here, mister?"

Glen ran a huge hand through his dark mane. "We were traveling with a group out of Independence, headed toward South Pass and then onward to Oregon. We lost an axle, just here. The wagon master confiscated our oxen and told us to leave our possessions and bunk in with someone else, but I refused to leave my tools. Without them, we'd starve wherever we ended up. He said they'd be back for us soon. That was five weeks ago by my reckoning."

Stacy shook her head. "Was your wagon master Lassiter?"

"Did he send you, then?"

"Hell no. Lassiter's a snake. He won't send nobody. He'll just say you fell sick along the way and he gave you a proper Christian burial."

Glen's eyes clouded with anger and his grip tightened on the hammer. "Nasty dobber. I'll be sure to correct him if ever I see him again."

"I'd pay good money to witness such a spectacle." She waved at the hand-built cart. "What's your plan, then?"

He pointed to an anvil crouching beneath the wagon's husk. "I'll load my tools and whatever else will fit and pull this cart back the way we came. Then try again next spring."

"You're a blacksmith, then?"

"The finest," said Maddie with pride lighting her eyes.

Stacy smiled. A blacksmith with an anvil could come in handy on a journey of two thousand miles. Horseshoes, harness buckles, and yokes all had a way of falling into disrepair under such continuous duress. "What if you could continue west? Would ya?"

"In the beat of a heart."

She turned and began walking toward her horse. "Wait here then, no more'n three days. I'll come back for ya. If I don't, then I'm probably shot and won't be comin'."

As she mounted, she found them watching, seemingly puzzled by her suggestion.

"No offense, lass, but the last person who said they'd return told us a tale."

Stacy stretched her spine. "I am Stacy Blue, blood daughter of

Cornelius Blue and the Shoshone nation. My promises are like your anvil there. They do not bend. I'll return within three days or meet you beyond the pearly gates."

She touched the brim of her cap and urged her mount into a loping gallop. Glen and Maddie waved at her, cautious hope crowning their sunburned faces.

CHAPTER TEN

WITH THE WAGONS BRIEFLY AT REST IN A SANDY CRUX BETWEEN a pair of low rises of grass, Paynter listened intently to Stacy's report, right after Gus and Cornelius roundly chastised her for running off into such a risky venture. She dismissed them as if they were residue she'd scraped off her boot and continued talking seemingly without inhaling a breath. Jake brushed past the part about the abandoned family to focus on logistics.

"You figure they'll hit us at dusk, then?"

"Seems so to me."

He studied the sun. "Then we got maybe six hours."

Lucien had seemed content to pursue a path of willful disregard—of ignoring the gunmen in hopes they wouldn't attack. Stacy's report, though, appeared to rattle him. "What do you suggest, then? Circle up the wagons and wait?"

Gus chuckled. "I don't think that's what Paynter has in mind, Mr. Ashley. He means to meet them head-on."

Lucien lifted a palm toward Jake. "I forbid it. We must establish a defense and keep our forces together."

Jake swung his gaze slowly to the man. "Did you fight in the war, Mr. Ashley?"

"I did not. I was needed in other capacities. Why?"

"Because you sure talk like you did. But if you had, you'd know an exposed and indefensible position when you saw one."

Ashley bowed up as if to fight, clenching and unclenching his fists. Cornelius touched his shoulder. "I wouldn't, Mr. Ashley. Just take a moment to consider his reasoning."

Ashley glared at Jake but crossed his arms. "Let's hear it, then."

Jake motioned to the settlers, who watched the parlay from

a distance with wringing hands and nervous pacing. "See those folks? Men, women, children, babes in arms?"

"What of them?"

"When Quantrill sacked Lawrence during the war, he ordered the killing of two hundred men and boys, nearly all unarmed. Sally was one of those pulling the trigger. If he can march into a proper town and gun down dozens, what do you think he'll do to a small band of wagons isolated on the prairie?"

Lucien's expression went slack like a busted rope. He blinked at the settlers. "What exactly do you propose, then?"

Jake tossed his head toward Stacy. "What's between us and where we're headed, maybe three hours yonder?"

"A dinner plate. Flat as a drunken sailor."

"No washes? No rises?"

Stacy touched her chin and lifted her eyes upward and to the right. "Well, there's Muddy Creek. Winds like a snake back on itself, and the banks are thick with cottonwood and scrub. They gotta cross it somewhere."

Jake nodded approval. "That'll do. But we need to decide where that happens. We need to give 'em someone to chase after."

"You're lookin' at her."

"No, ma'am." Gus crossed his arms. "It ain't right to send a woman to do that job."

"Now you gone and stepped in it," said Cornelius with a half smirk.

Stacy planted a finger in the center of Gus's chest and set her jaw. "Then we can't send you, can we? And I already told you, I can ride faster'n any two of you. My grandfather picked my calico special from his herd before he died and called the spirit of the wind to bless it."

"Is that right?"

She withdrew her finger. "That's right." Her eyes grew wistful. "I swear, sometimes when I'm ridin' him, his hooves leave the earth and he flies."

Gus chuckled. "What do you call this wondrous beast?"

"He ain't got no name. You can't name the wind."

Lucien shook his head. "I agree with Mr. Rivers. And he should go instead."

All eyes turned toward Paynter. He grimaced. When had he become the final judge and jury for every decision of the group? He didn't care for it but appeared to have no choice in the matter.

"Stacy will go, then, and bring 'em on a line toward the train. We'll meet 'em in the middle at Muddy Creek. Just give us a rifle shot a few miles out so we can intercept your course. And stay out of range. Sally's good with a long gun, so that's about half a mile."

The smile that stretched her face promised to ache if she held it too long. "Got it. Now, who all's gonna be there to meet me?"

"The three soldiers, Gus, and me."

"No," said Lucien firmly. "I go. You stay. We can't have you roaming loose on the plains with your sordid history."

Jake pursed his lips and nodded. "Excellent idea, Mr. Ashley. I'll stay behind with the settlers and your sister while everyone who can ride and shoot travels ten miles into the wilderness."

Lucien's face clouded as he considered the notion. His lips grew into the beginnings of a respectable snarl. "I've changed my mind. You come with us."

"If you insist."

"But your wrists remain bound, and you carry no weapon."

Jake frowned at Lucien in the manner of a wolverine biding his time. He didn't relish the idea of riding into armed conflict without freedom of movement or a means of defense. However, he couldn't very well stay behind. Nobody knew Sally like he did. Without him, they'd all probably die. With him along, maybe only most of them would get killed.

"Agreed," he said finally. "But we should tell them what's goin' to happen."

Lucien followed his pointed hands to the growing knot of

settlers who had inched closer until nearly within earshot. "They don't need to know."

"They do. You can't cover this like whatever else you're hidin.'"

Lucien threw up his hands. "You tell them, then. If they lose heart, the fault will be yours."

Jake approached the gathered men and women, who were fronted by Emshoff, Roberson, and Rosalyn.

"What can you tell us, Herr Paynter?" said the German.

Jake halted eight feet away and worked his eyes from person to person, gauging their collective states of mind. They were afraid, that much was clear. But they also seemed determined, which came as no surprise. Only determined souls would set off across a hostile continent with no assurances of survival or prosperity. The hope that sustained such grit could put up one heck of a fight when cornered. Jake was counting on that.

"It seems you already know that professional killers intend to raid this expedition." Many heads nodded. "So I'll give it to you plain as milk. Some of us are riding out to stop them. If we're lucky, we'll kill enough to turn 'em back. If not…" He let the alternative hang in the breeze of their imaginations for a few seconds. "They'll catch up to you by nightfall, and angry as a wounded bear."

The settlers exchanged shocked glances before numbing acceptance began remolding their expressions. Rosalyn nodded grimly.

"And if that happens? What should we do?"

Jake shook his head. "Every man, woman, and child must choose for themselves in that moment. Whether to cooperate and cede power to them, or fight back with your life in the balance. Whether to go quietly or with a shout of defiance."

"What would you do?"

"I'd shout. I'd fight. But that's just me."

She dipped her chin with seeming gratitude. In times of trouble, people preferred disquieting candor over calming evasion. He'd come to learn that lesson well.

"Thank you," said Emshoff. "We will do what we can. We will do what we must."

"I know you will."

Jake spun on his heels and went after his mare. By the time he'd finished untying the tether from the tailgate, everyone had gathered around his horse. Stacy was already disappearing southward toward the horizon, her long braid flying as her horse grew wings. He mounted and nodded to Gus.

"Take us out, sir."

The former buffalo soldier wheeled his horse around and set a track southwest across a boundless plain toward the unseen Muddy Creek. Lucien slipped past him on his finely bred stallion.

"I'll lead the way."

The three soldiers joined him. Jake pulled his mount alongside Gus's buckskin and rolled his eyes in disgust. Gus just grinned. "Better this way. Then I can't be blamed when this all goes to Hades." He let Lucien gain another ten yards before reaching behind into his saddlebag, retrieving a familiar revolver, and handing it to Jake.

Jake grinned like a kid with a piece of taffy. "You kept it for me."

"Like you asked."

He perused the piece, a British-made Kerr's Patent single-action five-shot revolver, forty-four caliber. The only remnant of his time in the Confederate forces. "Loaded?"

"Five shots, caps and all."

Jake stuffed the revolver into his belt and pulled his shirt over the butt to conceal it. "Thanks."

"Couldn't let you stumble into battle without at least a fightin' chance. Even though that seems to be your preferred method."

"You know me too well, Sergeant Rivers."

He prodded the mare to make up ground on the others. Though he questioned his chances of surviving the day, the lump of cold metal pressing against his gut gave him at least a modicum of hope. Most days, a modicum proved more than enough.

CHAPTER ELEVEN

MUDDY CREEK LIVED UP TO ITS DESCRIPTIVE NAME AND WAS every bit the winding serpent Stacy had claimed. It carved a lazy cut through the Nebraska sod, often doubling back on itself only to veer again toward the distant Missouri River where it would offer itself to the mother waters. The soil along the banks was sawdust-soft, swallowing the horses' hooves with every tremulous step. A riot of stunted trees and bushes coated either side of the creek, clinging to the capricious run of water while warding off the ever-encroaching prairie. With the utmost of care, the band slipped through the foliage and across the creek. They circled into a loose knot, six riders waiting for a banshee called Miss Blue to come screaming up from the south.

"Spread out along the creek but stay against the trees," said Jake. "Blend in with the foliage. Watch for dust plumes, reflections, anything. Give a shout if you spot something."

As the band scattered, Lucien followed Jake. "I'll be keeping an eye on you."

Jake waved his manacles. "Afraid I'll go back and have high tea with Miss Ashley?"

"You're not allowed to speak her name," he said with more believable menace than Jake had heard from him before.

"Point taken."

They drifted up the creek together on horseback for several minutes in silence. Jake briefly wondered if Lucien would put a bullet in his back to solve his prisoner problem, eliminate his sister's distraction, or just for spite. He dismissed the notion, though. Lucien wasn't the kind of man to commit atrocities in public. He would bide his time and do it privately, quietly, and by someone else's hand.

"Why'd you kill your captain?"

Lucien's unexpected question ruined the blessed silence. Jake glanced away from the horizon. "I'll tell you if you let me know why Sally and his men are so keen to slit your throat and raid your wagon."

"I don't know why."

Jake had suffered many liars before. Lucien seemed like a proficient one, and his denial would have convinced most people. However, Jake had heard some of the best liars in the civilized world during the war, and compared to them, Lucien was second rate.

"I'm guessin' it's money. Everything comes back to dollars at some point. And judging by the deep ruts your front wheels lay down, I'd say gold, and plenty of it."

Lucien's face went ashen before he recovered his bluff. "You think mighty highly of yourself, don't you, Paynter?"

"No," he said. "I'm a bad man whose done terrible things. On the contrary, I don't think much of myself at all. Something you should try, maybe."

Lucien set his jaw and turned away to stare at the horizon, coiling for a torrid response, when he froze. "There. See that?"

Jake followed his pointed arm and waited until he saw it. A flash of light on the horizon, too regular to be accidental. He smiled. Stacy signaling, no doubt. The banshee was on the fly.

"Rally here!" Lucien called, an order repeated down the creek. Within minutes, the others had gathered along the far bank with the wall of brush shielding them from the approaching riders. As they moved in a line up the creek, a distant shot rang out, confirming Stacy's approach. They continued until she was coming at them on a straight line. A blur of horses perhaps a half mile behind her marked Sally and his men hot on her track. Jake motioned along the creek.

"Tie off your mounts, spread out, and find a position. Me,

Gus, and McQuaid will take the first three in line, one, two, three. Everyone else open up on the rest of 'em."

Only then did Lucien notice the revolver Jake had pulled from his belt. "Who gave you that?"

Jake laughed. "Sally did, seven years ago. I intend to reacquaint him with it."

Lucien appeared ready to order the weapon confiscated. But to his credit, he said nothing and instead followed Jake's instructions. Meanwhile, Jake found a position where the creek bellied toward the riders, putting him forward of the point where they would likely cross. They'd move right in front of him, exposed and unaware of his lurking menace. He tied the mare away from the creek and hurried to the water's edge in a crouch. Bracing himself against a ragged cottonwood, he waited, cursing again the heavy manacles binding his wrists. If the conflict devolved into fists and chokeholds, he'd be at a heavy disadvantage. He pinned Stacy in his gaze as she approached. Her former confidence had dissipated into barely restrained panic as she glanced repeatedly over a shoulder at her pursuers. Her horse slowed dramatically when it hit the soggy soil along the creek and she nearly lost her seat. However, she and her mount pressed through to the safety of the trees. Confident someone would share the plan with her, Jake swung his attention to the approaching band and winced. They were more spread out than he'd hoped. He wedged his bracing elbow against the cottonwood's trunk and slowed his breathing.

"Five shots," he whispered.

When the first rider was halfway across the creek, Jake put a bullet through the man's temple. He tumbled lifeless from his horse onto the near bank, a human sandbag flailing to a permanent rest. A second and third shot from the trees brought down the next two riders before they could comprehend the fate of their comrade. One fell dead, while the other clambered into the brush on the far bank, cursing loudly at whoever possessed the unmitigated gall to shoot him.

The last four riders reined their horses to an abrupt halt while firing blindly into the opposing trees. Jake lined up the man nearest him, exhaled a breath, and squeezed the trigger. The bandit's hands flew to his newly ventilated neck to suppress the spray of blood. Jake watched with detached horror as the man slouched slowly over the mane of his confused horse until his arms fell to a dangle alongside the animal's neck. Jake blinked with the recognition of an expired life, something he'd seen so often as to become something of an expert on the matter. Every man's death was different until the fire went out. Then they were all the same. He tore his eyes away from the grim spectacle to find the remaining three riders wheeling about in a tight circle of retreat. One was a big man with a shaggy beard like a sprung bale of cotton. Sally.

In a flash of prophetic intuition, Jake knew what would happen next. Sally would return to Missouri, livid as a stirred-up rattlesnake, and round up as many men as he could gather before striking west again. When he tracked down Ashley's train, he would slaughter them all. Every man. Every woman. Every child. He'd stage it to look like a massacre at the hands of the Cheyenne or Sioux. He'd carry Rosalyn into the pit of darkness with him before snuffing her life, take whatever Ashley was carrying, and depart to rape, pillage, and murder elsewhere. Stirred by the apocalyptic vision, Jake glanced first at his frightened mare pulling at the restraining bush some thirty yards distant, and then at his revolver.

Three shots remaining. Three devils in flight.

Before he could formulate a plan, Jake was atop his mare and bursting across the creek, perhaps four hundred yards behind the pursued. He dug his heels into the mare's ribs, hoping her inherent hostility toward him would lend strength to her undersized frame. A mile flew by, then another, and another. Little by little, the mare slowed as her breathing labored. The already tired horses of the bandits suffered similarly, for they slowed as well, and the gap tightened. Then, as one, Sally and his men circled around to face Jake a hundred yards distant. Jake cocked the Kerr and risked a glance behind to find himself alone. One against three. With no time to think, he dropped from the saddle of the halting mare, raised his revolver with both hands, drew a bead on the middle rider, and pulled. The startled man tumbled backward from his horse, clutching his erupting chest. The other two halted their intended charge. Sally bellowed across the distance, shaking the knee-high grass with his wrath-of-God bass.

"Who the hell are you?"

Without answering, Jake began mounting again. In reaction, the riders turned and fled. After pressing the mare forward a hundred strides, Jake settled her into a trot. What had begun as a desperate chase had evolved into a patient but relentless hunt, and he the wolf. Thoughts of the settlers, Gus, and even Rosalyn slipped into the unseen grottos of his mind, a shed skin, as a familiar red haze blossomed up to fill the void. Sally must be stopped, and through savage means. The well of violence he harbored deep in his core seemed satisfied to fuel his slow-burning rage and drive him forward into the fall of night. The wolf called, and he answered.

CHAPTER TWELVE

GUS LEVELED HIS SPENCER CARBINE AT THE INJURED BANDIT'S face and caressed the trigger. This was usually the moment where sloppier folks ended up dead. He took special pride in his attention to detail, though.

"I will interpret so much as an involuntary twitch from you as hostile intent and remove a portion of your head," he said coolly.

The man curled half of his top lip until it disappeared into a red moustache while he explored Gus's face as if to measure the claim. After a few seconds, he extended both hands away from his sides while letting his revolver spin to dangle from a finger by the trigger guard.

"Set her down, slow-like."

The man laid his weapon carefully in the mud alongside the creek.

"Now, stand up."

"Can't."

"Why?"

"Got a bullet in my thigh."

"I don't care. Stand up and back away."

The prisoner stood, wincing and grunting as he rose, favoring his wounded leg with a one-footed shuffle until he nearly fell into the creek. Gus rose from beside the tree he had reached after a dash across the creek, never allowing the barrel to stray more than an inch from dead center of the bandit's forehead. He covered the twenty yards to the man, stooped to recover the discarded revolver, and flung it into the creek.

"Now, why'd you hafta do that?" the man whined. "That there

was my favorite piece. A by-God Starr forty-four caliber. Won it in a poker game, then shot the loser with it when he had second thoughts."

"I'm havin' second thoughts right now. So you best do as I say."

"What now, then?"

"Move slow across the creek."

"On a busted leg?"

"Or as a dead man. Your choice."

He sighed and hopped through the water with further grunts of pain. When he reached the bank, McQuaid and Muñoz grabbed him none too gently and flung him down on his back. McQuaid pulled a Dragoon and pressed it into the man's cheek just below his left eye socket. "My finger's itchy. Just give me a reason, lickspittle."

The man cut his eyes toward the tip of the barrel. "I'll kill you before this is over, bluebelly."

McQuaid managed to cock his weapon before Gus nudged him aside. "Not yet, Corporal. He needs to spill his secrets first."

"Go to Jericho, mister," said the man.

"You first, Ketchum."

The prisoner's vinegar abated as he narrowed his eyes at Gus. "Do I know you?"

"Not a bit. But I know you. Got real acquainted with the spur on your right boot a couple nights back while you were trying to relieve yourself. If I'd been a more cautious man, you'd be dead already."

Ketchum's narrowed eyes widened and he frowned. "What do ya want, then?"

Lucien came stomping up just then with Stacy dogging his tail. "We want answers. Who sent you? Will they send others? I need names."

"Are you Ashley?"

"Yes."

Ketchum smiled and placed his hands behind his head as if set-tling in for a warm afternoon's nap. "Go hang, Ashley."

Lucien planted the tip of his boot in Ketchum's temple to demonstrate his objection to the suggestion. The bandit snuffed like a candle and his head flopped to one side in insensibility. Lucien spun toward Gus and McQuaid.

"Where's Paynter?"

"Gone," said the corporal. "Shot down two and lit out after the others."

"Lit out? He gave chase?"

Gus shook his head at Lucien. "You seem surprised."

Lucien scowled. "I didn't figure him for the kind of man who'd put himself in harm's way for others."

"You're as wrong as a five-legged dog, then."

Lucien waved a dismissive hand and pointed to McQuaid. "Ride after him, Corporal. No doubt his 'chase' is a fabrication. He'll be headed for parts unknown by now."

The young soldier straightened and looked down his chin at Lucien. "My orders, sir, are to protect you and yours. Paynter was dumped on us last-minute. I don't figure Senator Ashley or General Bartlett would have me chase him across the plains and leave your train undefended."

Lucien furrowed his brow, perhaps surprised by McQuaid's newfound mettle. Gus always found it amusing how a jackass could bring out the gumption in even the meekest of men.

"Besides," said Gus, "his run solves your biggest problem."

"And that would be…"

"Miss Ashley's unhealthy curiosity about him."

Lucien's face went redder than usual. "My sister has no more interest in that man than she would a cockroach."

"Whatever you say."

Lucien paced away, kicking Ketchum's head again in the pro-cess, and circled back. "You go then, Mr. Rivers."

Stacy snorted disdain as Gus folded his arms. "I will not. I done hunted him down once against the cries of my conscience and will not do so again."

"You'd let a killer run free?"

"We're all killers, in one way or another. Some do the deed with their own hands." He leveled a glare at Lucien. "Others order it done. It's killin', just the same."

Lucien raised a hand as if to slap Gus. He didn't so much as flinch, hoping Ashley would give him a reason to break the skin of his knuckles on the sharp edges of the man's face. Perhaps Lucien saw the peril of Gus's gaze, because he turned abruptly to squat beside Ketchum. The restless palm found the prisoner's cheek instead. He slapped him a second time to rouse the bandit from his stupor.

"Land's sake. Stop hittin' me."

Lucien grabbed Ketchum's collar with both hands and lifted his head six inches off the dirt. "What's Sally planning? Tell me or I'll leave you here for the coyotes."

Ketchum blinked to sort out his vision. When he did, his narrow focus fell on the man hovering over him. "You wanna know what Sally's plannin'?"

"Damn right."

"I'll tell you, then, 'cause you asked so nice. He'll be back, if only to taste of that sweet sister of yers."

Lucien rocked Ketchum's head to the side with another slap of his palm and growled. "Watch your tongue."

Ketchum smiled again through blood-stained teeth. "He'll make you watch. Then he'll flay you a bit, just enough to keep you alive and in agony, and he'll stake you to the dirt for the sun and the insects and the varmints to have. That's what Sally's plannin'."

Lucien thrust Ketchum back into the dirt and stood up. "You're more of a snake than Paynter said."

The prisoner blinked twice as his bloodied expression

reorganized into bland confusion. "Paynter? Jake Paynter? Ain't he hung?"

When Lucien walked away, Stacy strode over to the man. "He ain't hung. He's with us, and right now, Sally's no doubt lookin' over his shoulder to find Paynter doggin' him like Death on his horse."

Ketchum's eyes hardened with concern. "Paynter's here? He's after Sally right now?"

"That's what I said. Don't hear so well, do ya?"

Ketchum sat up and rubbed his swelling cheek absently, staring at nothing. He seemed mildly distressed. Gus sliced a length of leather from the tether of a dead man's horse and used it to bind Ketchum's wrists. As he tightened the knot, he looked into Ketchum's vacant stare.

"Paynter frightens you, don't he?"

He engaged Gus's eyes. "So what?"

"Why? You ride with some hardened men."

Ketchum chuckled. "Sure, but Paynter is the worst of the lot. You shoulda heard what he done outside Fayetteville before he turned coat. Sally told me all about it."

Stacy appeared abruptly and planted a boot in Ketchum's ribs, stealing his breath. "You'll not speak of Mr. Paynter. You're a liar, anyway."

The bandit eyed her defiantly. "Trusting him will be your last mistake, missy."

"Not that it matters now," said Lucien impatiently. "He's in the wind, and we have two months of trail ahead of us. McQuaid."

"Sir."

"Take Mr. Ketchum into custody. We'll haul him back with us to use as leverage should Sally return."

Ketchum laughed derisively. "You don't know Sally very well, then. He don't negotiate. Not even for his own kin."

Lucien appeared to ignore him. Muñoz motioned to one of the dead men. "Should we bury them?"

"Leave them where they lie," said Lucien. "As a warning to any others who mean us ill."

Muñoz shrugged and helped Evans lift Ketchum to his feet. As the three soldiers set about putting the prisoner atop his horse for the journey back north, Gus turned to find Stacy corralling one of the dead bandit's horses.

"Starting a herd, are ya?"

"Nope." She strung out the tether and mounted her calico with an adept leap that won his approval. "I'm going after the blacksmith and his wife and babe like I promised."

Gus didn't know Stacy very well, but he'd already come to recognize her don't-cross-me expression. He mounted up. "I'm comin' with ya, then."

"I don't need no nursemaid." Her tone was defiant, but her eyes spoke relief.

"Nevertheless." He looked to Lucien. "We'll catch up. Don't wait for us."

Lucien turned away. "I never intended to."

Gus and Stacy trotted north with the spare horse, settling into a comfortable pace and an uncomfortable silence. By God, she annoyed him sometimes. He glanced back over his shoulder to the prairie south of the creek, wondering if he'd ever see Paynter again in this life. He faced forward again, resigned. If he didn't, he hoped at least his friend would find freedom from those who wanted him dead and the demons that hounded his soul.

CHAPTER THIRTEEN

THE WORST KIND OF PREY ARE THOSE POSSESSING OF CLAW, fang, and horn. When they turn to fight, hunter and hunted alike are bound to suffer. This immutable fact honed the edge of Jake's determination to razor sharpness. Once Sally and his remaining man stopped running, someone was sure to die.

As the sun slipped toward the western reaches, Jake trailed at a distance, watching when he could see them, tracking when he couldn't. His quarry had opened up some breathing room with a burst of their horses, but had settled into a trot as their weary mounts lost a step. Jake didn't much care. He had two bullets left and intended to use them. He'd catch them this side of the Missouri River, one way or another.

When his mare stumbled and lunged, probably from a prairie dog hole, he threw his hands forward for balance. The manacles dug into his wrists, raw now from the incessant bounce of the ride, raising a curse to his lips. No matter how this ended, he swore to lose the irons, even if he had to fight someone to the death for that privilege. He looked up from his wrists to find the shadows growing long enough to give even the smallest of trees an acre's sway over the unbroken ground. Sally hadn't slowed his pace, so Jake continued to match it even as the sun's bloody orb vanished with a whisper. Darkness fell quickly until he lost sight of the ground beneath the mare. She stepped tentatively from shadow to shadow as if each might conceal an ankle-snapping steel trap. When she stumbled again, he reined her to a stop.

The conjoined outlines of two riders faded into darkness near a solitary tree in the distance. He marked the location of the tree in the map of his mind and slid from his horse into knee-high grass.

After a moment of disorientation, he crumpled to the earth still clutching the mare's reins. She tugged at them a few times before abandoning her complaint to forage on whatever was within reach. Too weary to sleep, Jake lay in a languid stupor while trying to remember who he was. The stupor eventually gave way to waves of fitful sleep punctuated by panicked awakenings to find that the ghosts were not really there, only to repeat the cycle. Sometime in the small hours of the night, his troubled mind and body called a wary truce and settled into a pitching slumber.

Jake woke with a start to a meadowlark's song, a bugle call unique in all creation. He pushed up from the dewy ground to find that his Kerr had replaced the mare's tether during the depths of night. He sat up to find her grazing calmly not twenty steps away, perhaps hoping he had died. He brushed grass and soil from his damp cheek and rose to stand. During his unconscious state, the sun had managed to traverse the far side of the world and was gaining on the eastern horizon. He rubbed his eyes and found the lone tree in the predawn gloom. The red haze, which had abated to a fine mist during the night, flowered again within him, demanding his lethal services. *Time to move, Paynter. Time to kill.*

The mare eyed him with disappointment as he approached. She stepped away when he attempted to mount, forcing him into a foot-hopping chase that culminated in a haphazard landing on the saddle horn. He leaned toward her flicking ear.

"Save your piss and vinegar for later. We'll need it."

He lined her up toward the solitary tree and urged her into a high-stepping trot. She huffed complaint but did as he asked. As the light grew, he nudged more speed from the mare until she settled into a loping gallop. From time to time, she'd turn one white-rimmed eye toward him as if to ask, "Are you sure about this?" Jake's answer remained the same every time. To be unsure was to beg an appearance of the Reaper and a final sentence.

Jake spotted his quarry before they saw him. He rode toward

the men with a steady revolver and high hopes of riding through their camp before they realized his presence. No such luck. Sally's remaining man raised a shout and fired a reckless shot in Jake's general direction. However, the death of his accomplices must have lain heavily on the man's mind for he leaped onto his horse without gathering his bedroll and fled. Sally followed within seconds. Jake held his fire. He needed to make his two bullets count, and blazing away atop a galloping horse was a sure recipe for wayward shots. As the mare thundered through the cold camp, Jake took the liberty of spitting on the abandoned bedroll, just for spite. Afterwards, he collapsed his world again to the narrow corridor of grassland separating him from the fleeing men and pushed the mare for more speed. She was undersized, but by Harry, she could run.

Sally's companion was the first to panic. After a dozen glances over his shoulder to find the gap closing, he wheeled his horse about and raised his rifle. Jake sent a bullet through his throat, rudely interrupting the man's attempt at homicide. He was still writhing in the grass and gasping his final breaths when Jake flew past. Suddenly bereft of his rider, the outlaw's horse fell in behind the mare, seemingly unable to abandon its headlong journey on such short notice. Jake snorted. Momentum was a powerful force, often outliving rational thought. He was well-acquainted with its effect on him, even if subconsciously. He'd been driven by it ever since fleeing from his cruel brothers, carried more by winds of fortune than by any grand design. Now, momentum propelled him along the Big Nemaha back toward Missouri in pursuit of a monster with hopes that his own monstrousness was up to the task.

An hour on, Sally's patience apparently snapped. Before Jake could contemplate the motion, Sally was turning in his saddle as his horse skidded to a sideways halt. Jake raised his Kerr to let loose his final shot as a puff of white smoke erupted from Sally's weapon. A blaze of fire lit Jake's left hip, dropping him into a leaning crouch.

Grimacing, he looked up to find Sally swearing and shaking the ruined hand that had stopped Jake's bullet short of his forehead. He cradled his rifle and grabbed the hand, cursing in agony.

"Dammit, Paynter! Look what you did!"

Sally slung the rifle over a shoulder, turned the mount one-handed, and resumed his run. When the mare began to follow, Jake stopped her. He was out of bullets and the fire in his hip finally screamed loud enough to garner his attention. He pressed the wound with his hand and brought it away soaked with blood. Even if he doubled back to retrieve the dead man's weapon, he'd bleed to death before catching Sally again. Sliding from the saddle with a grunting wince, he found the unattended stallion watching him with question, ears perked as if waiting for a reasonable explanation. Jake turned away to study the wound. Sally's shot had laced a six-inch channel along the top edge of his pelvis that seemed determined to leak every drop of blood from his body. Though it was not a shot to a vital organ, he had seen a dozen men expire of such wounds during the war, bleeding dry before needle and thread could be applied. The human body did not fare well when depleted of blood, and his was draining like a tumbled bucket. He removed his bandana and stuffed it into his pants over the wound. It was, however, a temporary measure. What he needed was a fire, and right quick.

As he limped toward the strange horse while pressing the wound, the animal became abruptly shy and began to step backwards in a slow-moving dance.

"Easy, boy. Easy. Not gonna hurt ya."

The stallion took him at his word and halted. Jake began rummaging through its saddlebags, praying for matches. He hadn't prayed in a long time, which made him feel like an unworthy prodigal, deserving of nothing. The bags held no matches, but God rewarded his brief show of piety with flint, steel, and a long knife. After collecting dry grass, twigs, and several sticks, Jake settled onto a bare spot along the bank of the river and began striking the flint with steel. Three dozen times he did so, even while his gaping wound bled unattended to soak his leg. No luck. He mopped his brow and tried again, knowing that to stop was to die. After another dozen strikes, the grass blazed to life. He lifted the wad of grass and gently breathed encouragement until it produced a respectable yellow flame. He set it down carefully and began adding grass, twigs, and finally sticks. By the time he pushed larger limbs into the hungry fire, spots had begun to float before his eyes and his fingers had grown cold. He set the blade of the knife into the flame, dropped his pants, and lay down beside the fire, willing himself not to fall asleep.

His thoughts drifted chaotically, a drunken sailor of reasoning. The mare's huff of breath on his face drew his eyes open. She glared at him with condemnation, reminding him that he was dying. He blinked into awareness and retrieved the knife. The handle was hot, but no match for the blade. With an intake of breath, he pressed the hot steel against the gash. A scream of ruined rage emerged from his chest, dissipating into a plaintive weep. He shook his head violently and brought his focus again to the wound. Blood still ran unabated from half of it. He set the blade back into the flame and clenched his fists in agony while counting.

"One, two, three…"

Upon reaching thirty, he pulled the blade again, scorching his fingers in the process. He curled his other hand into a fist, clenched his teeth, and pressed the knife again to the flowing wound. He expelled a string of screaming curses that melted into an agonized cry as he held the blade in place until the odor of burning flesh invaded his nostrils. When his hand began to shake violently, he lost the knife and collapsed to the soil with a defeated moan, certain of his final demise.

The meadowlark woke him for a second time that day. *Surely not the same one,* he thought while clawing up from the black pit of unconsciousness, *but wouldn't that be a grand notion if it were?* His eyes creased open to find himself unmoved since his self-inflicted medical procedure—cheek planted firmly in the dirt, hat crushed beneath his temple, raw manacled wrists lumped together at his waist, pants still around his knees. When he shifted his legs, his left hip stabbed him with an insistent reminder of its tortured state. With deliberate movements, Jake stumbled to his feet. The blood rushing from his head threatened to return him to the dirt, but he resolutely clung to balance until the vertigo passed. Both horses raised their heads from foraging in the tall grass beneath riverside trees, to regard him coolly. On determining that he was no longer a corpse, they returned to their respective tasks.

Jake inhaled a deep breath and twisted to examine his wound. As he expected, it was a pulpy disaster of the first order, a train wreck of mangled skin and dross. Morbid juices seeped from the mass of scorched flesh, but his life-sustaining blood seemed content to pass the wound by without seeking exit. He touched the wreckage, wincing as he did so. Stupid idea. Pulling up his breeches proved a daunting task. Blood from his wound had plastered the crumpled arrangement firmly to his left leg. He pried it loose, with each exertion eliciting a sharp complaint from his hip. When he managed to finish the job, he noted with disappointment the ruined nature of his breeches. Between twin bullet holes and a tub of blood, they weren't fit for mopping a dirt floor, let alone for traveling.

He rounded up the Kerr and the knife, flint, and steel, which lay scattered about the still-smoking fire where he'd discarded them one by one during his frantic act of self-preservation. With tools in hand, the momentum of the past twenty-four hours belched the last of its steam in a dying sputter. He froze like a neglected monument, staring vacantly into the far distance. Freedom lay beyond virtually any horizon. An hour in any direction and he would become a forgotten man, dissolved into the endless landscape to emerge from the chrysalis at his pleasure into a new existence.

A new existence. A new life. But what kind of life?

With yawning solitude beckoning, recent memories crowded in to shove it rudely aside. Gus's ridiculously persistent optimism in the face of relentless misfortune. Stacy's insistent interruption of his stubborn isolation. The Emshoff family's casual acceptance of him as a hero-in-waiting instead of a dangerous criminal. And Rosalyn, too-naive Rosalyn, who showed him the same courtesy she might offer a gentleman, as if not realizing the enormous gap between him and civility. The memories stirred to life the apocalyptic vision of the horror Sally would visit upon them after he returned with more men, firepower, and retribution.

"No."

The single word, discharged by latent emotions Jake had believed long dead, put his feet in motion. He collected both horses, stowed his collection of tools, and mounted the mare with a grimace and a curse. After tying the stallion's reins to the mare's saddle horn, he prodded his mount west along the Big Nemaha. With her belly full and a few hours of rest, she seemed less hostile than usual. Jake knew the feeling. He pulled a hunk of jerky from his saddlebag and began to chew, mapping in his mind the route that would return him to the wagon train. First, though, there was a dead man ahead who was no longer in need of his bedroll, rifle, or breeches. And Jake was not a man to disregard unexpected windfalls or proper pants.

CHAPTER FOURTEEN

STACY'S PLAN TO MATCH GUS SILENCE FOR SILENCE HELD FOR probably an hour before her annoyance rejected further waiting.

"Why'd you insist on coming, anyway?"

Gus flashed a wide grin that set the planes of his face into a pleasing geometry, not that she'd noticed. "Don't ya mean 'Thank you, Gus, I appreciate your company, Gus,' or somethin' resembling that?"

"No," she said with rising inflection, "I meant what I said. I bet you don't think I can handle this on my own."

"Not true."

"Then you probably just want a share of the credit for retrievin' those poor folks."

"Similarly untrue. You ain't so good at guessin' my thoughts, Miss Blue."

She huffed at him. "And why would I be? I barely know you. And stop callin' me Miss Blue, for land's sake."

He laughed and turned his eyes upon her. "I'll stop callin' you Miss Blue when you tell me what Stacy's short for."

"Never. It's just plain Stacy."

"Really?" Gus shook his head and tsked. "I thought for sure a man called Cornelius would think up a more extravagant name for his daughter. 'Plain Stacy' seems a mite mundane."

She gave him her best death stare. "It's Stacy. Nothin' more."

"As you wish, Miss Blue."

She gritted her jaw and stared ahead. If he weren't so handsome, she'd spit in his eye. As it was, he might be digging out a wad of sputum before the day was over. "You never answered my question. Why'd you come?"

"For the pleasant company, of course. And I stand by that, despite yer best intentions to deprive me of such."

"Doesn't 'pleasant company' cut both ways? Or am I just a trained circus bear here for your amusement?"

"You do amuse me, Miss Blue. That I admit."

And so it went for mile upon mile, Stacy trying to pick a squabble with Gus but mostly failing. In the meantime, she managed to share with him something of her life since the age of seven, riding one wagon train after another with her father for twelve years. Some to California. Some to Oregon. Some to the wilderness of the various territories. Though she loved the excitement of the slow-moving trains of prairie schooners, it was the rides back to Missouri that pleased her most. They would return to the Wind River country, to the Shoshone people of her mother. Sometimes they'd stay a week, other times all winter. Her grandfather taught her to ride—truly ride—and tan hides, chip flint, and hunt the elusive antelope. The Shoshone women would wag their tongues, accusing her grandfather of raising a boy. He would always counter with simple logic. "I am making a Shoshone," he would say. "Mind your own lodge."

Only after spilling her closely guarded memories did she regret her runaway mouth. However, Gus made for an easy listener. He just nodded and smiled, as if he knew something she had clearly missed. In return for her candor, he spoke of his days in Alabama chopping cotton from sunup to sundown since early childhood. Of the community of the enslaved, of their customs and solidarity. He didn't mention what happened after. Though curiosity ate at her, she couldn't bring herself to let go of her feigned disinterest to probe further. He was singing her an old spiritual from his childhood when the last verse died in his throat. He raised a finger toward the horizon.

"There, I reckon."

Stacy craned her neck to spy the scavenged wagon in the

distance, rotting in the hollow below a grassy ridge. As they approached, the giant reappeared with his hammer, a latter-day Thor guarding his tiny, wrecked kingdom. When Stacy raised a hand in greeting, a smile split his face.

"The wee lass has returned!" he called out. The utter surprise on his face was unmistakable. She halted her calico and vaulted from the saddle.

"As promised."

"I'm pleased you're not shot."

"As am I."

Maddie emerged from behind the wagon with the babe in arms. The little girl watched Stacy with cautious interest, perhaps hoping for another round of biscuits.

"This here's Gus Rivers," Stacy said as he dismounted to join her. Gus offered the blacksmith a hand and the Scotsman shook it heartily.

"Glen Dunbar. Maddie, my wife, and baby Lily."

Gus touched the brim of his hat and dipped his forehead. "Ma'am."

Stacy noticed that Maddie wore a similar expression of surprised relief, and chuckled. "You seem mighty astonished to see us."

The woman blushed. "I suppose we are. After what happened before, my faith in human decency has suffered a blow." Then she smiled. "But I have never been more pleased to be wrong."

"And look," said Stacy while waving to the extra horse. "We've a fine stallion to pull your cart in your stead. Unless you prefer to do the luggin.'"

Glen laughed heartily. "I accept your kind offer, lass. I'm a large man, but your horse makes six of me. He'll put to shame my feeble efforts."

"Is your cart ready for travel, then?" asked Gus.

"Let us hope."

Gus helped Glen put his hope to the test as the two of them muscled the heavy anvil into the cart while Stacy strapped the rigging to the spare horse. Glen had reconstituted the wagon straps into a harness that draped over the horse's back while suspending a pair of tongues on either side of the animal. The tongues were wrapped in canvas strips from the bonnet to prevent wood and leather from abrading the horse's sides. She finished to find Gus and Glen bent double with hands on knees, gasping from the exertion. Gus raised a finger without looking up.

"How much…" He inhaled another breath. "…does that thing weigh?"

"Twenty-one stone," said Glen.

"In American."

"Three hundred pounds."

"Land o' Goshen. That's a load."

Glen stood up to put his hands atop his head. "We're lucky I traded the four hundred pounder for the smaller one in St. Louis."

With demonstrations of virile manhood completed, Gus and Glen began loading less burdensome tools of the blacksmith trade onto the cart. Stacy followed Maddie to retrieve the rest of their baggage from beneath the ruined wagon. It wasn't much—some clothing, meager food supplies, one half-empty sack of cornmeal, and cooking implements. While Stacy moved most of it to the cart, Maddie retrieved a large black leather bag and lugged it from the wagon with one hand while clutching Lily in the other.

"What's in the bag?" Stacy said.

Maddie smiled obtusely. "A collection of just-in-cases."

"Weapons?"

"Oh, no." She laughed. "We don't carry guns."

"No?"

"Glen swore off them after the war."

Stacy cocked her head. "What could you do if someone means you harm?"

She laughed again. "Have you not seen my husband when he wields his hammer?"

"Yeah," said Stacy with a smile. "I guess I see your point."

With everything the Dunbars possessed settled onto the makeshift cart's platform, Glen and Gus covered it with another section of canvas bonnet and began securing the material with a chaotic assortment of rope and leather raided from the bones of the wagon.

"Think she'll hold?" asked Gus.

Glen stood tall, seeming to scrape the sky, and held up his palms. "I built her with these two hands. She'll hold for a thousand miles."

"Undiluted confidence is a beauty to behold," said Gus. "But before we put her to the test, you should christen this here ship."

Glen pursed his lips and looked to Maddie. She gazed at the cart, her eyes going soft. "We should call her *Reliance*. For we relied on the word of a good stranger to rescue us, and we must now rely on this cart to transport us to a new life."

Glen smiled and nodded agreement. "*Reliance* it is, then."

With vessel named, Stacy and Glen boosted Maddie astride the calico and handed up Lily.

"She's the swiftest horse west of the Mississippi," said Stacy, "but I'll lead her to keep her from takin' flight. We'll set an ambitious pace. With luck, we'll catch our expedition before dusk tomorrow, assumin' they leave without us. Which I reckon they will."

Maddie's eyes filled with tears. "Thank you, Miss Blue. You've restored my soul."

"It's nothin'."

"How come she gets to call you Miss Blue but I can't?"

"Shut up, Gus Rivers."

He smiled again in that way she wished he wouldn't. "We take turns riding the buckskin, me, you, and Mr. Dunbar."

"No need. I can walk."

"Just say 'thank you,' Miss Blue."

"You wish."

The motley party set forth toward the west with *Reliance* in tow as the sun reached its daily zenith. Stacy led the way with tether in hand. For some reason, she felt ten feet tall.

CHAPTER FIFTEEN

THE STIR OF ANXIOUS VOICES ROLLED UP THE TRAIN TOWARD the lead wagon until Rosalyn turned to explore the reason for it. Families walking alongside their rigs pointed southeast with agitated concern. She swiveled her gaze to scan a prairie so flat, a person could see all the way to St. Louis if not for the dust. Her darting eyes came to rest on a lone rider approaching in the distance, leading a second horse. One of Sally's men?

"Rosalyn," said Lucien from her side. "Fetch my rifle."

She hesitated before retrieving his weapon from the jockey box and taking it to him. He lifted the rifle to peer down the sight at the rider.

"Who is he?"

"Can't tell yet."

Two minutes passed as the traveler gained on the now-halted train, when suddenly the Emshoff children began jumping up and down with ear-piercing squeals. Rosalyn instinctively strode toward the rear of the train, compelled by disbelief. The reports of Paynter's departure had come as little surprise, given his death sentence. Surely he wouldn't blithely surrender his newfound freedom. She joined the Emshoffs and soldiers as the wayward prisoner approached, his wrists still draped in irons.

"Herr Paynter," Mr. Emshoff called with astonishment. "You have returned."

Paynter stopped his horse and eased from his saddle with grunts of pain. He leaned his head against the saddlebag briefly before facing the collected group of settlers and soldiers. "I brought back an extra horse. The rider had no further use for it."

Rosalyn blinked with dawning surprise. Paynter had returned of his own volition, despite knowing that a rope likely awaited him at the end of the journey. But why? He had nothing to gain, but his very life to lose. McQuaid saved her from asking the too-invasive question.

"Why the heck'd you come back?" said the corporal. "We figured you was halfway to Mexico by now."

Paynter stared at McQuaid, seemingly confused by the question. "I've been asking myself the same for two days."

"What's going on?" Lucien's disapproval interrupted the stilted reunion as he sailed with fury into the conversation. "What happened out there?"

Paynter handed the horses to Privates Muñoz and Evans and limped forward toward the group, clutching a hip with one hand.

"You're injured," said Rosalyn with concern as she reached toward him. Lucien yanked her back, raising her ire. He ignored her malicious glare.

"Explain what happened, Paynter. Do not leave us guessing."

"Can I get some water first? Throat's parched from the ride."

Three farmers rushed to offer him canteens. He took a long draught from one, wiped his mouth with the back of a sleeve, and closed the container before returning it to his eager benefactor. He yanked a thumb over his shoulder.

"Three of 'em cut out from Muddy Creek, but you already knew that. I gave pursuit. I felled the first one just a couple of miles out. But the other two kept movin', one of 'em Sally."

Paynter relayed the rest of the story with blunt detachment, reporting the events as if a casual bystander rather than a critical participant. The chase into the night. The conflict at dawn that downed another bandit. The final encounter with Sally.

"I failed to bring Sally down and he escaped." His conclusion dripped with disappointment. "And he laced me good with a lead plum." Paynter touched his hip to show where he'd been hit. "Just a flesh wound, though. I collected what supplies I could and came back."

Lucien, who had been listening with folded arms, dropped

them to his side. "Why'd you return, then? You had horses, weapons, supplies, and a two-day head start."

Paynter glanced at Rosalyn and held her eyes before allowing his to fall away. "Because of what's coming."

"What's coming?" said Rosalyn.

He faced the east. "The Devil on horseback with all his minions."

"Explain," spat Lucien.

"You don't know Sally. The man would walk a mile on hot coals to exact retribution for the smallest slight, and he knows no compassion. We thwarted his attempt to rob this train. We obliterated his entire party and sent him packin', short a finger or two. He'll be back, and with a vengeance. He'll bring as many men as he can convince, buy, or threaten, and enough firepower to flatten a brigade. I expect two dozen men. They won't leave us alone until none are left breathing."

When Paynter faced the group again, he must have seen the panicked distress painted on every face. Settlers mumbled fearful dismay while exchanging terrified glances. He held forth his hands, still connected by a length of chain.

"I know it sounds like the end of all things, and I apologize for my frankness. But we need not tuck our tails and wait for the inevitable. We need not cower like rabbits in a warren."

Mr. Emshoff stepped forward. "Are you suggesting we can fight them?"

Paynter nodded with an amused smile. "I suppose I am. Which is why I came back."

"So you can fight them?"

"Yes," he said. "And so I can teach all of you to fight them. Our only hope lies in numbers and superior strategy."

Lucien waved his hands. "Do you actually believe a band of farmers can stave off the remnants of a Civil War raiding party for weeks on end?"

"I do. So long as Sally doesn't bring more men than we can repel. And so long as we can wear down their numbers until most turn back. Then we tackle what remains with what's left of us."

"We're with you," said Roberson as he approached to plant a hand on Paynter's shoulder. The action released a dam of restraint. Within seconds, two dozen men and women mobbed Paynter to offer their belief. Lucien's hand on Rosalyn's elbow was the only impediment that prevented her from joining the huddle. In the midst of the well-intentioned horde, Paynter seemed desperately uncomfortable, a trapped wolf searching wildly for an avenue of escape. Lucien dispersed the gathering by releasing her elbow and wading in to stand six feet from Paynter.

"Corporal, relieve the prisoner of his weapon and return him to the rear."

McQuaid failed to move, his jaw setting grimly.

"No," said Paynter. "I'm finished with the manacles. If you insist that I wear them, then shoot me now. I will not take another step in these irons."

Before Lucien could erupt, McQuaid stepped in to Paynter with the key and unlocked the manacles. After they fell away into the soldier's hands, Paynter rubbed his wrists one at a time.

"I did not give you permission to do that, soldier," said Lucien.

"With all due respect, sir, he is my prisoner, not yours. Besides, we need these for Ketchum instead."

Paynter narrowed his eyes. "Ketchum is here?"

"He was leg-shot at Muddy Creek. We brought him back."

"For what?"

"To use as leverage if Sally shows up again."

Paynter frowned and shook his head slowly. "You shoulda left him to die. Now, you have a snake in your cabin, and he'll bite you the moment you turn your back. And Sally? He doesn't care a lick for anyone. He's a man accustomed to destroying the innocent without a second thought. Imagine his disregard for the guilty."

Lucien grunted. "By your own admission, aren't you no different?"

Paynter's eyes grew hooded. "I never grew accustomed to it."

Rosalyn wondered what he meant by his remark. What he'd done, and why. Her good sense told her to leave well enough alone, to give Paynter a wide berth. At the moment, though, she was a poor pupil. She detected in Paynter a spark of something good, perhaps even spectacular. She was determined to explore it, unearth it, maybe help it grow.

"One more condition," said Paynter to Lucien and McQuaid. "I keep my Kerr and the Henry rifle I picked up."

Lucien shook his head violently. "Not possible. You're a killer."

"I am. And other killers will be comin' with the sole intent of murdering this entire party—men, women, and children. You need a killer on your side, Ashley. And you need one armed to the teeth."

Lucien stewed for a bit while glaring at Paynter. Then he addressed McQuaid. "Very well. He is your prisoner and your problem now, Corporal. If he causes anyone grief, I will make your life utter misery when we arrive at Fort Bridger."

McQuaid bowed up. "Heard and understood, sir."

As Lucien retreated past Rosalyn, he yanked her arm to drag her away.

"Would you unhand me?" she said with affront. He ignored her protest until they had walked well away from the knot of humanity toward their wagon.

"Listen to me, Rosalyn. We still have time to escape this nightmare."

"What are you saying?"

"If we cut loose an ox or two, we can load them with the most important valuables and slip away in the night. We can ride double on my horse until I might purchase another."

Rosalyn stared at her brother aghast. How had she so effectively missed his slide into complete self-absorption? "You're suggesting we abandon these people to Sally and his men? To save ourselves?"

"Exactly."

She ripped her arm from his grasp and stood with hands on hips, a new Colossus of Rhodes standing firm over the Nebraska prairie. "I will not. You can flee if it suits you, but I will remain. I will fight. Your horde of gold cannot buy my soul, Lucien, as it has apparently purchased yours."

His eyes went wide briefly. "You put your trust in the wrong man, little sister. It will be your undoing."

When he stomped away, Rosalyn was left to consider his claim. With some regret, she failed to dismiss it as impossible.

CHAPTER SIXTEEN

PAYNTER'S HANDS SEEMED TO FLOAT, LIGHT AS FEATHERS NOW free of the irons. He found the need to reeducate their fine movements as he cleaned his Kerr after they'd set up camp for the evening beside the first three trees he had seen all day. The Emshoff children leaned over his shoulder with whispered interest, apparently fascinated by the disassembly and reassembly of the piece.

"What's that?" said the littlest one, whom everyone called "Lisbet" and usually with a bit of pique.

"A hammer."

"Doesn't look like a hammer."

"That's what it's called. I didn't think up the name."

"And what's that?"

"Cylinder."

"Silly what?"

Her older brother, Otto, patted her head. "Cylinder, silly goose."

"Oh."

Such was Paynter's lot until riders came up from the south. Even with the dimming light, he recognized the distinctive calico and buckskin belonging to Stacy and Gus, respectively, although the rider of the calico wore a dress. He stood and ambled into the encompassing grass to meet them. When Stacy, who had been leading her horse, saw him, she dropped the tether and ran toward him with a chaotic jumble of hops, skips, and whoops.

"Paynter! You came back!" He winced, sure she would try to embrace him. However, she veered aside at the last second, circled him, and landed facing him, dancing backward to match his steps. "Well, I'll be dipped. You came back."

"Seems so."

The wonderment of her expression gave way to right proper chagrin. "Wait. Why'd you come back?"

"Hold your horses. I don't want to explain it more'n once."

When the colliding parties met, Gus raised a hand before shaking Paynter's. He held the handshake while turning over Paynter's wrist and cocking one eyebrow. "No irons?"

Jake grinned. "My terms for staying."

Gus grunted intrigue, released his hand, and waved toward the newcomers. "We found our wayward souls. That's Maddie Dunbar and baby Lily up there, and this here's Glen Dunbar, blacksmith-at-large. And he brought his very own twenty-one-stone anvil."

Paynter assessed the strapping young man whose shirt strained to contain his muscled shoulders. He looked the part of one who pounded a hammer against iron from sunup to sundown. In the cavalry, every troop of ninety-five carried along at least two farriers who handled shoeing and other light smithing needs while on the range. Such men were worth their weight in gold. Jake extended a hand and paid for it with a couple of crushed fingers.

"Jake Paynter."

"Glen Dunbar. Pleased to make your acquaintance."

The Scottish accent brought back memories of his grandmother, the woman who'd raised him until she passed before his sixth birthday. She talked like that.

"You built this cart?"

Dunbar lifted his chin with pride. "I did, sir."

"Well done. And don't call me 'sir.' We're about the same age, and unlike me, you possess important skills. Just Paynter will do."

Jake turned to walk alongside the man as they resumed the final steps toward the Emshoff wagon. "Can you fight?"

Dunbar cut his eyes at Jake. "I'm done with firearms, if that's what you mean. Had enough of that during the war."

"Union?"

"Eleventh Pennsylvania Infantry. And you?"

"First Kansas Colored Volunteers. That's where I met Gus. Blackburn's Raiders before that."

Dunbar grunted. "Never heard of Blackburn."

"Confederate."

The man's brows shot up. "Ah."

They walked in silence for a moment before Dunbar turned to him. "I may not be keen on guns these days, but I can wrestle a bull if I have to."

Jake chuckled lightly. "There may be call for that before this is over."

Seconds later, the cart rolled up on the Emshoff wagon, which still formed the butt-end of the train.

"Lisbet," said Jake. "Put down the revolver."

The little girl complied while Otto and the other sister, Dora, elbowed her with I-told-you-so expressions. Mr. and Mrs. Emshoff came around from the far side of the wagon to meet the newcomers. Within thirty seconds, Mr. Emshoff had invited the Dunbars to camp with them all the way to the Idaho Territory.

"I don't know," said Maddie, now dismounted. "It would be an awful inconvenience to you."

Mrs. Emshoff's hands found her hips. "Wie sagst du das auf Englisch? We…insist."

She nodded firmly one time in the universal code for *It has been decided, so let it be done.*

The Dunbars offered effusive thanks and worked out the logistics for transporting four children and two families' worth of stuff between a wagon and a horse-drawn cart. Jake had his hand-me-down bedroll from the dead bandit, so he was content to sleep in the open or settle beneath the Emshoff wagon when the heavens spat rain.

By the time negotiations concluded, a mob had crowded around the wagon. Soldiers, Lucien and Rosalyn, Cornelius, the

Robersons and Savoys, and a dozen others Jake could not yet name. As only the worst of friends could do, Gus thrust Jake onto center stage and told him to dance.

"What's the plan, Paynter? I assume that's why you came back."

"What makes you think I have a plan?"

Gus laughed loudly. "You always got a plan. Sometimes it's short on details and other times downright horrifying. But you always got one. Let's hear it. Everybody's waitin.'"

Gus folded his arms and grinned, no doubt fully aware of Jake's dislike of attention. He glanced at Lucien to find him ready to shut down the entire assembly. Jake sighed heavily.

"Well, Holy Christmas. All right. But you asked for it." He leaned his back against the wagon's sideboard to spare his hip unnecessary agitation. "To start, this crew stands little chance against the wrath of Sally and his gang of cutthroats. Let's get that perfectly straight."

Many nodded, startled. Good. He had their attention.

"We, however, have numbers. By my count, maybe thirty men who can fight..." He held up a palm to Stacy, who was working up a protest. "And a decent number of women who can pull a trigger as well as any man. Some better." He nodded at Stacy, mollifying her for the moment. "Maybe forty fightin' adults, then. We also have a respectable number of rifles, muskets, revolvers, knives, hammers, pitchforks, and cast-iron cooking implements. Anything that can be fired, swung, stuck, or thrown is a weapon. We got plenty, I'm thinkin'. What we lack, we can make more of. Spears, pikes, and the like. We need to assess our ammunition, though. Firearms without fire are no better than clubs."

McQuaid lifted a hand. "I wasn't supposed to say nothin', but desperate times. We got two kegs of black powder and a thousand rounds of shot packed into Savoy's wagon—multiple calibers, half in paper cartridges. And plenty of wadding and percussion caps to boot. The U.S. Army paid him eighteen dollars transport fee, and he agreed not to smoke any tobacco in his rig for the duration of the trip."

Jake's smile overflowed its well-maintained banks before he brought it under control. "You're a hero among men, Corporal."

McQuaid ducked his head with a grin. Jake slapped a palm twice against the wagon behind him.

"We also got eighteen fortresses on wheels. Though they ain't walls of stone with guard towers and boiling oil and moats, their wooden planks can provide cover and create a perimeter difficult to penetrate. And we have seventeen horses, which means we can saddle up our own little cavalry."

As Jake ticked off their list of military assets, every face brightened. Except for Lucien's, but his skeptical scowl faded a few degrees. Jake inhaled a deep breath to drop the bad news.

"None of it," he said with a cavalry lieutenant's authority, "is worth spit unless we know how to use it properly. And right now, we don't know our head from our tail."

His audience grew restless, exchanging worried glances and perhaps growing agitated by Jake's whipsaw explanation. He spared them the agony while throwing down a faded gauntlet.

"Our job, then, is to rectify our shortfalls as best we can. Way I figure, Sally'll need several days to attend to his wound, collect his men, and outfit 'em. Then he'll need to run along our trail for a while at twice our speed to catch us. Meanwhile, we keep moving west at a hard pace to open up distance. That gives us about ten days, maybe twelve, before he shows up on our flank. And he'll bring at least three times his previous force."

He let the daunting numbers circulate through collective minds before continuing.

"We have that much time, then, to turn a bunch of civilians into a military troop. Nothing less stands a chance."

"McQuaid can make the necessary arrangements," said Lucien. "He's the ranking soldier, after all."

Every eye turned to Lucien, regarded him as if he'd just pro-claimed himself Queen of England, and then turned to face Paynter again. Mr. Emshoff nodded at him.

"Where do we start, Herr Paynter?"

Before he could answer, Lucien moved to the center of the group. "You can't put a federal prisoner in charge of this. That's madness."

Emshoff glared at him coolly. "Herr Ashley. One does not send a sheep to kill the wolverine. One sends a wolf."

Rosalyn tugged on Lucien's sleeve. "It is what we must do. Surely, even you can see that."

Lucien exhaled an exaggerated breath. "If we must. However, if this affair spirals into tragedy, we have only this decision to blame."

Jake shook his head, smiling wryly. "Don't fool yourself, Ashley. This is already a tragedy. We're just tryin' to cover it with enough frosting to make it palatable."

CHAPTER SEVENTEEN

EVERY ENDURING CIVILIZATION IN HISTORY HAD LEARNED that an effective defense begins with the building of a walled fortress. In the absence of brick and mortar, the prairie schooners were the answer. Every night for at least the next ten days, the settlers would need to practice building a makeshift fortress from their wagons as rapidly as possible. A sudden arrival of the enemy would leave no time to stake out a circle in advance and then fill it with slow-moving vehicles. To that end, Jake rode up and down the line all day, wagon by wagon, providing detailed instructions to the owners about what they would do at day's end when he gave the signal to circle up. The farmers listened carefully and nodded understanding, threatening Jake with a false sense of security. He knew better, though. The gap between understanding and experience is measured in miles, not inches.

"They ready for this?" asked Cornelius as he rode alongside Jake just ahead of the Ashleys' lead wagon.

Jake shielded his eyes against the sun, which was drawing very low on the horizon. "What do you think?"

Cornelius heaved the remnants of his tobacco twenty feet off the trail. "Nah. I predict the grandfather of all fiascos."

Jake wanted to disagree, but his good sense was nodding too hard to do so. "This far enough, then?"

Cornelius squinted at the sun and then scanned the landscape. He spurred his horse off to the right. "I believe this will do. Loose the hounds, Mr. Paynter."

"Check your watch."

Cornelius examined his gold pocket watch. "Seven-oh-four precisely."

Jake pulled his revolver from his recently recovered holster and fired two shots overhead. According to his instructions, the first nine wagons were to reach Jake and cut an immediate ninety-degree right turn. The first five would pass Cornelius's horse and make another sharp right turn. Meanwhile, the last four wagons in the train would wait until the train halted and then make a ninety-degree right turn as well, and meet the lead wagon as they came together. The resulting formation would make an approximate box shape. Finally, each owner would steer their respective oxen alongside the adjacent wagon at the last second to draw the rigs as near to one another as possible, head to butt. Though the animals would be stuck together like blackberry jam, it was the simplest formation possible, and merely a starting exercise in the following of instructions and the guiding of rigs.

That was not at all what happened.

Ashley's Conestoga and the next wagon made decent turns around Jake. The third, however, nearly ran him over as it cut the angle. The next two followed suit, while the sixth swung too wide and doubled back on the seventh to compensate. To avoid a collision, the seventh wagon circled to the right until meeting the eighth, whereupon all three ground into a nose-to-tail stalemate. Meanwhile, the remaining wagons kept coming at a breakneck pace, driven by the panic of those who respond to change by refusing to alter course. One after another, the trailing rigs peeled off to the right and left to avoid smashing their oxen into the seven-eight-nine logjam. At some point, the four that were supposed to form the bottom of the box decided they had waited long enough and turned sharply, but in the opposite direction before realizing their mistake and swerving back toward the train.

When the dust settled and each rig ground to a necessary halt, Jake surveyed the damage. Thirteen wagons had created an island of knotted mayhem with teams of oxen facing in all cardinal directions. Some were trapped entirely inside larger loops. The remaining five that had been leading the train formed a similar knot some thirty yards distant, less entangled but fully exposed, nonetheless. Jake put his face in his palm and muttered words typically reserved for the worst of occasions. He looked up as Cornelius arrived at his side.

"A fiasco, as I predicted."

"How long'd it take?"

Cornelius checked his watch. "Eighteen minutes."

A dam of frustration broke inside Jake. He rode to a spot equidistant between the two islands of stranded vessels and waved his arms. "Everybody! Come here! Right! Now!"

Forty or so adults and a few children shuffled away from the wagons to mill around him. Most wore sheepish expressions. When they had gathered, Jake peered down from the mare at the assembled group and shook his head.

"I honestly don't know what to say. If we had practiced for a month to make the most intractable mess possible, I don't believe we could've done better than this." He lifted his arms in opposing directions to indicate the two piles. Most eyes found the dirt.

"How long again, Mr. Blue?"

"Eighteen minutes."

"Eighteen minutes," he repeated, "to render this entire expedition unfit for travel. Damned impressive!"

He let their shame hang in the silent breeze for ten seconds. Then he exhaled a loud breath. "If we are to survive what's comin', we need to form up within three minutes. Our box must be absolute perfection, with no gap bigger than what a horse can jump through single file. This…" He waved his hands again toward the wrecks. "Is how we all die."

His audience stared at their collective feet, thoroughly cowed. Even Lucien. Satisfied that he had made his point, Jake clapped his hands together and gathered calm. "Look at me."

They glanced up as if children expecting a visit to the woodshed.

He forced his frown to recede as best he could. "I shoulder the blame for this. Perhaps I was too sloppy in my instructions. Maybe I was too lofty in my expectations. So, tomorrow I'll do better. And I expect the same of you." He looked to Cornelius and Stacy. "Go help 'em sort out their rigs without someone getting crushed. Form up some kind of perimeter so we can corral the horses."

"On it," said Cornelius.

Jake prodded the mare out of harm's way and watched the untangling of wagons and oxen with dismay. Ten days was not enough. Before he could descend into a morass of hopelessness, Gus rode up alongside him.

"Not too bad."

Jake peered at him with incredulity. "Pardon? Not too bad?"

"Nobody died. No oxen were injured. Everybody tried. Not too bad."

Jake snorted. "We got no chance." Gus peered at him until Jake met his eyes. "What?"

"Remember how we was in '62 when the regiment formed? Black soldiers, white officers, and only you and a few others with any actual fightin' experience? Remember that?"

Jake did. What a collection of misfits they all made—men escaped from slavery, poverty, marginality, brutality, or all of the above, and a junior officer straight out of the Confederacy with a new blue coat and not a foggy notion of how to lead men. He remembered his hopeless dismay at the time, so akin to his present emotion. Two months later, they had defeated a larger force in their first engagement, the model of discipline under fire. Jake chuckled.

"Yep. I do. Thanks, Gus."

"That's my job now. Keepin' your head straight."

"A thankless job, to be sure."

"You know it."

———————

"Ketchum's wound is festering."

The grim assessment from Muñoz drew Jake's attention from his humble supper at the Emshoff wagon that had been tangled with another until a half hour earlier. The soldier stood framed against the remains of the day, blue sky fading into gold behind his suspendered shoulders. Jake nodded at him from his seat in the grass. For once, he just wanted to eat supper in peace without having to solve a problem.

"You gotta take the ball out," Jake said. "Or hack off the leg. Otherwise, it'll kill him soon enough."

"I'll do it."

Jake looked up to find Maddie Dunbar hovering. He stood and brushed off the seat of his breeches. "You will? You've done this before?"

"Not exactly, but I've seen it done a hundred times in field hospitals and on battlefields."

Realization hit Jake. "You were a nurse."

"Still am."

Glen stepped up beside his wife and draped a large arm over her slender shoulders. "That's how I met her. At Gettysburg. There I was, lying in a bloody row with a thousand other wounded, waiting for treatment or last rites, thinking I'd never rise from that cursed ground. Then I saw her." He looked down at his wife with eyes misting. She returned his gaze and hugged his arm. "An angel on earth, drifting from man to man to offer a tourniquet, a suture, a comforting word. When she came to me, I vowed I'd never let her go."

"And he didn't. We exchanged addresses and found each other after the war."

Glen pinned Jake with an earnest gaze. "If she says she can, then she can."

Mrs. Emshoff, who had been apparently trying to follow the conversation, waded in. "Ich helfen. I help."

The German woman folded her arms to brook no disagreement. Jake nodded. "Right. Let's go do this, then. Gus?"

"Yep."

"You, Glen, and Mr. Emshoff can hold him down while Mrs. Dunbar and Frau Emshoff do the work."

"He ain't gonna like it."

"Don't much care."

After Maddie retrieved her mysterious leather bag, the makeshift medical team made their way to the wagon belonging to the Flanagans, an older couple whose children had died of disease or violence one by one during the war. Mr. Flanagan couldn't hear anything less than a bolt of lightning striking his head and Mrs. Flanagan talked incessantly. Taking on Ketchum as an unwilling guest had been a boon to Mrs. Flanagan, for now she knew her conversation was not wasted. When Jake peered into the wagon's bed, he saw Ketchum shackled to a tiny bare spot on the floor, curled into a ball and drenched with sweat. The outlaw spied Jake and smirked.

"Come to see the caged animal?"

Jake ignored him. "Gus, Glen. Lay him out on a blanket in the grass."

As they removed Ketchum from the wagon, Maddie went to work boiling water on the Flanagans' fire and setting out instruments while Mrs. Emshoff patted down the grass and laid out a blanket. Stacy, who had ambled up for the show, watched Maddie. "Where'd you get those doctor tools?"

"Doctor Nathan Green from the field hospital gave them to me when he retired after the war. He said if I was going west, I'd need them."

"They look downright dangerous."

Maddie laughed. "They are, in the wrong hands."

Ketchum complained as they moved him, not quite

understanding what was about to happen. When they laid him flat and Glen began removing Ketchum's pants, the bandit understood.

"Git yer hands off me!"

"No, sir," Glen said as he yanked the breeches painfully away from the wound in Ketchum's thigh. "The lead must come out."

Ketchum swiveled his head side to side, perhaps looking for a doctor. "Who's gonna do it?"

"Mrs. Dunbar," said Jake. "With help from Mrs. Emshoff while Mr. Dunbar, Gus, and Mr. Emshoff pin you down."

His face grew an expression of incredulity. "You're lyin'!"

"Afraid not."

Ketchum hugged his chest and shook his head. "I ain't being tended to by a couple o' women, a negro, and a mob of fer'ners. Won't have it."

Jake smiled menacingly. "Good. We'll do it my way, then."

"What's your way?"

"I'm gonna hack off your leg with a tree saw."

Ketchum swallowed hard and looked at his would-be doctors again. "I suppose just this once. But don't never tell no one."

He fidgeted while Maddie and Mrs. Emshoff boiled cloth, horsehair sutures, and a pair of bullet forceps.

"Ready now," Maddie said. "Hold him tight. He's bound to pitch a fit."

Glen pinned the man's arms to the grass above his head while Gus and Emshoff each sat astride a leg. Maddie inhaled deeply and plunged the forceps into the wound. Ketchum screamed murder and arched his back while Gus and Emshoff rode legs that thrashed like a pair of unbroken broncs. The frenetic motion forced Maddie to dig around inside the wound while Mrs. Emshoff mopped away blood until Ketchum passed out. Within seconds, she produced the lead ball with a wide smile.

"There we have it." She set aside the slug and forceps to retrieve a curved needle and horsehair thread.

"Pinch it tight," she said to Mrs. Emshoff while demonstrating. The woman nodded and squeezed the ragged edges of the wound together. She had clearly done it before. With adept movements, Maddie sealed the wound with a suture while Stacy watched on with amazement.

"I'll be dinged. You're fast."

"I had lots of practice."

When she finished, the men loaded Ketchum back into the wagon and shackled him again to the floor. Jake watched with a smirk. "I think I prefer Ketchum best when he's passed out."

When Jake hopped down, his hip lodged a formal complaint. Maddie saw him grimace. "Let's see it, then."

Jake considered ignoring her, but Glen loomed behind his wife with eyebrows raised in challenge. He sighed and pulled his breeches down at the hip. She probed the wound with a light touch before engaging his eyes.

"You did well, Mr. Paynter. It would've killed you for sure." She stepped away to retrieve a bottle from her sorceress's bag. "Apply this to the wound in the morning and evening."

"What is it?"

"A magician never tells. Just do as I say. Or I can have Glen do it for you."

The right side of Jake's mouth lifted in a half grin. "I can manage, Doc. Thanks."

As he made his way back to his bedroll in the shadow of the Emshoff wagon, he spun the small brown bottle in his hand. It had been a long time since anyone had given him a gift.

CHAPTER EIGHTEEN

GUS HAD LIVED LONG ENOUGH TO RECOGNIZE A POISONOUS snake when he saw one. Ketchum was every bit a timber rattler, coiled up and waiting for the right moment to strike. When it came to the crawling kind, you either stayed out of its way or cut off and buried the head. He supported the former but prepared himself for the latter.

"He's gotta go," Gus said to the huddle of lingerers. The fade of day left every face in shadow. Stacy nodded agreement while Glen frowned. The big Scotsman hadn't seen Ketchum in action, so he didn't know the mortal danger of carrying him along, chained or otherwise.

"We can't very well abandon an injured man in the middle of nowhere," said Glen. "It doesn't seem proper."

Stacy folded her arms. "'Course we can. He'll turn on us first chance he gets as sure as I'm standin' here. I say we give 'em the extra horse and three days' supply of food and send him on his way. It'd be more consideration than he woulda given us if we hadn't handed his gang their proper comeuppance at Muddy Creek."

Glen was seemingly considering Stacy's plan when Lucien finally had enough. "No. He stays. If Sally shows up, we need all the poker chips we can muster."

Gus knew in his gut that Lucien was dead wrong. Sally wouldn't care an iota about Ketchum. He was the sort of man who expected absolute loyalty from others but offered none in return. "So you don't believe Paynter, then?"

"Not as far as I can spit. He's a killer who will hang when we reach Fort Bridger. He'll do anything to spare himself that fate, even lie or deceive those who know him best."

When Lucien pinned him with an accusatory glare, Gus began gathering up a heated response. A loud call interrupted his attempt.

"Mr. Ashley!"

The huddle turned to find a dozen settlers approaching, representing probably half the families in the train. Mr. Savoy appeared to front the group. They gathered around with hats in hands and exchanging nervous glances. Lucien waited no more than five seconds before losing his patience.

"What is it now?"

Savoy narrowed his eyes and jammed his hat back on his head. "If you must know, we are all concerned about what's comin'. This Sally fella sounds like a cutthroat of the worst kind and now he's mad as spit. You saw what happened earlier when we tried to make…what was it called?"

"A defensive formation," said a farmer called Tillison.

"Yeah. A defensive formation. Instead, we made about the biggest pile of wagons I ever seen, with one team of oxen staring up the backside of another." He exhaled a frustrated breath. "Despite what Paynter thinks, we're not soldiers. We can't fight against them who've waged war and still mean to."

"What's your point?" said Lucien coolly.

"Well…" Savoy removed his hat again. "We thought maybe you could negotiate. You seem to have something they want real bad. Maybe you could just give it to 'em and they'd leave."

Lucien stared the man down with pale blue eyes. "Never."

"What's your plan, then? To save us all?"

"I'd like to know the answer to that question as well."

Gus turned to find that Rosalyn had come up behind him. She stood with folded arms and fiery determination, challenging her brother. Lucien locked eyes with her, and they exchanged an unspoken conversation they'd likely had before. Several times.

"You worry too much, sister." He faced the settlers, dismissing her as if she were still a tagalong from childhood. "All men can be reasoned with. I can't imagine Sally would burn an entire wagon train for spite. No one could be that monstrous."

Gus's gut curdled. Lucien was definitely wrong about that. He'd seen worse many times over—enough to understand that the darkest corners of the human soul seemed capable of atrocities that would make even God turn away.

"Listen, people," Lucien continued, "I think I really know what's happening here."

The settlers crowded nearer during Lucien's pause, drawn by the gravity of his smooth intonation and the promise of understanding. The man smiled and spread his hands.

"It is my belief that Mr. Paynter is in league with the bandits. After all, he rode with many of them during the war. He knows them."

Rosalyn's folded arms found her hips. "What are you suggesting?"

"Just this. I believe Paynter made a deal with Sally and Ketchum back in Missouri. He'd gain our trust and deliver us all to Sally in the end. In return, he'd be a free man."

Stacy threw her hands up before Gus could. "That makes no damn sense. How do you explain him shooting four of 'em? And coming back when he coulda run? Huh? How do you explain that, Mr. Ashley?"

Lucien's smile went cold. "Simple enough. We only saw him shoot two. For all we know, he chased the others to make a show of it and let them go. And why would he return, you ask? For a share of the plunder, of course. It's not enough to be free when you can steal another man's possessions first."

"And the wound to his hip?"

"No doubt self-inflicted, for show."

Stacy's nostrils flared dangerously. "You ever put a hot knife to yer skin before? If not, I'd like to show you how it feels."

"Look, Miss Blue." His tone indicated he was done explaining to her and his next words were for those he might convince. "All the evidence points to Paynter's complicity in this affair. He is wanted for the murder of an army captain. He is no different from Sally. He is to be feared, not trusted with the lives of your families."

When Gus saw a few of the farmers beginning to nod in favor of the poisonous logic, his well-maintained dam of restraint collapsed and sent his mounting anger surging toward Lucien. "You don't know a blessed thing about Paynter and yet speak as if an expert on the man. You may be an almighty senator's son, but every word from your mouth just now couldn't be more wrong."

Lucien's initial surprise melted into a canny smile, an alligator waiting in the tall grass. "I see. Well, *Gus.*" He spoke the name with barely concealed disdain and a veiled promise of future retribution. "Perhaps you would care to enlighten us, then. About your Mr. Paynter."

"Gladly." He expelled the word with enough force to push Lucien back a half-step. Gus moved toward the farmers while gathering calm. He knew that if he spoke in anger, some wouldn't hear it. With the warmth of a western sunset, he flashed a smile and nodded slowly.

"Your suspicion is understandable. Your doubt is prudent. Please allow me to lay those to rest, once and for all."

"We're listening," said Savoy.

Gus put his hands behind his back, the way he used to when explaining a difficult assignment to the men under his watch. "It is true that Paynter joined up with Confederate raiders when he was seventeen. It is also true that he rode with them for months, and did regretful things. All true."

"There is your evidence," said Lucien. Gus pinned him with a dangerous glare before resuming.

"I don't know exactly what he did. But I do know this. Something happened. Somethin' that tore him from his foundations. Somethin' that scarred his soul." Gus lifted his eyes to the afterglow of sunset that still lingered on the horizon. Paynter had said little of those days early in the war, as if speaking the words would cast him adrift from humanity. As it was, he was holding on by his fingertips. "All I know is that he quit his outfit one day and headed north. In Kansas, he joined up with a new unit, the First Kansas Colored Volunteers, as a sergeant. How he managed that, I'll never know. They musta been desperate for anyone with experience who'd march with us, I suppose."

Gus returned his thousand-yard stare to the captivated farmers. "That's where I met him. I didn't like him much at first. The only time he spoke was to growl or holler or berate, and still not much more'n a kid. But then I got to know him. That's when I began to understand that he was *with* us. Really with us. That he would die for us, because we were in it together and we were all he had. And right now, this wagon train is all he has."

Savoy nodded, perhaps wanting to shed his doubt. Wanting to believe. "Are you sure, Gus? That he'll fight for us?"

"No doubt." Gus rubbed his chin, calling up painful memories that burned his thoughts and begged to be reburied. "It was '63, the heat of the summer. We were ordered into the Cherokee Nation to meet a rebel force that outnumbered us by double. Place called Honey Springs, though I didn't see no honey. Wasn't a man among us who didn't fear he'd be buried there. When we engaged, the general ordered us to attack in the midst of a rain squall across a muddy field. But the enemy wasn't havin' it. They beat us back with the ferocity of a starvin' dog and poured lead on our retreat."

He rubbed his eyes with one hand, recalling the chaos, the cries of dying men, the thunder of artillery.

"Colonel Williams was shot, so I helped him fall back toward our defensive line. When I looked over my shoulder, you know what I saw?"

Everyone shook their heads expectantly.

"Paynter and a few other soldiers returning for the wounded. Lifting them from the mud and the blood and the muck. Dragging them through the fire to safety. That's when I knew."

"Knew what?" said Rosalyn. Her eyes shone with tremulous hope.

"That's when I knew that whatever Paynter did before he found us didn't matter anymore. Whatever fire consumed him forged him into somethin' new. Somethin' better. You ask why he came back? Well, I'll tell you. Paynter'd rather die than leave behind those that are with him. And right now, we are with him. I trust him. You should too."

Gus looked into the eyes of every farmer and knew he'd won Paynter a reprieve. Lucien, on the other hand, seemed beyond convincing.

"He looks after his own self-interest. His self-preservation. He doesn't care for anyone but himself."

"Wrong again. He doesn't care about himself at all. He gives himself away to others, without hesitation, without question, and without expectation of favors. Unlike most other men I know."

When Gus aimed those last words at Lucien, he was inviting a row. Hoping for it, in fact. Rosalyn spared everyone the spectacle.

"I trust you, Mr. Rivers," she said, "and I believe in Mr. Paynter. The alternative is hopeless despair. Aren't we all here because we hope for a better life? For a brighter future? Without that, we should begin digging one another's graves in this prairie sod and leave the future to those with more courage."

Her show of support for Gus and Paynter brought a stir of assent from the gathered settlers. They folded together in animated conversation and began drifting back toward their wagons. Lucien, however, eyed his sister with a promise of a private set down later.

"I said it before, Rosalyn. You waste your faith on the wrong man. He will only disappoint you. Men like him always do."

She marched away with chin lifted as if not hearing his claim, and he followed, clearly agitated.

"A fine speech," said Stacy to Gus. "And I mean it. I almost threw my hat and whooped."

"Thanks. Always had a knack for it, for better or for worse."

"For better this time, Gus Rivers. For better."

CHAPTER NINETEEN

THE FIASCO OF THE PREVIOUS DAY HAD PAYNTER QUESTIONING his decision to return. Personal history had taught him that the price of caring was usually a painful burn. As Stacy marched toward him in the early morning light, he suspected she intended to stoke the fire.

"Paynter. We gotta talk."

He rubbed grit from the corner of his right eye, stretched his shoulders, and cocked his head toward the vacant prairie while recalling the memory of trees. "Let's walk, then."

They had only wandered ten steps from the wagons when Stacy leaned close. "They was about ready to shackle you up again last night after what happened yesterday."

"I'm not surprised. If you have to blame someone, might as well blame the outlaw. He's a dead man anyway, right?"

Stacy punched his shoulder, raising a sting. "Enough with the 'woe is me.' This is serious."

He rubbed his upper arm and gave her an annoyed grin. "Right. So, what happened?"

Stacy told him. About the concern of the farmers. About Lucien's accusations. About Gus's defense. To his surprise, he found more discomfort with Gus's words than with Lucien's. What Lucien said, however, raised his ire. He was growing weary of being misunderstood. After Stacy finished, they walked in silence as he chased around loose thoughts in his head. Should he have kept riding after shooting Sally? Should he leave now and never look back? These questions troubled him for the space of a minute before he arrived at a reasonable conclusion.

No.

If he abandoned the expedition now, then everything Lucien accused him of might as well be true. Everything Gus said of him would become a lie, well-meaning but nevertheless untrue. He stopped to stare at the endless horizon as the sounds of the awakening train echoed across the emptiness.

"Well?" Stacy, who didn't seem a fountain of patience, had lasted about as long as she could. "Whadda ya think?"

He turned around and began retracing their steps. "I think we need to refine our defensive plans."

"Refine?"

"Add some nuance."

She smirked. "By nuance, you mean complication. Right?"

"Yep."

"I don't know." She shook her head and waved at the wagons. "You saw what happened yesterday. Now you want to throw a spanner into the works. Is that a good idea?"

Jake chuckled. "Likely not. But we have no choice. We can't coddle these folks. We need to challenge them."

"You think that'll work?"

"These are hardy people. Bold people. Adventurous people. They will rise." His thoughts drifted back to the early days of forming a regiment from men who'd never been soldiers and knew nothing more than tilling the soil. "I've seen it before."

"So now what?"

"Fetch your pa. We need a collective meeting before we roll out today."

Ten minutes later, Cornelius had assembled representatives from each wagon beside Lucien's Conestoga. Many of their faces waited with half-formed winces, probably expecting another berating for the previous day's woeful performance. Cornelius motioned to Jake.

"The right honorable gentleman from St. Joseph's jailhouse has the floor."

Jake stepped forward. "I've noticed that most days, your wagons roll out in a similar order, each following the same wagon they always follow. I've noticed that the order holds even when we split into columns."

The settlers exchanged nervous glances as if they'd been caught stealing cookies from Grandma's pantry.

"Let's make that a rule," he continued. "Now, line yourselves up in order of procession."

The representatives from each wagon milled about for a minute while forming into the order into which they'd settled. Lucien folded his arms and scowled, but took his place at the left end of the line.

"Now," said Jake, "raise your hand if you know the cardinal directions. East, west, and the like."

A few glanced from side to side first, but within seconds, all had raised their hands.

"Now leave your hand raised if you can count to four."

All hands remained aloft.

"Again, leave your hand raised if you know the difference between left and right."

Several grinned while all held their hands steady.

"Good! It seems you all possess the acuity to form a proper wagon box. I'll admit that working in fives and fours might've confused you, so we're gonna both complicate and simplify the maneuver. No odd numbers this time."

The hands drifted down as he walked to the head of the line.

"Mr. Ashley, your wagon is North One. Got it?"

Lucien just glared at him, so he slid right to the next man. "Mr. Fowler, you are North Two. Understand?"

The grizzled man narrowed his eyes but nodded. Jake slipped down the line, numbering the next wagons North Three and Four, and the next four as West One through West Four. He skipped the next two, much to the concern of Mr. Janssen and Mrs. Flanagan. The last eight wagons he numbered South One through Four and East One through Four, ending with the Emshoffs' rig. He walked back to the head of the line, ignoring Mrs. Flanagan's raised hand and worried expression.

"Sound off in order. Tell me your direction and number."

Lucien rolled his eyes. "North One."

"North Two," barked Fowler.

And so on, skipping again over the middle two, until reaching the end. He returned to Lucien. "Again, but faster. I want you to call out as fast as I can trot down the line."

They repeated the roll call, finishing as he reached Mr. Emshoff. "Better. Better. Now, remember your direction and number. Tell it to your family members so everyone knows. Have them repeat it back to you at least twice a day."

He stepped back toward the middle to address everyone while Mrs. Flanagan energetically pumped her hand. "When we form up a box, your direction identifies which wall of the box you form. All North wagons make the north wall. All West wagons make the west wall. And so on. Your number dictates the order of your lineup in that wall. The anvil cart sticks with the Emshoff wagon. Understand?"

A mass of head nods allowed Jake to finally turn his attention to the clearly agitated Mrs. Flanagan and the puzzled Mr. Janssen. "As for the middle two wagons, you have a special job. When the box forms, your rigs will occupy the middle. All ammunition will be moved to those wagons. When the box closes, women and children will run for those wagons. There, they will dispense ammunition, load weapons, tend to the wounded, and try to beat down any fires. The men will occupy the outer wall."

"And me, by hooky."

"And you, Stacy. There, they will shoot any adversary who

strays too near. If anyone penetrates the wall, they will shoot, stab, bludgeon, or otherwise remove the intruder from the fight. Does everyone understand?"

Reluctant head nods forced Jake to repeat the plan. Twice. When he was certain they understood, he kneeled to the dirt with a grimace from his aching hip and motioned them closer. He retrieved the knife that had saved his life and drew eighteen dashes in the dirt alongside a rut.

"Three moves, just like checkers. Three moves to close the box. Now pay attention."

The farmers crowded around, jostling one another until everyone could crane a neck enough to eyeball his diagram. Jake waved a hand along the dashed line.

"Each dash is a wagon. Now watch. Move number one."

He erased the first four dashes and made four more at a right angle away from him. "All North wagons turn right sharply and from the same spot. Do not turn until you arrive at that spot. Then turn like a bad peach. Everyone else keep moving forward. Don't stop. Don't slow down.

"Move number two. After finishing, and by God, I mean finishin' the first move, North wagons turn sharply again to the right. West wagons do exactly as the North wagons did in move number one. Turn right. At the same dang spot. Meanwhile, Janssen and Flanagan—you turn your rigs right into the center of the forming box, side by side. Make sure you get inside the box. All the way. Everyone else—move forward. Don't stop. Don't slow down.

"Move number three. The East wagons, the last four. Turn sharply right and go until you meet Ashley's rig. Meanwhile, everyone tighten the box. Pull your oxen inside as best you can. Got it?"

A few head nods, some blank expressions. Paynter explained it again. And again. And one more time. By his fourth run-through, they seemed to possess the concept. He stood, sheathed his knife, and brushed dirt from his hands.

"Now," he said deliberately. "How many left turns does the plan entail?"

"None," said Roberson.

"Exactly. So if I see a single left turn, I will shoot you in the head." When some faces went ashen, he smiled. "Relax. It was a joke. I'll shoot you in the leg. Now git."

―――――――

Jake spent the rest of the day riding up and down the column of oxen and wagons as they trundled across the prairie, asking questions.

"What's your direction and number?"

"What's your job during move one? Move two?"

"Which direction are you supposed to turn?"

"Which hand is your right? Show me."

By the time the sun neared the horizon, Jake had spoken more words in a day than he had in the previous year. His mouth and brain drooped with exhaustion. Cornelius rode up alongside him.

"Now, Paynter?"

"Seems as good a time as any."

As with the day before, they rode ahead to mark the point of the first turn. When the first wagon approached the spot, Cornelius cupped his hands to his mouth and shouted, "Form up! Wagon box!"

With much more precision than the day before, the wagons made the turns and in the correct direction. Jake watched with fascinated horror, though, as the procession ground to a halt twice before restarting. However, they managed to create a shape remotely resembling a box, although with gaps too wide.

"How long, Mr. Blue?"

Cornelius peered at his watch. "Thirteen minutes. Maybe twelve and a half if I'm generous."

Jake inhaled deeply and exhaled. Too long. Too sloppy.

"I know what you're thinkin', Paynter."

Jake turned to find Gus at his side. "Oh?"

"Yep. You're thinking they took too long and the box is too sloppy. That about right?"

Jake just grunted.

"But," Gus continued, "it's a box. Don't worry about the time. They'll get better. And don't worry about the gaps. We'll show 'em how to tighten the box at the last."

Jake sighed. "I suppose you're right."

"'Course I am. 'Bout time you admitted it. And you may be a jackass at times, but you're a right fine instructor when lives are on the line."

"'Course I am. 'Bout time you admitted it."

CHAPTER TWENTY

Stacy saw them coming first—far sooner than Jake had predicted. As she rode watch some two or three miles south of the slow-moving caravan, her mind dwelled on many things. Lucien's continuing hostility toward Paynter. Gus's speech. Paynter's plan. The much-improved but too slow circling of the wagons the previous night. The repetition of the prairie further dulled her senses, feeding her a steady diet of yellow grass, gray-green sage, and faded blue skies until every direction seemed a doppelganger of every other. The sporadic buzz of locusts should have warned her of what was to come, but she failed to listen. In her numbed distraction, she didn't notice the riders until she could nearly count their numbers—at least thirty. Cursing her inattention, she spurred the calico at breakneck pace across that same monotonous terrain toward the vulnerable train. Jake met her a few hundred yards out.

"Riders! Riders!" she shouted. "Thirty at least!"

He spun his mount without a word and barreled toward the head of the train with Stacy hot on his tail. He fired his Kerr at the sky one time. Fifty pairs of eyes locked on him.

"Form up! Form up! Riders comin'!"

Cornelius surged forward to mark the first turning point while Paynter raced for the second. Stacy joined Paynter at the second turn. As the wagons flowed around her at a pace disgruntling to the oxen, she stood in her stirrups to watch the large party approach. After a couple of minutes, Paynter abandoned his job as a turnstile and drifted toward the oncoming mass.

"Stay there," he called to her over a shoulder.

Stacy's surging curiosity gave her no choice but to disobey his instructions. She shouted to the mounted Mrs. Janssen. "Caroline! Come mark the turn!"

When Mrs. Janssen arrived, Stacy joined Paynter even as Gus rode up. She peered at the approaching party, disregarding Jake's scowl of reprimand.

"I'll be mud wallowed," she whispered within a few seconds. "Pawnee."

When the three of them formed a stopgap between the riders and the circling train, the Pawnee stopped, their horses spread in a loose line. They watched with curious interest and amusement as the box closed. When the activity stilled, one raised a hand, a man whose face was lined with years.

"Hello the house."

Jake returned the gesture. "Hello the riders."

"May I come over?"

"Suit yourself."

He dismounted with a second man and walked toward them. Stacy followed Jake's lead and climbed off her horse. Gus joined them. When the two men closed within ten feet, they halted. Both sported the buckskin leggings, shaved skull, and brushed top comb favored by the Pawnee. The burnt bronze of their faces spoke of weeks under the sun without shelter. When the men squatted and sat, Jake, Gus, and Stacy matched their position. The older man tapped his chest.

"I'm Charles Buck. This is Scuddy Set La. We were returning from a hunt and saw your dust far from the main trail. Are you lost?"

"No," said Jake. "Your English is better 'n mine."

The man laughed good-naturedly. "That ain't saying much, mister." He motioned to his comrade. "We were scouts for the Union, Scuddy and me. My grandfather met President James Monroe in Washington when I was waist tall. He taught me the white man's language from my youth. I've had plenty of practice since then."

Stacy relaxed a bit as she eyed the hunting party. The Pawnee likely meant them no harm. Which was good, because they appeared well-armed with rifles and bows. Jake nodded toward the man.

"I ain't never met a president. So, what can we do for ya?"

Charles tossed his head. "We have plenty of meat. Some corn meal would warm my belly if you'd make a trade."

"Of course." Jake turned toward McQuaid, who stood next to the nearest wagon with wide eyes and rifle in hand. "Measure out two gallons of cornmeal from whoever wants fresh meat in trade."

McQuaid jumped to comply. By the time Stacy turned back toward the riders, Set La was returning to meet another man who carried a small deer over his shoulder. The group stood in stilted silence as the trade goods were brought forth and exchanged. Charles broke the stalemate.

"Where are you headed? Unorganized Territory? Idaho? On to Oregon or California?"

"The first," said Jake. "Fort Bridger."

"Why a wagon box? This is Pawnee country."

When Jake hesitated, Stacy stepped into the conversation. "My father leads this train. We fended off an attack of bandits a few days back."

Charles seemed surprised. "What kind of bandits?"

"The leftovers from raider units, Union and Confederate both."

"Fascinating." He rubbed his chin. "They usually don't venture this far west. You must be expecting them to return."

"With a vengeance."

He turned to Set La for a brief exchange in the Pawnee language. The other man chuckled, causing Stacy to bridle.

"What's so funny?"

Set La shook his head. "I believed the white man's war among themselves was finished. Perhaps it will return."

"Is that what you want?"

Set La and Charles cocked their heads at one another.

"No," said Charles. "But during the war, outsiders left us alone. Now, they come again in large numbers, like a swarm of locusts from horizon to horizon. They trample our lands, given us by the Union under treaties signed by the president. The railroad will only add logs to the fire."

He turned to sweep his arm from left to right.

"When I was a boy, we numbered tens of thousands. We roamed between the Mississippi and the Rocky Mountains. Now, we live on a small reservation, only a few thousand of us remaining." He cupped his hands together. "We live in a box, like your wagon box there. Waiting for another attack. It is no way for people to live. It is no way for a child to grow."

Charles dropped his hands, sadness crowning his amiable features. The silence stretched for ten seconds until Stacy grew uncomfortable. Paynter grunted commiseration.

"I wish I could help. But the government wants to hang me, so I doubt they'd listen."

Charles's eyes widened and his soft frown became one of deep consideration. "What's your name, mister?"

"Paynter."

Charles's eyes went wider, and he exchanged a silent gaze with Set La that spoke of recognition. The other man nodded. "Niineeni' howouuyooniit."

"Niineeni' howouuyooniit," Charles repeated.

Paynter's face adopted Charles's disappearing frown. "What does that mean? Niineeni' howouuyooniit?"

The older man laughed as he rose to his feet. "It is you. But you should ask the Arapaho about it. You may encounter them soon enough."

Without explanation, Charles and Set La turned to go, waving as they went. "Good luck, Paynter."

The men rejoined their party, mounted, and trotted off from

the direction they'd come. Paynter's frown persisted. He looked at Gus quizzically.

"Don't ask me," said Gus. "I don't speak Pawnee or Arapaho."

"Stacy?"

"No notion. Didn't recognize the phrase at all. It's not Shoshone, anyway."

Paynter grunted again as they fetched their horses and walked back toward the train. Stacy's father was waiting astride his mount, his moustache turned up slightly in what promised to be a grin beneath the bushel of hair. "Paynter."

"Cornelius?"

He lifted his pocket watch above his shoulder and tapped the face of it with a finger. "Seven minutes."

The worry appeared to leak from Paynter's face and one side of his mouth twitched upward. "Seven minutes. Huh."

Stacy and Gus exchanged a glance behind Paynter's back. *We got a chance*, it said, *if we can keep Paynter's head on straight.*

CHAPTER TWENTY-ONE

JAKE LEANED AGAINST THE EMSHOFF WAGON WATCHING THE stars congeal into a map of points scattered across a void much grander than the one on which he traveled, while considering names. Orion. The Big Bear. The Little Bear. Cassiopeia. Niineeni' howouuyooniit. Why had Charles and Set La called him that? And from the Arapaho? From there, his thoughts turned to the wagon box. Though seven minutes was good progress, it remained a recipe for disaster. An armed band the size of the Pawnee hunting party would have cut most of them down before they could've mounted a respectable defense. And even if they managed to cut the time in half, he still hadn't prepared them for the fighting afterward. There was much to teach, and the days slipped by like springtime snow melt, irretrievable and far too fast. His morose thoughts threatened to draw him into that familiar well of isolation.

"Mr. Paynter."

He turned to find Rosalyn approaching slowly with a bundle of cloth cradled in both hands. Whereas the wagon circle had made them neighbors before, the box separated them by three wagon lengths. Her presence, then, was no accident of proximity. He squinted in the darkness and removed his hat. "Miss Ashley."

"We've extra cornbread again, if you're so inclined."

"Does your brother know you came?"

"No." She laughed, the sound of tinkling crystal. "He thinks I'm visiting the Robersons."

"He won't like it if he learns the truth."

She put one hand on a hip. "Do you plan to tell him?"

A grin threatened to capture his lips, but he beat it back. "No."

She reached him and thrust the bundle toward him. "Then take this."

He accepted her offering and unwrapped the cloth. Inside, like a bar of gold, sat a large square of cornbread still warm to the touch. He lifted it to his nose and inhaled. "Do you mind?"

"Not at all."

He broke off a piece and popped it into his mouth. It tasted like sunshine. "Good cornbread. Got a little somethin' extra. What is it?"

"My secret."

He nodded and ate another piece. "Fair enough."

She shifted from foot to foot as he finished the bread. "You seemed a million miles away just now," she said. "Watching the stars."

He licked the crumbs from his fingers, unconcerned about etiquette. He didn't think she'd mind. "I reckon I was. Somewhere off the shoulder of Orion."

Her eyes sparkled with curiosity in the reflected firelight of the Emshoffs' campfire. "You know your constellations."

"A few. My grandmother taught me when I was young, though she called the Big Bear 'the Plow.'" He looked to the array of stars riding higher in the sky than they would all year. "She'd sometimes steal me away from the eyes of my father, and we'd slip into the cane fields to watch the night sky and share shortbread and secrets. She'd like this, I think."

Rosalyn edged nearer, watching the same part of the sky. "You must miss her."

He nodded. "She was the only mother I ever had, 'til I was six, anyway. Then it was just my father and older brothers."

His voice went colder than he'd intended. She seemed not to notice, or pretended not to, anyway. "I also lost my mother too soon," she said. "Father was always too occupied with being important, so it was just Lucien and me most of the time. I know you don't care for my brother, but he's always protected me."

Jake grunted a breath. "Which is exactly the reason he cares little for me, I'm sure. If I had a sister, I wouldn't allow her in the same county as me."

She turned her face toward him until he met her gaze, shadowed as it was by the night. "Mr. Paynter, surely you aren't as bad as you think."

He frowned and blinked slowly. "I am, Miss Ashley. On at least that subject, your brother is right."

"Oh." Her eyes fell. "Would you prefer I not speak to you again?"

He almost said yes, without thinking. However, his restraint gave him a moment to consider the question. That was all the time he needed. "No. I would not prefer that."

A smile curled her lips, which was more reward than he could've ever hoped for. The guardian within him that kept watch over his destructive inner fire whispered caution. Whispered that he should send her away. That he should forget her existence. For once, he didn't listen. They watched the stars in silence for a time, she seemingly content just to dwell in the small crease between a moment ago and what comes after.

"Miss Ashley," he said finally, not meeting her eyes.

"Mr. Paynter?"

"What's your brother hiding? It has us all in dire straits."

Her breath caught and she crossed her arms tightly. Her attention drifted to whatever lay beneath her feet in the darkness. "I can't…"

Without thinking, he lightly touched her shoulder, freezing her erupting fidget. He pulled his fingers away gingerly. "I understand. I'll take it up with him. I won't drag you into this."

She peered up at him for the space of a few heartbeats. "Thank you. Good evening."

As she walked away, the void stretching above him seemed a little emptier than before.

CHAPTER TWENTY-TWO

JAKE BIDED HIS TIME UNTIL THE NEXT EVENING. THE BEST WAY to trap a snake in the grass was to remain still as a stone and wait for it to move. The wagons had formed up in under six minutes, infusing him with a sliver of hope. In his confidence, he waited in the shadows of the Ashleys' behemoth for Lucien to return from his rounds of visitation. He didn't need to wait long.

"Tell me what you're hiding, Mr. Ashley."

The senator's son jumped with a start as he rounded a corner of the Conestoga. "Paynter. What are you doing here?"

"My apologies. I didn't realize my question was so unclear. So let me ask again more specifically. Just how much gold are you carryin' that Sally would drag his men across half the West to get it?"

"I'm not carrying any gold."

Jake knew he was lying. Few men could maintain eye contact when so boldly fabricating the truth. Lucien was no exception. His eyes flicked left to right and back again as he spoke. Jake closed the few feet that separated them, his voice a low growl.

"Don't play coy with me. You endanger everyone here. Gus. Stacy. The Robersons. The Flanagans. The Emshoffs. Your own sister." He let that last one hang between them for a few seconds. "You should let us know what we might be dyin' for. It's the least of your obligations to these people."

Lucien seemed to unlock from his surprise. "What do you care, Paynter?"

A fair question that he continued to struggle to answer. "Let's pretend I don't care. But let's just say that if I'm gonna die before I hang, I'd strongly prefer to know *why*."

It was only then that he noticed the others, likely drawn by the intensity of the exchange. Gus, Roberson, Savoy, and Glen had filtered to the edge of the conversation.

"It's a fair question," said Gus.

Lucien glared at him. "I owe *you* no explanation."

"You owe me, though," said Roberson, suddenly agitated. Two more farmers drifted into the circle. "You promised we'd be safe when we joined this here expedition. You stood on that soapbox in St. Joseph and swore us an oath. Now, you refuse me an answer as to why my wife and two children might get shot by an outlaw?"

"Calm down, Roberson. You shame yourself."

The revolver was out before Jake could flinch. Roberson's shaking hand leveled the weapon at Lucien, who, to his credit, refused to cower. "Put the gun away, Mr. Roberson."

"Answer the question." Roberson's fury seemed only to mount. Though a part of him hoped the farmer would pull the trigger, Jake knew it would crush Rosalyn. He stabbed out a hand and tore the revolver from Roberson's grip so abruptly that the farmer stared in disbelief at his empty fingers before yanking his eyes toward him. Jake gently lowered the hammer and returned the weapon to Roberson.

"Save it for Sally and his men, Mr. Roberson."

The farmer let his arms fall as the revolver dangled from slack fingers, seemingly ashamed of his outburst.

"I could have you shot," Lucien said to Roberson. Jake wheeled on Lucien.

"I could step aside just as easily. Tell these men the truth, Mr. Ashley. Next time, I won't intervene."

"Tell them." Rosalyn's voice cut through the tension as she joined the huddle, her jaw clenched with determination. "Show some courage. Show some faith. You've asked as much from these people. You owe them that and more."

Lucien directed a burning glare at his sister that extinguished over the course of a few tense seconds. "Very well, then."

He stood tall and faced the farmers. "As you well know, this expedition is one of the last before the transcontinental railroad completes. New York to San Francisco in a week. By this time next year, every eastern slick with an ample measure of greed and a bagful of money will be riding in a sleeper coach to the territories or Oregon or California to leverage away the businesses of people who walked two thousand miles to get there. The year after that, there will be few grand fortunes to be made. Only crumbs from the table. You decided right to join me. This may be the little man's last chance for glory."

The farmers nodded, seemingly captured by Lucien's vision. Bile rose in Jake's throat.

"As for me," Lucien continued, "I plan to intercept their game. I've brought enough gold to start an empire strong enough to block them out."

Savoy scratched his jaw. "Just how much gold?"

"Let's just say a significant sum."

"Why didn't you just tell us about it?"

When Lucien failed to answer, Rosalyn did. "He was afraid you'd leave us for dead on the trail and take the gold."

Roberson grew a look of affront. "What do you take us for? Criminals? Ain't right. Ain't right at all."

"I see that now," said Lucien with little apparent shame. "But a man can't be too careful when it comes to money. People perform terrible deeds for things that shine."

"Like murder a wagon train for it?" said Jake.

"Yes. That."

Jake rubbed his chin. "I wonder, Mr. Ashley. Where'd you come up with so much gold? It's not exactly readily available these days."

"It doesn't matter."

"Oh, it does. In fact, I happen to know that most of the gold floatin' from hand to hand right now was confiscated from the Confederacy at the end of the war. A man with legal authority—a senator, say—could collect a large supply without much record of it and send it west to disappear into the wilderness only to emerge as something resembling a business empire."

Even in the dim light, Jake saw Lucien go red with rage. Rosalyn turned on her brother with indignation. "*Confederate* gold? Taken illegally? Is that what we carry?"

"You fail to understand. It doesn't matter now where it came from. It only matters what the gold will become."

Jake shook his head. "You are the one who misunderstands. If that's Confederate gold, then Sally doesn't want it just to have it. He wants it because he believes it's his, and that you took it from him. He's comin' to take back what he believes you stole." He chuckled darkly. "At least now we know why he'd go to such lengths to stop this wagon train. At least now we know for sure he's coming back, and right soon."

With that pronouncement, the farmers turned to melt into the firelit night to huddle beside their families. Rosalyn glared at her brother before striding away with shoulders hiked in anger. In their absence, Lucien faced Jake, Gus, and Glen.

"As I said, it doesn't matter now. What will happen will happen." He looked away from Jake to engage Gus and Glen. "If you help keep this train safe, I'll be sure to reward you."

Gus laughed quietly. "We don't need your gold, Mr. Ashley. We protect these people because it's only right. Not everything can be bought with thirty pieces of silver. Or gold."

"Well stated," said Glen as he crossed his brawny arms.

Lucien shook his head. "That's not been my experience. All people have a price."

Jake turned to walk away, leaving the conversation to Gus and Glen. He knew that what Lucien said was true. All people have a price. But he also knew that every man has a breaking point. He had reached his years before and no amount of gold could modify his course.

————————

The depths of night gave birth to an epic thunderstorm that might've made Jake miss Texas if not for its deadly intentions. Rolls of distant thunder dwelled in the background until a cataclysmic crash yanked Jake from the halls of sleep. His eyes met with darkness until a web of lightning raced across the sky from corner to corner, shattering the glass of the night. The accompanying peal of thunder propelled him to his feet. He lifted his nose into the wind and smelled the rain before the first drop touched his face. Within seconds, a gusting blast pushed him two steps backward and the buckets of heaven turned over. All around him arose the groans, complaints, and shouts of folk roused from slumber to find the roof caving in.

As his traveling companions huddled beneath tents and wagon beds to escape the onslaught, Jake's thoughts turned to the creek fifty steps from the wagon box. It had channeled no more than a foot of meandering water when they'd crossed it earlier. But its flow was from the southwest—the direction of the thunderstorm. He pulled his hat low against the driving rain and splashed through the deluge toward the creek. He was ankle deep when another eruption of lightning revealed his worst fears. The sleepy stream had swelled to four times its earlier width, force-fed by a torrent barreling down on the wagon train. He closed his eyes to recall the lay of the land as they had formed the box. They'd come across a roll of ground and crossed the hollow of the creek to circle up on the other side—at the edge of another rise! He began shouting into the darkness as he ran.

"We gotta move! We gotta move!"

Cornelius met him, sagging under the weight of water. "It's the creek, ain't it?"

"We shoulda known better," he hollered. "This place will be a river in ten minutes!"

Jake raced from wagon to wagon and tent to tent, yanking people from cover. "Hook up your team! We gotta get out o' this draw yesterday!"

Between Cornelius and him, they managed to instill sufficient panic to launch the entire party into frenzied, rain-soaked activity. Jake helped several families hitch their teams and thrust them toward the adjacent rise with instructions to find high ground and stay put. By the time the last of the wagons had lurched into motion, the creek had spilled its banks and filled the hollow with nearly two feet of rushing water. Cries and shouts in the darkness gave way to flashes of light that revealed a dozen rigs mounting a gentle slope that had already become a quagmire. Mothers and fathers drove oxen with abandon while dragging children from the muck toward higher ground. Wagon wheels swerved left and right with each lurch of the teams as vicious winds tore at the bonnets. Jake slogged through knee-deep water to find his blanket washed away and the mare yanking her tether free of the stake. He dragged her toward the trailing wagon, where a voice shouted imperatively in the darkness.

"Gehen sie! Jetzt!"

Emshoff. Jake pulled alongside the shadow sludging through the flow. "Where's your family?"

"In the wagon," yelled Emshoff.

Jake leaped from the mare. "Get 'em out! Take the mare and get 'em uphill!"

"But my wagon…"

"Go, I said!" He snatched the willow switch from the German's hands. "I got it."

Emshoff ducked away to follow Jake's orders. He carried Lisbet through the now thigh-deep current toward the rise as his wife pulled the terrified Otto and Dora along behind. Jake began lashing the oxen with the switch, who lowed in terror from the thunder and rising waters. After a dozen steps, the animals began shifting sideways. Jake looked back to find the shadowy hulk of the wagon rotating into the current, dragging the oxen with it. For an instant, his darker nature whispered in his ear. *Leave the wagon. Let the waters claim it. This is not your fight.* But another voice some-where deep inside reminded him that unasked, the Emshoffs had shown him kindness and filled his belly. They had pried him from the morass of isolation to call him friend. They had challenged him to rise above his guilt and lead the way. And more than any-thing, Jake wanted to be the man they saw instead of the man he was. Determination surged in his gut. He leaned into the yoke of the lead oxen to add his weight to the churning bulk of the ani-mals, resolved to ride the rig until it washed away, and hoping to swim free.

The point of no return approached as the tail of the wagon slipped farther downstream. Thoughts of how he might unhitch the oxen rampaged through his head when suddenly he became aware of others around him. There was Gus, lashing the yoke with a rope tied to his horse's saddle. And big Glen Dunbar, pushing the ox behind him. And Emshoff, Roberson, and a dozen others massing along the sides of the wagon to heave it from the rushing current. Seconds passed—a dozen yammering heartbeats—then a wheel found purchase. And then another, and another. The team bulled slowly forward, rising from the water by inches and then by feet. He continued his desperate push with tunnel-vision intensity until the oxen topped the rise and pulled the wagon to a stable position.

As he sank to his knees, the mud met him, welcoming and cold. He kneeled, his chest heaving and legs shaking. Only upon lift-ing his head did he realize the storm had passed, blowing out as fast as it had come. In its wake, the moon owned a pristine sky clear as winter ice. He found the other men around him on the muddy turf, fighting to regain collective breaths. A familiar feeling overtook Jake—the kinship of banding together in battle to overcome a superior foe. The feeling had been absent since the end of the war. Its return on a nondescript rise in the vastness of a bland prairie among the ranks of homespun farmers surprised him. The mud beneath his fingers abruptly felt less cold, less final. He shook his head in disbelief.

"I'll be damned."

He resumed his feet and stretched his shoulders, wondering. For a week, he'd considered the wagon train's odds of repulsing Sally and his men as no better than thin. But now—maybe. Just maybe.

CHAPTER TWENTY-THREE

ON THE SEVENTH DAY, GOD RESTED. FOR JAKE, THE SEVENTH day after fighting off Sally's first attack proved the most laborious yet, the previous evening's battle against nature notwithstanding. What did the proverb say? No rest for the wicked? With Grand Island and the Platte River in reach, the still-soggy train set out early and moved at an anxious pace. Grand Island was little more than a scatter of houses and shops owned mostly by German immigrants, but the railroad had reached there just weeks earlier. After two weeks of wide-open prairie, the settlers seemed anxious for a taste of civilization, no matter how insignificant. Even if it was just a humble cluster of buildings and a few people called Schmidt and Müller. But first, they had to cross the Platte.

Jake turned over his feisty mare to Mrs. Janssen, who rode with the ease of a cavalry officer, and helped the Flanagans drive their oxen. Mrs. Flanagan poured an unending stream of information, anecdotes, and opinions into his left ear as they walked. He tried to discourage her with a steady diet of one-word replies, but she wasn't having it. At one point, he caught Mr. Flanagan grinning at him. Only then did Jake wonder if the man really couldn't hear or if he had concocted the most brilliant and elaborate ruse ever to avoid talking to his wife. He sighed and put his head down while driving the oxen forward.

When the river and a huddle of whitewashed buildings on its far bank came into view, Jake began breathing easier, and not just for the impending peace and quiet. He knew Sally wouldn't attack them near a settlement, and Fort Kearny lay just two days upriver. For a while, then, he could lay his burden down. Just a little while, though. As the trail approached the river, the ruts began to scatter. It seemed previous expeditions held a variety of opinions on where best to cross. The decision wasn't an easy one. The Platte at Grand Island was less a river than a series of creeks, streams, and marshes held loosely together by gravity and slight rolls in the landscape. An inch deep and a mile wide, folks said of it, for good reason.

"Pull her this way," Cornelius called to Lucien. The big Conestoga began to curve toward the left. The wagon master clearly knew his approved spot for crossing. As the train began to bend toward the river, Jake soon saw Cornelius's logic. Under normal circumstances, the Platte all but disintegrated into four or five separate streams, none more than thirty feet wide and a couple of feet deep—an easy set of crossings. The previous night's storm had driven a deluge through the channels, doubling the depth and rendering the banks a morass of mud. Cornelius rode toward the place with the widest spreads between individual streams. If a wagon became mired in the muck, teams on the banks could help extract it with ropes.

The Ashleys' massive wagon was the first to hit the water. Because the rig was built for just such crossings, the oxen pulling it barely lost a step as the vehicle cut through the stream like a righteous plow. The remaining wagons struggled a bit more. Nobody seemed accustomed to fording streams with a loaded casket on wheels weighing north of a ton. At least they had oxen and not mules. Mules would have had plenty to say about wading into a river. Oxen just lumbered through as if the water didn't exist. When it came time to roll the Flanagans' wagon through the first cut, Jake noticed that the couple had climbed into the jockey box. Mrs. Flanagan waved happily at him. Now waist-deep in muck, he didn't feel much like returning the cordiality.

Over the next two hours, the train moved through one stream after another, five in all, to collect in a line on the far side of the

Platte. Gus walked up to him, soaked to the chest. Clearly, he'd been helping another family.

"Enjoying yourself?" Gus said.

"Immensely."

"Good. 'Cause you look like you could throttle someone right now."

"Do you care?"

Gus laughed. "No. So long as it's not me."

"I'll spare you, then."

"Mighty kind of you. Now, what's next? I doubt the good people of Grand Island would like us to tear up what passes for a main street with a hundred oxen."

Jake eyeballed the sun. Probably three o'clock. Enough time to settle and let the people walk down a real street for a change and perhaps barter for supplies. "There's no sense wastin' a day. Let's set up the wagon box just outside town in that grass field over there."

Jake turned the oxen over to a very pleased Mr. Flanagan and recovered his horse from Mrs. Janssen. She patted the mare's neck after dismounting.

"She's a fine animal. Where did you find her?"

Jake chuckled at the joke only he knew. "The army gave her to me, probably because nobody else wanted her. We're both army rejects, it seems. A match made in hell."

Mrs. Janssen cocked an eyebrow as he led the mare away. She probably thought he was not right in the head. Which he wasn't, most days. He mounted and rode up alongside Cornelius, who seemed to anticipate Jake's idea.

"Where should we plant it?"

"Just there." Jake pointed to the big patch of runaway grass, now going brown under the June sun.

"Yes, sir. That'll do. A finer kingdom of grass I've never beheld."

The two of them marked the turns as usual and Cornelius gave the signal. Though tired from the pressed march, a strange fire seemed to light everyone's eyes. They pushed their teams hard, made precise turns, and closed the gaps with urgency.

"Four minutes," said Cornelius as he snapped his pocket watch closed. "I think I might shed a tear."

Jake understood the sentiment. From eighteen minutes to four in less than a week. His pride threatened to swell before he remembered that they'd made no other preparations for an actual battle. He'd need to begin rectifying that soon, or the wagon box would be for naught. He turned his attention to the town not a hundred yards distant to find that a large knot of locals had congregated to watch the show. A mustachioed man waved a hand.

"Impressive execution," he called with an accent that had once been German. The Emshoffs sailed past him with children in tow, no doubt eager to converse with some of their former country-men. Lisbet slipped from Mrs. Emshoff's grip when she stopped to wave at Jake. Before he could restrain his hand, he lifted two fingers to return the wave. Her mother, who had turned to retrieve the child, lifted her lip in an I-saw-that-Herr-Heart-of-Stone smile before resuming her beeline for the town limit. Perhaps spurred by the Emshoffs' example, the train emptied within minutes as everyone crossed the field to reacquaint themselves with the feel of a town.

"This place won't stay small for very long."

Jake looked down to find Rosalyn beside the mare examining the under-construction train depot, her hand shielding her eyes from the sun's glare. He followed her gaze.

"Union Pacific, I hear." He dismounted to stand beside her. The ground beneath his feet that had seemed so solid for years abruptly lost its concrete nature. He wondered why.

"The railroad will change everything," she said. She smiled softly at him. "I wonder if anyone knows what's coming."

He rocked his head side to side. "I never seem to know what's comin'. Hopefully, other folks are better prophets than me."

She continued watching him, her thoughts inscrutable. "Would you care to join me for a walk about Grand Island, Nebraska?"

He considered the request long enough for her to grow visibly uncomfortable. "I better not."

"Why? Because of Lucien?"

"No." He motioned as if tugging a rope around his neck. "Because of this. Most people won't mourn my passing. I'd hate for you to feel any regret. Any hurt."

Her eyes teared up, and she swiped at them with the back of one hand. "Too late for that, Mr. Paynter."

As she strode away toward the town, the ground beneath his feet became water.

A night of restless sleep hadn't stilled the surface of the ground much. Ashamed of his weakness, he steeled his spine to view the collected settlers. Every adult in the train formed a crescent before him just beyond the wagon box, intent on what he would say. If he didn't know better, he'd think Lucien was jealous of the attention. Jake snorted at the irony. He'd just as soon become invisible. Instead, he lifted his palms to encompass the group.

"Everyone has a job when the moment comes. Every man. Every woman. Every child. Those who can shoot will operate a weapon from the protection of an assigned wagon. That's rifles, muskets, revolvers, shotguns—anything that throws lead shot. We'll need the stronger men to also carry a long pike. If any horse or rider attempts to enter the square, they get the pointy end in the chest. We need nurses to tend to the wounded. We need runners to ferry ammunition and loaded muskets between the middle wagons and the defenders. We need older children to herd younger children into the safety of those same wagons. Finally, we need folks ready to douse the flames."

"Flames?" said Mrs. Savoy, her face ashen.

"They will attempt to fire the wagons. We must account for that."

Their faces went as grim as he'd hoped. He needed grim right now, and somber and sober and a little frightened. Nothing engaged learning like fear of the alternative. Still, compassion stirred within him despite his best efforts to ignore it. Against his better instincts, he offered a final word.

"Those men that are coming for us? They're mostly loners, like me. They follow Sally only to serve their own interests. But you all are different. You look out for one another. You help one another. You fight for one another. That makes you better than them. And over the course of time, better wins more often than not."

A dozen head nods and a general lifting of spirits followed his words. He wondered if he'd offered too much false hope, but shrugged. Too late now. With his speech finished, Jake released the crowd to their respective wagons and went to find the mare. Stacy drifted up beside him.

"You can sling a phrase like a politician when you feel like it."

"I never feel like it."

She laughed before growing somber. "How long do you figure we have?"

"Seven days, I'm thinking."

"How do you reckon so precisely?"

Jake had given that question much thought and was confident in his calculation. "Fort Kearny lies two days upriver. They won't hit us between here and there. Too many witnesses. The army typically patrols a two-day perimeter around its forts. Once we get three to four days past Fort Kearny, we become fair game. We'll rest a day or two at the fort. So, seven days, give or take."

She gazed at the ground while seemingly considering his mathematics. "Are you sure they'll come for us?"

"Certain of it." He pointed to a lone rider in the distance, outlined against the predawn light. "They got a scout watchin' us right now."

Stacy grimaced and involuntarily touched the knife at her belt. The motion brought a half grin to his lips. What they lacked in experience, they made up for in grit and determination.

CHAPTER TWENTY-FOUR

"ME? DU WILLST MICH?"

Mrs. Emshoff pointed at her nose with disbelief while her husband chuckled. Jake just nodded and offered a smile of reassurance. "Yes. You. I want you in charge of the middle wagons when the fight begins. Protecting the children. Organizing the ammunition. Directing treatment of the wounded."

She continued to stare at him as if waiting for the joke. "But my Englisch. It is bad."

"Maybe, but your spine is made of steel and you give orders like a field general. Like a Kommandant. You have seen war before. Mrs. Dunbar will be your right hand because she has witnessed the same. When everything seems bleakest, the two of you will stand. This I know."

She nodded slowly, her jaw slightly agape, beginning to believe. Mr. Emshoff leaned to kiss her cheek and whisper inaudibly into her ear. She blushed and pushed him away with a wide smile as he belted out a laugh.

"I'm taking that as a 'yes'?" said Jake.

Mr. Emshoff wiped a tear from his eye, his cheeks still stretched in a grin. "She will do it, Herr Paynter. Mein Kleiner Kommandantin."

"Very good." He dipped his forehead at Mrs. Emshoff. "Now, go make your plans with Mrs. Dunbar."

She gave a single, sharp, neck-rattling nod, spun smartly on her heels, and strode away as if to invade Hell itself. He cocked his head at Mr. Emshoff. "Has she always been such a firecracker?"

"Oh, no," he said. "I have tempered her."

Jake grinned dryly as he and Mr. Emshoff began collecting

those who could shoot. That group included most of the men, Mrs. Janssen, and two other women. Gus and Stacy already held the jobs of scouting for the approach of adversaries. Each morning, they disappeared into the grass to watch the eastern and southern flanks, and returned before nightfall, tired and with a new report. He didn't want to distract them from that critical task by loading them with responsibility after a long day's ride. That meant pressing others into leadership, reluctant or otherwise. When the fight came, though, he knew Gus and Stacy would lead anyway.

"Corporal McQuaid."

"Yes, Lieutenant?"

Jake frowned at him. "I ain't that anymore. Not since the Green River."

"Sorry, Paynter."

He waved a dismissive hand. "I need you to organize the infantry. Catalog our firearms. Figure out who can handle what. Who has experience with what. Assign two shooters to every wagon, and do your best to put a long gun at every location. Make an inventory of ammunition. Align the ammunition with the weapons, and store the appropriate rounds in each wagon. Got it?"

McQuaid's eyes had gone wider and wider as he listened to his assignment. Five seconds after Jake finished, he nodded twice and turned to his men. "Private Muñoz, Private Evans. We got our work cut out for us."

"The rest of you work with Corporal McQuaid to sort out the weapons." He turned toward the German. "Make sure the young soldier doesn't get overwhelmed."

"As you wish."

Jake risked a glance at the Ashley rig. Lucien had seemingly relinquished all planning to others and focused instead on the defense of his wagon. Jake found Rosalyn watching him. When she took a few steps in his direction, Lucien grabbed her arm none too gently.

"Fill the water barrel, sister. It's running low."

She glared heat at him before shaking her arm free and returning to her wagon. Jake frowned with concern. He didn't find Lucien's actions surprising. But he hated that Rosalyn was trapped in her brother's web of poor decisions.

Jake breathed a soft curse and went looking for the blacksmith. He found him loitering behind his wife as she huddled with Mrs. Emshoff in the throes of planning. Jake tapped his shoulder.

"Let's walk."

He led Glen inside the square, occupied by thirty riding horses, draft horses, and milk cows. As they dodged mildly annoyed livestock, Jake swept his hand around the perimeter. "Riders will try to jump the tongues and chains to gain the interior. Your job is to make sure they pay for the incursion."

Glen grunted understanding. "Are you asking me to shoot them?"

Jake recalled what the man had said about laying down his firearms after the war. "Only as a last resort. I want you to recruit three or four of the strongest men to guard the interior. We'll make long pikes and lay them in each gap. If a horse charges, raise the pike. Make 'em jump through it."

Glen grew a dark smile, perhaps surprised that the war he'd left behind had caught back up with him. "A regular William Wallace, then."

"If that's what it takes." He motioned toward Dunbar's cart. "Hit them with your hammer, if you must. Sling your anvil at 'em. Pull them from the saddle and throw fists at their heads until they stop movin'. Whatever it takes." He paused and lowered his voice. "Your wife and little one will depend on you not to fail. This makeshift keep must not fall."

Glen peered back at him, clearly affected. "You think it will come to that?"

"I do."

The blacksmith nodded slowly, his eyes filling with intent. "I'm thinking iron tips on the pikes might make them more effective."

"Good man."

He meant the compliment. Glen *was* good. As were Gus, Emshoff, and Stacy, and nearly everyone he'd met. All good. That worried him, though. The coming fight would undoubtedly prove nasty—the kind of nastiness that shocked and appalled good people into indecision. What he needed were a few bad men to counter the pure malice that was certain to come. For now, though, he'd have to fill that role for everyone.

The arrival at Fort Kearny just prior to sunset the next evening proved cause for celebration for most. Not for Jake, though. The stop marked the one-third point of his journey to swing from a rope at Fort Bridger. Just one step nearer to a final reckoning that had been coming for seven years.

As he surveyed the fort from horseback, he noted yet again how unpresuming it was. When folks from back east heard "fort," they expected a daunting defensive fortification with walls of stone or log pickets, guard towers, cannons on the wall, a moat filled with spikes. In other words, all the trappings of a proper medieval castle, American-style. What they usually got was a collection of buildings that a herd of buffalo could wander through without meeting resistance. Fort Kearny was no different. Approximately thirty wood-frame and adobe buildings huddled around the tree-lined perimeter of an expansive parade ground. Minor earthworks provided a minimal buffer between the buildings and the prairie, and even those had been constructed only during the height of tensions with the local tribes a few years earlier. What it lacked in military charm it made up for in function. Due to its position on the Oregon Trail, Fort Kearny had become a major resupply point for westbound settlers. The fort commander was commissioned to sell supplies at no profit, and often gave away food in cases of hardship. No wonder the farmers eyed it like a candy shop.

"Ready?"

Cornelius's question drew him from his well of thought. "Yep. Looks like a good stand of untrampled grass just north of the fort."

With target in sight and the candy shop beckoning, the party formed a wagon box in three minutes and twenty-eight seconds from gunshot to closing of ranks. An unspoken agreement passed between Jake and Cornelius to withhold the time lest the settlers become complacent.

"We always stay a day," said Cornelius. "We could wait longer, maybe outlast Sally and his men. Maybe they'll leave."

"No," Jake replied. "They won't leave. We can't outlast them. If we convinced the commander to send a guard detail with us, Sally would wait until the soldiers reached their range and turned back. And we can't stay here. The army doesn't abide wagon trains sitting idle, consuming supplies, blocking the trail. They'll move us along whether we want to or not."

"So, stay a day and leave?"

"That's the way I figure it. Besides, if the worst happens, the nearer we are to this place, the better chance any survivors have of finding help. Sally's going to attack, no doubt. The sooner it happens after we leave here, the better it is for us."

Cornelius nodded. Though worry painted his face, he remained resolute. One does not travel four thousand miles of trail every year for two decades without possessing a mountain of resilience. Jake only hoped that this journey would not be the wagon master's last.

By early afternoon, the families of the train had managed to resupply, dispatch mail back to loved ones, and generally wander the

parade grounds. As they collected back at the wagons, Jake sent
them to school. All those with muzzle-loading guns went with
Gus, who drilled them in the rapid loading of powder and shot
both standing and kneeling. Jake had taught Gus on a Prussian
musket six years earlier. Now, Gus could reload three times for
Jake's every two, fulfilling the adage that "poor is the pupil who
does not surpass the master." Mr. Emshoff acted as his aide in
the muzzle-loader brigade, given his experience loading Austrian
muskets during the war against the Dutch.

Meanwhile, McQuaid drilled those with breech-loading rifles
and revolvers on methods of maximizing their effectiveness when
under duress. Firing intentionally and not wildly with a space to
breathe between shots. Working with adjacent wagons to set up
crossfire for riders who approached too closely. Firing in alter-
nation with the man or woman at your side to maintain a steady
drumbeat of shots. Crouching behind the wagon wall between
firings and when reloading, changing position between each shot
so as not to telegraph to the attackers a precise source of the next
volley. Keeping ammunition within arm's reach. And so on. But
first, they had to pile the possessions to the interior side of each
wagon to clear a space wide enough to duck into without putting
all the cargo weight on one set of wheels.

With firearm training covered, Jake turned to the protection
of the interior of the box. They collected spare wagon parts from
the fort and began fashioning them into long pikes, twelve feet in
length, with metal tips courtesy of Glen. The butt end of each pike
was fitted with a metal hook so it could be driven into the earth
with an energetic swing. The anchors would render the pikes less
movable when horse and rider rode into them. They also fash-
ioned shorter spears with skinning knives strapped to the end,
like bayonets. These were for close-in skirmishes should the battle
come to that.

While helping Glen, Jake kept an eye on Mrs. Emshoff. Like a field commander, she drilled the children and remaining women in a combination of English, German, and indistinct cursing. Over the course of two hours, she had them converging on the central wagons in seconds, and setting up the nursing unit, ordnance supply chain, and fire brigade in under a minute. Jake smiled with satisfaction. His instincts about a person were not always right, but in this case, they proved dead accurate. His uncharacteristically high spirits helped keep at bay the dark reality that nipped incessantly at his heels, a hellhound intent on dragging him into the abyss. Sometime during the next few days, these people would engage a highly skilled and brutal force of men with guns whose sole malicious aim was the destruction of the wagon train and everyone associated with it. How could a ragtag collection of farmer families stand against such evil and survive, let alone triumph?

CHAPTER TWENTY-FIVE

DEATH IS PATIENT, GIVEN ITS LORDSHIP OVER TIME AND distance. As a result, it wouldn't come riding in until two weeks after the wagon train had left Fort Kearny behind. Moving steadily westward, the convoy passed the divide of the North Platte from the South Platte, hewing to the former, with no sign of raiders. Gradually, the prairie began whispering warning of the mountains to come as it sprouted ranges of low hills in the distance, some of which crept perilously close to the river. Prairie grass slowly surrendered elbow room to tufts of hardy green sage sprouting in bunches atop the more inhospitable patches of ground.

When Jake's seven-day deadline passed, many settlers began to believe that Sally no longer gave chase. Not Gus, though. He knew the promise of wealth made men capable of most any horror. He'd steadfastly clung to his instincts that death was coming, but its spectral presence after fifteen days of respite still felt like a punch to the gut. It manifested as a smear of dust on the eastern horizon, the sure sign of a large party. With Fort Laramie still four days ahead, the appearance of Sally and his legion could prove disastrous.

"I'd better go see," he told Paynter. The words had no more than left his mouth when Stacy horned into the plan.

"I'm goin' with you."

"You shouldn't. This'll be dangerous."

She glared at him as if she intended to burn him to his boots with her eyes. "I'm going. You can stay behind and cower if you like."

He grinned. He liked her best when she was puffed up like an alley cat, ready for a fight. If she was to come along, that's the Stacy he'd need.

"Suit yourself. Stock up on cartridges and caps and let's go."

After a minute's preparation, they mounted up and turned toward the southeast. Cornelius cut them off, bringing their horses to a halt. His firelit eyes pierced his daughter. His moustache twitched, matching the deep worry of his eyes. After a silent moment, he wheeled his horse away. "You be careful, Anastasia Evangeline Blue."

She cut her eyes at Gus and spurred her calico ahead, daring him to catch up. When he did, he looked at her sidelong with a relaxed grin.

"Don't say it," she said.

"Oh, but I have to."

"I'm warnin' you."

"Threat duly noted and discarded. Anastasia."

She whipped her head to glare at him again. "It's Greek, you know."

Her discomfort with such an ostentatious name amused Gus. He continued to grin in complete defiance of her seeming intention to glare him into submission. "Why Greek?"

"By the Lord Harry, I don't know! My pa just likes Greek. Always has." She stared ahead and pouted for a bit. "It means 'resurrection.' Ma liked it too. She fancied the idea of somethin' dead coming alive again."

Stacy lapsed into silence, studiously avoiding his eyes. After letting her stew sufficiently, he nudged his buckskin next to her horse and reached out a hand. She peered at it, then at him.

"Augustus Rivers," he said. "Pleased to meet you, Anastasia."

Her brow furrowed and her frown wavered before she reached to shake his hand. "Augustus? Really?"

He adopted an expression of faux affront. "It's Latin, you know. Means 'majestic.' I suppose my mama liked Latin. When she'd tan my misbehavin' hide, I swore she was speaking it."

"Majestic," she said with dripping sarcasm. However, a smile captured her face and refused to let go for a quarter hour. As the smear of dust became more apparent, her smile faded.

"What happens if we fail?"

Stacy's question took Gus by surprise. She didn't seem one to second-guess anything. Seldom wrong but never in doubt. He hesitated before responding, though, because the same question had plagued him for days.

"I've been in a dozen pitched battles by now," he said finally. "Every time I was still breathin' at the end, I shook my head in disbelief. Don't know how a man can stand in a field crossed by ten thousand bullets and miss every one of 'em. Regardless, there are only two ways out of this—livin' or dead. If we succeed, it'll be the former. If it's the latter, then we won't care so much. Corpses are very agreeable, in my experience."

When she exhaled loudly, he wasn't sure if he'd offered comfort or consternation. However, he had only a moment to dwell on it. Tension abruptly filled the air between them like a sticky liquid when the riders came into view, following a feeder stream on a perpendicular line to Gus and Stacy, mostly obscured by the patchwork of scrub that clung to the water's edge. They rode single file, a serpent slithering along the border of the creek in search of prey. Flashes of black and brown and gray gave form to their numbers.

"What do ya reckon?" said Gus. "Thirty?"

"Forty, at least." To her credit, her voice did not quaver.

They altered course to shadow the band of outlaws. If the men noticed them, they gave no indication. Within minutes, though, the group split in two, one remaining on the parallel course and one circling languidly toward Gus and Stacy.

"They're gonna hit the train from two directions," she said.

"Seems about right." He jerked a thumb over his shoulder. "You ride back fast and tell Paynter what's comin'."

"What about you?"

"I'll watch for a bit and then join you. Now git."

She nodded grimly. "Take care, Augustus. Don't die on me."

"And you, Anastasia."

Contrary to her nature, she left him with the last word and spurred her horse away toward the now-distant wagons. Once he became certain she wouldn't watch him too closely, he urged his horse toward the advancing group of about twenty men. Gus spun all sorts of tales in his head for why he rode toward the enemy rather than away. Maybe he could ascertain Sally's plan. Perhaps he could slow him down a little, or feed Sally's overconfidence. Mostly, though, Gus fell back on his military training. When overwhelmed by an oncoming enemy, someone must guard the retreat. Stacy was retreating, so he would form the rearguard.

Even from a distance, he recognized Sally's runaway blond beard. He reined his buckskin to a skidding stop two hundred yards away and pulled his loaded carbine from its sheath. Sally held up a hand to halt his men. The last time he'd attacked the wagon train, his men had been picked off like flies from a horse's haunch. His actions spoke of newfound caution. Gus cupped a hand to his mouth.

"What do you want, Sally?"

A smile split the big man's beard, obvious even from far away. His voice boomed in response. "Just give us the gold and no blood will be shed. You have my word."

Gus would sooner believe his mama's outlandish folktales than a word the man said. He shifted in his saddle, straightened, and called out again. "Fine. We'll see what we can do. But no bloodshed, promise?"

"Ah swear on my mother's grave."

Gus wheeled his horse around and kicked it toward the wagon train at a stiff gallop. He'd heard enough stories about Sally to know his promises were as hollow as an empty keg. Including the story about how he'd shot his own mother when he was twelve.

CHAPTER TWENTY-SIX

WHEN STACY CAME FLYING BACK TOWARD THE WAGON TRAIN, A bolt of purpose bounding across the expansive prairie, Jake was certain Gus was dead. Why he thought this he didn't know. They'd survived a version of hell together, so why now? As she drew closer, though, her expression wasn't one of grief, but of determination. He exhaled the breath he hadn't known he'd been holding and met her at the train's midpoint.

"Paynter, Paynter," she said, nearly breathless, "they're comin' and…"

"Hold a minute, little sister," he said with a palm raised. "Wait for the others and then tell it one time."

They waited only a half-minute before Lucien, the soldiers, and Cornelius joined them, all on horseback. The wagon master drew up beside his daughter and reached to squeeze her hand without a word. She flickered a smile at him before the stone determination returned.

"Go ahead," said Jake.

Released from her constraints, she hurtled through an explanation like a colt that had slipped its halter. About coming across the men. About the splintering into two groups. About the count. Although Jake had expected a large number of men, hearing forty clenched his gut. Only then did he realize he'd been holding out false hope for a smaller army. No such luck. During the telling, everyone had begun glancing nervously toward the east. It was McQuaid who saw Gus first.

"Look there."

Jake turned to find his old friend burning Stacy's trail, no less determined. When he joined the group, he cast a long look back the way he'd come. After a moment, he nodded and faced the group. "Must be bidin' their time. If they had a notion, they'd have followed hot on my heels and been arriving any minute. I reckon they're that certain how this'll turn out, or at least they talked that way."

"You got that close?" Stacy's question was an accusation.

"Close enough. We hollered across the distance and Sally made an offer."

Paynter's scalp crawled with those words. "Let me guess. A negotiation that avoids violence."

"Exactly. Turn over the gold and no one suffers."

"Out of the question," blurted Lucien. "I will not hand over a single bar to armed bandits."

Jake shook his head. "Let me spare you the moral dilemma, then. Sally is sellin' snake oil. He means to eradicate this party whether you hand over the gold or not."

Lucien seemed almost relieved. "Are you certain?"

"You asked the commander at Fort Kearny for more escorts. What did he say?"

"He said, and I quote, 'Three soldiers are as good as thirty.'"

"Why'd he say that?"

Lucien frowned, perhaps disgusted by recalling the unfruitful conversation. "He didn't believe my claim. He refused to entertain the notion that gangs of raiders survived the war intact and had the audacity to raid wagon trains between Fort Kearny and Fort Laramie."

Jake dipped his head in agreement. "That's right. And I've no doubt Sally knows this. Maybe he's even promised the commander a windfall should he look the other way. I don't know. But I do know this. Sally believes he will overwhelm us at little cost to him or his men, and that he'll ride away a wealthy man. But the only scenario in which he keeps his newfound wealth with no one the wiser is where we all lie dead in the tall grass."

"What do we do, then?" For all his bravado and calm under fire, Lucien sounded uneasy for the first time. A glance at the others found expressions of equal concern.

"We do what we've trained to do. We trust our efforts and brook no doubt. Second thoughts tend to become last thoughts when you're runnin' through a fire. You must believe in yourself, all of you, and follow the plan. No one is comin' to save us. All we have is one another."

He cut his eyes in turn at every rider in the circle until he found understanding, acknowledgment, agreement. This was the way of soldiers. Nothing else existed beyond the moment before them, the mission before them, the mountain before them. Survive the moment, execute the mission, and climb the mountain. Every alternative ended in defeat, disgrace, or death. He knew that the second they broke the circle, events would kick into motion that could not be called back. The manner in which they broke the circle would go a long way toward dictating how those events progressed.

"Let's not waste a moment, then. Gus and Stacy, set up a patrol eight hundred yards out. McQuaid, run one last inventory on the ammunition. Cornelius, be prepared to mark the first turn of the box."

"Why not form up now?" asked the wagon master.

"This is flat ground with plenty of room for attackers to approach. Hard to defend." Jake pointed forward along the river. "We need to make those hills ahead. High ground along a steep bank will give us an advantage. It'll be harder for Sally to attack uphill."

He motioned to Lucien. "Ashley, ride the column and warn everyone to stand ready to form up and fight."

"And what of you?" said Lucien. "What will you do now?"

Familiar darkness had already begun to settle into Jake. The wolf had begun to awaken, to stir and stretch and sniff the air. It was only a matter of time before he slipped his cage.

"I'll ride at a distance for now. I'm fixin' to kill a lot of men. It's best I not be too near people that I care about right now."

Without waiting for comment, he kicked the mare into motion and rode into a funnel of isolation polluted by the red haze from which would emerge the beast that could not be satisfied.

CHAPTER TWENTY-SEVEN

CERTAINTY IS OFTEN THE FIRST STAGE OF A JOURNEY INTO failure. Jake had learned that lesson well, but Sally had seemingly missed some of that same education. When the attackers began their approach during the last gasp of daylight, they trotted their horses at a leisurely pace. Even from a distance, Jake could see the jubilant interplay among them as they already counted the gold they'd soon share. *Good,* he thought. *Just how we want them.* Meanwhile, he doubted everyone and everything except the Henry in his hand and the darkness in his soul. He'd always trusted the wolf to bring him through the fire and had been well rewarded for his loyalty. As if he had a choice.

Jake shaded his eyes to find the train crawling along the crown of a tiny hill overlooking a thin branch of the Platte cutting its own trail north of the main channel. Though not a spectacular rise, one side fell precipitously into the river, effectively blocking an angle of attack. They wouldn't do better. He raced the mare toward the wagons, pointed the rifle he'd borrowed from the dead man skyward, and squeezed off a single shot. The wagon train reacted immediately by assuming the frenzied energy of a kicked-over ant hill, but a frenzy with the precision of a well-oiled steam engine. Every ox picked up a step as their owners encouraged a faster pace. As Jake watched the two groups of riders approaching, one from behind and one from ahead, every wagon made the turns with a practiced sharpness he'd not thought possible even a few days earlier. When faced with impending death, most people panicked and let chaos rule their thoughts and actions. Others, with no reasonable explanation as to why, adopted an air of cool detachment that transformed them into efficient machines intent on staving off imminent destruction. As one, the settlers had become the latter. If he hadn't been so embedded in the clutches of the beast, and himself so coolly detached, he might have felt pride in their actions. Instead, he only saw the necessary path to survival forming into a box of bonneted wagons.

By the time the riders had approached to within six hundred yards, the box had closed. And in their swaggering confidence, Sally and his men had allowed the box to form atop the daunting ridge, ceding the settlers an excellent defensive position. Jake covered the final distance and slipped the mare between a pair of oxen and the butt of an adjacent wagon to enter the square. Because they'd had no time to unhitch the oxen, the central area had become a crush of animals jockeying for space. Women and children were still threading their way through the herd toward the central wagons. Meanwhile, Mrs. Emshoff had jumped atop one of the jockey boxes to direct movement, shouting in German but making her point clear with dramatic hand movements. Jake grimaced at her exposed position until Maddie thoughtfully jerked the woman from her perch. He began threading his way among the stack of animals while continuing his cold study of the approaching units. Their pace had slowed, perhaps over surprise that a fortress had bloomed in the grass once occupied by a vulnerable line of wagons. The surprise didn't last long, though. Sally fired a shot into the air, sending the two units galloping toward the defenders. Jake smiled with dark satisfaction. Rather than maintaining splits and riding in a uniform front, the attackers bolted ahead with individual aspirations, creating a spread between the first and last riders and bunching horses into uneven knots. Apparently unaware of the danger posed by their disorganization, they bore down with the tactics of raiders, shouting of joyous murder and firing wild shots to instill fear. The stratagem usually worked. Not this time.

"It's yours, McQuaid!"

The corporal nodded at Jake and watched the approaching

horde close to within two hundred yards. The wild shots of the
raiders began connecting with the wooden sides of the wagons
as splintering crunches. Then one hundred yards. Still, McQuaid
waited. When the lead riders reached to within fifty yards, he
shouted the command.

"Fire! Fire!"

The initial volley of defensive shots rang out in rapid firecracker
succession. Three men fell from their horses and others slumped
in their saddles. Another volley seconds later brought down two
more. The ferocity of the defense had the immediate effect of
driving the attackers around the wagons instead of through them.
Unfortunately for Sally's men, the two groups chose to veer toward
the same side adjacent the river and collided in a jumble of horses
and men.

"Crossfire! Crossfire!" yelled McQuaid.

Cascading volleys of shots began sounding from three walls of
the fortress. More men fell, dead or wounded. Meanwhile, Jake
stood in his stirrups and began dropping the raiders from their
saddles with a succession of trigger pulls from the rifle. One. Lever
down, hammer back. Two. Lever down, hammer back. Three.
Lever down, hammer back. Four.

The mass of riders bolted down the river's embankment in
spontaneous retreat. Some of the wounded found riderless horses,
while others stumbled into the river clutching a collection of sur-
vivable or mortal wounds. In the hanging dust of the aftermath,
Jake counted twelve bodies lying still or dying in the grass. He fell
back into his saddle and squeezed his way out of the box.

"Sit tight!" he shouted while urging the mare toward the
embankment. Sally had already found the far side of the river and
had turned to face the embankment. When he saw Jake, he raised
his rifle. Jake mirrored the action and held. After a few yammering
heartbeats, Sally lowered his weapon and shook a ruined fist.

"You can't stay put forever, Paynter! You're trapped. We'll

starve you out! We'll burn you out! This only ends one way, and you know how!"

Still in the grip of the red haze, Jake's mind performed cold calculations. Sally was right about the trap. Any attempt to send for help from Fort Laramie would likely fail. They had enough food for weeks, but enough water for only a few days. Meanwhile, the animals would go thirsty without access to the river. Four days, maybe five. They could hold out no longer than that. He eyed the expanse of grass surrounding the wagon box. A well-placed wildfire would put them in immediate and dire straits. That seemed the more pressing problem. Then the wolf whispered to him—a notion, an idea.

"Sally!" he shouted. "Let's settle this between you and me! With or without weapons! Your choice!"

The big man shook his head and laughed. "I ain't stupid, Paynter. We got the upper hand. We'll just sit here and bide our time while you think about it."

In a lightning movement, Jake raised his rifle and put a bullet in the forehead of the grinning fool riding the horse next to Sally's. In response, the raiders wheeled around to find a camping spot well out of Jake's range. As they moved away, he counted. Twenty-nine, some wounded. Still too many. He returned to the wagons to survey the damage, detached, as if calmly determining if a paw had been severed in the trap. Other than gouges and holes where bullets had struck the wagons and bonnets, the rigs remained sound. One ox lay groaning with blood pooling from its belly. Before Jake could do it, Gus reached the animal, said something into an attentive ear, and ended its misery.

"Anyone shot?" Jake called out.

Maddie stuck her head out of a wagon bonnet. "Got one with some cuts from flying wood splinters. Not much else."

As the defenders emerged, Jake recognized their general euphoria of not only having survived but having defeated the enemy soundly in the first battle most of them had ever joined. This worried him greatly. No soldier really learned to fight until having been beaten savagely. The specter of another loss made for better fighters—more resolute, more clear-eyed, more vicious. The easy victory had created a false sense of what was to come next. And in his experience, too much early success was always a prelude to disaster.

"Hold your positions, then. Sally's just gettin' started." Everyone froze and watched as he circled the box. "The next attack will look very different from this one. Don't get comfortable."

As he made eye contact with several defenders, his heated gaze fell upon Rosalyn. She stood unharmed with a shotgun cradled in her elbow, staring at him with concerned questioning—whether over his physical health or mental state, he could not know. He nodded nonetheless, and then separated himself again from civil humanity to prowl the high bank along the river, lying in wait.

CHAPTER TWENTY-EIGHT

JAKE'S WARNING SHOUT YANKED STACY FROM THE DEEPEST OF slumbers that sometimes precedes the morning after a sleepless night. She rocked to her feet, stumbling like a Saturday night drunk. For a few seconds, she forgot where she was and why Paynter's shout should be so alarming. Then the details of the past hours came to her in a rush of awareness. The attack the previous evening, and how they'd sent the enemy packing. Paynter's absence as he patrolled the perimeter like a hungry predator. Gus's planning and direction filling the void as they picketed the oxen outside the box to create another layer of obstruction. A cold dinner devoid of campfires as everyone huddled under wagon beds to avoid the wandering horses inside the square. And the children, all sixteen of them, packed inside the central wagons into cubbyholes, nooks, and crannies for protection against a sudden onslaught of bullets.

Jake shouted again as his horse leaped a wagon tongue to circle the interior of the defense, no more than a shadow in the predawn. "You got thirty seconds! Take your positions!"

The roughly wakened defenders scrambled into their assigned locations even as shots began popping from the surrounding darkness, closing fast. Stacy jumped into a wagon alongside a corn farmer named Earl Havens. He nodded grimly and ducked with eyes wide when a bullet thwacked the wagon bed. When Stacy peeked between the rim of the bed and the bonnet, she spotted nothing distinct. Shadows in the darkness. Vague forms moving in and out, left and right, highlighted for an instant behind the flash of a muzzle before falling dark again. And screams, some of rage, some of fear, some of pain. She raised her Lefaucheux and fired a blast into the night, hoping to find an elusive target. Two seconds later, a bullet ripped through the bonnet inches above her head. She crouched low, remembering Corporal McQuaid's training. She moved positions, reloaded by feel, popped up to shoot blindly, only to crouch and move again.

While rising for a fourth shot, a steady flame not thirty feet away immediately drew her eye. She stared in wonder, confused. When the flame became an ascending arc, she aimed at the flame's origin and pulled the trigger. Her eyes cut swiftly upward toward the streaking glow leaking through the bonnet as the flame sailed over, an intentional comet seeking the interior of the box. The glow halted and flashed bright, all at once. Without thinking, she leaped from the wagon bed, rolled to her feet, and raced toward a flaming wagon with only two thoughts in her head. Children. And black powder. When a mountain rose before her, she grabbed it with both hands.

"Get the powder, Glen! I'll fetch out the children!"

She stepped up on the tongue of the Janssen's flaming wagon and leaned into the bed. Eight children were screaming in terror, including a five-year-old holding Lily Dunbar. Stacy snatched up the baby and marshaled the children from beneath the burning bonnet while Glen manhandled the heavy kegs of powder from the bed. Several women were attempting to douse the flames but were losing the battle in dramatic fashion. With the rescued children in tow, Stacy ordered out the younglings in the second wagon some fifteen feet away in case another incendiary breeched the box. She herded the collected children beneath the second wagon as the inferno of the first spit waves of heat at them. Above her in the second wagon's bed, Ketchum was screaming in abject terror, begging not to be left chained inside a tinderbox, pleading for his miserable life. To her back, her newfound charges cried loudly with fear of the violent unknown, while baby Lily wailed with terror in Stacy's arms. Unable to think, she lifted Lily to her shoulder and rocked her. Memories flashed. A young mother from South

Carolina had tried to teach her a lullaby on a journey two years earlier. Stacy had resisted the attempts mightily and would've sworn she didn't know the words. But like a roll of thunder across the plains, they came from a distance into her mind and began to settle on her lips even as she watched the horror of the battle unfold.

"Hush up, baby, don't say a word," she sang into Lily's ear, "Mama's gonna buy you a mockingbird."

A farmer wearing a straw hat staggered out of his wagon, clutching his chest. He stumbled toward the center before crumpling to the dirt to lie still.

"If it can't whistle and it can't sing, Mama's gonna buy you a diamond ring."

A rider attempted to leap through a gap between two wagons, only for the horse to become impaled by a pike lifted by a farm boy no older than fifteen. When the fallen horse pinned the rider, the boy's father drove a pitchfork through the man's neck.

"If that diamond ring turns brass, Mama's gonna buy you a looking glass."

Tears began rolling down Stacy's cheeks and into the baby's soft hair as a second rider breeched the gap to cut down a woman with a saber as she tried to spear him. Mrs. Janssen. Glen yanked the man from his horse and killed him with two crushing blows of his fist before adding a third in contempt.

"If that looking glass gets broke, Mama's gonna buy you a billy goat."

A woman with her sleeve ablaze fell back from the flaming wagon crying while two others tried to extinguish the flames with their bare hands.

"If that billy goat runs away, Mama's gonna buy you another today."

Two men dragged a third man into the box, shouting for Maddie to do something as she pressed her hands against the gushing wound of yet another man.

With no more words to recall, Stacy repeated the lullaby over and over as mayhem reigned inside the wagon box. People running, people shooting, people falling, people dying. At one point, Paynter flashed before her on his mount, shot a bandit the moment he stepped from cover, and raced again into the darkness with a reverberating howl. So intent was Stacy on the carnage assaulting her eyes that she didn't hear Lisbet's cry until Otto yanked her shirt.

"Miss Stacy, Miss Stacy. Lisbet!"

She turned to find Lisbet's face ashen as the little girl watched blood spread along her skirt in the blazing firelight. Stacy thrust Lily at Otto, who scooped up the child. She pulled up Lisbet's skirt to find a wound in her upper thigh oozing dark blood. A stray bullet. Guilt plagued her. She should have left them in the safety of the wagon bed. She pushed the little girl to her back and clamped a hand around the wound as Lisbet whimpered. She turned to Dora.

"Find me a bandana, a belt—anything I can use for a tourniquet." Seconds later, a bandana appeared under Stacy's nose. When she had tied it high on the little girl's thigh, the bleeding slowed but did not stop. She clamped her hand again on the wound.

"Don't worry, Lisbet. We'll fix this."

She regretted lying to a small child, but needed to keep everyone calm despite the shouts, cries, and gunshots that continued to saturate the air seemingly in all directions. As the bubble of violence continued to encompass them, she prayed for the first time in years. Prayed as she had never prayed before that the violence would end for the sake of the children. As the chaos of predawn gave way to dim light in the east, the sounds of conflict petered out slowly. Stacy remained focused on the little girl, afraid that if she looked away, she'd lose her, and perhaps find everyone else dead as well. Suddenly, Mrs. Emshoff was there, followed shortly by her grim husband, then by Maddie. Stacy slid aside and stood to let them attend to the little girl.

"Will she survive?" Her voice emerged as a choked whisper.

None of them answered. A presence to her left drew Stacy's attention. Paynter stood stock-still with a spray of blood across his face, his knuckles bloody and a gash on his arm, studying the attentions to Lisbet while drawing heavy breaths through flared nostrils. His jaw was a piece of iron, his eyes as hard as granite. Everything about him cried rampaging death.

"What's happened out there?" she asked him.

His eyes did not leave Lisbet while he spat words through gravel as if barely able to master human speech. "They retreated. We lost Private Evans, Mr. Havens, Mrs. Janssen, and Savoy's boy, Jeremy. Others wounded." He stood for two minutes in silence, methodically reloading powder, shot, and caps into his revolver without once looking at his hands. Then he squatted beside Maddie. "Will she live?"

"I don't know, Mr. Paynter. I'm sorry."

Mrs. Emshoff released a sob, driving Paynter again to his feet. He let loose a guttural snarl that raised the fine hairs on Stacy's neck, leaped astride his mare, and raced out of the box with revolver raised. After a minute, shots began echoing in the distance, five in all. Then true silence fell, broken only by the early morning breeze, the groans of the wounded, and a lone meadowlark nearby. Stacy tore her eyes from the little girl and wandered away aimlessly, wondering if she'd ever see Paynter again in this life.

CHAPTER TWENTY-NINE

THE SUN HAD RISEN TO QUARTER SKY BEFORE JAKE'S RAGE abated enough for him to walk again among innocents. His risky lunge into the lair of the surprised enemy had left two more lying cold on the earth, but Sally still commanded nearly two dozen men by Jake's count. Worse, their steep losses had not seemed to convince them to leave. Greedy men operated by a strange mental calculus that allowed them to callously set aside the dead in anticipation of a larger share. The successful raid seemed to convince Sally's band that their strategy of attrition would ultimately net them a fortune in gold.

With some semblance of mental order restored, Jake slipped the mare into the wagon box. Two dozen pairs of eyes watched him carefully, each marked by haunt, loss, and numbing terror. They had all performed a similar calculation and arrived at the same conclusion. The wagon train would not survive the raiders' repeated attacks. Jake dismounted to let the mare dig at the trampled grass for her breakfast. He slowed while walking past Mr. Janssen, who sat next to the ashes of his wagon while holding the hand of his dead wife and staring into the abyss, as if he could somehow change fate. Jake looked away and met the approaching Gus, Glen, and Lucien. Gus raised a hand.

"We should talk, Paynter."

"We should."

The four of them walked over to the Conestoga for conversation. Those not already attending to the wounded and the dead gave them a wide berth, clearly understanding the need for privacy. The men squatted in a tight circle, looking to Jake. He rubbed the bridge of his nose.

"What are the losses, Gus?"

"Five dead now. Six wounded. Five oxen down, and one horse. One wagon lost and another damaged."

Five dead. When he'd left, the count had stood at four. He steeled his nerves for what he must ask. "Lisbet?"

Gus's expression remained blank. "Still breathing, barely. Mr. Gillam expired an hour ago. The rest seem like they might survive. Until the next raid, anyway."

Jake inhaled deeply and nodded. He pinned each man with a bleak stare. "We won't survive another assault. They'll break our will. When that happens, we're finished."

Three nodding heads told him that they'd all figured the same.

"Which is why," he continued, "we can't allow another raid to happen. We must take the fight to them."

Lucien appeared stunned by the suggestion. "But their numbers are too many. They are too well armed."

"It can work." Gus's determined enthusiasm countered Lucien's doubt. "At Island Mound, we advanced on foot against a mounted force twice our size. They splintered in surprise and confusion. That allowed our cavalry to flank 'em and force a retreat."

That day remained seared in Jake's memory, not so much for the victory but for the valor of men in the first battle of their lives fighting like seasoned warriors of old, pressing resolutely against an unbeatable foe until the adversary turned and fled.

Glen grunted agreement. "The strategy has worked many times before. My family hails from Falkirk, not five miles from Bannockburn. Four centuries ago, Robert the Bruce faced an English army three times the size of his own. Knowing that he could not survive repeated attacks from such a force, he instead charged the field with everything he had. It blew apart the enemy positions and dissuaded the survivors from staying around. We could do the same."

"I'm not sure." Lucien was clearly unconvinced. "We are not Union soldiers. We are not, what's his name, Robert the Bruce."

"True," said Jake, "but we have two things in common with both of those events. Our enemy is overconfident, and we are desperate. When sufficient quantities of desperation and hubris collide on the field of battle, desperation always wins. Always."

Lucien stared aside at the milling farmers, his face painted with worry, before facing Jake again. "What's the plan, then?"

"Their predawn assault worked so well that they will almost certainly repeat it. So instead, we will assemble our best fighters and ride through their camp after nightfall, after they've had a little time to fall into their liquor and aren't thinkin' straight. We'll steal as many horses as we can and scatter the rest."

"Won't they just attack us again, but on foot?"

"Not if we aren't still here."

Glen's eyes lit. "You mean to move the wagons at night, then?"

"Yes. On to Fort Laramie at a hard pace, maybe make it in three days. We have wounded to care for. Supplies and animals to replace. And perhaps the commander at Fort Laramie will be more inclined to send troops out after raiders than his counterpart at Fort Kearny."

"We're gonna need to prepare to move," said Gus. "Bury the dead. Load the wounded. Consolidate the oxen."

"That's your job, Gus. You and Cornelius. Then at nightfall, you and I will ride out with Stacy, McQuaid, Muñoz, and Emshoff."

"And me," said Glen stoically.

"I thought you were finished with firearms."

"I'll make an exception. Wouldn't want to disappoint the Bruce."

"And I'm coming as well." Lucien's pronouncement was adamant. When Jake cocked his head askance at the man, Lucien scowled. "I know you think I'm just a spoiled senator's son, kept out of the war because of my father's connections. But I am not a coward. I am not afraid to fight for what's mine. And I will not stand by while outlaws threaten Rosalyn. So I'm coming with you, by God."

Jake considered Lucien's demand. He was a snake, no two ways about it. But he'd shown no evidence of cowardice, and even a snake will fight for its own. "All right, then. You're with us. But don't even think about tryin' to negotiate with Sally once we start. Any agreement with him is a death warrant."

"I realize that now."

"Good. Now let's get to our business. We've wagons to prepare and a raid to plan."

Jake stood from his squat, his hip still complaining about the surgery he'd performed on it weeks earlier. Maddie's cream had helped, though, just as she'd promised. Thoughts of the nurse dragged his attention to the makeshift hospital beneath the Flanagans' wagon. Four people lay stretched out beneath it, including a small figure surrounded by her family. Maddie, Rosalyn, and two young women attended to the other wounded. Jake clenched and unclenched his fists several times before walking toward the medical ward. Somber eyes met him when he crouched to examine Lisbet. The little girl seemed to be sleeping, her eyes closed and features slack, her skin the color of cold ash. He looked to her parents. Mrs. Emshoff refused to meet his eyes, but Mr. Emshoff did.

"She has lost much blood, Herr Paynter."

Jake returned his attention to the little girl, watching her unmoving form for perhaps half a minute. Spontaneously, he reached to stroke her forehead.

"Rest, little one," he whispered.

Her eyes flickered open to blink at the wagon bed above her before focusing on Jake. She mouthed "Mister Paynter" without speaking, smiled, and lifted two fingers to wave. He instinctively returned the gesture, losing himself for a moment. But only a moment. Then the vision returned, of another wounded child from a different time and place long ago. Another child who looked to him for hope, for salvation, not realizing who he really was. He stood abruptly and walked away, pressing his temples in an attempt to will away the unwelcome images. A hand on his elbow interrupted his efforts. He opened his eyes to find Rosalyn at his side, her forehead creased with worry.

"Mr. Paynter."

He lowered his hands and returned her concern with a woeful gaze, unspeaking. She honored his silence before opening her mouth once, twice, but closing it again. Her third attempt bore fruit.

"Things will turn out for the good. You'll see."

"You can't know that." And he meant it. Those who said "all things turn out for good" hadn't seen what he'd seen. Hadn't done what he'd done. Sometimes, malice and evil so perfectly filled up a space that good could find no path to slip inside. He wanted to be wrong about that, but had yet to find evidence of it.

"You are right," she said. "I can't *know* that. But I can hope. What do we become, then, without the hope that the worst in this ugly world can be resisted, can be rectified, can be overcome?"

"You become me."

He tapped the brim of his hat and walked away. Hope didn't banish the visions. Hope didn't erase the evil. Hope didn't keep him alive. And for the next few days, he'd need every ounce of reality he possessed to keep himself breathing and all those with him. What he didn't need was Rosalyn's hope trying to infect him with false promises. He *wanted* it, yes. But he couldn't afford the luxury.

CHAPTER THIRTY

THE SUN HAD BEEN AN HOUR GONE WHEN THE AD HOC CAVALRY marshalled their forces for the mission. Jake studied his force—Gus, Stacy, Lucien, Glen, McQuaid, Muñoz, and Emshoff—while dumping a mound of forty-four caliber rimfire cartridges into his saddlebag and stowing the Henry.

"Wait up."

Jake turned to find another man limping toward them, leading a horse. Before the newcomer could blink, Jake jerked out his Kerr and pressed it into his temple.

"Ketchum," he growled. "What are you doing?"

Ketchum lifted both hands. "Easy, Paynter. I didn't escape, if that's what you're askin'."

"He's with me," said Lucien.

Jake cut his eyes at Lucien with bewilderment before glaring again at Ketchum. "You're with Sally, not with Ashley."

"Not true," he said. "I got no love for Sally. He's a dark-hearted son-of-a-bitch. But I do love gold, and Mr. Ashley pays in advance."

Jake lowered his gun to glower at Lucien. "You bought his loyalty?"

"And why not?" Lucien waved toward the wagon train. "We're mostly a mob of farmers. Ketchum knows war. We need all the help we can get."

Jake flung his weapon into its holster with disgust. "It's a mistake, Ashley. He'll sell us out first chance he gets."

"I think not. Gold is a powerful motivator."

Jake mounted the mare without a word, prompting the others to imitate him. Roars of merriment and drinking could be heard from Sally's men even though they'd chosen a camping spot a mile downriver. Jake led his raiding party down the embankment and across the Platte, each armed with repeating rifles, revolvers, and spare ammunition. The bandits outnumbered them three to one, but Jake counted on the dual effects of surprise and alcohol to swing the advantage. They didn't plan to stand and fight. They only hoped to separate the enemy from its means of launching further attacks.

Low-hanging clouds concealed the gibbous moon and wrapped them in a cloak of night as they wheeled a wide arc to the south to come up into the belly of the enemy camp—and the picketed horses.

"They got 'em staked in a line a hundred feet south of the camp," Gus said with his voice low. He'd scouted the camp three times in six hours, the last time just after sundown. "Only one sentry, though. Cocksure sons of guns."

Jake twisted back to address the shadows on his tail. "Wait here for a count of three hundred. Then come fast. Meanwhile, I'll go introduce myself to the sentry. And watch Ketchum. If he says two words, shoot him."

Jake spurred the mare away toward the glow of an overly large and raucous bonfire. He hadn't counted on a friendly breeze from the north putting him downwind of the horses but was grateful for simple miracles nonetheless. He slipped into a dry gully that would carry water into the river during the rainy months and dismounted. The low position would prevent his silhouette from appearing above the black earth. He led the mare to within fifty feet of the sentry before dropping her tether. The guard was facing the campfire, probably lamenting the fact that he had to work while others drank his share of the whiskey. Jake leaned his cheek against the mare's nose, willing her to silence, before ducking away toward the oblivious man with his knife at the ready. The absence of the wolf continued to bother him, but did not prevent him from puncturing the man's throat from the side. He caught the staggering sentry between two mildly concerned horses, laid him down, and put a hand over his mouth as the man tried in vain to shout through an air passage filled with blood.

"Shh," said Jake. "It'll be done soon."

He held his hand in place for perhaps ten seconds until the sentry stopped moving. *No more than a boy,* he noticed. How'd he fallen in with such a hellish crowd? But then Jake remembered that he had sold his own soul at the tender age of seventeen. He stood up to fetch the mare, but found her watching him from ten feet away. He grunted and began cutting the picket rope.

When Gus clambered up beside him, he whispered, "Cut the lines. Tell everyone to take at least two. As many as we can. We'll drive the rest south onto the prairie."

For a half minute, all went according to plan. Before a drunken outlaw showed up.

"Hey, Bowles," the drunk called while staggering toward the pickets. "Sally wants to know if…"

The man swayed to a halt when he nearly stumbled over the sentry's body. He jerked his head left to right and fumbled a gun from his hip. "What the hell?"

Someone shot the outlaw before Jake could silence him with his knife. The gunshot had the effect of drawing the bandits like an avalanche toward the dissolving pickets, shouting with alarm as they came. Cursing, Jake sheathed the knife and drew his revolver.

"Grab what you can and ride! Don't wait for me!"

He leaped astride the mare and sliced her through the advancing party, Kerr cracking as he went. He spun a circle and came again from the side. Most of the bandits milled aimlessly around the broken tether line or chased shadows in the darkness. None had managed to corral a horse. He knocked down two men with kill shots and the mare crushed the ribcage of a third as she ran through him. He circled again, pulled from his shirt the bottle of moonshine donated by Mr. Flanagan, and raced toward the campfire. He tossed it into the flames as he passed. The resulting explosion showered dirt onto his hat as he forded the river. That was the signal to Cornelius to begin the march. The mare dug her way up the far embankment, lifting Jake above the mayhem. He watched as disoriented men flashed in and out of the firelight, looking for someone to fight. They seemed sorely disappointed. Then, somewhere in the darkness, Sally lifted a roar as a Goliath from the valley.

"Paynter! You're a dead man! Dead!"

Jake dismounted and sent the mare away from the embankment to graze. He returned with his Henry and a saddlebag containing sixty cartridges, settled into the tall grass, and sent a shot into the murk beyond the campfire.

"Down!" shouted three men at once.

He sat cross-legged, stretched his neck, and began counting. When he reached two hundred, he squeezed off another shot and then moved positions. For the next three hours, Jake repeated the maneuver—waiting, firing a shot, moving, only to wait again. Occasionally, someone would take a blind potshot at him, never coming within ten feet of hitting him. Once, a brave soul crossed the river upstream in an attempt to ambush Jake. He waited until the man's shadow appeared on the embankment before sending him back into the river forever. Upon reaching the final bullet, Jake stopped counting. All remained quiet for another several hours short of a sporadic curse or a shout in the distance. When the horizon began to fill with light, he lay prone in the grass with his rifle stretched before him. Vague figures moved around in the brush, darting from position to position only to lie still again. The campfire had long since surrendered to the ashes. Jake held his position until he was certain of the truth.

Not a horse in sight.

No, not one.

He exhaled a slow breath and shot the man who'd spent the

last hour maneuvering toward the river for a clean shot at Jake. He spun away from the embankment and caught up with the mare, who had found a nice patch of grass well away from the gunfire. She cut judgmental eyes at him before allowing him to mount.

"Move along, princess. We got a train to catch."

Rare elation filled his chest when they reached the former location of the wagon box and found it empty save for the burned hulk of the Janssen wagon and another abandoned, half-burned. He removed his hat while passing five crosses driven into the turf, mildly relieved that the sixth still eluded the Reaper for now. Jake followed the fresh wheel tracks above the Platte with Chimney Rock in his sights and passed the natural landmark four hours on. The rock punctuated one end of a range of proper hills that gave evidence of the landscape ahead. A dome of earth sprouted a spire of rock that towered three hundred feet above the river basin, a compass earnestly pointing toward the gates of the West. It took him another two hours to draw up alongside the Emshoff wagon. Mr. Emshoff waved with euphoria, despite having driven his oxen on foot all night and well into the day.

"You survived! Sehr gut!"

"And Lisbet?"

Mr. Emshoff's expression darkened. "Still fighting. She's a warrior."

When he looked up, Jake finally noticed the herd. Gus and Stacy rode up to meet him, smiling, no doubt amused by Jake's surprise. "We brought away fourteen in the first run," said Gus. "Then Ashley and I circled back to round up four more. With the extras from their dead friends, I figure there's no more'n a dozen horses left behind. If they can catch 'em."

Jake cocked his head. "Mr. Ashley went back with you?"

"Shocked me too," said Stacy.

"Probably wants to sell 'em to the fort."

"Maybe," said Gus. "But I believe him. He ain't no coward."

Jake shook his head "You're not gonna go trustin' him now, are you?"

"Not on my mama's blessed memory."

"Good."

The rear flap of the Emshoff wagon flap flipped open to reveal Glen, shirtless but with his wide chest wrapped in a bloody bandage. When Jake narrowed his eyes, Glen laughed.

"Somebody got lucky with a shotgun. That's all. It didn't hurt."

Maddie, who had circled around from the side with Lily slung from her chest, shook her finger at Glen. "Is that why you cried like a baby every time I removed a pellet?"

"I didna cry, wife." He threw on his shirt and stepped down from the wagon. "And I'm finished *resting*. Can't sleep a wink in a wagon bed that bounces like a rubber damn ball anyway."

"Crybaby."

He squeezed Maddie to his injured side. "I'll show you crybaby. Just a few wee scratches."

She giggled. "You've nothing to prove to me, husband."

Jake turned his eyes away in ache, not knowing where the pain had come from. Had his father ever loved his mother that way? Had either of them felt that way for him? He urged the mare ahead until he caught up with Cornelius riding alongside the Ashleys' wagon. Rosalyn's eyes went wide.

"Mr. Paynter. You came."

"As I promised."

She cut narrowed eyes at Lucien, who looked away. Apparently, he'd placed a different wager and lost.

"Best I can tell," said Jake to Cornelius, "they've not many horses left and will need to chase them across the prairie. 'Course, once they catch the first, the others'll come quicker. How much rest do the oxen need, do you reckon?"

The wagon master tipped his hat back. "A few hours. Long

enough to eat and drink and stand still for a bit. Then we move again before dawn."

Jake knew the plan. They hoped to push ahead on a hard march. With some luck, they'd be too near Fort Laramie for Sally to chance another raid. But he also knew that Sally didn't entertain the same logic most men did. That fact, and the ten strangers riding bareback in buckskins who'd been shadowing him for the last hour, kept him alert despite his lack of sleep.

CHAPTER THIRTY-ONE

AFTER PAYNTER RODE AWAY, ROSALYN WHEELED ON LUCIEN.

"Did I not tell you he would return? Did I not?"

He glared at her balefully. "Do not gloat, sister. It doesn't suit you."

"I am not gloating. I'm simply reminding you that despite your high regard for your opinions, you are sometimes wrong."

Lucien snorted before frowning. "I will admit misjudging him, but only a little. He has proved helpful."

"Helpful? Merely helpful?" She crossed her arms as they walked. "If not for Mr. Paynter, we'd all lie dead above the river thirty miles back. If we had survived even that long. His ideas and actions have preserved us all, you included."

"If not for Paynter, Mr. Sally would not be in such a murderous mood. We would have found a means of coming to an understanding with Sally, I'm certain." He nodded toward the jockey box, under which was stowed hundreds of gold bars.

"I think you overestimate Sally's humanity."

"As you overestimate Paynter's. They are the same."

"And yet you freed Ketchum and wooed him with a bar of gold?"

Lucien shook his head. "Ketchum is a mercenary. I own him now just as surely as I own these oxen. But Paynter belongs to no one. That makes him dangerous. Not that it matters, though, for he'll get what's coming to him and soon."

Rosalyn allowed the cryptic pronouncement to tumble through her mind before she pinned her brother with a hard stare. "Just what are you saying, Lucien? What will become of Mr. Paynter if he sees us safely to Fort Laramie?"

Lucien set his jaw, clearly not wanting to answer. When she elbowed him, he finally met her eyes. "The same thing that was to become of him all along. He will hang. If not at Fort Laramie, then at Fort Bridger as the army demands."

Her blood went cold. "You *want* to see him hang, don't you?"

"Yes."

"Why?"

"We've already discussed this. He thinks you are someone within his reach. As if a man like that could ever be worthy to even grovel in the mud where your shoes have trod."

She believed his reason, for he'd said it already. But there was something more. Something personal. Though she loved her brother, she knew him to be a supremely selfish man. What would raise such resentment in a man so dedicated to self-service and a crafted public image?

"You're jealous," she said with surprise. His furtive glance confirmed her suspicion. "Jealous because he has earned the respect and admiration of everyone in this train. Jealous because he knows precisely what to do while you offer no plan."

His hand shot out to clutch her forearm painfully. "Watch your words, Rosalyn. You disrespect me."

She twisted her arm away. "You disrespect yourself. To be envious of a man who saved your life and mine. Who came back twice to help us when he could have fled to freedom."

Lucien's cold glare warmed slowly as he apparently adopted a new tack. "Yes, he did save us. I admit it. But to what end? What sort of man would put his life in jeopardy to help strangers and ask for nothing in return?" He paused. "Paynter wants something, I tell you. His freedom, yes, but more. That is why he stays. And he will take what he wishes if we let him, as a criminal must. He's a killer. You must never forget that."

Rosalyn had heard enough. She spun on her heel to stride toward the rear of the train.

"Where are you going?" shouted Lucien.

"To let you lead this train alone for a while, as you so desperately wish."

She continued walking until reaching Paynter as his horse ambled next to a wagon at the midpoint of the column. He touched the brim of his hat.

"Miss Ashley."

She turned to walk with him. "My brother says you should hang, even after everything."

"He's not wrong."

She flashed her eyes up at him, affronted on his behalf. "Surely, you must believe deep in your soul that you are redeemable, no matter what you've done?"

He seemed to consider her question for a moment. "Just one problem, Miss Ashley. I ain't got no soul. Not anymore."

She walked along in silence before reengaging him. "At least promise me one thing."

"And that is?"

"When we near Fort Laramie, you will run. You will leave and save your life. If not for yourself, consider doing it for me. And for Gus. And for Stacy and all of us."

He nodded slowly. "I will consider it. Now, if you'll excuse me, I need to speak with that war party over yonder."

She blinked and watched him amble his horse toward a clutch of riders atop a low ridge in the distance, who she'd not seen until just then. War party? She broke into a trot as she returned to the front of the train, alarmed and heartbroken.

CHAPTER THIRTY-TWO

IN JAKE'S EXPERIENCE, ARMED MEN ON HORSEBACK shadowing his movements were either allies or adversaries. In the absence of context or information, the line between the two trended toward invisibility. As he rode warily up to the men holding the ridge above the wagon train, he leaned heavily toward guessing adversary. The nearer he drew, the heavier he leaned. These were grim men, battle-hardened men, intentional men. This was not a social call as had been his meeting with the Pawnee.

"What are we doin', Paynter?"

Surprised, he spared a glance to find Gus and Stacy trailing him closely and the wagon train drifting to a halt, everyone watching with fearful fascination. "Go back to the train."

"Shut up," said Stacy. "We ain't turning back. You should know better by now."

"I do. I had to try."

"Who are they, do you suppose?" said Gus.

"Don't know. Sioux, maybe? Or Cheyenne?" Both tribes had been at war with the government until two months earlier, led by Chief Red Cloud of the Oglala. This concerned him greatly, particularly given the abrupt appearance of the men. In every conflict, some were always reluctant to lay down their weapons when hostilities paused. Sally was evidence of that.

Gus and Stacy settled their horses on either side of the mare as they rode the remaining distance toward the watchers. The ten men formed a line that closed to a semicircle when Jake, Gus, and Stacy halted ten feet from the center man. Like the others, he wore his hair long, twisted into a pair of braids pulled forward, one over each shoulder. Whereas the others wore a single feather cocked to the side or no feather at all, the man in the middle sported a head-dress marking him as a war chief. Several of the men displayed a distinctive tattoo in the middle of their bare chests—three spots in a horizontal line.

"Arapaho," said Stacy. Jake cut his eyes toward her.

"You certain?"

"Yeah." She tapped a finger three times across her chest to indicate the tattoo markings. "Absolutely."

Jake recalled what Charles Buck had told him in Nebraska—his cryptic remark about meeting the Arapaho soon. His concern grew. The Arapaho had allied with the Sioux and Cheyenne in Red Cloud's war, and these men were clearly battle-tested fighters. The opposing parties studied one another for nearly a minute in silence broken only by comments from the gathered horses as they got to know one another.

"Do you speak English?" Jake asked finally. The war chief continued to pin him with his unwavering gaze, his lips a thin, unmoving line.

"Enha ne tagwa?" Stacy's question—*do you speak Shoshone?*—met with the same silent study. Another minute lapsed as the horses grew restless, apparently having finished their conversation.

"I guess we have nothing to talk about, then."

The man next to the war chief turned his head to speak in low tones. The leader nodded once, never allowing his eyes to leave Jake. The other man met Jake's eyes.

"You are Paynter?" The question in English caught Jake off guard. "The one who kills white chiefs?"

Jake blinked with surprised unease. However, he fully understood the man's point. "Yes."

The war chief grunted recognition. "Niineeni' howouuyooniit."

Jake cocked his head upon hearing the name again. He looked back at the second man with question, who in turn shifted his attention toward Gus. "You are the buffalo soldier?"

This question came in a blend of Shoshone and English. Gus caught the gist enough to nod. Jake shifted his mindset into his limited command of the Shoshone language to ask a question. "Who are you?"

"I am Two Wolves." He motioned to the leader. "We follow Yellow Tree."

Jake had heard the name while serving at Fort Bridger, and later from the Shoshone. Yellow Tree carried a reputation for relentless prosecution of battle against those who threatened his people. He had occupied a center position in Red Cloud's war against the government to stop wagon trains from overrunning land protected by an earlier treaty—a treaty now broken. This realization brought Jake a minor measure of relief. If Yellow Tree had wished him dead, he would already be cold on the ground. But what did he want? Why did he and his men shadow the train? Jake let his eyes wander over the horses ridden by the Arapaho. Many wore battle scars, and all seemed weary. Hard winters without shelter took a heavy toll on the horses who were the lifeblood of the plains tribes. A young warrior, probably no older than seventeen, eyed the herd the wagon train's cavalry had liberated from Sally's men, and a motive occurred to Jake. He met the eyes of Two Wolves.

"Are you on a trail of war?"

"No." Two Wolves glanced at Yellow Tree, who made a small hand movement, before he faced Jake again. "Red Cloud makes a treaty with the white chiefs. We walk a different trail for a time."

Jake looked at Yellow Tree. "We have many horses. More than we need. We took them from men who want us dead."

Two Wolves appeared to repeat Jake's words to the war chief. Yellow Tree lifted an eyebrow without turning away from Jake and spoke words Jake did not understand. Two Wolves translated.

"Yellow Tree says the men who want you dead will die before you. He means respect by this."

Jake furrowed his brow and glanced at Stacy, who lifted both eyebrows at him, almost mocking. He dipped his forehead. "Please thank Yellow Tree for his respect. Please tell him that his people grow strong under his leadership. Tell him we would like to make a gift of ten horses."

Before Two Wolves could translate, Yellow Tree held up a hand and spoke two English words. "Five only."

Trying not to betray surprise, Jake met Gus's eyes. Gus nodded as he wheeled his horse around. "On it."

With a few words of instruction from Two Wolves, four of the younger warriors kicked their mounts after Gus. Jake did not watch them and hoped nobody in the wagon train would decide to become a hero at the worst possible moment. He instead returned Yellow Tree's gaze, unblinking, while awaiting Gus's return.

"You are Shoshone." Two Wolves spoke the words to Stacy in the Shoshone language.

"I am. My mother's father was Many Horses. He gave me *this* horse."

"We know of him. Does he live?"

"No. He joined his ancestors two winters ago."

"Good for him."

Jake mostly followed the exchange. Many Horses' name was still on the tongues of the Shoshone when he had wintered with them. Only then did he realize he should have asked Stacy about her family before. His habit of keeping people at arm's length prevented such questions from crossing his lips, a necessary evil for maintaining isolation. The next question from Two Wolves, again for Stacy, stirred him from regret.

"Do you travel with the white people freely?" Two Wolves nodded toward the wagons.

"I do."

He nodded, but with a why-would-you frown. Yellow Tree spoke again, but this time to Paynter, and still in the Arapaho language. Two Wolves translated.

"He asks why those men want you dead."

Jake chuckled uncharacteristically. Why indeed? What could he say that might not draw further interest from the warriors? The truth, he decided. To hell with it. "We carry gold. They want it. They will kill everyone for it."

Yellow Tree snorted derision, again without translation, and spoke at length.

"Yellow Tree is amused," said Two Wolves finally. "Those men would kill you for gold. You cannot feed it to your family. It will not warm you when snow is deep in the valleys. It is good only for decoration. Those who kill for decoration are not truly men, but beasts."

A half smile touched Jake's lips. "I agree. It is the thinking of a madman."

The thump of hooves marked the return of Gus and the four young warriors, each pulling a horse. Gus approached Yellow Tree and offered the tether of the one he pulled, a tall chestnut stallion. "Please tell Yellow Tree the buffalo soldier wishes to offer a gift. I mean respect by this."

Yellow Tree accepted the tether and handed it to the man on his other side. Then he nodded to Two Wolves, who addressed Jake.

"Yellow Tree offers freedom for Niineeni' howouuyooniit. We will prevent any from following."

Again, Jake tempered his surprise. Why would a man he didn't know make such an offer to a stranger? "Give Yellow Tree my thanks. But I have promised to protect these people from those who hunt them. I must stay."

Without waiting for translation, Yellow Tree walked his horse backward six steps and spoke a command. As one, the men turned their mounts and trotted away. Jake watched for a moment before calling out.

"Two Wolves! Does Niineeni' howouuyooniit mean 'one who kills white chiefs'?"

The warrior paused to look back at him, a cryptic smile on his face. "Watch the trail at your back, Niineeni' howouuyooniit."

He turned, gave two sharp cries which spurred his horse ahead, and rejoined his band. Jake watched as they traveled northwest until disappearing over a low hill. He shook his head with disappointment. It was enough to be known as a killer by everyone he knew without suffering that indignity from complete strangers. When he turned to face Gus, his old friend just laughed while Stacy frowned with bewilderment.

"What just happened?" she said.

"I don't know."

Gus laughed again. "I can't tell if you just made new friends or new enemies."

Jake still wasn't sure either. Allies? Adversaries? An answer was beyond him, though an inkling was beginning to stir. "Most people I know have been both at one time or another. Why would Yellow Tree and his men be any different?"

"Speaking of enemies, Lucien is mighty angry about you giving away horses while gettin' nothing in return. I believe he wants to tell you all about it."

Jake urged the mare back toward the train. "Doesn't mean I have to listen."

CHAPTER THIRTY-THREE

As promised, Lucien was waiting for Jake when he rode back up to the train, which had begun to lumber forward again. Jake dismounted and faced him with arms folded. "Well? Let's have it."

Lucien was seething. "Did those people intend to attack us?"

"I don't believe so."

"Did they demand horses?"

"No. I offered."

Lucien threw up an exasperated hand. "Why in God's name did you do that? Those were ours, collectively. The decision was not yours to make."

Jake gathered a curse and stored it away for a later time. "We don't need 'em. Maybe they do. They gotta feed their families when this is all over, just like us."

Lucien shook his head with clear disdain. "If you keep giving away our property to every vagabond that shows up, we'll arrive empty-handed at our destination."

"They weren't our horses to begin with. What does it matter if we give a few away?"

"It matters immensely. We keep what we earn, and we risked our lives for those. We killed for those."

"That's not why we did it. We killed to stay alive. To preserve those we care for."

Lucien snorted. "You miss my point entirely. Besides, what kind of moral derelict would take something without giving in return? Answer me that."

Jake swallowed a disdainful laugh. "I don't know, Mr. Ashley. Perhaps you might explain how you came by the gold in your wagon. Perhaps you might tell me what you gave in return."

Lucien bristled. Jake felt that the man might try to punch him. He hoped so, a little, so he could leave Lucien in a bloody heap on the side of the trail. However, Lucien restrained himself, which saved Jake having to explain to a disappointed Rosalyn why he had pummeled her brother half to death. The man seemed to gather calm before responding through gritted teeth.

"My father came by that gold fair and square."

"Is that so?" Jake grinned lazily. "I'll bet those bars have 'CSA' stamped on each and every one of 'em. How did your virtuous father…" He spat in the dirt. "…come by so much Confederate gold 'fair and square'? I wonder."

"That is none of your concern, Paynter."

Jake nodded and frowned. "Yeah. I thought so. Not so different from your so-called vagabonds."

Lucien waved at the ridge the Arapaho had occupied minutes earlier. "We are nothing like them. They are savage. Uncivilized. Killers."

"Sounds like most people I know. At least the Arapaho are true to the welfare of their people. Not like Ketchum and his ilk who'll swap loyalties for a bar of gold."

When Lucien grew a wicked smile, Jake knew what was coming. The man let the accusation wallow in his mouth before speaking it. "Swap loyalties? Like you did during the war?"

If stares could kill, Lucien would already be gasping his final breaths. Jake inhaled deeply, tamping down the red haze. "I did nothing for profit."

"Then why? Why'd you do it? Why abandon one side for another?"

Jake turned to walk away. "To save what was left of me."

As he led the mare toward the rear of the train, unwelcome memories crowded around him, a dense and malicious fog clinging to his awareness, invading his senses. Reminding him of how it all went wrong. Forcing him to recall the dark day he fully lost his bearings.

"Shoot him, Paynter," said Blackburn, his eyes twin pools of righteous fire as he extended the Dragoon butt-first to Jake. The new boy. The seventeen-year-old runaway seeking glory and respect.

Jake cut his eyes between the offered revolver and the frightened man on his knees at Blackburn's feet, bound, gagged, and bloodied. The man stared pleading holes through Jake until he looked away in discomfort. "I don't know, Captain Blackburn."

Lightning flashed behind the captain's eyes. "Shoot him, by God. Shoot him or I will shoot you."

Jake glanced at Sally, who loomed behind Blackburn while wiping fresh blood from his saber. The big man impaled him with his dead-eyed stare that generally preceded savagery. "I'll open you up, boy. Who are you with? Us? Or him?"

Sally nodded toward the terrified prisoner. Jake blinked and accepted the weapon from Blackburn with a trembling hand and stepped up to the bound wretch. As he extended the barrel toward the man's head, the prisoner's muffled cries became more desperate and he clenched his eyes shut, squeezing trails of tears down each cheek. Jake pulled back the hammer and touched the trigger lightly. All he had to do to please Blackburn was pull the trigger. All that stood between him and the respect of the other raiders was a gentle squeeze. A flick of the finger, nothing more. Try as he might, though, he could not still his trembling hand. When he glanced up at Blackburn, he expected fury. Instead, the fire of the man's eyes had tempered to a warm flame. He offered Jake a sympathetic smile and placed a comforting hand on his shoulder.

"I know, Paynter. It's a hell of a thing to take another man's life. To play God. But I want you to look at him good."

Jake looked at the man, who had allowed one eye to open with desperate hope. He seemed a pathetic figure, past middle age with a pot belly and a thinning scalp that only emphasized his shaggy sideburns. His family already lay dead in the house. Except for his young daughter. She was somewhere behind the house with Blackburn's lieutenants, but she'd die when they were finished with her. Jake didn't particularly want to be the one to end the man's life, shattered though it may be. It was as if Blackburn heard the whispers of his innermost thoughts.

"I know he don't seem like much," said Blackburn. "But you have to understand. This man is a sympathizer. He gives succor to the enemy. He takes food from the mouth of your family. From the mouth of your mother."

"My mother is deceased, sir."

"Of course, of course." Blackburn's tone was dead calm, as if quieting a spooked stallion. "But what would she say if she were here now? Hmm? I think she'd tell you to do your duty. I think she'd tell you to protect your family. To preserve your way of life. To take care of you and yours."

Jake didn't much care for the family he had left, and didn't particularly enjoy his recent way of life, but Blackburn's words were like a drug, numbing his mind, seizing his thoughts, offering the comfort of oblivion. He swayed on his feet, overcome.

"Shoot the man, young Jake. Shoot the man, and all will be well. I promise."

In that moment, he wanted nothing more than to be free of indecision. He wanted nothing more than all to be well, to earn the respect that had always eluded him. As Blackburn's siren call stole his reason, Jake pressed the barrel again to the prisoner's forehead and pulled the trigger. He blinked at the violence of the slug exiting the barrel, but not before the executed man's last thoughts became apparent on his face. Shock. Dismay. Resignation. All in the brief moment that lay between the seconds. Then he fell over dead, a significant portion of his brain matter liberated from his shattered skull onto the earth beneath him.

"That's a good boy," said Blackburn as he retrieved his weapon from Jake's frozen hand. "You did well. You did right."

When the raiders mounted up a few minutes later, Jake knew he'd *crossed a great divide into a dark and dangerous country. A place he'd never seen before, one that lived only between storybooks and nightmares. He had no idea how far he'd journey into that country but would soon learn.*

CHAPTER THIRTY-FOUR

EXHAUSTION SET IN AFTER THE LONG NIGHT AND TWO MORE days. Jake suggested they press onward in darkness, but he was outvoted by the weary and the overly optimistic farmers. Everyone had apparently taken notes when Jake had described the radius of army patrols as two days. When the train crossed that invisible line marking the supposed patrol boundary and into the Unorganized Territory, they had begun to breathe easier again. To speak in other than hushed tones again. To laugh again. Refuge was near, and Sally could not touch them. Jake considered this point of view disastrously incorrect, but clung to the hope that he was the one in the wrong. Gus's uncharacteristically stoic demeanor informed Jake that at least he was not alone in his caution. The remnants of the most brutal units of the war were nothing if not unpredictable. Sally would storm Fort Laramie if he thought he'd survive the attempt.

With Jake's objection noted and dismissed, the train formed into its now customary box at dusk to set up camp. Within half an hour, a dozen campfires had been set, with beans in Dutch ovens casting an aromatic net over the nomadic fortress. When the Emshoffs and Dunbars invited him to share their fire, he did for a time. However, he couldn't get past the hole in the gathering where Lisbet should have been, asking difficult questions and stirring up minor trouble. The little girl occupied a small nest in the wagon bed, mostly sleeping from fever. Maddie's concern over her survival hung like a pall over the conversation, reeling them back into silence time and again. The strain of the awkward social situation proved too much for Jake.

"I thank you for the grub, Mrs. Emshoff. Especially the rye. Danke."

"Bitte schön, Herr Paynter."

He took his leave and scanned the dark skies. A million stars stretching from edge to edge of night's vast canopy informed him that no rain was imminent, so he moved his bedroll away from the camp to exist in his natural state—alone. The exhaustion that he'd denied for two days finally came to visit with sweet promises of oblivion, and soon rendered him deeply asleep. There were no dreams. At first. Then the grass was filled with serpents, flicking their probing tongues. And a shout in the night. And a cry.

He sat bolt upright, his heart racing. Another cry, and another. He was on his feet in a flash of reaction and racing toward the encampment, the Kerr clenched in his right hand. Had he reloaded it? He couldn't recall doing so since leaving the valley of death where he'd pinned down Sally's men all night. Stupid. He'd let complacency invade unnoticed, making him no better than the farmers he'd so harshly judged. An unusual glow of light led him to the far side of the wagon box where many of the travelers had gathered. The scene he came upon unfolded like a manic vision before him. Sally stood with eight men in a semicircle facing the wagons. The rest of his army had apparently hightailed or passed from this life. Before them on hands and knees with rifles to the backs of their heads were some of his party. Mrs. Roberson. Mr. Cawthon. A young girl called Meg. Mr. Emshoff.

And Rosalyn. At Sally's feet.

Two torches held aloft by Sally's men illuminated the scene in flickering firelight, causing shadows to dance and obscuring the features of the prisoners. Jake slipped up to the corner of a wagon and inspected the Kerr's chamber. Two chambers loaded. He lifted his eyes as Sally began to speak.

"Let me tell y'all how this will go. We're gonna wait here not so patiently while you collect everything that shoots and pile it right here in front of us. If you dawdle, we start killin' your friends. If you raise a weapon in our direction, we'll kill you and then start killin' your friends." He scanned the wagons. "Paynter. I know you're here. Show yourself and I'll think about not shootin' this pretty little lady."

Jake madly began performing the mathematics of survival. He could shoot Sally dead, and in the process ignite a gun battle that would surely kill Rosalyn. He could slip away, but that would probably kill Rosalyn too. He could step forward, which would likely result in both her death and his. The calculation had no solution, because more than anything, Sally was a dark angel of death. This would not end without the Reaper riding through with a broad scythe, harvesting settlers and outlaws alike with energetic and indiscriminate swings of his blade. When Sally pressed the rifle muzzle into Rosalyn's hair and pulled back the hammer, Jake stepped into the light with his Kerr pointed at Sally's forehead. He did not recall making that decision, but his feet moved anyway. Sally smiled wickedly.

"Why, there he is! The man of the hour." He lifted a bandaged hand from his weapon and waved it at Jake. "You owe me two fingers, Paynter. And some men."

"Let them go," he growled.

"I reject your proposal." Seemingly undisturbed by Jake's pointed weapon, Sally turned his attention to the gathered settlers. "What'd I tell ya? Weapons here, now! You got 'til the count of fifty. Go!"

The crowd scattered like ants under a sudden cloudburst, running to gather weapons. Jake shook his head and groaned. It was a terrible mistake. He spied Gus, Stacy, and the soldiers to his left, who were apparently following the same line of reasoning. If he could signal them somehow to open up on Sally's men all at once, then maybe...

"I need your weapon, Paynter." To make his point, Sally pulled Rosalyn up by the hair, eliciting a startled cry from her, and wrapped an arm across her neck. He gripped his rifle with one hand—the one with its full complement of fingers—and leveled it at Jake. "This very second. Same goes for y'all standing over there in the shadows."

Jake knew he shouldn't comply. Compliance was a death sentence for some or all. Rosalyn was shaking her head, telling him not to do it. The wolf cried for blood—anybody's. Gus stood ready to follow his lead and attack. Nevertheless, for the second time in seven years, Jake laid down his weapon voluntarily.

"Kick it this way. Hands where I can see 'em at all times."

When Jake did so, Sally smiled again. "Not so hard, right? If you'd been this cooperative all along, we'd not be in such a contentious mood."

The unintended but to-be-expected consequence of Jake's capitulation was the defeat of the others. Gus, Stacy, McQuaid, and Muñoz tossed their weapons toward the raiders. One outlaw scuttled forward to gather them up. Within seconds, other weapons began piling up ten feet in front of Sally, forming an altar of firearms suitable for ritual sacrifice.

"Now," said Sally, "what shall we discuss?" He turned to the man beside him. "Whadda ya think, Bert? What should we talk about?"

"The weather maybe? Oh, wait. How about let's discuss the gold Ashley took from us."

"Fine suggestion, sir. First rate." He turned to face Lucien, who stood in the middle of the gathered settlers, his face a mask of stone. "See here, Mr. Ashley. I'm not a greedy man. I'd settle for half of what you got and then leave you be. Or I can shoot your sister, slit your gullet, and take all of it. However, far be it from me to decide on yer behalf. I'll give you thirty seconds to think it over. Take your time."

Jake wasn't quite sure what to expect. If anyone could exchange the life of a loved one for the lure of riches, Lucien seemed to be that man. When he remained silent as the seconds ticked by, the wolf began whispering to him again, forcing him to determine if he could reach Sally before Rosalyn died.

"Half." Lucien's harsh proclamation brought Jake back to the present. "Half, and no more."

"Excellent decision, Mr. Ashley. I knew a senator's son would understand such a gift despite his loss of leverage." He turned to the man beside him again. "Didn't I say that, Bert? That Mr. Ashley would choose prudence over glory?"

"You did. Not a half hour ago."

Sally motioned toward two of his men. "Accompany Mr. Ashley to his fine Conestoga and relieve him of half his hoard. Take back two of our horses and load 'em up. Pronto."

Everyone, including Jake, remained locked in place as the three men left to undertake the task of enriching Sally. Meanwhile, Mrs. Emshoff to his left stared a hole through Jake. *What will you do about this?* that stare asked. *Why will you not fight?* it accused. He wondered the same. Sally settling for a portion when he could have all was inconsistent with his character and history. Was it his lack of men? Or did he intend to ignite a slaughter regardless? But every time the wolf pushed Jake to the lip of the precipice of violence, one look at Rosalyn in Sally's grip pulled him back. He had never wanted to feel this powerless again.

"Tell me, Bert. Whacha gonna do with your share?"

Bert flashed a gap-tooth smile. "Well, I figure I'd stay at one o' them fancy hotels. You know. The kind where they bring a hot bath to yer room."

Jake stood like a statue, torn, as Sally and his men discussed how they'd spend their spoils. It was then that Jake noticed Ketchum's absence. He'd expected him to rejoin Sally. Or even maybe help the settlers. The snake had clearly chosen to stay out of it to preserve his own skin. He should've shot the man when he'd had the chance.

The snort of a horse drew his attention. The two bandits led a pair of horses laden with heavy saddlebags as Lucien followed behind, appearing dejected.

"That's a lot more than half," Lucien said.

Sally laughed. "My apologies. My boys are a bit uneducated. Countin' and 'rithmetic ain't their strong suits."

Lucien seemed about to erupt. However, he wisely bit back the bulk of his malice. "You got what you came for. Give me my sister."

"Fair enough," said Sally. "But there's one more thing I need before I release my new friends here."

"What's that?"

Sally waved the rifle barrel that had been pointing at Jake the entire time. "I need Mr. Paynter."

"What for? Was he in this with you?"

Sally hurled a guffaw at Lucien. "With us? Oh, hell no. He shot half my men."

"Then what will you do with him?"

"What won't I do? Maybe peel back some of his skin, see what makes him tick. Maybe drag him behind a horse for a few miles. I don't know. I'll think of somethin' amusing."

As Gus began to step forward, Jake saw how it would end. A barrage of shots into the gathered settlers. Maybe Sally dead. Probably Gus dead. And Stacy, and Rosalyn, and Emshoff, and…and…

"Stop, Gus," he said firmly. "Everything's all right. It's a good trade. One for five."

"But, Paynter…"

"I've decided." He stepped toward Sally, who seemed a little surprised by the surrender of the man who'd nearly cost him everything. When he stopped five feet away, he held a hand to Rosalyn. "Hand her over, or so help me God, I will end your life before the last breath exits my body. You know I will."

Sally blinked, produced a smile that did not reach his eyes, and pushed Rosalyn toward him. When she tried to embrace Jake, he shoved her behind him. "Go to your brother."

Without a word of permission, the other prisoners jumped to their feet and ran to their loved ones. Mrs. Emshoff gathered her husband into a crushing embrace before turning haunted eyes toward Jake. He gave a half smile and shrugged. Then Sally clipped the back of Jake's head with a rifle butt. A sea of stars swam across his vision as he stumbled to a knee. When he looked up, Sally was standing over him, joyous.

"We're gonna have a high time, you and me."

Two seconds later, Burt fell between them with an arrow bisecting his throat. To Jake's right, another man fell, and then another. Shots began ringing out, from the darkness, from the wagons. In his addled state, Jake struggled to understand what was happening. Before he could collect his senses, Sally's burly arm encircled his throat. "I'm gonna kill you now, Paynter. You did this."

Jake clutched the man's arm, wrestling in vain to dislodge it. The stars began to swim again. A shape barreled into them both, sending them sprawling. As Jake attempted to inhale a breath through his liberated windpipe, he watched fascinated as Mr. Janssen plunged a knife into Sally's left eye.

"You killed my wife, you son of a bitch."

He pulled out the knife and shoved it through Sally's temple. The raider's remaining eye seemed bewildered and mildly amused, dead as it now was. Jake stumbled to his feet, searching frantically for the next battle, the next assault to beat back. He found none. Each of the bandits lay unmoving or moaning in agony. Movement from the shadows tore his attention from the carnage to find Yellow Tree entering the pitiful light of the dropped torches, a ghost of a man with a bow in his hand. Two Wolves came behind him while other vague shapes lingered in the darkness beyond. Yellow Tree knelt calmly beside one of the dying men and brought a club down with a single stroke that shattered the man's skull. Two Wolves quieted the other in a similar fashion. Jake glanced at the settlers to find them pressed against the wall of wagons, frightened, perhaps wondering if the battle had only just begun. Meanwhile, Yellow Tree rose and faced Jake.

"Niineeni' howouuyooniit," he said. "Your enemies lie dead."

Jake stared in disbelief. "They do. You have my thanks."

"I offer freedom once more. A life for a life. You ride away with us."

Jake nearly accepted the offer. He almost rose to mount the mare and disappear into the night. But "nearly" and "almost" were powerful words that neutered actions, that forever altered trajectories.

"I can't. I must stay."

"Why?"

"I don't know."

Yellow Tree gave a single, slow nod. "Then it is done."

The war chief spun away and melted into the darkness as suddenly as he had come. As Two Wolves turned to follow, Jake leaped forward to grab his arm. The warrior eyed Jake's hand with disdain until he released his grip.

"Two Wolves," he said. "Niineeni' howouuyooniit mean 'one who kills white chiefs'?"

The man's eyes remained hooded, but his jaw softened with empathy. "No. It does not."

"What, then?"

Two Wolves tossed his head with a lean smile. "You stopped the slaughter of Yellow Tree's people at the Green River. Niineeni' howouuyooniit means 'he is merciful.'"

With that he was gone, and Jake was fairly certain he'd not see the man again. For perhaps a minute, he watched the void where the Arapaho warriors had disappeared, trying to reclaim himself from the long unyielding darkness. Failing that, he turned back toward the wagons.

CHAPTER THIRTY-FIVE

EARLY THE NEXT MORNING, JAKE, GLEN, AND GUS SET ABOUT burying the dead bandits in a shallow mass grave thirty yards outside the wagon box. Lucien wanted to leave them for the carrion eaters, but Jake wouldn't have it. He needed them buried. He needed Sally beneath the dirt. He needed this to be over. The three of them, stripped to the waist, established a steady rhythm of biting the earth with spades and tossing it aside. They worked in silence for a time.

"Mr. Janssen walked away in the night," said Glen after a while.

"Whadda you mean?" said Gus.

"He woke me and Maddie and gave us his dead wife's shawl. He asked us to watch over it after he left. We asked where he was going, but he didn't know. Last I saw, he was leading his horse north."

"There's nothing much to the north except Sioux country."

"He knew that. He seemed like a man looking to get lost."

Jake understood. Sometimes the only way to shake the demons of the past was to leave them behind and find a lonely place. Jake's demons had proved more diligent than most.

"Maybe we should go fetch him back," Gus said. However, the tone of the comment was rhetorical. Gus above all people knew the value of disappearing for a time.

"No," said Jake. He muscled another spade of sod from the earth. "He needs a new path. Even if it kills him. His old path is a dead end, anyway."

They resumed digging until the pit seemed large enough for nine bodies. Jake and Glen began lugging the bodies one by one to the pit and tossing them inside as Gus started filling the hole again behind them.

"Janssen has a point, Jake."

Jake looked up from the body in his hands at Gus's comment. He'd never heard Gus utter his Christian name before. Whatever his old friend had to say, it was important. He tossed the body into the pit and stood with hands on hips, gathering his breath. "What point is that?"

"It's early in the day. Nobody is paying much attention to you right now. I could gather your belongings, pack your horse. You could slip over that hill and be gone before anyone reckons what happened. I'll not run you down. Neither will Stacy or Cornelius, or the soldiers. Lucien ain't got the gumption."

Jake considered the suggestion while walking with Glen to fetch the final body. Sally's. The same notion had entered his thoughts repeatedly throughout the night. Twice he'd stirred from his bedroll to do just that. Each time, though, he'd settled back in for reasons he could not identify. Now, in the light of day, the reasons were beginning to manifest. To congeal into substance that might be handled and examined.

"Let me think about it, Gus."

Jake lifted Sally's legs and Glen manhandled the big man's torso. He stared into Sally's dead face, which still wore an expression of bewilderment, and wondered how he'd look when he died. If it came at the end of a rope, at least he'd see it coming. At least he'd not look like Sally. There was a simple appeal to greeting death on the open road with an empty hand and joining it for the final ride into an undiscovered country. To see it coming and find final solace in that.

They heaved Sally into the pit and resumed shoveling. The sun had cleared the horizon by the time they finished the job, and they shone with sweat. Jake mopped himself down with a bandana and donned his shirt. So deep was he in his thoughts that the press of the gun barrel to the back of his skull caught him completely off guard. A second barrel pressed into the middle of his back informed him of the gunman's identity. He touched his hip, found it bereft of his holster, and extended both hands, palms open.

"Ketchum," he spat. "What's this about?"

"Hold your horses. And don't move a muscle. I'll relieve you of your brains or your kidney if you turn on me. You know I can."

"I know."

When Jake chuckled, Ketchum snorted. "What's so funny?"

"Nothin'. Just stray thoughts about seeing what's comin'."

He waited only a moment before Lucien walked up with McQuaid. Lucien shoved the familiar manacles toward the corporal. "Shackle him, soldier."

McQuaid pushed the irons away. "What are you talkin' about?"

Lucien lifted his spine in a show of authority. "We liberated Mr. Paynter for a time because he was useful to our expedition. Now that the danger has passed, his usefulness has come to an end. From here on, he is only a threat or at risk of flight. Shackle him and take him on to Fort Bridger as you were ordered to do."

McQuaid's face clouded. Others began drifting up, realizing what was happening. Stacy held her shotgun in both hands while Gus's hand rested on the Colt at his hip. Mr. Roberson gripped a rifle and seemed ready to kill if necessary.

"What in the name of Jess and Joan are you doing?" said Roberson. "He saved all of us. He traded his life for my wife's. I won't let you bind him. No, sir."

"I stand with him," said Mr. Emshoff as he stuffed powder, ball, and wad into his musket. His wife appeared ready to fight Lucien with her bare hands.

Rosalyn ran up, breathless. "Lucien! What are you doing? This is unconscionable!"

To his credit, Lucien did not flinch at the flood of defiance. "Be reasonable, folks. This is a matter of law and justice. It is not ours to decide."

"The hell it ain't," said Gus as he whipped out his revolver to point at Ketchum.

A dozen other barrels lifted to find as their targets either Lucien or Ketchum. Behind Jake, Ketchum sucked in a breath and the pressure of his two barrels lessened. Gus looked Jake dead in the eye.

"Go, my friend. I already saddled your horse."

"Yes," said Stacy. "Do as Gus says. He's right this once."

"Run, Jake." Rosalyn took two steps toward him before stopping with hands that seemed uncertain of what to do. "Save yourself. For us. For me."

Lucien singled out Gus with his glare. "You will pay a price for this, boy. You'll hang instead of Paynter for aiding the escape of a federal prisoner."

"I saw him render no aid," said McQuaid. "Way I recall, Paynter slipped out in the night."

Roberson grunted. "That's what happened, for sure."

The others nodded and hummed agreement. A warmth Jake had not felt for a long time seeped into his chest. The same he remembered from sitting in the cane fields with his grandmother mapping the stars. These people were giving him a chance to be free. To continue the search. To seek what was lost, to the ends of the earth if necessary.

However.

If he ran now, he would validate everything Lucien claimed of him. A man out for his own interests without regard for the needs of others. A man willing to discard loyalty for a momentary advantage. A fugitive from the law, always on the fringe, always looking over a shoulder, always jumping at noises in the night, always waiting for death to come from his blind side, unnoticed, unheard, without warning.

He couldn't live that way. Not any longer. With some surprise, Jake found that he wanted his day in court to defend his name and become worthy of the friendship offered by those defending him now. He needed that day like he needed the next breath of air.

"I will not run. I will face the accusations with whatever dignity I still possess."

Murmurs of disapproval swept the group. Gus shook his head as if he'd expected as much. Stacy stomped a foot and strode away in anger. Rosalyn just stared at him with dire disappointment, wiping her eyes with the back of a hand. He tore his gaze from her and extended his hands toward McQuaid, wrists together. Lucien shoved the manacles at the corporal.

"Paynter has more sense than the lot of you."

McQuaid eyed the irons as if he just vomited them up before yanking them from Lucien's hands. He walked to Jake and began to shackle his wrists. "I'm sorry."

"I know. You're just doin' your job. And I'm doin' mine. No hard feelings."

When McQuaid finished, Lucien nodded with a look of grim satisfaction. "Show Mr. Paynter to his horse and tether it to the trailing wagon again. McQuaid, you'll join Private Muñoz as his escort. We don't want the prisoner to entertain a change of heart."

Rosalyn stepped up to her brother and laced his cheek with a palm. "Have you no shame?"

She stormed away. A startled Lucien rubbed his cheek before eyeing Jake with hatred. "You turned her against me, didn't you?"

"You did that all by yourself. You needed no help from me."

Lucien's face grew redder still before he erupted. "Well, what are you waiting for, Ketchum? Show him to his horse, and earn your damn pay for a change."

When Lucien walked away, Ketchum laughed quietly. "He's a temperamental sort, ain't he? But he has lots o' shiny gold. And I'm like an old raven in that way. I love me some shiny things."

He nudged Jake with the barrels, leaning him into motion toward his horse. The cold manacles, absent for weeks, bit into his wrists, reminding him with every movement of what he'd just surrendered.

CHAPTER THIRTY-SIX

STACY'S RAGE WITH PAYNTER FOR NOT RUNNING SUSTAINED her until they arrived at Fort Laramie. When soldiers belted Jake from his horse and hauled him away to the stockade, her anger shattered. She found a lonely place away from judging eyes and shed her grief as a river of tears.

Afterwards, she fell into a fog of work for days. Replenishing supplies from the fort's stores. Helping her father repair damaged wagons. Assisting Maddie in the treatment of wounded animals. Anything to keep at bay the fact that she'd failed to save Paynter. She listened to updates from her pa—of how the fort commander had doubted their story. Of how her pa had ridden out with soldiers to show proof of what had happened. Of Colonel Blaine's shifting plans for Paynter. But mostly, she remained lost in the mists of regret. It took a reprimand from Gus after almost a week to clear the air.

"You gotta look in on Paynter," he said. "They won't let me pass."

"Why me?"

He folded his arms and frowned. "Don't 'why me.' You're eaten up with what's happened to him, just like the rest of us. If you don't look after him now, you'll carry that regret forever. Believe me. I know."

The thought of doing something—anything—stirred her immediately. She cut her eyes at Gus, skeptical. "What makes you think they'll let me in?"

"'Cause you're a woman and not dangerous, as far as they're concerned." He grinned. "They'd be wrong about that, of course. You're as dangerous as a cornered polecat."

Stacy couldn't help but catch Gus's infectious grin, but it faded as she furrowed her brow. "What about Miss Ashley? What if I took her with me? Hard to turn away two women."

Gus shook his head. "She's been workin' on that for days. Managed to finagle two meetings with Colonel Blaine to ask for a visit with Paynter. She might be wearin' him down too. But Lucien's been keepin' her confined to the wagon, mostly. When he does let her out, he sends Ketchum to ride herd."

Stacy scowled. "We'll see about that."

The combination of Stacy's righteous indignation and Rosalyn's persistence did the trick. Within twenty-four hours, they'd won permission from Colonel Blaine for a visit and convinced Ketchum to look the other way for an hour. A bottle of Lucien's whiskey sealed each deal, unbeknownst to him.

"They won't let me in," said Gus as he approached the stockade with Stacy and Rosalyn.

Stacy huffed. "We'll see about that too."

When they arrived at the door, the on-duty officer leveled an accusatory finger at Gus. "Not him. You two may pass."

Stacy was in the midst of gathering up a vivid protest when Gus touched her arm. "I told you so. Let it slide, Anastasia. Or you'll be left out here with me while Miss Ashley visits Paynter."

His use of her forbidden name reeled Stacy back to her senses. "Just ain't right."

"Nevertheless."

Stacy snorted her feelings and joined Rosalyn in stepping through the door of the stockade behind a blue-uniformed guard, a pimple-faced boy who looked like he wondered how he'd joined the army for adventure and ended up watching prisoners in the middle of a howling wilderness. The interior proved surprisingly cramped and dark, a far cry from the freshly painted white exterior. As Stacy's vision adapted to the narrow space, she counted four cells. The disillusioned boy led them past three empty cells to the final one. Paynter lay on his bunk with hands folded over his chest and staring at the ceiling, as if practicing for his funeral. When he saw Stacy and Rosalyn, he swung his feet over the edge of the bunk and sat up.

"Ladies."

Stacy scowled at the adolescent guard hanging over her shoulder. "Can we get some privacy? Or would you like me to break yer nose?"

A startled look crossed the boy's face and he retreated to the cell block door to wait while Stacy speared him with a fortitude-melting glare the entire way. Then she nodded. "Stay put."

When she looked again at Paynter, his face had grown a half grin. "Still a model of how to make friends, I see?"

"I got enough friends. Don't need new ones."

"That I understand." He shifted his eyes toward Rosalyn, who stood aside with fidgeting hands. "How long have I been in here?"

"Six days," she replied.

"Hmm. Seems longer."

Stacy watched Rosalyn put her trembling hands on the bars of the cell, her tongue apparently locked as she stared at the floor between Paynter's boots. Realization struck Stacy like a wayward branch. Miss Ashley liked Paynter. And not just as a friend. Stacy swallowed a snort, wondering how a fine lady like her had fallen for a condemned man of wretched repute. Regardless, she understood the appeal. Despite his concerted efforts to push people away, Paynter couldn't help but draw everyone. He was a brilliant and deadly flame, and they the unsuspecting moths.

"How they been treatin' ya?" Stacy asked to break the silence that had descended in the cell block.

"Well enough." The purple bruise beneath his left eye spoke otherwise.

"Sorry you didn't run when you had the chance?"

Paynter gazed at the still-silent Rosalyn. "I got no regrets. What's going on out there? My gracious hosts won't tell me anything."

Stacy elbowed Rosalyn, hoping she'd get the message. The woman peered at Stacy briefly before understanding lit her eyes. She faced Paynter again. "Colonel Blaine initially disbelieved our story. He found dubious our claim of repeated attacks by a large band of white raiders. He was incredulous that a wagon train made up mostly of farmers managed not only to withstand the raiders but to obliterate them, and with help from forces he considers hostile. However, my brother's invocation of our father's name compelled him to listen."

"Does he believe you now?"

"He has no choice," said Stacy. "He sent a troop with my pa to the scene of the last two attacks. They found the bodies, the graves, the abandoned supplies, the ruined wagons, and rotting oxen. They followed footprints east for a few hours lookin' for stragglers and discovered a couple o' bandits with arrows in their chests. Looks like whatever's left of Sally's men are hoofin' it back to Missouri and trying not to get killed along the way."

Jake cocked his head slowly at Stacy, his shadowed eyes invisible but for a glint of the pupils. "What kind of arrows?"

"They didn't say, but I think you know."

Jake grunted seeming approval. "So you made them true believers?"

"We did," said Rosalyn. "We gave you most of the credit for our survival, hoping it would sway Colonel Blaine to treat you kindly."

Jake rubbed his cheek and winced. "Perhaps you should reconsider your persuasion skills. I don't think it worked."

"I am not surprised. The colonel can't seem to forget the

charges against you. Your killing of a fellow officer appears more offensive to him than Sally's attempt to murder an entire traveling party."

When she fell silent, Stacy knew there was more that Paynter should know. He seemed to understand as well and nodded. "Stacy. What's she not telling me?"

"We believe," she said, "that Colonel Blaine will send you along with us when we leave rather than hangin' you here without a trial. But just barely. And we're pretty sure he means to exact a price from you before he lets you leave."

"Yeah," said Jake. "I think he's just warming up to that task now. Thanks for the warning, though. I'll be sure to make 'em earn it."

Stacy grimaced. If she didn't know any better, Paynter sought the abuse, coveted the pain. Why else would a man surrender to an authority that hated him and then proceed to provoke a beating with every word from his mouth? He stood from his bunk, terminating her line of thought. He failed to move for several seconds other than the clenching of his fists.

"Lisbet?" The name emerged as a ragged whisper.

Rosalyn pushed her forehead against the bars. "Fort Laramie boasts a fine surgeon from Boston, which Maddie Dunbar verified. He was able to remove the ball from Lisbet's thigh bone, difficult as it was. He says she will recover as long as infection doesn't set in over the next few days."

Stacy watched as relief swept over Paynter's face. He exhaled and sat again on his bunk. "That's good. So, how long does that leave us here?"

"Another week, perhaps. Long enough for the injured to prepare for travel."

"So no one's turning back?"

"Not a soul. They've sacrificed too much to get here, endured too greatly to retreat."

"Good. That's good."

Listening to the civil conversation between Rosalyn and Paynter finally pushed Stacy past her limit. She slapped the cell bar in front of her. "Goshdarnit, Paynter. I wish you'd listened to us. But you don't do much listening, do ya?"

"No, not much. It's always been my downfall. But promise me somethin' when this is all over."

Stacy stepped away from the bars, not wanting to think about what came at the end of the trail. "Fine. What?"

"Take care of the mare for me. I worry she'll get lonely without someone to hate."

"She's not alone in that," said Stacy as she strode toward the cell block door.

CHAPTER THIRTY-SEVEN

A JOURNEY INTERRUPTED IS A JOURNEY FOREVER UNFULFILLED. The only solution was to stand again, lean into the wind with intention, and continue. In service to that truth, Gus rode up and down the line of wagons in the twilight before dawn, assessing readiness. Were all the teams hitched up? Had anyone failed to pack a stray item? Did everyone have sufficient water and supplies for the next leg of the journey to Fort Bridger? When he'd come to a satisfactory answer to all those questions, he positioned his buckskin near the stockade and waited.

The sun had breached the horizon before the stockade door opened. Two burly soldiers dragged a half-limp Paynter from the building and on toward the wagons. The stockade officer shot Gus a "hands off" glare before slamming the door shut. Gus nudged his horse along behind the soldiers as they hauled Paynter across the parade grounds like a fresh carcass. When they reached a point twenty yards from the Emshoff wagon, the men unceremoniously dumped Paynter into the dust and motioned to Corporal McQuaid.

"The prisoner is yours," one said.

"What's left of him," said the other. They shared a laugh as they returned toward the fort. Gus dismounted and lifted Paynter from the dirt. He winced upon seeing the mass of bruises, the eyes nearly swollen shut, the dark lines and splotches where blood had dried repeatedly. More blood dripped from his raw wrists beneath the manacles.

"For the love of God, Paynter."

Paynter pushed Gus's hands away without a word and stumbled toward his horse, which waited impatiently behind the Emshoff wagon at the end of the familiar tether. Stacy sidled up alongside him with concern.

"What'd they do to you?"

He ignored her and continued to shuffle forward. When he reached his horse, he tried to mount but fell onto his backside in the process. Gus lifted him again from the powdered earth and, despite resistance, helped him reach the saddle. Stacy planted herself in front of Paynter's horse.

"Talk to me," she said with too much anger. When he looked away into the distance, she stamped her foot. "Did you at least make 'em earn it?"

His nostrils flared, but his eyes remained fixed on the horizon. "Oh, yeah. They earned it. Now go away, little sister."

Stacy spat in the dirt and stomped away. Gus hurried after her and grabbed an arm. She wheeled to face him, her expression one of righteous but wounded fury.

"What happened to him? Did they break him?"

Gus laughed, but softly. "No, he's not broken."

"How do you know?"

"I just know. A broken man is never that determined to hate everyone."

"He hates us now?"

Gus lifted a finger to brush the tear on her cheek, causing her to freeze. "No, not really. He just does this from time to time. Whenever he becomes isolated, whenever he thinks his death is near, he starts shedding friendships like a snake changing its skin. He removes himself and can't be reached."

"Why does he do that?"

"To protect himself. To protect his friends from retribution over associating with him. To protect us from pain when we lose him."

"He's given up, then?"

"No, I don't think so. Just give him time. He'll come around by the time we reach Fort Bridger. He'll need us then, so have faith."

She peered at Gus with a hopeful frown that served to intensify her large, determined eyes. By the Lord, she was something!

"Thanks, Gus. You're a good friend."

"And you, Miss Blue."

She smiled and slipped away to retrieve her horse. Gus glanced back at Paynter to find him still fixating on the horizon. He didn't know what his friend was looking for, but prayed he'd find it before they reached their final destination.

In the face of repeated and brutal beatings, Jake had retreated into the iron fortress of his inner mind where it was safe, where the wolf might be kept at bay, where he could survive and treat his wounds. Now that the beatings had ended, he found escape from the mental fortress far more difficult than the entry. Prisons were like that. Regardless of the dismal despair within, a prison slowly possessed the inhabitant until the prisoner forgot how to exist outside of it. After a week inside, Jake had thoroughly forgotten the direction to the gate.

In his locked state, he became a spectator rather than an active participant, a man-shaped husk that rode when the mare moved, ate when food was put before him, and slept on the first empty spot he could find. So deep was his silence that McQuaid didn't bother to shackle him to a wagon wheel at night. Sometimes Ketchum would drop by to heckle him, but Jake barely noticed. The outlaw might as well have been a ghost. From his box seat in the theater of activity, Jake watched people move in and out and the wagon train roll along. On the first day, the procession continued following the Platte toward the northwest. Gus, Stacy, and Rosalyn stayed away for the most part, as if having been warned. When they tried speaking to him, he often ignored the overtures but sometimes added a grunt or a word. After three days, he realized his efforts to keep everyone at arm's length had created a remarkable ache within he'd never felt before. The walls of his iron fortress seemed taller, thicker, darker. He spent hours on end trying to discern what had changed, but came up baffled time and again.

On the fourth day, Lisbet's face appeared in the flap of the Emshoffs' wagon for the first time since they'd left Fort Laramie. He blinked on noticing how much she'd thinned during her recovery. Her mischievously innocent smile, however, had not changed a bit. She locked eyes with him and the smile faded. Perhaps she noticed that he had gone elsewhere. Maybe it was the bruises or his grim demeanor. Regardless, she studied him for a long time, her tiny brow knitted with concern. Finally, she lifted a hand and waved two fingers. Though his right hand twitched, he did not return the greeting. Within seconds, a look of affront rippled across her face. She lifted her chin and swept closed the flap. Another unusual sensation seized him in the aftermath. Regret.

Over the next several days, the wagons crossed creek after creek before veering south across the North Platte and into the Sweetwater River valley. They followed the Sweetwater day after day across a landscape strewn with sagebrush and antelope but largely devoid of people other than those who appeared in the distance and rode another way. Meanwhile, everyone continued to avoid him, including Lisbet. By ten days into the outbound journey, he was stewing in his isolation rather than reveling in it, marinating in the juices of dismal memories, old scars, and persistent ache. He wanted out but couldn't quite locate the key. On the twelfth day, they reached Independence Rock.

"Cornelius says we'll rest a day here," Gus said to him. "Not that you care."

Jake cut his eyes at him, trying to think of what to say. Nebulous thoughts nearly found words, but never quite coalesced. He did manage a nod, though. Gus lifted one eyebrow in response, maybe recognizing that Jake had begun working to escape his prison, before riding away to help guide the formation of the wagon box—Jake's old job. When the box formed, Jake dismounted and turned the mare out to graze. He trusted that she'd stay nearby. And if she ran? Well, good for her. He scraped away a small sagebrush beneath the Emshoff wagon and settled in to watch his fellow travelers abandon the train for the dome of rock. Independence Rock protruded from the otherwise featureless plain as if an enormous whale escaping the confines of the Sweetwater River. He watched Stacy clamber up its side to stand atop the dome more than a hundred feet above the plain and spin a circle with arms wide. Others joined her, starting with Gus. Rosalyn's green skirt flared in the breeze as she shielded her eyes to peer into the hazy distance. Ketchum hovered behind her, too near. The urge to join the party seized him briefly until he rocked to his knees. A minute passed, then another, and he settled back into his hole. He resumed his surveillance as everyone began carving their names in the massive granite dome alongside thousands of other names belonging to those who had passed by over the course of decades.

Two hours later, Mrs. Emshoff brought him supper, as she had for two weeks. This time, though, he held her eyes for a moment and dipped his chin. She returned the nod and retained the good sense not to say anything about it. He ate mechanically, like a reaper harvesting wheat. When it grew dark, he scraped away a second sage and curled in to fill the space until he drifted into sleep. He awoke several times during the night to the serenade of coyotes or calling of night birds. Perhaps that was the reason he slept well past sunrise for the first time in six years.

"Mr. Paynter."

A little finger poking his improved but still-tender cheek dislodged him from sleep. He cracked his eyes open, freeing them from the grit gluing them shut. Lisbet squatted near his head. When she lifted two fingers to wave, he returned the gesture. A smile split her face and she grabbed his hand.

"Come with me."

Jake was a man who liked to know what he was agreeing to, what he was about to do, what he was in for. Whenever someone asked him to go somewhere, he usually needed some questions answered first. This time, though, he said nothing. He found his hat and crawled from beneath the wagon bed before the little girl led him toward the rock dome. Though her limp was pronounced, he marveled she could walk at all. The astonishing resilience of young bones remained a mystery to him. As they walked, Jake ignored the wide-eyed stares of those he passed. When they reached the rock, Lisbet released his hand and produced an enormous knife from the confines of her skirt. He recognized it as the one he'd used to cauterize his hip wound what seemed a lifetime ago. How she'd gotten hold of it, he hadn't the foggiest notion. She held it up to him until he accepted it. Then she pointed to the rock face before them. He leaned forward to find a light set of scratches that looked a bit like the spelling of the name "Lisbet."

"Put yours next to mine," she said. Then she lifted her little hands. "I don't know how to spell 'Paynter.'"

Jake stood unmoving for several heartbeats as recollection stirred, a wrenching blend of good and bad. "Okay."

He leaned a knee against the stone and carved his name, digging it deep. Lisbet watched with fascination. When he finished his name, he began working on hers, rounding out the letters and increasing their permanence. Sweat dripped from his brow before he finished and stood. The little girl ran her fingers over both names and smiled.

"Does this say 'Paynter'?"

"No. It says 'Jake.'"

"Jake? Is that you?"

The promise of a future smile tugged at his lips. "I reckon it is."

CHAPTER THIRTY-EIGHT

OVER THE RUN OF DAYS AFTER DEPARTING INDEPENDENCE Rock, Jake continued his slow emergence from the confines of his fortress. A nod of the head here. A string of words there. When Glen Dunbar showed up with a pair of padded cuffs to wear beneath his manacles, Jake even managed to express his thanks and ask after Glen's family. This act seemed to liberate Gus, for he began riding alongside Jake for an hour or two at a time, talking to him but not expecting anything in return. In appreciation, Jake gave him a nugget of conversation now and then.

The journey out from Independence Rock required nine crossings of the Sweetwater over the span of a week until each wheel, hoof, and shoe was caked with seemingly impervious high plains mud. However, spirits were high because of what had slowly risen from the haze to dominate the southern horizon. A set of majestic tabletop mountains—the Oregon Buttes—marked the entrance to the saddle of earth that gave passage over the continental divide at South Pass. Cornelius called an early halt to the train just before noon, a few miles shy of the pass. The butt end of the Wind River mountains beckoned to the north, snowcapped even in late summer. Swaths of green on the lower slopes gave way to rocky heights where breath grew short and nights frigid—a realm of bighorn sheep, grizzly bears, and bugling elk unchallenged by men.

"South Pass City's that a-way a bit." Cornelius pointed north. "If you need anything, this is it until Fort Bridger. Be back by sundown. Don't make me come lookin' for ya."

Jake was prepared to settle into another hole when Rosalyn invaded his isolation. She had an affinity for that, it seemed. "Mr. Paynter."

He watched her walk up, wearing the same memorable green skirt she'd worn atop the rock dome. "Ma'am."

She seemed tentative, maybe a little nervous. Not like before. Was that his fault? She finally broke a stretching silence. "Some of us are riding into South Pass City for a look. Care to join us?"

He tried to say no, but the stubborn word resisted his attempts. He settled for dissuasion. "What would my keeper say?" He tossed his head toward Lucien.

"I've already beaten him down. He says you may go so long as McQuaid minds you."

"And I already agreed," said McQuaid.

Jake looked over a shoulder to find the corporal waiting astride his horse. Jake sighed in surrender. "I reckon."

Rosalyn hurried to retrieve her horse, as if a delay might allow Jake to change his mind. Which was prudent in light of his misgivings about agreeing to go. Before he could renege, though, the small party consisting of Rosalyn, Lucien, Gus, Stacy, the Emshoffs, and the Dunbars was making its way toward South Pass City. While Glen and Maddie shared a horse, the rest rode alone. Jake was impressed with how well Rosalyn managed her mount. She'd clearly spent hundreds of hours in a saddle.

Whereas much of the journey had been short on the presence of people, the approach to South Pass City proved different. The discovery of gold two years prior had transformed the sleepy stage and telegraph station into a swelling tent city of miners, prospectors, charlatans, and fools, numbering some two thousand souls. Tents and shanties clung to every square foot of dirt and shattered hillsides that surrounded the main street, engulfing the few more permanent structures that comprised the original town. The rush of people reminded Jake of St. Joseph, but tighter, muddier, and more ramshackle. He wondered if a stiff wind might blow everything away, leaving behind a grimy mass of humanity to bemoan their loss. As their little band rode toward the town center, the mostly male eyes watched them pass. Watched the women, anyway, each of whom was striking in her own way.

When they came to a halt at the general store, Jake was prepared to remain astride the mare and mind his own business. Gus would have none of it.

"Go on in, Paynter. Reacquaint yourself with civilization."

"This ain't civilization."

"What're you sayin'? Disparaging this fine metropolis. Why, keep that up and you might offend somebody."

"I offend most people most of the time, so nothin' new there."

Gus's continued prodding finally forced Jake from the mare. The horse eyed him as if warning him not to start trouble. He gave her a nod of compliance. "Let's go, McQuaid."

He and the corporal followed Lucien and Rosalyn before realizing that the others had gone exploring instead. He grimaced and stepped through the door anyway. What greeted him was a narrow space packed to the tall ceiling with everything a prospector might need and a thousand things he didn't. The aproned storekeeper raised a hand from across the crowded space as they entered.

"Hello, strangers." He beat his way toward them, slicking back his hair while perusing Rosalyn as if she was a fresh-baked pie. "New in town or just passing through?"

"Likely the latter," said Lucien. "But that depends."

"On what?"

"Business prospects."

"Then your timing is excellent, given the recent act of Congress."

Lucien grew a smile like a cat watching a bird. "So they passed it, then."

"What passed?" asked Rosalyn.

"The Wyoming Organic Act. This place is now square inside the new Wyoming Territory. It'll become a state before you know it."

Her eyes narrowed. "You expected this. Father must have told you."

"Perhaps."

The revelation wasn't lost on Jake. If a man wanted to carve out an empire and ascend to power, what better way than to influence the rise of a territory to statehood. And if someone possessed, say, a few hundred pounds of gold, his influence could range far and wide. When Lucien launched into deep discussion about future prospects with the storekeeper, Rosalyn drifted away to peruse the merchandise with McQuaid and Jake in tow. However, once he'd seen one flour sack, pickaxe, or lantern, he'd seen them all. After rounding the store, they rejoined Lucien, who had just finished his impromptu discussion with the shopkeeper. When they returned to the street, the others were waiting with the horses. Glen wore a big smile.

"Mr. Dunbar," said Rosalyn. "You seem pleased."

"That I am."

"Why, may I ask?"

His smile widened. "They've only one blacksmith here, and he died two weeks ago. God rest his soul."

Rosalyn tilted her head. "Does that mean…"

"We're staying," said Maddie. "Glen will set up shop here. The town is growing like a willow in water."

As the group rode back toward the wagon train, Glen discussed his plans with everyone. He had it all figured, it seemed. Though happy for the Dunbars, Jake would miss them. They'd shown him true and undeserved kindness. Stacy seemed a bit glum as well, but also wore the look of a proud parent. She had been the one to pluck them from the wilderness to deliver them here. Her pride was well earned.

"What about you, Mr. Emshoff?" Jake was surprised that he let the question escape his lips. He had become well aware of his growing regard for the German family. Usually, he maintained the good sense to keep his feelings buried.

"What's that, Herr Paynter?"

"I mean, will you stay here as well?"

He stroked his chin and nodded. "We are considering it, but only after."

"After what?"

"After we speak on your behalf at the trial."

The simple pronouncement struck Jake silent. They barely knew him. They certainly did not know the things he'd done. How could they speak on his behalf? That question would keep his thoughts occupied for much of the next several days.

CHAPTER THIRTY-NINE

THE NINE-DAY JOURNEY FROM SOUTH PASS TO FORT BRIDGER afforded Jake much-needed time to fully return to the realm of the living. Midway through the final leg, the wagons reached the treacherous Green River, whose waters ripped through the landscape under the force of snowmelt racing down the Rocky Mountain slopes. Jake knew the river well. His flight from military justice had begun above the same river basin nearly a year earlier when he'd refused a command. An array of ferry operations along the less dangerous stretches provided the means for transporting wagons, animals, and people across the surging waters. With the coming of the railroad and inevitable decline of business, most of the operations were likely to disappear inside of two years. For the time, though, Jake marveled at the audacity of the entrepreneur who'd tackle such a daunting task. Their particular ferryman, a weather-beaten man called Carl, moved all sixteen wagons across with a steady stream of chatter and without incident. Even the massive Conestoga proved only a minor inconvenience.

"You ever lost anyone?" Jake asked as he rode over on the final crossing with the soldiers and the Emshoff wagon.

"Oh, sure," said Carl. "Lost two last month. One tenderfoot from by-God New Jersey decided he didn't need to tie down the by-God wheels and turned his by-God rig into a less-than-serviceable raft. It didn't float for long, but she was a good ship while she lasted." He burst into laughter at his own story, perhaps having waited for a while to tell it. Jake had to admit that he found some humor in it.

"And the other?"

"Oh, that one. My fault. Mea culpa."

"How so?"

"I let 'em overload the raft, owing to a ragin' hangover. Lordy, did I have some kind o' headache. Only one drowned, though. Grandma, I think. We saved all the kids."

Jake glanced up to find Lisbet, Otto, and Dora watching him from the bonnet flap. He scanned the sides of the raft and decided they'd be fine and he wouldn't need to swim after anyone. After reaching the far side of the river, the train formed up, bid Carl the ferryman good fortune, and rolled on toward Fort Bridger. Once there, the remainder of the train would head toward distant Boise while Jake would become intimately acquainted with the end of a rope.

On the final day of the journey, with no last will and testament, Jake began bequeathing his few possessions to those who could use them.

"I cannot accept the rifle," said Mr. Emshoff. "You will need it after the trial."

"I may not last long after the trial," said Jake. "And a Henry rifle is a far sight better than a musket, even one of the good Austrian kind. Sixteen shots without reloading. No more standin' straight up under fire to ram black powder down the barrel and hopin' it don't explode in your face."

"It is too much, Paynter."

"Beans. I only owned it a short while anyway. Get it from Gus first chance you get. He's been keeping it safe for me."

"Nothin' for me, then?" Stacy's wide smile told him she was pulling his leg. That made the surprise all the better.

"I want you to have the Kerr. Gus'll give it to you."

"Your revolver?" She seemed incredulous. "I ain't never owned a handgun, let alone one of the best kind."

"You deserve it, Miss Blue. You're good people."

She turned away abruptly and rubbed her eyes. "Must be the dust."

"Yep," he said. "The dust."

He studied Emshoff and Stacy for a bit as they seemed to experience an odd blend of gratitude and despair. Both failed to meet his eyes for more than a second or two before examining their hands, or the dirt, or the horizon.

"One little favor, though."

Stacy looked at him finally. "Yeah?"

"Make sure Rosalyn gets the mare. She needs a horse of her own, and she'll take good care of the girl."

He withheld the rest. About how he hoped she'd lift up his memory when she rode the mare, if only from time to time. Although he'd always expected to fade from recollection soon after his passing, now that the end was likely near, such an outcome seemed bleak. The prospect of at least one person remembering him brought a small measure of solace.

"Sure," said Stacy. "I'll do that. But only if…if…"

"I know, little sister. I know."

———————

Fort Bridger was as unimpressive as Jake remembered it. It huddled on a plain a few miles shy of butting mountain ranges that guarded two approaches, surrounded by sage, scattered pines, and creeping despair. The compound appeared more typical of a military fortress than Kearny or Laramie, ringed by a ten-foot wall of vertical logs containing a double gate wide enough to pass two horses side by side. The cluster of buildings inside, however, seemed barely adequate to house the cavalry troop assigned there, a crowded island of security in a sea of hostility. As the wagon train rolled to a stop in the scrub outside the walls, a trio of buffalo soldiers came out on foot to meet them.

"Paynter. Am I sorry to see you."

He glanced down to find now-Sergeant Stubbs watching him

with a frown drooping his heavy moustache. "Feeling's mutual, Stubbs. I see you got some new stripes."

"Yep." He tapped the stripes on his shoulder. "These belonged to Gus before he mustered out. I inherited the position."

"Congratulations. You'll make a good sergeant."

Stubbs dipped his forehead in thanks. "Speaking o' Gus, we heard it was him who ran you down all the way out 'n Missouri. That true?"

"Afraid so. Though I thank him for it now."

"Thank him?"

"Anybody else woulda shot me on sight, especially with my gun aimed at the blank spot between his eyes. He just looked at me and said, 'You can shoot me or come with me, but this is the end of it either way.' I went with him, of course. Can't shoot the man who's saved your life at least three times."

Stubbs shook his head with seeming disappointment. "Still, I can't believe he brought you back."

Jake's eyes found Gus still mounted forty feet away in mumbled conversation with Stacy. He was watching Jake with a grim demeanor wholly uncharacteristic of him. "Don't blame Gus. He did what he had to."

The corporal's frown disappeared into a wide grin. "Oh, I don't blame 'im. It was his plan all along to set you loose along the way."

Jake narrowed his eyes. "He planned that?"

"Yep. Guess he changed his mind."

Jake thought back to the several times Gus had tried to send him away and failed. "He didn't change his mind. I was just too insensible to take what he offered."

"Speaking of insensible, I have orders to bring you to the fort commander, Colonel Huxley. We best go now before he finds yet another reason to put me on latrine duty."

Jake inhaled deeply and dismounted. McQuaid and Muñoz joined him in following Sergeant Stubbs through the gate of the fort. Jake couldn't help but admire the gallows dominating the muster grounds, tall and whitewashed to gleam in the sun, the smell of fresh paint still lingering on the light breeze. Someone had put some loving craftsmanship into its construction. The small party ambled past the instrument of death to the commandant's office, an unassuming log square with a tin roof. Stubbs rapped on the door.

"Enter," boomed an impatient voice. Stubbs opened the door but did not step inside.

"The prisoner, as requested, sir."

He grabbed Jake's sleeve and pushed him through the door. Jake came to a halt five feet inside the office when he saw Blackburn standing beside the seated Colonel Huxley. Blackburn smiled like a jack-o-lantern and the fire of his luminous eyes burned brighter.

"Well, looka here! It's our old friend Paynter come to the family reunion. Oh, how we did miss him in his absence!"

"Pipe down, First Sergeant," said Huxley as he examined Jake. The colonel had replaced the previous commandant after Jake's run, so he'd never laid eyes on him before. He wondered what manner of man was in charge of his trial. A legalistic man? A compassionate man? A dutiful man? A thoughtful man? The colonel pursed his lips, rubbed his bald scalp, and then shook a finger at Jake.

"I expected a giant, given the tales told of you, Lieutenant. But now I see you're just the miserable, traitorous dung heap I should have anticipated in light of the charges against you."

The harsh assessment answered all of Jake's questions. He was going to die, and soon. As if to confirm that conclusion, the man rose from his chair, straightened his coat, and peered into the depths of Jake's eyes.

"You will surely hang, Mr. Paynter."

"I expect so."

The colonel grunted assent. "We'd start your trial immediately, but I must wait for the officers from other installations to round out the court-martial panel. But don't worry. They'll be here soon enough. And in our magnanimity, we've even provided counsel for you, though we are not required by military law to do so."

Blackburn bit back a snicker, clearly amused by those last words. The reaction told Jake everything he needed to know about his supposed representation.

"Very kind of you, sir," he said.

The commandant's grin melted into a frown. Perhaps he'd expected fright, or groveling, or resistance. Jake refused the man the satisfaction of anything other than aggressive unconcern. Colonel Huxley motioned to Blackburn.

"See the lieutenant to his luxurious accommodations. And make sure he doesn't suffer an accidental gunshot wound along the way."

"Yes, sir." Blackburn produced his familiar Colt Dragoon and poked it into Jake's ribs. "Turn around, turncoat. Let's go."

Jake did as Blackburn said without comment. He knew the man searched for any reason whatsoever to put a bullet through his back. His only comfort came from the fresh scar decorating Blackburn's chin in roughly the shape of a rifle butt.

CHAPTER FORTY

WHEN GUS PULLED UP A CHAIR IN THE BARRACKS AND straddled it backwards, the men of K-Troop crowded around him, hanging from bunks and clutching the pine rafters to gather near. The gleam of lantern light reflected the collective sheens of faces moist from cloistered heat. The close proximity was a necessary evil, for the topic of conversation could get any of them whipped should the white officers catch wind of it.

"We heard rumors," said Stubbs, "of some nasty doins' out on the prairie. Let's hear it."

Gus draped his arms over the back of the chair and clenched his fingers together. "All right. It went this way."

He began with the capture of Paynter in Missouri, and how Paynter had given himself up without a fight. From there, his narrative followed the journey of the wagon train through the Nebraska grasslands, including the first fight with Sally.

A private interrupted the telling. "The lieutenant put down three of 'em?"

"Four. He put down four of 'em and took two of Sally's fingers for good measure."

"Damn."

"But wait. That was just his opening act."

The soldiers pressed closer, if such was possible, living and dying on Gus's every word, every turn of a phrase. When he told of how Paynter trained the settlers to fight, heads nodded all around. They knew their former lieutenant as a fair but tough teacher, a man who accepted nothing short of perfection when preparing troops for battle. When he began speaking of that first nighttime assault by Sally's small army, some men exhaled surprise.

"Then what?" Gus looked up to find Private Jefferson, one of his incorrigible favorites, leaning over the end of a high bunk, his expression flush with anticipation.

"Then Sally and his men hit us hard. And they was fit to be tied."

He told them of the second attack, the one that robbed the lives of five of their company, but how the defenders beat back the assault.

"Musta' been a sight to behold," said Stubbs.

"It was. I saw farmers gun down professional gunmen. I saw boys spear hardened soldiers. I saw a blacksmith break a man with his bare hands, and a farmer's wife take down a horse and rider. And I saw a young woman pull a mob of children from a burnin' wagon and guard them against stone killers." Thoughts of Stacy's heroics had been burned into his memory, a permanent etching to commemorate her courage. "Yep. It was a sight to behold."

Stubbs shook his head. "It seems surely dire, though. There's no way a party could survive more attacks like that."

Gus pointed a finger at the newly minted sergeant. "Exactly our logic. So, you were listenin' when I talked tactics."

"No choice, Sergeant Rivers. You never stopped talkin' long enough to breathe sometimes."

Everyone laughed, perhaps to bleed tension from the room. Gus lifted his hands to call for discretion. "Hold it down. Don't want nobody checkin' up on us, do we?"

Heads shook in agreement with the sentiment and the room grew as still as a morning lake. Stubbs lifted a palm. "How'd you stop 'em, then?"

"They couldn't seem to keep from underestimatin' us, so we used that against them."

He told about the night raid, of stealing the horses and mustering out the wagon train while Paynter kept what remained of Sally's men pinned down. He recounted the strange encounter with the Arapaho party. He spoke of Sally's final act of aggression, and how Paynter gave himself up—again. And how the same Arapaho came to their aid.

Stubbs shook his head in disbelief. "Why'd they do it? The Arapaho. They been fightin' us like wildcats for most of two years."

"I don't know exactly. But I have an idea."

"What're ya thinkin', then?"

"Later, maybe. I need to think on it some more before the trial."

Stubbs's brow grew a deep divot as he frowned. "You think they gonna let you testify?"

Gus laughed before restraining the sound. "Oh, hell no."

"Then you ain't crazy. You know we tried to speak on the lieutenant's behalf after he shot Cap'n Sherrod, but they sent most of us away and beat the rest into silence. They didn't wanna know anything. They only listened to Blackburn, and him knocked cold for most of it. He called Paynter a coward, afraid to fight, and they believed him. Slick-talkin' bastard."

"Yeah," said Gus quietly. "I know." He still felt the lashes on his back administered by Blackburn when he tried a second time to tell the story of what happened above the Green River. They'd mustered him out a week later, withheld his back pay, and told him to bring back Paynter if he wanted what was owed him. Gus had gone along, but had hated himself for it. He'd tried to make it right by helping Paynter escape, but the man was as stubborn as an untended cowlick. Gradually, he'd come to terms with the truth. Paynter meant to clear his name or die at Fort Bridger. He'd leave as an exonerated man or in a pine box. Given the army's disinterest in the testimony of those who'd actually witnessed the event, Gus's bet was on the pine box.

"So, that's it?" Stubbs's question came across as bitter. "He dies while we shut our traps other than to say 'Yes suh' and 'No suh' and 'How high suh.' Is that all?"

Gus stood from the chair and swiveled his gaze to encompass

the sixty-odd men who weren't presently on guard duty. "No. That is not all."

Stubbs grew a wicked smile. "Now there's the Sergeant Rivers I know. Whatcha thinkin'?"

"I'll help him escape if it comes to that. But..." He held the word and looked several soldiers in the eyes. "If you get caught aiding a fugitive, you'll face a firing squad. Except without a trial. I can't ask any of you to risk that much. I only ask that you look the other way when the time comes. That's all."

The room fell deeply silent, a collective held breath, a lingering anticipation. Then Private Jefferson coughed out a derisive laugh. "Aww, hell, Sergeant. We ain't gonna sit on our tails and do nothin'. We gonna help."

"Got that straight," said someone.

"Damn right," said another.

Despite the morbid topic, Gus couldn't help but grow a broad smile. "Thanks, men. I've never been prouder of a bunch o' ragtag misfits in all my life."

Jake stood on his bunk to peek through the slit of a window high on his cell wall. Though night had fallen, the glow of lantern light leaked from the barracks of K-Troop and home to his former charges. He wondered what they'd say of all this, if allowed. Through the open gate, he could just make out the vague outlines of wagons beyond the edge of the fort grounds, campfires dotting the landscape beside the rigs. He'd expected Lucien to move on after the first day, but three days had come and gone with no movement and no visitors. What were they waiting for? Most were bound for Boise with a long journey still ahead. Every day at Fort Bridger was another day wasted.

"You practicing for the hanging?"

Jake turned around to find Blackburn grinning at him. "Pardon?"

"I was just wonderin'. Thought maybe you was practicing jumping off a block. Making the break clean and quick."

Jake stepped down from the bunk without a word. He folded his arms and leveled a heated stare at his first captain. The man who'd molded him into an efficient killer. Blackburn's grin faded before he chuckled mirthlessly.

"Still laconic, I see. You know what that word means, huh? Laconic?"

"Yep."

Blackburn's grin returned. "Step to the bars, prisoner. I want you shackled before I visit you inside."

Jake complied and placed his wrists through the bars. When the stockade guard had shackled them to his satisfaction, he unlocked the cell and allowed Blackburn to step inside. Jake backed away, and they circled one another briefly as if repelled by an invisible force.

"What do you want?"

"What, Paynter? No cordialities?" He pointed to the bunk. "Sit yourself. Let's have a little chat."

For a moment, Jake was seventeen again and under the charismatic spell of the firebrand who called himself Captain Blackburn. He sat. The man smiled and leaned against the far wall of the cell.

"We had some high times, Paynter, you and me. You remember that little town in Missouri that laid out a spread for us? What was it called?"

"Neosho."

"Neosho. That's right. Too bad we had to kill some of 'em."

Jake growled. "We did more'n that."

Blackburn shrugged. "I like beautiful women. What else can I say? She wanted me, I could tell."

"Didn't seem to me like that at all."

Blackburn leaned away from the wall. "What would you know

of it, kid? Are you one of them dandy boys who likes his bunk time with other boys? I couldn't rightly tell, what with you abstainin' from the spoils."

Jake continued to glare. How had he ever placed his faith in this man? He could nearly smell the rot of Blackburn's soul. "I like women. Just don't much care for rape."

"It weren't rape! I told you. She wanted me bad. They all did. I was just doing my duty as protector and overseer of the good people of southern Missouri. Just like you."

"I ain't like you."

Blackburn frowned and shook a finger. "That's where you're wrong, Paynter. I saw with my own eyes the things you did. There's not an inch of daylight between us, no matter what story you tell yourself."

When Jake looked away, Blackburn laughed. "See? You're relivin' it now, aren't you?"

Jake was. The vision that had plagued him for years roared back with a vengeance, of that Missouri night in late '61 when his soul had departed his body.

"Burn it all!"

Captain Blackburn's cry drove the men of his small raiding party from their horses to comply. Fresh from the heat of conflict and with the smell of blood still filling his nostrils, Jake grabbed a lit torch and set fire to stacks of wheat dotting the fields, not thinking, just lighting them up and watching them burn.

"Paynter! Barns and sheds, boy. Over there."

Jake followed Blackburn's outstretched arm to the cluster of small structures clinging to the edge of the freshly harvested field. He shuffled through the thatch and leavings toward the first building, a small barn, and put the torch to it. Then he slipped to the second, perhaps a tack shed. When he stepped to the door, he heard inside a muffled cry. His hand went still and his ears pricked. No other sound. "Nobody inside," he told himself, knowing it was a lie.

"Move it, Paynter!"

At the sound of Blackburn's command, he lit the shed. The old, dry wood blazed up as if soaked in kerosene. Within seconds, a chorus of screams rose up inside, howling with terror. Rather than tearing open the door as he should have, he stumbled back to watch, mumbling. "There's no people. There's no people."

The screaming rose to a crescendo as the fire consumed the structure. When it had become fully engulfed, the door burst open and a small figure raced out, burning like the torch in his hand. When the figure fell near his feet, Jake threw away the torch and began beating the flames with his bare hands and rolling the body in the dirt. The flames abated even as the shed began collapsing onto the now-silent chorus inside. He stared at the body beneath him, a negro child, burned beyond recognition of gender. The child's eyes, which had been closed, opened with cloudy retinas to stare at Jake. A hand lifted, grasping, touching his cheek as breath choked from the child's throat.

"That you, Papa?" The croaked question hammered Jake through his gut, like a mortar shell had passed through his liver and taken his insides with it. The child gasped another breath and fell still.

"Looks like you burnt 'em all. Damn, Paynter. You're a beast."

Jake blinked and looked up from the dead body to find Blackburn standing over him with approval. He released the child from his burned hands, stood, and pushed past the captain.

"Where you goin', Paynter?"

Jake ignored him. He stumbled into the field, breaking into a shambling run. When he reached his horse, he mounted it without touching a stirrup and spurred it into motion due north.

"Paynter!"

He shut his ears, shut his head, shut his heart, and rode until he could ride no more.

"Paynter!"

Jake glanced at Blackburn standing in his cell. "What?"

"Didn't you hear me? I asked you a question. Why'd you turn coat? You a coward?"

Jake was on Blackburn in the blink of a gnat's eye, his hands closing around the man's throat. It took three guards to drag him off. When Blackburn had recovered his breath, he stood and rubbed his raw neck.

"Hold that man."

The guard's complied, and Blackburn began beating Jake until his brain stopped working.

CHAPTER FORTY-ONE

BECAUSE HIS OUTER CELL WALL FACED THE MAIN GATE, JAKE had a bird's-eye view of the arriving members of his court-martial panel. Or a prairie dog's view, anyway, given the narrowness of the hole in his cell that some might mistake for a window. He counted the arrival of ten men over the course of two weeks, all wearing officer's insignias, from Fort Laramie and Fort Phil Kearney. The fact that they'd ridden hundreds of miles across the territory threatened to impress Jake. More than that, it telegraphed the direness of his situation. Authorities didn't go to such lengths without intending to kill a man.

More puzzling, though, was the continued presence of three prairie schooners beyond the gates. Several days after he'd entered his cell, a commotion drew him to the window in the early morning to find Cornelius leading away thirteen wagons on a line toward distant Boise. Three wagons, however, had remained firmly in place, including the Conestoga belonging to the Ashleys. The distant figures of children identified the other wagons as belonging to the Emshoffs and Robersons. And then there were Gus and Stacy, still camped alongside the Emshoff wagon, which proved head-scratching. Gus should have collected his backpay by now, and Stacy should've gone on with her pa. But here they were, still.

He stepped down from the window with thoughts of Rosalyn breezing through his head, hoping she'd stayed for him and then hoping she hadn't. Had they all decided to make a go of it in the new Wyoming Territory? He couldn't say because he was allowed no visitors. Even Blackburn had remained scarce after beating Jake half to death. His ribs were only just now healed enough to allow a deep breath.

As if thoughts of Blackburn had summoned him from a pit of darkness, the man's voice sounded near the stockade door. "Here to see our guest."

Jake retreated to the back wall as the click of boots approached. Blackburn wore a grin even as he sauntered into Jake's view.

"There he is, the man everyone's talkin' about. How ya been, Paynter?" He put a finger to his cheekbone and frowned. "Those bruises don't look so good. You run into somethin', did ya?"

Jake remained quiet with arms folded loosely as he leaned against the block wall. Blackburn draped his hands through the bars and watched him for a time, seemingly content to observe Jake in captivity, a penned wolf falling slowly into despair.

"You shouldn't have turned," the man said finally. "You left us high and dry out there in the south of Missouri. After you ran, a few more got ideas about leavin' until I put a couple of bullets to good use. Nobody left after that. Fear's the best motivator, don't ya think?"

"Not especially," Jake mumbled.

"What's that? Not especially? Tell me, then. What motivates better'n fear?"

Recollections of a band of determined farmers fending off and destroying professional killers filled his mind. Sure, they had been terrified. Heck, he'd been terrified. But their courageous stand had been motivated by conceptions far loftier than fear. Family. Friends. Hopes. Aspirations. Dreams that might carry forth through their children, generation upon generation, lifting them upward to a higher plane, a steady arc toward a better life and gentler existence. That's why they stood. Not from fear.

"Answer the question, Paynter. What's better than fear?"

Jake shook his head slowly. "You wouldn't understand if I told you."

Blackburn grunted. "Well, I beg to differ. Folks'll agree to most anything when they're afraid. The more afraid they are, the more they'll fall in line."

The conversation abruptly wore on Jake. "What do you want, anyway?"

Blackburn grew a look of faux enthusiasm. "Well, now that you ask, I suppose I ought to tell you the good news. The last of your jury has arrived just now from Fort Phil Kearney. They're none too happy about having to ride four hundred miles just to hang a man. I'd say they seem ready to return as soon as possible. Whadda ya think about that?"

Jake leaned forward from the wall, dropped his arms, and stepped to the middle of the cell. "I think you should step inside with me, right now. No weapons. No shackles. No guards. Just you 'n me, here and now, and see what happens."

Anger flashed across Blackburn's face. Jake knew the man couldn't abide goading without resorting to violence. For a moment, he imagined his hands around Blackburn's neck one more time. One last time. When Blackburn inhaled a deep breath, Jake knew he'd lost that chance.

"I don't think so. Not now, anyway. But I will leave you with some confidential information concerning trial tactics. You listening?"

"Go away."

"That's the spirit. Let me help dampen that a little. Colonel Huxley will be the presiding officer, and he already despises you like a boil on the butt. So, there's that for starters. And he's decided to disallow any testimony from the rank and file. Only mine will be considered, given I was the only surviving white officer. You can't trust the rest of 'em. And do you know what I'll say?"

"Go away."

"You do?" Blackburn chuckled. "I thought so. I'm gonna tell them the God's honest truth. That you gunned down Captain Sherrod in cold blood, unprovoked and without cause, simply because you were gutless and hated his authority. And then you knocked me down and ran. That's my testimony."

Jake grunted a laugh. "You're a liar and a cutthroat and a coward, Blackburn. You always were and always will be. May your false testimony damn you to the inferno. Now, go away."

Blackburn's grin faded and he withdrew his arms from the bars. "Too bad, Paynter. I was hopin' we could rekindle old friendships, if only for a moment. Seems like you're more interested in dying alone. See you soon, then."

As he began stepping toward the stockade door, Jake approached the bars. "Wait."

"Oh?"

"Colonel Huxley said I had counsel. Who is it?"

Blackburn belted a laugh. "You don't know? No? Why, I'm your counsel. Whadda ya think we been doin' here? Consider yourself counseled."

Blackburn walked away still laughing, enjoying immensely the irony of the joke. Jake retreated to his bunk to wait and to keep the wolf confined. This wasn't the moment for the wolf and the red haze. This was the time for rational thoughts, logic, and clear-eyed engagement. He knew he was going to hang, sure as snow buried the mountains in winter. He only hoped to speak his piece, reveal the truth, and clear his conscience the best he could before the rope snapped taut.

CHAPTER FORTY-TWO

As the daughter of a politician, Rosalyn had learned to do at least one thing supremely well—argue passionately without turning allies into enemies. She used that particular skill to great effect as Lucien once again berated her for their continued inhabitation of Fort Bridger.

"The end of summer is already upon us, Rosalyn." He paced back and forth beside the Conestoga, waving his hands in wide arcs for emphasis. "Should we leave tomorrow, we'd not arrive in Boise until October with no time to settle in before the first snows. And who would guide us there?"

"Stacy Blue knows the way. I am certain Mr. Rivers would accompany us in exchange for a reasonable fee."

He wheeled on her. "Are you daft? Three wagons crossing more than six hundred miles of wilderness under the guidance of a woman and the protection of a former slave? The absurdity of it stretches belief."

She bristled and stiffened her spine. "Perhaps the idea stretches your belief because you lack imagination, brother."

"My imagination lacks for nothing, particularly when compared to your absence of good sense on the matter. Your infatuation with a criminal has condemned us to remain here for the duration of the winter."

Though she wanted to lash out with a denial, she could not. Her self-narrative of wishing to offer testimony on Paynter's behalf told only half the story. He drew her, despite the training ingrained deep within her. He was exactly the sort of man a well-bred woman should avoid. But the depths beneath his hardened exterior cried out for exploration. She forced a smile and touched Lucien's sleeve, a crafted maneuver intended to lower the animosity of the conversation. Another parlor trick learned from her father.

"You are not wrong regarding my motivations. But you are also not right regarding yours."

"What do you mean?"

"I mean only that you had already decided to forego Boise and remain here in the new Wyoming Territory. I could see it in your eyes as we departed South Pass City. The vision of what you could accomplish with your gold in a grand moment of new opportunity. How you could rise to power, how you could own a significant piece of what is to come. You wore it like an expensive suit, obvious for all to see."

Lucien stared at her briefly before pacing away a dozen yards. He paused for a time with his back to her before returning. He exhaled a measured breath. "Perhaps you are right. You often know me better than I know myself. I'll admit that plans have been crystalizing in my thoughts, given the circumstances. The gold rush and growing population from nearly nothing. The coming of the railroad that will open the territory to new money. The wide expanse of inexpensive, available land just there for the taking for those bold enough to grasp it. In Boise, we'd be latecomers. Here, we are still among the first. And we have the most gold."

Rosalyn nodded, a bit surprised over the ease of which he'd admitted the truth. The thought of staying in Wyoming unsettled her, though. If Paynter were to hang, how could she stay? If not stay, where would she go to escape the dismal knowledge of his death? She nudged away her disquiet and smiled again at Lucien.

"The Emshoffs and Robersons are committed to returning to South Pass City when the trial is finished. Will we travel back with them, then?"

"I think so, now that we have spoken with one another on the matter. We will be gone by the end of the week, I believe."

Her smile fled. "End of the week? That soon?"

"You don't know?"

"Know what?"

His face lost all expression. "The last of the court-martial panel arrived just an hour ago. The trial begins tomorrow."

"I see." A knot formed in her stomach, a fist clutching her entrails. "When will Mr. Emshoff, Stacy, and I provide testimony, then?"

Lucien shook his head in that patronizing manner that had so enraged her when she was younger. "There will be no testimony. We were not present when the crime was committed. We did not witness the events in question. Colonel Huxley has dismissed any character witnesses as superfluous to the trial."

Rage rose within Rosalyn, a wave of righteous wrath that threatened to sweep away the complacent and unsuspecting. "We will see about that!"

"Where do you think you're going?"

Rosalyn ignored his question and grabbed a surprised Stacy by the hand as she passed by. "Come, Miss Blue. We've a battle to fight."

Stacy's initial surprise melted into determined enthusiasm. "I do love to fight."

They flew through the muster grounds to arrive at the colonel's office. The pair of guards at the door froze when she and Stacy stomped up the steps, likely unprepared for a frontal assault by two women. Rosalyn threw the door wide. Colonel Huxley yanked his eyes from the stack of paper before him to stare and blink. He stood and rubbed his bald head, smoothing back the ghost of hair that had quit his scalp years ago.

"Miss Ashley. What a pleasure."

"Please sit, Colonel. And you've met Miss Blue?"

He plopped to his seat, seemingly bewildered. "We've been introduced, yes."

"Excellent. No need for further introductions, then." She

seated herself in one of the two chairs before the colonel's desk and invited Stacy to do the same. Stacy sat, removed her forage cap, and draped her long braid forward over one shoulder, a habit that had formed since her encounter with the Arapaho party.

Huxley steepled his fingers and leaned forward with a glint in his eye. "What can I do for you ladies? Some tea, perhaps? Coffee? I can have shortbread brought from the mess, if you like."

Rosalyn lifted her chin in a motion of genteel dismissal. "This is not a social call, sir. We have come for a purpose."

Huxley leaned back in his chair, frowning. "And what would that purpose be?"

"I just spoke with Mr. Ashley, and he informed me that testimony from Miss Blue, Mr. Emshoff, and me has been disallowed. Imagine my surprise at such a disclosure. However, I am certain he just misunderstood, as he does from time to time. Surely you would not prohibit testimony that might speak to Mr. Paynter's character. After all, this is the United States of America and he is entitled to a fair trial under the protection of the Constitution, is he not?"

Huxley rocked back and forth in his chair, his eyes blank. "It is you, Miss Ashley, who misunderstands. This is neither the United States of America nor is this a trial."

"What do you mean?"

"This fortress lies in a U.S. territory where the military is the law. This gathering is a military court-martial, not a jury trial. The rules are vastly different. Lieutenant Paynter is not entitled to counsel. We may call whichever witnesses we deem necessary. As such, we will only hear from those who were present when the crime occurred. And correct me if I'm wrong, but I do not recall from the notes that you, Miss Blue, nor the German were with the Tenth that day above the Green River."

Stacy leaned forward, as her father had taught her, pressing Huxley further into his chair. "Your notes are correct, sir. However, you just now claimed that you may call whichever witnesses you deem necessary. I appeal to you in no uncertain terms to allow the character testimony from those who witnessed it from Mr. Paynter on the journey here. His actions were nothing short of sacrificial and extraordinary."

Colonel Huxley casually reached for a cigar, cut the tip, and lit it while leaving the room in pent-up silence. He glanced at Stacy. "Care for one?"

"I do not smoke."

"Not even a peace pipe?"

Rosalyn placed a hand on Stacy's arm to restrain the forward lean. She didn't need Stacy to erupt, despite the thinly veiled slight. Not yet, anyway. She smiled at Huxley. "About our testimony. Will you allow it?"

He cocked his head side to side. "Why? The lieutenant will hang regardless of the testimony given. Everyone knows what he did. He admitted it. The facts are a matter of record."

"Because he deserves to be heard. I don't know exactly what he did, or why. But I refuse to believe his actions were without reason, without conviction. Such a narrative is out of place from what I've witnessed of his character. He is, at his core, a decent man."

"Lieutenant Paynter is a cold-blooded killer, miss. Everyone seems to understand this but you."

"I disagree. He has killed, yes, but only when provoked. The cold-blooded killer you describe would have left us all to die, or worse, made a deal with Sally to profit from our deaths. Mr. Paynter stayed. He fought for us. He risked his life for us. And for what? He did not earn his freedom. He did not earn any coin."

Huxley blew smoke in her face and sighed heavily. "I don't know why he stayed. However, I can assure you there was no altruism in his actions. He wanted something."

"What, then? What did he want that would outweigh his freedom? His life?"

Huxley's eyes wandered to her waist and back, lingering on her breasts. "I wonder."

Rosalyn folded her arms across her chest in self-defense. "Regardless of his reasons, Colonel, he deserves character testimony."

"No." He shook his head slowly. "But perhaps I might be persuaded into a change of mind in return for certain favors."

Rosalyn felt all expression drain from her face. "Favors? Such as?"

"My wife died three years ago. I haven't had the company of a woman since I arrived here three months ago. I'd prefer you." He motioned toward Stacy. "But she'd do."

When Stacy sprang to her feet, Rosalyn did not restrain her. Stacy pointed a finger at the colonel's nose. "You're a rattlesnake. Where I come from, we shoot rattlesnakes."

Huxley grinned. "Are you threatening me, Miss Blue? I do like a woman who fights back. Makes for interesting nights."

Rosalyn stood to join Stacy on her feet. "Since you respond so well to threats, Colonel Huxley, let me offer one. Imagine what would happen to the fort commander who raped the daughter of a U.S. senator hand-selected by General Ulysses S. Grant and appointed to his post by President Johnson."

"I'm not gonna rape you."

"Of course you won't, and you will not lay a finger on Miss Blue either." She clasped her hands together, exuding calm. "My father doesn't know you. I, however, am his beloved only daughter. He would be most displeased to learn that an army colonel offered justice in exchange for sexual favors with said beloved daughter. I'm sure General Grant would hear of it shortly afterward. He has an only daughter too, you know. Nellie. Lovely girl, perhaps thirteen years old."

Huxley's face grew red, as if a boil about to explode. However, he inhaled a deep breath through flaring nostrils. He bit his next words through gritted teeth. "Fine. You, the half-breed, and the German. For all the good it'll do you. Now, leave my office. If you please."

Rosalyn knew that the best way to undo a victory was to lord it over the beaten. She grabbed Stacy's arm and dragged her from the office. When they had walked from earshot of the guards, Stacy peered at Rosalyn.

"They're gonna hang him no matter what we say."

"I know." She walked another dozen steps. "So, how is Gus's plan coming along?"

"He's got it mostly worked out."

"Good. Tell him to finish planning. Paynter doesn't have much time."

CHAPTER FORTY-THREE

THE PAIR OF RANK-AND-FILE PRIVATES WHO ESCORTED JAKE from the stockade to the mess hall did so with blank expressions. He recognized one—Private Jefferson—as the subject of many a diatribe from Gus when he was acting sergeant. As they neared the mess, which was to double today as a courtroom, Jefferson leaned near to whisper.

"Keep the faith, Lieutenant. You ain't alone."

The encouraging words had a shocking effect on Jake. He hadn't realized how low he'd sunk until that moment. The offering from Jefferson refilled some of his nearly depleted reservoir of determination. "Thank you, Private."

The escorts walked him into the mess hall to a chair positioned against one wall. Jake sat and draped his manacled wrists between his knees.

"Dismissed," said Huxley. The privates saluted and left. Jake turned his attention to the sea of blue uniforms arrayed before him behind two long tables pushed end-to-end, facing an empty chair. Thirteen army officers, a blend of cavalry and infantry from three different posts. The most common facial expression was one of disdainful curiosity. Besides Huxley, he recognized only one—his former Second Lieutenant, Henry Stallings, now elevated to First Lieutenant of K-Troop. He appeared uncomfortable and failed to meet Jake's eyes. Colonel Huxley occupied the center position as presiding officer. They were otherwise alone, with the exception of a noncommissioned white officer, Sergeant Ayers, who apparently served in the role of bailiff.

"Colonel, you offered counsel," said Jake. He knew that his

counsel was Blackburn, a farce, but wanted to poke the colonel. Huxley simply smiled.

"Ah, yes. In my oversight, I appointed counsel who turned out to be the chief witness for the army. My mistake. Would you like another counselor?"

"I would not."

"Very prudent." He lifted a gavel and rapped the table. "Let the proceedings commence, then."

The colonel pushed back his chair, rose to his feet, and lifted a pair of papers from the tabletop. He scanned them briefly before beginning to read.

"The charges against First Lieutenant Jacob Paynter are these. That he willfully disobeyed a direct order from a superior officer, to service his own cowardice, in the highlands above the Green River basin on 27 October 1867. That he dissuaded the collected members of Tenth Cavalry K-Troop from carrying out the officer's orders under threat of violence. That he willfully and in cold blood murdered said superior officer, Captain William C. Sherrod, without provocation. That he assaulted and wounded First Sergeant Ambrose T. Blackburn on that same occasion as the latter attempted to subdue him. That he fled his post, again with threats of retaliation against the members of Tenth Cavalry K-Troop. For these crimes, the court-martial will determine his guilt or innocence, and any such punishment that may result from guilt, up to and including hanging by the neck until dead."

Huxley sat and motioned to the sergeant. "Fetch the witness."

Within moments, Ambrose Blackburn entered the room and saluted the officers. Sergeant Ayers held a Bible to him and swore him in. Jake wondered if Blackburn had ever opened a Bible before, or given any meaningful thought to the words inside. He grinned at Jake as he swore to tell the truth and only the truth. When Blackburn had settled into a chair, Colonel Huxley motioned to him.

"First Sergeant Blackburn. Will you recount for the court-martial the events of 27 October 1867 as they pertain to the criminal offenses of Lieutenant Paynter?"

"Gladly, sir. Happy to perform my duty." As Blackburn leaned back in his chair, Jake couldn't help but consider the irony. The man had waged a brutal war against the assembled officers up until three years earlier. However, a shortage of volunteers for the Plains Army and a character affidavit from an influential Confederate supporter had allowed Blackburn into the military he formerly opposed, and as a noncommissioned officer, no less. Jake knew him, though. He saw in Blackburn's eyes the mild disdain he held for his so-called superiors. He knew Blackburn felt himself above all of them. His show of humility was just another of his charismatic performances given for the purpose of pursuing some benefit.

"We arrived above the Green River basin around midday," said Blackburn. "It was hard to tell the hour because snow had been falling for a time. Anyway, Sherrod had on good authority from his Crow scouts that a large hostile force had gathered in the basin. He sent Paynter and a couple of others to confirm the report, and they indeed found a large Indian gathering. When Sherrod ordered Lieutenant Paynter to lead the charge into the draw to press an attack against the hostiles, he refused the order."

"Did he say why he refused the order?" asked an infantry captain.

"Yes, sir. Said he didn't want to fight a larger force. Said he was afraid of dyin.'"

"Carry on, then."

"Yes, sir. After refusing the order, Paynter threatened to shoot any colored soldier who followed the order. Then, he shot Captain Sherrod without warning. When I tried to subdue him, he struck me with his rifle butt."

"Did the blow render you unconscious?" asked Huxley.

"No, sir. I was woozy, to be sure, but I saw what happened next. Paynter threatened to kill anyone who tried to stop him. He rode off for parts unknown before I could do anything."

"And there were no other white officers present?"

"No, sir. Lieutenant Stallings was sick with fever back at the infirmary."

"With Captain Sherrod dead and you disabled, who was the ranking officer?"

"Sergeant Rivers."

"And he is colored?"

"Yes, sir."

A cavalry lieutenant nodded vigorously. "It only stands to reason, then. Colored officers have been instructed to obey the orders of white officers without question. Lieutenant Paynter's orders, then, could not be disobeyed."

"That's how I see it," said Blackburn with satisfaction.

While the officers asked the witness a few more questions, Jake stared at the floor. Very little of the testimony was true. Sure, he'd killed Sherrod and assaulted Blackburn, but nothing else aligned with reality. When they ushered Blackburn out, Jake was certain they'd ask for his version of events before finding him guilty and hanging him. However, that was not to be the case, but for a surprising reason.

"We have a slight change of plans, gentlemen," said Huxley. "The court-martial will recess until tomorrow, at which time we will hear three character witnesses on behalf of Lieutenant Paynter, after which he may speak for himself."

The disbelief on the faces of some of the jurors surely matched Jake's expression. "Character witnesses?" said one officer. "Do you jest?"

Colonel Huxley seemed abruptly uncomfortable and absently shuffled the papers before him. "I realize that such witnesses are uncharacteristic of these proceedings, but who are we if not magnanimous? If we can offer the accused a sliver of hope, is it not our Christian duty to do so?"

The officers seemed to accept his argument, but barely looked Jake's way when Sergeant Ayers fetched the privates to escort him back to his cell. On the return journey, one thought occupied his mind. How had Rosalyn convinced Colonel Huxley to hear character witnesses? For he knew it had been her. No one else possessed the right combination of good will, determination, and political clout to succeed in such an ostentatious endeavor.

CHAPTER FORTY-FOUR

As Jake lay on his excuse of a cot deep in the night while staring at the ceiling, he considered the elusive nature of truth. The best lie wasn't a blatant fabrication. The best lie was the truth twisted, and the more subtle the twist, the more convincing the lie. Blackburn's testimony had covered most of the ground on which the truth stood. However, he'd stirred the pot just enough to alter the story completely, replacing elements of nobility and self-defense with savagery and brutality. It was the man's skill at warping reality that had drawn Jake, a refugee from a hateful home, to the promise of a better way and a higher purpose. It had taken him only a few months to sort through the labyrinth of words to the ugly truth beneath. It had required the devastation of a personal moral collapse for him to walk away.

The creak of door hinges drew him from the depths of his tortured mind into the immediacy of the present. Soft footfalls approached to reveal two figures, shadowy in the absence of lamp light. He rose to perch on the edge of the bunk, waiting. The clink of a careful turn of the key made clear the stealth of the visit. Had Blackburn come to finish him? His hands spasmed and his body tensed for a death match.

"Paynter."

The whisper of a familiar voice bled his tension in a breath. "Gus? What are you doing?"

He stepped inside the cell and whispered to his accomplice. "Jefferson. Go watch the door."

"Yes, sir."

Gus stepped across the open space to join Jake on the edge of the cot. "I ain't supposed to be here, just so you know."

"I ain't either, but here I sit."

Gus chuckled softly. "Yeah, I know." He bumped Jake's shoulder with his. "What's on your mind?"

"Not much. Been mostly thinkin' about truth."

"Hmm. A right good subject, considerin'. Sergeant Ayers waded too far into his bottle tonight and started talking. Sounds like there weren't much truth told at the trial today."

"Nope. Not much."

"Too bad." He clenched his fingers together. "Sad to say, I'm eight years a grown man and haven't seen much in the way of truth. Pure truth, I mean. It's always tainted, somehow. Infected, like gangrene in a wound."

"I've seen it before."

"You've seen pure truth?"

"The purest truth." Jake closed his eyes. "The Camden Expedition, spring of '64, southern Arkansas. I remember we were all hungry—more than usual. The belly to the backbone kind of hungry. White troops. Black troops. Didn't matter. We were in bad shape and gettin' worse."

"I remember."

"Major General Steele sent Colonel Williams with the Kansas First and the Eighteenth Iowa to forage the countryside for food. We showed no mercy, taking from folks who had little to give, all for the sin of living on the wrong side of the border. Then we came upon a widow with six small children, and we took her last hog. I remember how she looked at us. The despair. Like we'd just murdered her children, which we likely had by takin' food from their mouths. But I also remember you, Gus. How it ate you alive. How you just kept tellin' anyone with ears that it wasn't right. Remember?"

Gus was quiet for a moment. "I do."

"And then I remember that night, watching you walk out of camp drivin' that hog and carrying a sack of flour or beans or rice over your shoulder."

"It was rice."

"Right," said Jake. "You came back an hour later empty-handed. Just enough time to walk to that widow's farm and back again. Am I right?"

"You are."

Jake nodded and patted Gus's knee. "That was the purest truth I ever witnessed. You goin' hungry to do for another who was weaker, less able, less fortunate. Pure truth, Gus."

"I don't know about that."

"Well, I do. That's what I cling to. That maybe truth can find a way despite the forces massed against it."

Gus heaved a sigh that petered out before reaching the cell bars. "Seems like they gonna hang ya, regardless."

"Likely."

"Do you have any regrets, then?"

Jake knew Gus was talking about his repeated decisions to stay with the wagon train instead of bolting for freedom. However, he sat atop a mountain of regret formed long before his forced journey from St. Joseph, built grain by grain, boulder by boulder. "I regret a great many things. I regret not helping you return that hog."

"At least you didn't stop me."

"I suppose so. But more than that, I regret what happened the next day. How I retreated from the field at Poison Springs and left our men to be butchered, even the wounded."

Gus shook his head. "Don't, Paynter. We were both shot up good. Weren't much we could do while leakin' blood all over the earth."

"We should've anyway. What good is it to live while regret crushes the life out of you? Most days, I wish I'd stayed and died fightin' for something bigger than myself. But I didn't stay that day. I'll regret it 'til my last breath."

Gus exhaled a sigh. "I don't disagree. It haunts me too. I wake in the night sometimes…" He rubbed his face with both hands. "But tell me. If you had more time to make amends, to atone for what you've done or didn't do, would you?"

It was a good question—one Jake had contemplated for a very long time. He had spent most of the past seven years trying to do just that, knowing the candle of his life could be snuffed out at any moment. "I would."

Gus put a hand on Jake's shoulder. "I'm pleased to hear you say so, 'cause I've made arrangements for just that. For more time."

"Arrangements?"

"Sergeant Stubbs has your mare waiting beyond the fort grounds, with weapons, ammo, and supplies. Private Jefferson has agreed to let me hit him on the head to knock him cold. Truth be told, I've always wanted to knock him upside the head. Then you walk out. Jefferson's story will be that you picked the lock and attacked him before runnin'. You'd have a four or five-hour head start."

Gus's plan didn't surprise Jake. He'd assumed that something was afoot. But the fact that so many others would risk hanging to gain his freedom threatened to overwhelm his senses. He didn't want anyone placed in that position. He wanted to tell his story to the court-martial. He wanted the truth to at last see the light of day.

"I can't, Gus. I need to tell them what really happened."

"Won't matter." Disappointment dripped from Gus's voice. "Not this time. You should go, my friend. You should run."

"No." Jake stood from the cot. "To run now is to confess a lie. I'm weary of runnin'. I've run too many times before and I won't run just now. Can you understand?"

Gus stood and shook Jake's hand. "I understand. Not happy about it, but I understand. You want to save your soul instead of your life. And that's also pure truth."

Jake was left alone inside the locked cell to dwell on the past, knowing that his future might not see another nightfall.

CHAPTER FORTY-FIVE

THE QUARTERMASTER'S CLOCK TICKED RELENTLESSLY, reminding Rosalyn of how long they'd waited since Mr. Emshoff had been escorted to the mess hall to offer testimony.

"How long's it been?" The question from Stacy interrupted minutes of nervous silence as they sat alone in the otherwise empty commander's office.

"Nearly half an hour."

"Is that good?"

Rosalyn wondered the same. "I hope so. The fact that they've not finished with Mr. Emshoff might indicate a willingness to listen."

"I hope yer right."

Two more minutes ticked off the clock before Sergeant Ayers opened the door. "Miss Ashley. The court will see you now."

She rose, smoothed her skirt, and followed the sergeant out the door. Mr. Emshoff stood away from the path to the mess hall, but his eyes held warning. When she veered toward him, Ayers chased after her.

"Witnesses are not allowed conversation," he said. "Follow me."

She turned on the sergeant, who couldn't be much past nineteen. "I will speak to Mr. Emshoff. You may drag me into the court if you wish, but I would not advise such a course of action."

He held up both palms. "Just be quick about it and don't tell no one."

She nodded and turned to Mr. Emshoff. "Did they listen?"

His persistent frown had already answered the question, but she needed details. "No. I was given little chance to speak. They assumed me loyal to Herr Paynter for helping my children. Instead, they asked *me* questions."

"What kind of questions?" The fine hairs on the back of her neck stood on end.

"Did Mr. Paynter promise me anything in exchange for testimony? Money. Protection. Not to harm my family. Why was I so intent on helping a prisoner, a criminal? Did I hope to use him for my own purposes? Why was Mr. Paynter so friendly with my wife? Were they having an affair?"

Rosalyn shook her head in irritated disbelief. "They asked you those questions?"

"And more. They asked why I came to the United States. Did I intend to sow sedition? Was I loyal to this country? They did everything but call me an enemy. And when they'd finished, they dismissed my unspoken testimony as unreliable and sent me away."

Rosalyn stamped a foot, now furious. "What did Paynter do?"

"Nothing. He stared at the floor the entire time. Like he was not surprised."

Rosalyn turned again to Ayers, seething. "Take me in, Sergeant."

By the time she stepped into the makeshift courtroom, Rosalyn had tamped down the flare of anger, molding it into cool determination. As she entered, the thirteen officers stood and remained standing until she found her chair. Most eyed her in a way indicating they'd like to know her better—outside the courtroom. She decided to use that to her advantage. She spared a glance for Paynter, who sat to the side with his eyes impaling the floor beneath his feet and his jaw flexing.

"Gentlemen, Colonel Huxley," she said. "I offer a good day to you and my gratitude for hearing my testimony."

Colonel Huxley pulled at his collar, betraying nerves. He was still apparently wary of what she might say of Paynter—or of him.

"Miss Ashley," he said. "You brighten our gathering with your lovely presence. As we have met already, I will turn over the session to Captain Beekman. For fairness, as you know."

"Of course," she replied, while understanding the maneuver.

Huxley was taking the coward's way out. Captain Beekman rose and circled from behind the tables to stand before her.

"Miss Ashley. Might I first say what a fine figure you cut in that dress. Beautiful women are as scarce as rain at western military posts."

She glanced at Paynter to find his eyes flicker up to stare death at the captain before again finding the floor. She smiled at the soldier. "Thank you. Now, are we here to discuss my attire or will you instead hear my testimony?"

The captain laughed and winked at her. "The latter, Miss Ashley, I assure you. Now, as you may know, Lieutenant Paynter is accused of cowardice, sedition, assault, murder, and abandoning his post. All very serious crimes. Would you like me to recount the details of his actions?"

"That will not be necessary."

"Fine, then. What do you offer to counter the obvious indications of the accused's miserable nature?"

She began to suspect the captain had been trained in the law and had argued before juries in the past. His swaggering confidence and backhanded insinuations were the product of much practice. However, this was not the first time she had faced such a man.

"I will begin with the initial gun battle against Mr. Sally and his outlaws."

She described in detail how Paynter had warned of the outlaws' intentions, had led the preemptive attack, and had given the wagon train a long reprieve to prepare for what came later. She focused, though, on his return—how he'd rejoined the settlers of his own free will. Beekman listened intently while massaging the point of his chin and pacing back and forth. When she finished with her account, he stopped to face her.

"Per your testimony, Lieutenant Paynter did not return with the others, but instead rode on toward the east. I wonder. Was he perhaps in league with Sally and intent on joining up with him? And did Sally subsequently cut Paynter out of the spoils?"

Oh, yes. Captain Beekman was a trained snake. "That would not explain why he led the attack that waylaid Sally's party, killed four of his men, and wounded Sally in the process."

"And you witnessed all of this? His leading of the attack? His wounding of Sally and the killing of Sally's men?"

She clenched her jaw. "No. But Miss Blue witnessed some of it."

"Then whatever you offer is hearsay, is it not?"

She tried to keep the anger from seeping into her demeanor. "May I offer, then, testimony of events I did witness?"

Captain Beekman's face broke into a magnanimous smile. "But of course, Miss Ashley. We are waiting on pins and needles, aren't we, gentlemen?"

The officers chuckled and a few whispered among themselves. This seemed just an amusement to them. Rosalyn straightened her spine further until vertebrae popped. "He devoted himself for weeks to training us to defend ourselves. To preserve, to fight, to win. When the second wave of attacks came, he fought courageously for us. He risked his life for us. He did not run, even though on several occasions he had opportunity to do so. He asked nothing in return from anyone at any time, other than to be free of his shackles." She risked another glance at Paynter. He had not moved. "Is that not direct evidence of sterling character?"

Captain Beekman folded his arms and nodded. "Perhaps, perhaps. Or maybe it is evidence of simple lust."

"Pardon?"

"Mr. Ashley, your brother, seems to believe Lieutenant Paynter is, shall we say, sweet on you. Perhaps his actions were motivated by hopes of a romantic encounter."

The accusation lifted Paynter's chin as he bored holes through the captain with his eyes. In that moment, she was certain of two things. Paynter cared for her. And he wanted to throttle Beekman for asking the question. Still, it did not explain all that he'd sacrificed.

"That is absurd," she said. "Mr. Paynter rebuffed most of my attempts at friendship. He never sought me out, but rather pushed me away."

Beekman smiled. "So, Miss Ashley, you tried to befriend the accused? Are *you* perhaps sweet on *him?* Is that why you testify on his behalf?"

She could feel her face flushing and cursed it for doing so. "No, Captain. I testify because it is right and honorable."

"I'm not so certain," he said while addressing the officers. "She seems compromised." He regarded her again. "Did Lieutenant Paynter compromise you, Miss Ashley?"

She began to rise from her chair in anger. "He most certainly did not! What manner of gentleman would ask such a question of a lady?"

"Forgive me," he said with sticky-sweet calm. "Legal matters are often stressful and confusing. The fairer sex is sometimes not quite up to the task."

Before she could erupt, Huxley brought down the gavel. "I believe we've heard enough from the witness. She's dismissed. Sergeant Ayers, show her out."

When the sergeant grabbed her arm, she prepared to resist. However, her eyes locked with Paynter's. He shook his head subtly, his face devoid of emotion. She inhaled a breath and followed Ayers from the mess hall, trying not to call down fire on the so-called court.

Rosalyn seemed as if she might spit nails when she sailed from the mess hall past Stacy. She said not a word, but only shook her head with an expression of frustrated rage. Stacy's nerves erupted more as she followed the sergeant inside. The gathering of officers watched her with appraising eyes until she took her seat before them. Paynter didn't even bother to look up at her. Before she knew what was happening, a captain approached and stood nearly in her face, looking down at her along the bridge of his nose.

"Miss Stacy Blue?"

"Yes."

"Is it true you are half Indian?"

Dread knotted her gut, like what she'd felt just before Sally had attacked the train. She'd heard the same words and tone too many times before. Her jaw clenched. "Yes."

"And did you serve as translator for the Ashley expedition upon encountering a bloodthirsty Arapaho war party?"

Irritation bubbled up within her, displacing the nerves immediately. "They were not a war party. And one of 'em spoke good English."

"Not a war party, you say?" The captain bobbed his head back and forth as if considering her claim, though the levity on his face was purely patronizing. "But they attacked the wagon train in darkness with bows and rifles, did they not?"

"No. They attacked Sally's men."

"Why? Why'd they do that?"

"To help us."

The captain smiled and paced before her slowly. "I can't help but wonder. Why'd they help you? They've been at war with us for years."

"I don't know. Maybe you should ask them."

The other officers exchanged smiles, as if knowing what was coming. Stacy tensed in her chair. The captain circled the open space once before planting himself solidly three feet from her, leaning forward with barely concealed aggression. "Miss Blue, are you in league with the Arapaho?"

"I don't know any Arapaho."

"That might be true. Maybe." He leaned nearer still. "However, are you sympathetic to Indians in general? Given that you are one yourself?"

Stacy knew she should be quiet. Should shut her mouth. But she couldn't catch her anger quick enough to hold the words inside. "What would you do if someone took your land and your wild game and threatened your children? Would you just stand by like a coward and do nothin'?"

"Then you *are* sympathetic to the Indians."

"I…"

The captain had already turned to the colonel. "As the witness is hostile against the U.S. government by her own admission, I believe we may safely disregard any intended testimony from her."

Colonel Huxley already had the gavel raised and brought it down sharply against the table. "Agreed. The witness is dismissed."

Stacy leaped from her chair. "Why, you den of desert rats! You shame yourselves and all decency under heaven."

"Sergeant Ayers!" shouted Huxley. "Remove the witness from this chamber by any means necessary."

Ayers cracked the back of his hand across Stacy's cheek, wobbling her knees. He caught her upper arm and began dragging her toward the door.

"Niineeni' howouuyooniit," she called out. And then in Shoshone, "Tonight you run. Stand ready."

She did not see Paynter's face to know if he had understood.

CHAPTER FORTY-SIX

THE OFFICERS OF THE COURT-MARTIAL EXCHANGED SELF-congratulatory chatter after Stacy was manhandled from the mess hall. Good riddance, they said. The audacity of the woman. Meanwhile, Jake whispered quietly to the wolf to lie still. Now was not the time. When the officers had finished backslapping, Colonel Huxley gaveled the meeting back to order.

"Last order of the proceedings before we adjourn for verdict," he said. "By rule, Lieutenant Paynter may speak on his behalf. Or he may waive that privilege." He addressed Jake. "Do you waive the privilege?"

"I do not, sir."

"Very well, then. Do you have a statement?"

"Yes, but a question first."

Huxley drummed the table and pursed his lips. "Very well. Ask it."

Jake leaned forward and gazed at the colonel, willing himself not to blink. "Will anyone under my command that day, other than First Sergeant Blackburn, be allowed to testify?"

The colonel smiled. He must have expected that question. "We asked for their testimony, but they refused. A pity, that. But I suppose it was to be expected. They are inherently unreliable."

Jake tried not to react to the boldness of the colonel's lie. "Yes. A pity."

"Do you have a statement, then?"

Jake rose from his chair, his manacled wrists hanging before him. "My statement is this. I wish to give my account of that day above the Green River basin. The true account."

"We have heard the account already."

"With all due respect, sirs, you heard a tall tale conjured by a man whose gift at spinnin' stories has killed a lot of good folks. I know you see me as murderin' scum, a disgrace to the command chain, a stench in the nostrils of the army. I don't blame your disposition. I might feel the same if I'd heard only what Blackburn had to say. But as I am likely to hang, I ask only to tell my story. Afterwards, you may do with me as you please."

Huxley seemed ready to deny the request when Lieutenant Stallings spoke for the first time during the proceedings. "It is only right, sir. Any of us would wish the same. He is, after all, still a member of this regiment. Regardless of what he has done, we should live up to the standards we claim."

Several nodding heads appeared to push Huxley toward a decision. "Very well, then. The court-martial will hear Lieutenant Paynter's *version* of events. So long as he keeps them brief and to the point. And I reserve the right to silence him at any time."

Jake dipped his head toward Lieutenant Stallings. "Thank you, sir." He stepped forward from his chair two steps to close the distance between him and the men who would determine the course of the rest of his life, however many hours that might be. "We rode out to the Green River basin with orders to locate a reported band of hostiles. Tenth Cavalry K-Troop, under the command of Captain Sherrod, and a Shoshone scout, Darwin Follows the Wind. When we arrived, the captain ordered Follows the Wind, Sergeant Rivers, and me to scout the basin. We set out in the darkness of early morning on October 27, and soon found what we were lookin' for."

Jake peered down through the gathering fall of soft snow into the wash below his position atop the basin wall. Sprawled along the flat overflow between the river and the rise on which he perched was a large collection of lodges and cook fires, a few horses, and perhaps two hundred people. He whispered aside to Follows the Wind. "Who are they?"

"Not certain. But no horses wear paint."

Gus emitted a hum of understanding. "No painted horses. No war-riors present, then."

They continued watching in silence. Despite the muffle of falling snow, the sound of dog barks, laughter, and children playing rose from the camp below. Jake continued searching every form, every posture, every filled hand for signs of impending battle. After several minutes, he knew the truth.

"Women and children," he said softly. "And a few gray-hairs too old to fight."

"Where are the men, do you suppose?" said Gus.

Follows the Wind frowned. "They do not hunt. Not with winter upon us." He paused. "Raiding, I think. Into Ute land, or Mormon land. South, most likely."

Jake motioned his comrades back from their discreet overlook. As they retreated toward their horses left waiting a half mile from the river basin, Jake saw a column of blue emerge from the mist of falling snow. Gus cursed softly.

"They were supposed to wait for us to report. Why'd they follow our trail?"

One answer occurred to Jake, but he didn't want to think about it. By the time they reached the horses, the rest of K-Troop had arrayed itself just beyond. Captain Sherrod sat astride his tall chestnut at the front of the group like the point of a spear.

"Lieutenant Paynter. What'd you see?"

Jake waged a brief war with his desire to say nothing. To speak of emptiness in the wash along the river. He allowed his misplaced faith in his commander to nudge aside suspicions of what might come next.

"Women and children in lodges beside the river. No warriors."

"How many?"

"Two hundred or so."

The captain worked his jaw. "You are certain you saw no war-riors? That the camp is not a trap to lure us down to the river? That *a mounted force doesn't wait for us across the basin? You recall what happened to Fetterman and his men."*

Jake did remember. Everybody remembered. Less than a year earlier, a combined force of Sioux, Cheyenne, and Arapaho had lured a troop of eighty soldiers into a trap and killed them all in fierce fighting. The massacre had become a victory cry for the tribes but a call for revenge from the Plains Army. The lust for blood was exactly what worried Jake. He considered lying. To recant his report. To claim that he saw signs of a thousand warriors waiting. He paused too long in his indecision.

"Follows the Wind," said Sherrod sharply. The scout leveled his eyes at the captain. "Did you see any warriors of your enemy in the basin?"

Follows the Wind glanced at Jake, uncertain, but he was a straightforward man. "I did not."

Jake hoped Sherrod would turn away since there was no one to fight. However, by the time Jake mounted his horse, the column was moving again toward the valley. He pulled alongside the captain.

"What is your intent, sir?"

Sherrod clenched his jaw and said nothing as K-Troop closed the gap between their position and the basin. When they arrived at a long draw leading into the river bottom, Sherrod called a halt and dismounted. After Jake dropped slowly from his horse, the men took his lead and dismounted as well. Questions swirled through his brain like the flakes encompassing the troop. Did the captain want to see the encampment for himself before turning back? Sergeant Blackburn's change of mood should have told Jake what was coming. The man's eyes lit with fire and his movements became crisp and energetic. Like they always did before an anticipated bloodbath. Sherrod turned to his men and issued a quiet order.

"Check your weapons. Make sure you've a full complement of cartridges at the ready. And fix bayonets."

Dread gave way to dismay in Jake. He eyed the captain, waiting. After a few seconds, the captain faced him.

"*Tell your men to mount up and lead them into that draw. Burn everything. No prisoners. None left alive.*"

Jake twisted his head to one side. "*They are women and children, sir.*"

"*They are hostiles.*" His tone was sharp and short. "*Enemies of the United States. We will treat them accordingly. Mount up your men and lead them into that draw.*"

Jake skewered Captain Sherrod with a resistant glare. "*No, Captain.*"

"*Are you disobeying a direct order?*"

"*Yes, sir.*"

Sherrod strode toward Jake, yanking his revolver from his belt as he walked. Upon reaching Jake, he pointed the weapon at him with three feet of air between the end of the barrel and Jake's forehead.

"*Lieutenant,*" growled Captain Sherrod, "*you will obey my order or receive a bullet.*"

"*No, sir. I will not lead the men into that draw.*"

Jake relayed the rest of the tale to his judge and jury—of the captain's order to have him shot. Of the skirmish that ensued where he put Blackburn to sleep and shot the captain dead. From there, he lied. If the officers knew how K-Troop not only had let him go but had encouraged his escape, several others would surely join him on the platform with the hangman. If they knew how Follows the Wind had directed him toward refuge with his people, the scout would be shot on sight.

"Afterward," he finished, "I jumped on my horse and pushed it down the draw alone."

"Did anyone pursue?" asked Huxley.

"I don't know. Snow was fallin' fast by then. I didn't look back."

He took a moment to assess the expressions on the officers' faces. Some remained unchanged from before his testimony. Others had gone blank, ciphers of emotion. A couple, including Lieutenant Stallings, seemed genuinely disturbed. However, he couldn't read minds like some carnival fortune teller. He couldn't see into the hearts of men he barely knew. As he watched with dread resignation, Colonel Huxley leaned back in his chair.

"Anything else, Lieutenant Paynter?"

"No. Nothing else."

The gavel cracked against the table, echoing through the hall. "Then this session is adjourned." He motioned to Ayers. "Remove the lieutenant to his cell. We will recess for thirty minutes before reconvening to decide his fate."

Jake rose mechanically and walked ahead of Sergeant Ayers from the mess hall. His gaze found Ketchum lounging against a corner of the building with mirth in his eyes.

"Why the long face, Paynter?" said Ketchum. "They bent on stretchin' yer neck?"

"You still here?"

"Ashley's still got plenty o' gold, so, yeah."

Jake brushed past him without another word. The outlaw chuckled in his wake. "This is how it ends for men like us. You shoulda figured that by now."

Jake *had* figured it, a long time ago. He pinned his stare forward and followed Ayers into the stockade. When the iron door clanged shut behind him, he remained standing in the middle of his cell, wrists still shackled. There he stood, a forgotten statue of a lost civilization. Shadows through the slit of window spoke of the slow passage of the sun as it fell toward the west. The cell had grown dim when the cry of the stockade door sounded, followed by the click of boot heels. After a moment, Colonel Huxley's voice sounded at his back.

"First Lieutenant Jacob Paynter."

He didn't reply. Or move. The colonel cleared his throat.

"After a surprisingly spirited debate, the court-martial has found you guilty of disobeying a direct order and murdering the officer who gave that order. Although you *may* have acted in self-defense, we could not dismiss your corruption of the chain of command. As such, you are sentenced to hang after breakfast tomorrow."

Jake remained unmoving—not even a flinch. He'd expected this for most of a year. Huxley waited for a half minute before turning to leave. "If you wish a last meal, inform the stockade officer. And God have mercy on your soul."

The boots clicked away and the door closed with a reverberating thud. After the sound died, Jake walked to the cot, removed his hat, kicked off his boots, and laid down with manacled wrists resting on his belly. In the void of the end of all things, one question galloped through the recesses of his mind.

If he had the moment back again to do over, what would he do differently?

After a few minutes, he found an answer. *Nothing.* He would not change a thing. For once in his life, he felt no regret for what he'd done, for extending mercy. Sleep captured him shortly afterward and spirited him away into a night of mild, forgettable dreams.

CHAPTER FORTY-SEVEN

EVERY MOMENT OF AWAKENING IS DIFFERENT FROM THE LAST, driven mostly by circumstances. How deep was the sleep? What was the dream when sleep ended? Was the rest adequate or not? However, one class of awakening stood apart from all others—that instant climb from slumber to full vigilance, heart hammering, breath shallow, muscles tensed—driven by the distinct perception that something was horribly wrong. Sometimes, the instinct proved false, prompted by a vivid and disturbing dream. Other times, it told the truth of the need to act. Jake awoke in his cell to the shrill call of such a truth.

Within seconds, he was standing on the cot peering into darkness through the slit of window. Shouts emanated from the night, then a shot, and another. The gate stood wide open and the campfires that accompanied the three remaining prairie schooners had gone cold, providing no evidence of what might be happening beyond the walls. A bell began to sound, crying metallic alarm. A minute later, a line of soldiers rushed past his window in a state of half dress but armed. More shouts sounded, these from inside the grounds, followed by a volley of shots. An attack? On an army fortress in the depths of night? Such incidents on the western frontier had become as rare as blood steak.

Without quite knowing why, Jake stepped down from the cot and retrieved the knife from his boot—the one Lisbet had given him to carve his name in the rock. No one had ever bothered to search his footwear. He stuffed the knife into his belt, donned his boots, and grabbed his hat. When he returned to the window, all hell was breaking loose. Knots of fire dotted the muster grounds. Shots rang out from the soldiers in regulated bursts. The shouted orders of officers echoed through the night, angry and vengeful. A new arc of fire periodically sailed into the grounds, no doubt a flaming arrow shot from distance. He looked again through the gate toward the remnants of the wagon train, hoping his friends had found cover. It was then that he saw the fiery chariot coming for him. Knowing he was no Elijah, Jake leaped from the bunk and pressed his back against the cell bars. Light pulsing through the window grew in intensity until a shudder rocked the cell, staggering him. The back wall of his cell disintegrated into a wave of shattered blocks spilling across the floor, crushing the cot as a rolling wall of flame pushed into the space. A wave of heat and smoke drove Jake to his knees. From the accidental vantage, he saw the chariot for what it was—an army wagon loaded with burning hay. Within seconds, his choice became clear. He could suffocate in his cell or crawl beneath the wagon to freedom. Because of his death sentence, or maybe in spite of it, he chose the latter. The jumble of masonry bit his palms and knees as he clambered beneath the burning rig to emerge on the muster grounds beyond.

He stood, but immediately doubled over to cough smoke and crud from his lungs as the gunfire continued popping along the walls around him. When he returned upright, he swung at the figure before him, driven by pure instinct. He missed—mostly—as the man stumbled backwards.

"Easy, Lieutenant. It's me, Stubbs."

Jake stepped toward him. "What the hell is happening?"

"Didn't Stacy tell you?"

"What?"

"Stacy. She told you to be ready. This is your breakout."

Jake blinked with surprise. He hadn't really believed they'd try. And if they did, he'd expected something much subtler. "The wagon?"

Stubbs grabbed his arm and dragged him into the shadows of an adjacent structure. "It was the only thing heavy enough to break down the wall."

"But the fire?"

"I knew you might stay without some…convincing."

Jake nearly laughed at the sheer audacity of it. Before he could say anything, Stubbs tugged him into motion again as they made their way toward the gate. Muzzle fire lit the night to his right and left, but a void of night lay beyond the opening.

"Who's attacking the fort?"

Stubbs laughed again as he ran before Jake. "We are."

"Come again?"

They slipped through the unguarded gate and barreled into the sea of night-soaked sage. "Gus and a few troopers started a ruckus beyond the walls. The rest of K-Troop rallied to 'defend' the fort."

Stubbs stopped and dragged Jake into a squat. A quick glance behind showed that no one had followed. Gunfire continued unabated from the "attackers" and "defenders."

"Somebody could get shot in the confusion," Jake said.

"Maybe, if not for one thing."

"What's that?"

"The whole troop is in on the plan. Every shot is a mile too high."

Stubbs pulled Jake to his feet and pushed him farther into the darkness. "Run, Lieutenant. Don't look back. If you turn around, I'll fight you."

He stared at the outline of the sergeant for the space of a few breaths before dipping his forehead. "Thanks, Stubbs. I owe you."

Jake leaned into the night and began to run. He passed the vacant area no longer occupied by the remaining three wagons but had no time to consider the implications. The manacles popping up and down began rubbing his wrists raw within a minute, but still he ran. Three times he stumbled, crashing painfully into tufts of sage before rising to run again. His breaths were coming in great heaves when horse hooves pounded up behind him. He wheeled around, preparing for the final fight of his life.

"Jake!" The sound of Gus's voice liberated the violence from his stance. Outlined against the sky were three horses, one of them empty. A small figure catapulted from one and ran toward him. He raised his hands again in self-defense as his attacker sucked him into an embrace.

"You made it out."

Stacy. He let her clutch him for a few seconds before pushing her away. She stumbled back and punched his shoulder. "I'm mad at you, Paynter. You shoulda run a long time ago. Most days, you're not a smart man."

He couldn't help but chuckle between gasping breaths. "You're right. On all counts."

"Well, give me yer hands."

She grabbed a wrist and attacked his manacles. Only when they fell away did he realize she had the key. Surprise gripped him again. "Corporal McQuaid knows about this?"

"Hully gee, Paynter. Half of it was his idea."

Words failed Jake as the magnitude of the operation became apparent to him. Gus, Stacy, K-Troop, McQuaid—they'd all risked themselves to spring him, to deliver him from the end of a hangman's rope. Gus laughed at him.

"No matter how hard you try to make it alone, Paynter, those of us who care about you are gonna watch yer back. Get used to it. We even brought your mare."

Jake reached up to rub the horse's neck. "Sorry about that, old girl."

"She's fully packed," said Stacy. She pressed the belt containing his Kerr into his empty hand. "Your Henry rifle, cartridges, powder, shot, caps, bedroll, coat, provisions contributed by the Emshoffs and Robersons, and canteen."

He began strapping on the gun belt. "What if the colonel sorts out what really happened?"

Jake knew the answer to his own question. Aiding the escape

of a condemned fugitive could result in lashes, prison, or execution, particularly for the buffalo soldiers. The army's claims of fair and impartial justice rarely extended to men of color. Benefit of the doubt was for those of Jake's complexion, and they'd still sentenced him to hang.

"He won't sort it out," said Gus. "The men are unified and tight-lipped. Emshoff and Roberson owe you their lives. They'll take this to the grave."

"But what about Lucien?"

"He don't know a thing."

"Hmm." Jake finished buckling the belt and took ownership of the mare's reins from Gus. As if sensing his thoughts, Stacy grabbed his wrist and pushed into his hand a piece of paper.

"A letter from Miss Ashley, in case she never saw you again."

"She knows what's happening?"

"Most of it." Stacy punched his shoulder again, hard, just shy of leaving a bruise. "Dodgast it, Paynter. She likes you. Don't act so surprised."

He folded the letter and stuffed it deep into his pocket. "Thanks, Stacy. Gus. I don't know what to say."

Gus grabbed his shoulder and patted a cheek. "Just stay alive. We *will* meet again." He stepped back. "I don't know where you'll go, and I don't want to. The less I know, the better. But the Yellowstone country is to your back, straight north, in case you wondered. You got about three hours 'til dawn. Three hours until they come after you."

Jake swung into the saddle. He tipped his hat and spurred the mare into motion, heading north into the night. The staccato shots from the fort fell away behind him until the darkness absorbed even those to hold him in its embrace.

CHAPTER FORTY-EIGHT

THE BEST MEASURE OF LEADERSHIP IS HOW IT RESPONDS TO the unexpected, the unfathomable, the unfixable. After the false attack on the fortress, Gus could tell that Colonel Huxley was flailing mightily, changing his plan from minute to minute as he cast about for a way through. Gus had known it was only a matter of time before his turn in the colonel's crucible of uncertainty arrived.

"The colonel wants to see you."

Gus cracked an eye open and looked up from the bunk where he'd grabbed a couple of hours of sleep. Two buffalo soldiers stood over him, deeply uncertain. Their carbines in ready position informed Gus immediately as to the tenor of the colonel's "request." He pulled on his boots and tucked in his shirt before walking with the men onto the still-dark parade ground. They found Huxley surveying the smoldering remains of the stockade, hat clutched in hand, Lieutenant Stallings by his side.

"Sergeant Rivers, as requested, sir."

The colonel turned his attention to Gus. Even in the torchlit predawn, the scowl splitting the man's face was as plain as dry toast. "What the hell happened here, Sergeant Rivers?"

"You're askin' me?"

The colonel stomped forward to stand nose to nose with Gus and pressed a finger into his chest. "Don't play the happy imbecile with me. You know everything that goes on here."

"If you recall, sir, I was mustered out of the army and I been away six months. How could I possibly know everything?"

Huxley's scowl only deepened. "I can't rightly explain what occurred here last night. We were attacked, but by who? And why? They didn't take anything, didn't harm anyone. The only casualties were a hay wagon and the stockade, with one prisoner missing. Nothing makes sense."

Gus cocked his head nonchalantly. "Paynter is gone, then? I assumed he died in the fire."

Huxley turned away to face the ruins again. "There's no body. We've been digging through hot rubble for an hour, and nothin'. He's gone. Which brings me again to my suspicions that the attack had something to do with Paynter."

Gus was glad for the darkness. He didn't want the colonel to see how much he struggled to hide his amusement and maintain a fabrication. "Who would do such a thing? Attack an army fort at the edge of nowhere to free a loner condemned for murder? Seems mighty odd."

"I don't know. Maybe the Arapaho again. Maybe raiders seeking revenge. Though I can't figure how they managed to propel a burning wagon through the stockade wall."

"It is a puzzle, no doubt."

Huxley was still fishing about for an answer when a horse rode up behind them. Sergeant Blackburn vaulted from the saddle and saluted the colonel. "I found where he went. He run out in the sage maybe a mile, where someone met him with a horse. He headed north from there, alone. I didn't track the others."

A chill ran up Gus's spine. How had Blackburn managed to discern so much of the truth in near darkness? As if intercepting Gus's thoughts, Blackburn eyed him coolly in the torchlight. "I can track a ghost through a blizzard. Given enough time, I'll figure out who helped him."

The man's show of pure and focused leadership seemed to provide Colonel Huxley the impetus he needed to finally make a decision. "First Sergeant. Assemble a tracking party with provisions and plenty of ammunition. Pursue the prisoner as soon as you're ready. And I don't care if you bring him back alive or in pieces."

A smile crept across Blackburn's face. "Yes, sir. I'll do just that. And Rivers?"

"Blackburn."

"You're with me. It'd go a long way to makin' me believe you didn't have a hand in this fiasco."

Gus gritted his teeth. He'd chased Paynter down once before and his conscience couldn't bear another such show of disloyalty. If he declined, though, there was no telling what'd happen to the men of K-Troop. Not with Blackburn already on the prowl. "As you wish, First Sergeant."

"Good choice. And bring the Indian girl. We'll need a translator and Follows the Wind is nowhere to be found."

Gus turned and strode away to find Stacy—and to keep from strangling the man.

Sunrise found the tracking party miles from Fort Bridger and headed resolutely on a northbound line. Along with Gus and Stacy, Blackburn had included Lieutenant Stallings, two of the white officers who'd sentenced Paynter to swing, and Sergeant Stubbs with five buffalo soldiers loaded for bear. Gus prayed like mad that the troopers would keep silent about what they knew. But what choice did they have? A word from any one of them would condemn them all.

The small force advanced at a shocking pace behind Blackburn. He followed Paynter's faint trail at a trot, stopping only twice for a closer look at disturbed soil and brush. Paynter had spoken of Blackburn's ability, but Gus had thought it mostly the exaggerations of an impressionable young man. Now, he knew better. He motioned discreetly to Stacy, and they fell to the rear of the cavalcade by some thirty yards.

"He's headed north for sure," said Stacy. "Up the west side

of the Wind Rivers through the Great Basin and over the Gros Ventres into Yellowstone country. A man could lose himself for a lifetime up there."

"Sounds about right."

"You seem worried, though. Like he won't make it."

Gus shook his head. He reminded himself never to play poker with Stacy because she had already learned his tells. "I *am* worried. We're makin' too good o' progress. I doubt Paynter expected anyone'd be so hot on his heels."

She fell silent, apparently digesting his words. She pulled her calico nearer and leaned in his direction. "What does that mean? What ya got in mind?"

"You shouldn't have to ask."

She looked away with grim understanding. As they closed the gap to the main party, Gus measured again his willingness to kill to keep Paynter on the run. Ending Blackburn didn't bother him. The man had it coming in spades. The other white officers, though—that was a different question. He had no disagreement with them personally and would hate for the whole affair to come to an exchange of bullets. Anyone could die if that happened, including Stubbs. Or Stacy. And if he survived a shootout, he'd become an outlaw himself. When he had quit the cotton fields of Alabama and crossed the Mason-Dixon line, Gus had sworn he'd walk the straight and narrow to avoid becoming a fugitive ever again. But here he was, wrestling with just such a notion and savoring the irony. Some promises can't be broken and others can't be kept. The collision of the two could shatter a man.

CHAPTER FORTY-NINE

WHAT THE GREAT DIVIDE BASIN CLAIMED IN THE magnificence of its name, it made up for in numb monotony. For hour upon hour, Jake rode north through an unending landscape of rolling sage-covered hills and ancient creek beds, skirting knots of antelope who always managed to keep a half-mile buffer between them and him. The Wind River mountains that would funnel him toward the Yellowstone remained hidden by distance and haze somewhere ahead and to his right. Though he prodded the mare at a brisk pace, he took care not to burn her down. The gate to Yellowstone country lay four or five days onward. A rapid journey of that distance would kill a horse as surely as starving it would. Despite her antagonistic nature, Jake had grown fond of the mare. She was a fighter with a healthy dose of suspicion, qualities they held in common. He didn't want to destroy her over anything as base as panic or sheer stupidity.

As the sun rose to midday, Jake grew sleepy in the pleasant heat. His thoughts, so heightened since his early morning flight, grew languid and unfocused as a general torpor settled over him. Flashes of memory from his youth paid a call and settled in for a long, uncomfortable visit. His father laid out in his best suit on the dining table, unrecognizable after death had leached the ever-present rage from his angular features. His elder twin brothers, Edwin and Anthony, struggling for control of the sugar plantation, initially with words and then with fists. Their insistence that young Jake was dead weight, and their periodic attempts to make reality of the metaphor. Perhaps it was the heat, but one memory kept repeating, like an itch in the middle of his back he couldn't reach. He was fourteen again and kneeling in the cane fields, hoping to remain hidden until his brothers sobered up. The stifling heat of August just past sundown invaded his senses, laboring every breath as if he were inhaling water.

"*Come out, Jakey, Jakey.*" *His brothers' calls from the edge of the cane field were anything but congenial.* "*We got a new rifle we wanna show ya.*"

Bullets pinged into the stand of cane, striking earth or carving a staccato passage through the leaves, followed each time by uproarious laughter. Jake crouched lower while inching deeper into the field. The reek of fetid water collecting between the plants assaulted his nose until he could smell nothing at all.

Then the man came. Jake couldn't see him, but only heard him in conversation with his brothers.

"*Young mastahs. Can I help ya up to the big house?*"

"*Run along, Aaron. Back to the cabins.*"

Two more shots sounded through the cane, and another round of laughter. "*Jakey! Come out, boy.*"

"*Mastahs, I'm pleadin' with ya t' stop. He's your brother. He might end up kilt.*"

"*You tryin' to tell me what to do?*" *This from Edwin.*

"*No, suh. Jus' tryin' t' help.*"

"*You ain't helpin'. Now, git!*"

"*But suh…*" *Sounds of a scuffle ensued, and then a shot rang out. Even the crickets and cicadas fell silent in the aftermath of the weapon's report. Jake held his breath until his eyes swam, before Anthony spoke.* "*Dammit, Edwin. It'll run us twelve hundred to replace him. Why'd ya do that?*"

"*Leave me be. I need whiskey.*"

Retreating footsteps marked the departure of his brothers. Jake waited for a time until the stars had marched higher in the night sky before he ventured from his refuge. He found the dead man by stumbling over him. Jake put a palm against the man's cheek, finding it already going cold. He'd seen dead people before. He'd witnessed killing before. None of it had ever seemed to involve him, though. Until now.

"Aaron," he whispered. He hadn't even known the man, or his name. An overwhelming sense of obligation seized him. That he should do something for the near-stranger who'd died on his behalf. After minutes of wrestling with what to do, he simply rolled Aaron to his back and draped the cold hands across his belly. What else could he do?

A flash of sunlight drew his attention to water—the remains of a springtime creek. He slipped from the mare for a taste. It was mildly bitter but not fetid. Not like what had gathered between the rows of the cane fields. He took a long draught from his canteen, wiped his mouth, and topped off the container before letting the mare take her fill. He stood aside from her to shake away the dregs of the memory, but couldn't discard the sense that he should've done more. That his cowardice had made him complicit with everything he saw his cruel brothers do. A flash of anger revived him, shook him from the torpor. Who or what he was angry with he couldn't rightly say. He climbed aboard the mare and nudged her flanks.

"Git on, girl."

They moved on from the creek, from the memory, and back into the repetition of unchanging landscape heading north. Always north.

Jake rode past dark until he feared the next step might snap the mare's foreleg. He stopped her at a jumble of three boulders about the height of a man, pressed together by forces he couldn't fathom. He'd covered a good stretch—sixty, maybe seventy miles. If anyone trailed him, he'd seen no evidence in his repeated backward glances. That stood to reason. Tracking a single horse across a high desert was no easy task. Overconfidence got the best of Jake and he lit a small fire. He should've known better. A light source on the open range could be seen for miles, a beacon of stupidity. It was the surest way to attract attention, the last thing a condemned fugitive should want. However, another factor was at play—one he barely recognized. Rosalyn's letter had been smoldering in his pocket all day. Every time he had reached for the paper, he had withdrawn his hand. Now settled for the night, he became powerless against its call. The small campfire proved sufficient to make out the words as they flickered on the paper.

Dear Mr. Paynter,

I apologize for the forwardness of this letter, and pray you read it as a free man, not as a prisoner. First, let me offer my deepest gratitude for your actions to preserve us against Sally's men, despite my brother's resistance. He is a stubborn and difficult man, but not without finer qualities. I am thankful that your finer qualities proved more than equal to the task of overcoming the difficulty he presented. Even if he does not credit you with saving us, I do. Mr. Rivers informed me of the circumstances surrounding the shooting of your captain. Though I had prepared for the worst, to learn that you had sacrificed yourself for others came as no surprise. Despite what you seem to think of yourself, you are a good man. My brother's opinion cannot change that. A court verdict cannot change that. I only wish we had made introductions under better circumstances. I will cling to the hope that we might meet again someday. If not, I will carry cherished memories of you always. God bless, and stay alive.

Rosalyn Ashley

The letter hung limply in Jake's hand as he dissected the words. For weeks, he had tried to convince himself that her good opinion of him didn't matter. That it was a distraction, a nuisance. To see it written indelibly on paper in his hand shook him to his core. For any woman to consider him worthy of regard startled him. But for one like Rosalyn—refined, gracious, kind—to view him in such a light? It challenged his doubt.

The chaos of speculation chased him into sleep and ensured a restless night of waking to darkness before stumbling again into slumber. His final awakening drove him to his feet in panic. The sun had risen. In the shadow of the rocks, he had slept like a guiltless child well into the morning. Letting loose a string of colorful curses, he recovered the hobbled mare, loaded her up, and drove her from the camp at a hot pace. Upon reaching the first hilltop, he turned in the saddle to scan the basin behind him. A flash in the distance drained away all hope. On the far horizon, a line of horses traversed the downslope of a hill. Six miles? Eight? He couldn't tell. Though it was hard to know for certain, he determined that the riders were dressed in blue. It had to be Blackburn. Nobody else could've tracked him so well and so fast.

He spurred the mare onward, knowing what lay ahead. The Plains Cavalry rode the best horses the government could buy, bred for stamina, for distance. Despite her pluck, the little mare couldn't hope to keep pace with such monsters for another four days. They'd run him down on the desert, well short of Yellowstone country. He couldn't hope to stand alone and fight a band of soldiers he had trained himself. He'd die for sure. With no other choice, Jake set his mind toward the Wind River mountains. Another long day's ride would take him into the foothills and provide him a prayer of slipping from sight among the broken hills and valleys that gave entrance to the high country. He angled the mare toward the northeast and spontaneously patted the side of her neck.

"My apologies, girl."

She tossed her head and offered comment, likely an equine curse that he failed to translate.

CHAPTER FIFTY

THE MARE WAS STRUGGLING WHEN SHE AND JAKE REACHED the foothills of the Wind Rivers. She had pressed doggedly onward through the heat of the day and into the evening while the pursuit closed to within about three miles. When Jake could no longer see his pursuers in the falling dusk, he dismounted, cut sharply north, and led the exhausted horse along a mile-long flank of exposed rock stretching into a creek-cut canyon. Before long, moonless night fell proper, plunging them into a perilous enveloping darkness. In such conditions, they could step off a sudden drop and find themselves broken on rocks twenty feet or a hundred feet below. He found a reasonably level section of limestone and called a halt. His pursuers couldn't travel in darkness any better than he could, and he hoped the sudden shift of direction along trackless limestone would throw them off his trail. He sat down to lean against a boulder, vowing not to get too comfortable. He would move with the coming moon, because Blackburn would do the same. He blinked a few times, stretched, and let loose a yawn.

Jake woke, not remembering having fallen asleep. After a few seconds of disorientation, he yanked his eyes to the horizon to find a half moon rising, orange and low in the sky. The rock shelf on which he sat glowed in the moonlight, a collection of planes and shadows. He stood, rubbed the knot from his neck, and walked upslope. The shelf melted into a wall of rock some twenty or thirty feet tall. After hobbling the mare to keep her stationary, he traversed the wall for an hour before finding what he needed. As he unhobbled the mare again, she thumped his skull painfully to let him know just how she felt about the predicament he'd led them into.

"Just wait," he whispered. "You're gonna hate this."

The mare reluctantly high-stepped over a ruin of small rocks as he led her to a chute that cut upward through the wall. The going proved steeper than he'd anticipated. He pulled, pushed, and prodded the horse ever higher over rugged terrain until they reached the next shelf. He plopped to the ground to catch his breath as the mare huffed over his head. Below, he heard a voice, and then another. They were looking for him, but not too close. After a few minutes of rest, he led the mare farther north along the shelf until locating another chute suitable for traversing the next but shorter wall.

By the time the coming sun began returning color to the plain below, they had cleared three walls of stone and faced a gentle rise that appeared to lead to gentler progress beyond. After ascending the rise for a bit, he left the mare unattended and returned to scout the mountainside below. Within minutes, he spotted his trackers clearly for the first time. They were traversing up the mountain more than a mile down canyon from his position. He counted eleven, maybe twelve. More surprisingly, Gus and Stacy seemed to be part of the number. He assumed they participated under duress. Jake returned to his horse, mounted up, and rode her higher into the range. The pursuers were off his trail. If he was lucky, they'd never find it. Worst case, he'd gain hours—time he'd need to cross over the mountains into the Wind River country.

"Steady on," he told the mare. She didn't need much telling, though. With her head down and plodding strides, she carried Jake higher into the wilderness, two souls determined to become lost.

———

Jake had badly misjudged the raw power of determined hatred. As a result, the bullet that cracked the boulder beside him spewed a shower of tiny rock projectiles against his cheek. He snared his Henry and dove away from the mare, who reared and stumbled back up the deer trail they'd been following for half an hour. Jake, meanwhile, found what shelter he could—another boulder, barely large enough to conceal his body. He pinned his back to the rock with rifle at the ready to think. Since losing the pursuers early the previous day, he and the mare had made their serpentine way through the sky-hugging valleys that hatched an array of paths among the high peaks of the Wind Rivers. By nightfall, they would be descending. He'd not seen nor heard any sign of the trackers in more than a day. Until the bullet nearly ripped a channel through his skull.

"Hey! Paynter!" The voice from below rippled through him with a shuddering chill. Blackburn. "I got you dead to rights. Throw out your weapons, and maybe I won't shoot you just for sport."

Jake's mind remained a maelstrom of thought. How had Blackburn found him? Two realizations struck him in quick succession. First, Blackburn had taught him the strategy of laying down a serpentine course, but bending the pattern left or right over time. He'd known Jake would use it and had guessed the right direction of the bend. It was the second realization that lent Jake a small measure of resolve. Blackburn had used the word "I," not "we." He was alone.

"You're too predictable," shouted Blackburn from below. His voice echoed in the rocks, clear as a school bell despite the fifty or so yards separating their positions. He seemed in the mood to gloat. "You did just what I taught ya. I'd hoped that after all this time, you'd a' learned a few more tricks, but clearly you didn't. So, here you are, in my sights and nowhere to run. I'll put a slug through your brain before you get five feet in either direction."

Jake had to agree with the logic. His protective boulder was exposed, with no other cover for thirty yards in any direction.

However, Blackburn was wrong about one thing. Jake had learned plenty of new tricks since they had parted ways. In particular, he'd learned the art of strategic patience—of withholding an attack and waiting for an adversary to make a fatal mistake. The more confident the enemy of their superior position, the more likely they were to fall victim to the strategy. And Blackburn was nothing if not confident of his position.

"Predictability's somethin' I must've learned from you," Jake called. "I knew you'd leave the rest and come chargin' in alone. How long 'til the others catch up? An hour? Three hours? More?"

"Don't matter. I left a trail, so they'll be here in no time. I'll just make sure you stay put until they come."

"Not a bad plan." He paused. "But by my reckoning, we'll start losin' daylight in about three hours when the sun cuts behind the peaks. You sure everyone else'll find us by then?"

When Blackburn failed to respond immediately, Jake knew he had him worried.

"But you're probably right," Jake said. "Though I'd make a wager if I could. Like that wager you made with the mayor of Hoddsville. You bet half our horses against three head of cattle with a single throw of dice as the decider. Remember that?"

"Hell, yeah. It was a good bet."

"How'd ya know you wouldn't lose? The loss of half our horses would've left us walkin' ahead of the advancing Union forces."

Blackburn laughed, the tenor of it mildly patronizing. "Come now, Paynter. You know I'd never make a bet like that if I thought I'd lose. Loaded dice make for a good insurance policy."

"Even loaded dice can fall the wrong way from time to time."

"Sure, sure. But if they had, we'd a' taken the cattle anyway. After all, we had more men and guns than did the poor country saps of Hoddsville. Those are better insurance policies than a pair of loaded dice."

"I suppose you're right. Never seen evidence to the contrary."

Jake kept Blackburn talking. For his part, the man seemed happy to reminisce. He missed his days leading more than a hundred raiders with few constraints and no accountability. The fact that he was taking orders from far less experienced men clearly galled him, and speaking of past times with Jake proved a good outlet for reclaiming his former glory. And Jake just kept feeding him glory, one small bite at a time. Minutes stretched into an hour. When Blackburn's tone had settled into one of a man talking to a neighbor across a fencepost, Jake capitalized on his strategy of patience.

"Hey, Blackburn. Remember that girl in Clairmont? Callie Mae somethin'."

"Anderson." The clipping of the name indicated that Blackburn knew where the conversation was headed.

"Yep. Anderson. She was as pretty a girl as any of us ever saw. I remember you thought as much. You spent most of a week tryin' to woo her, to get her alone. But she'd have none of it. So you got numb drunk, took what you wanted from her anyway, and then choked the life from her. You were a real Romeo. Can't see how any of the ladies resisted yer charms."

"Shut up, Paynter. Not another word."

Jake straightened against the boulder and redoubled his grip on the cocked rifle, finger through the trigger guard. "Problem is, Ambrose, you're nothin' but a stone-cold killer. Always were. Always will be. And worse, you like it. Snuffing out a life intoxicates you like three shots of whiskey."

"I said to shut up." The anger in Blackburn's voice was palpable, a wave of heat emanating from the rocks below. "You're no less a killer than I am. I've seen what you did."

"You may be right. But then again, Callie Mae chose death over loving you, Romeo."

"Dammit, Paynter!"

At the utterance of his name, Jake spun his Henry over the

boulder, found blue, and fired. In his anger Blackburn had risen from cover to expose his head. Jake's shot went wide. Mostly. The bullet clipped the side of Blackburn's jaw, spinning him backwards to his belly with rifle flying. Jake hurtled around the boulder, raced down the slope, and planted a boot on the back of Blackburn's neck as he reached for his loose weapon.

"Pull back yer hand."

Blackburn withdrew his reach. Blood flowed freely from the lacing wound along his jawline. He cupped a hand over it to stem the bleeding and cocked an eye at Jake. "Go ahead, boy. Pull the trigger. You know you want to."

Jake pumped the lever, pulled back the hammer, and pressed the barrel of the Henry against the back of Blackburn's skull. His finger touched the trigger lightly. Every horror the man had visited on others galloped through Jake's brain. All the rot he had introduced into Jake's soul invaded his senses. The man deserved to die a thousand times for what he'd done. But what would change in the aftermath? Blackburn would be dead, for sure, but Jake would remain the same. Nothing as simple as murdering an evil man could fix what was wrong with him. Killing Sally's men had done nothing to reclaim his soiled soul. On the contrary, any small bend of his character toward the good had been the result of quiet mercies, tender words, small kindnesses. Never a fist. Never a bullet. Never a flame. His finger drifted away from the trigger.

"I may be a killer," he said barely above a whisper, "but I ain't a murderer. Not anymore."

Without a word, Jake mashed Blackburn's ankle until it twisted beneath his boot. With the man cursing in pain, Jake calmly collected Blackburn's discarded rifle and unattended horse and started upslope.

"Don't leave me here, Paynter. Damn you!"

"It's like you said. You left a trail. Everyone'll be here in no time."

Jake recovered the mare but mounted Blackburn's stallion to give his partner a well-earned rest. He ignored Blackburn's threatening calls until they faded into the expanse of wilderness at his back.

CHAPTER FIFTY-ONE

STACY HEARD BLACKBURN COMING THROUGH THE WOODS before she saw him. His string of curses tumbled down the mountainside like spring runoff from the permanent snowfields above the tree line. He limped toward them from a thicket of pines, leaning heavily against a makeshift walking stick, his shirt a field of black, drying blood. A mass of mangled flesh along the side of his jaw identified the source of the bloodletting.

"First Sergeant," said Lieutenant Stallings as he dismounted. "What in the name of the Almighty happened to you?"

Blackburn drew nearer as everyone left their saddles for the inclined earth. He remained unspeaking until all had dismounted, as if waiting for his audience to settle. "I found Paynter's trail this morning when I was out scouting. Didn't have time to come back for the rest of you, so I came on alone."

"I noticed." Stallings seemed less than pleased.

"Anyway, I tracked him all day, leaving a trail even a child could follow." Stacy winced at the thinly veiled insult, but the lieutenant remained stoic. "I was closin' in on the fugitive, nearly had him in my sights. But then he ambushed me. Shot me from a distance, but I ducked for cover and he ran off."

Several aspects of the brief tale struck Stacy as pure balderdash. Foremost among them, if Paynter had meant to kill Blackburn, he'd be dead. And she'd never seen Paynter run from a fight. Joyous mischief sent her sidling closer to the wounded man. "That so? He ambushed you?"

"That's what I said."

"Where's your horse?"

"Spooked when I fell off."

She nudged his walking stick. "What about yer rifle? That run off too?"

Gus chuckled at her back. One side of Blackburn's lip lifted in disdain. "I lost my rifle in the fall. Couldn't find it, so I came back this way."

"Couldn't find yer rifle? Musta' been one heck of a fall. Surprised you survived." She flashed him a smile. "I'd be happy to look for it. And yer poor horse too. Just point me in the right direction."

Blackburn's shell of civility cracked, revealing him for what he was. Fire lit his eyes and his face contorted as he snatched the front of her shirt. "I would peel you like an apple, girl. Have you and throw you away with the rest of the garbage. You'd be sorry you ever laid eyes on me."

Gus planted a fist in Blackburn's face before Stacy could. The man stumbled backward, releasing her shirt. Gus stepped between her and Blackburn, a tower of righteous menace. "Lay another hand on Miss Blue and I'll take it from you."

Blackburn rubbed his reddening cheekbone and trembled with rage. "I'll see you shot, Rivers."

"I ain't in the army no more. Remember? You're the one who made sure o' that."

Blackburn aimed his molten glare at Gus for a few seconds before wheeling toward Lieutenant Stallings. "We gotta go after Paynter. He's gonna hang, even if it kills me."

Stallings, who had watched in silence, shot a glance at the other officers—a what-do-you-think cock of an eyebrow. Stacy waded into the inquiry before they could form a conclusion. "Lieutenant. There ain't no way we catch Paynter today. And probably not tomorrow, now that he's got an extra horse." She tossed a mocking glance at Blackburn. "And two rifles."

"She's right," Gus added quickly. "By tomorrow night, he'll be in Shoshone country, and they call him friend. You told us yourself they just signed a treaty with the government not two months ago. You run an armed force onto their lands to take an ally from under their noses, it might not go so well. The government just put an end to Red Cloud's war. I doubt they want a new one just now."

Stallings looked again at the other officers. One of them shrugged. "I gotta get back to Fort Laramie. I ain't got time to start a war with the Shoshone with only half a dozen soldiers at my back."

"Hafta agree," said the other. "The fugitive ain't worth it. Let the Shoshone have him, I say. Or the winter. I don't much care."

Stallings turned his eyes toward Stacy. "You're half Shoshone."

"Yeah. What of it?" She expected something hurtful. Something nasty. The lieutenant surprised her.

"What's your opinion, then? Will Chief Washakie see this as a breach of treaty?"

A hint of smile touched her lips. "He will. He takes care of his own."

"You think he considers Paynter one of his own?"

"I wouldn't test him on that."

Blackburn stepped into Stallings's face. "But, sir. He'll be in the wind. We might never—"

"Shut it, First Sergeant." Stallings motioned to Stubbs. "Saddle him up with someone."

Blackburn threw down his stick. "I ain't ridin' with no…"

"Then walk, Blackburn! Your choice. I no longer give a damn."

Stallings mounted his horse without another word and turned it downslope. The other officers followed his lead, as did the rank-and-file. Stubbs lifted his chin and smiled at Blackburn. "You can ride with me. But watch yer hands."

Blackburn seemed ready to explode, but hobbled to Stubbs's horse and climbed up behind him. They turned to follow the others, who were already a hundred yards closer to Fort Bridger. Gus grinned at Stacy.

"Miss Blue. Shall we?"

"We shall."

She mounted her calico and fell in beside Gus's buckskin to trail the rest of the party. After a few minutes, she asked her nagging question.

"Do you suppose we'll ever see him again?"

Gus cut his eyes at her and nodded. "I think so. He's like a bad winter. He always comes back, eventually." He waved his hand toward her. "What about you? What'll you do now?"

"Too late to catch up with Pa. He's halfway across Idaho by now. No sense in goin' all that way just to hole up in Boise for the winter. Nope. Figure I'll winter in South Pass City where at least I know a couple o' folks. Maybe I can bunk in with the Emshoffs 'til I get settled. I got enough money to get me through to spring if I tighten my belt a notch or two. Maybe I can find a job mindin' stock."

"I figured you'd go to your ma's family for the winter."

"It's not been the same since my grandfather died. Besides, I reckon I'll leave Paynter in peace for now. If anyone needs a little peace, it's him."

Gus laughed. "I'd agree with that. He's been lookin' for it ever since I've known him. I wish him well."

"Me too," she said. "So, what about you, Gus? Where will you go now?"

Gus lifted his chin to the wind and squinted into the distance. "I'm thinkin' I liked the look o' South Pass City. Believe I'll give it a go for a spell. Especially since I know folks there."

When he glanced sidelong at her, she couldn't hide her smile, but didn't care so much this time.

CHAPTER FIFTY-TWO

THERE WAS SOMETHING ABOUT CRAWLING ACROSS THE ROOF of the world that restored perspective. The thinner air, the bluer sky, the crisper breeze, the knowledge that every direction eventually led downward to the lands of people, of problems, of potential. Jake's high-country seclusion allowed him to understand where he stood with Blackburn. He should've killed the man. Should've pulled the trigger when he had the chance. Enemies were like feral cats—if you kept feeding them, they'd keep coming back for more. And there was no better way to sustain an adversary than by wounding but not killing them, leaving them alive and more dedicated to vengeance than ever before. Yes—not ending Blackburn had likely ensured they'd meet again with the outcome less certain. The perspective of the world's rooftop, though, also brought Jake a new revelation. Three years earlier, he would've shot Blackburn without an instant of doubt. Three months ago, he likely would've done the same but with hesitation. Now? Something unseen in the deep recesses of his awareness had stayed his hand, had opted for mercy toward a man who deserved none. The cogs of his internal machine had shifted, and he didn't know exactly how.

The fall of night caught Jake and the two horses near a majestic thrust of rocky spires—a circle of teeth straining toward the heavens, standing as sentinels over inhospitable ground where even the spirited pines feared to tread. The waning of light gave way to an invasion of stars that marched across the sky to claim all four corners, lords and masters of creation for a few hours, brilliant in their collective reign. As he watched the drama unfold, Jake's thoughts wandered to the stars and beyond. His life swept before him, daring to be understood. The things he'd done and not done. The people he'd loved, those he'd hated, and the mass of humanity somewhere between that extensive gap. The men he'd killed in conflict, and there were many. And the few for whom he'd surrender his life to take back what he'd done to them. But mostly, he dwelled on the previous three months, on the gifts he'd given and those he had received. Eventually, sleep took him in her arms as she hadn't in years.

Morning roused him just ahead of the coming sun. After a cold breakfast, he moved the horses downslope to graze for a while, oddly unconcerned if anyone followed. For the moment, he felt untouchable, invisible. When he finally mounted the stallion again, the mare gave him a baleful glare. He laughed out loud.

"Jealous, girl? I didn't know you cared."

Despite her huff, she followed compliantly, drawn along by the tether wrapped around his saddle horn. After a brief search, he found a meager stream of water and followed its downward flow. The stream merged with another, and another still until they formed a proper creek. The creek gave way to a lively tumble of water that became a river, white and frothy as it pummeled the rocks on its headlong journey to a distant ocean. The river canyon deepened until passage became hard-fought ground that Jake and the horses claimed foot by perilous foot. So intent was he on the journey that he didn't see the man until he called out with high-pitched chirp. His eyes flew up to find a rider ahead, waiting. He paused only briefly before continuing toward him. The old man sat patiently astride a gray horse, his long white hair gathered into a pair of forward braids. When Jake had approached within thirty feet, he raised a palm.

"Hello, Beah Nooki."

The Shoshone elder raised a palm in reply. "Paynter. I came for you."

Jake closed the gap and halted his horses. "How did you know where to find me?"

"Old men know such things." His eyes twinkled with merriment. "The spirit takes the strength from the body and moves it here." He touched his temple.

"Did Follows the Wind tell you I might escape Fort Bridger?"

"That too." Without another word, he turned his horse and beckoned for Jake to follow.

They rode in silence as the sun crawled across the sky until the river broke free of the mountains to run unrestrained into the Wind River valley. Liberated from the rocky slopes, Beah Nooki settled his horse in beside Jake's and gave him a long, appraising gaze.

"You changed, Paynter."

Jake's ruminations from the previous night came back to him. He agreed, but how did the old man know? "Why do you say so?"

"When you left the people, you were as a man already dead."

"Dead?"

"Your body drew breath, but your head walked with spirits. Your eyes held no life." Beah Nooki faced ahead. "Now, I see you living."

Jake knew the statement was actually a question. "I *was* dead and didn't know it for a long time. But I've found reasons to live these past few months." A smile touched his lips. "All those reasons have names and faces."

The elder nodded and smiled. "My heart swells for you, Niineeni' howouuyooniit."

Jake peered at Beah Nooki in surprise. The Shoshone and Arapaho weren't friends. To hear the elder repeat the name the Arapaho had given him? "You've heard the story?"

"You did not tell us last winter what happened. After you left, Follows the Wind returned and told us. We told the Crow and the Blackfoot. The Arapaho told the Cheyenne, who told the Lakota and Oglala. Your story is among the nations now—the mercy you gave that day."

A chaos of emotion washed over Jake. Unworthiness. Guilt. Wonder. His face must've betrayed the maelstrom, because the old man laughed loudly.

"Come, Paynter. Winter with us again. Stay long, if you must."

"Thank you. I would be honored."

As he rode with Beah Nooki toward the small village hugging the banks of the Little Wind River, Jake shook his head in disbelief. For a dedicated loner with no friends, he carried a long list of people who cared for him, and for whom he had come to care. At least one inspired something more, if a man like him could even aspire to such heights. And as for the wolf? He remained quiet, seemingly content to rest for a time.

Get a sneak peek at
Jake Paynter's next adventure in
Devil's Ride West

CHAPTER ONE

July 1869, Wyoming Territory

INNER DEMONS STARVED OF AIR NEVER DIE FOR GOOD. JAKE
Paynter's demons returned with a vengeance when a pair of Texas
Rangers came for his head. Jake scanned the sweeping expanse of
blue sky overhead to find a hawk circling the broken hills of sand-
stone and sage that walled him on three sides. Satisfied, he turned
back to the task of setting a rabbit snare. Perhaps the bird knew
what he was doing and hoped to jump his claim. Disregarding his
potential rival, Jake shoved a stick into a soft patch of clover two
handspans away from the skirt of a juniper bush.

With deft movements, he tied a length of sinewy twine between
the bush and the stick, leaving a large loop suspended above the
clover. With luck, a jackrabbit in search of a tempting meal would
wander through the loop until the twine tightened around its furry
neck. As he stood, Jake brushed away mild guilt over condemn-
ing an innocent creature to the same fate he'd escaped the previous September. After all, a man had to eat. And the driven hunter
remained, the last vestiges of the wolf he'd only lately laid to rest.

Jake moved along the ridge of earth that followed a creek until
he found another lush outcropping of clover. His mind soon
drifted while he set another snare, content to inhabit solitude for a

time. Nature conspired to dull his senses. The pleasant touch of an early summer breeze. The warmth of the unobstructed sun. The scattered trill of birds drowning out distant calls of children at play somewhere near the village. Perhaps that was why he didn't sense them coming until it was too late.

"Stretch yer hands, Paynter. Slow-like."

The drawling voice from ten feet behind him snapped Jake back to reality. He didn't bother reaching for his revolver, which he'd irresponsibly left at the village. The knife in his hand wouldn't do him much good with a bullet in his head. Out of options, he did as commanded and raised his hands skyward.

"Stand and pivot," said a second voice with similar intonation.

Jake rose slowly and turned to face the strangers. Two men, both at least five years north of fifty and solid as stretched wire, faced him with confident wariness. One stood a head taller than the other. Matching mustaches framed straight-lipped determination. Twin Remington forty-fours gripped in steady outstretched hands targeted his chest. The shorter man lifted his chin.

"You gonna drop the knife, son? Or we gotta do this the hard way?"

Something in their aspect informed Jake that his run was over. That he was dealing with professionals who weren't likely to make a mistake. It was that realization that undoubtedly resurrected his demons for first time in nearly a year. The taller man seemed to sense what was coming because his eyebrows lifted with uncertainty. Too late, though. Jake flung himself from the ridge headfirst down the embankment and into the creek. His body bounced up from the rocky creek bed, and his legs were in motion when his feet found soil.

"Dog blast it!" one of the Rangers swore.

Without sparing a backward glance, Jake knew that to stop running was to die. The splashing of boots in the creek behind him gave evidence that one had taken to the water. The other raced along the embankment above him, no doubt. Jake dodged right as a blue screamer whipped past his ear. He clung to the narrow border between the water and the flaring embankment as it bent slowly to the right. Shouted conversation from behind and above identified the locations of both pursuers.

Left to his own devices, Jake might've run all day until one of the men got off a clean shot. His deepest instincts, however, had different plans. Without much forethought or so much as a glimpse at his adversaries, Jake scrambled up the embankment like a treed cat and launched himself at the startled man. A shot went wide beneath Jake's arm as he bear-hugged the taller pursuer and dragged him back over the embankment to land atop the second man in a pile of arms, legs, and desperation.

"Holy hell!"

The shout from the shorter man as he splayed face-first into the shallow creek spurred Jake into a frenzy of advantage. As he flung the tall man away, he came away with his revolver. When the shorter fellow rolled over to face him, Jake liberated his weapon as well, even as the man squeezed his abruptly missing trigger. With a Remington pointed between each set of eyes, Jake stood over the shocked men lying side by side on their backs in six inches of water and sand. Dark whispers urged him to end them, and quick, with a narrow tunnel through each forehead. While he was considering the advice, the shorter one leveled a glare at his partner.

"Dammit, Hyde. I done told you he was a runner. Didn't I say one of us should watch the creek?"

Hyde's forehead creased with disagreement. "Go to Hades, Chancellor. If you'd a' just shot him instead of chattin', we'd not be bathin' in this damn creek, now, would we?"

"Ain't never shot a man with his hands raised and never will."

"And you think I would?"

"Didn't say that. I know you wouldn't either."

"Damn right. Might've changed my mind, though, had I known I'd be lookin' at the wrong end of my own firearm."

"Can't say I disagree." Chancellor expelled a heavy sigh. "Can't believe it's come to this after thirty years."

Jake's predatory gaze faded into a pair of blinks when Hyde extended his left hand toward his partner. "It's been the time of my life, Chancellor."

Chancellor reached across his body to shake the hand. "A hog-killin' time, Hyde. The finest."

The warming display of well-worn camaraderie had the effect of beating back the darkness. Of freeing Jake's reason. A parade of shining faces slipped uninvited through his consciousness, calling to him. Gus Rivers. Stacy Blue. The Emshoffs, the Robersons, and others who had extended a hand of friendship at their own peril. And brightest among them, Rosalyn Ashley, the kindhearted sister of a man who wished him dead. With the emergence of mental quiet, Jake recovered long enough to study the men before him and to see what he'd missed before. Knee-high, pointed-toed boots. Holsters mounted high on the hips instead of slung low, for drawing while riding. Wide-brimmed vaquero-style hats. Beaten leather chaps. The familiar drawls. His brow drew down with recognition.

"You're Texas Rangers."

Hyde lifted an eyebrow. "We are. What of it?"

"Why'd you come for me? I ain't wanted in Texas."

Chancellor sat up slowly, showing both hands to Jake. "Fair question, son. I suppose it's just a matter of serendipity."

"Come again?"

Hyde sat up as well. "We're headed from down Austin way up to the Powder River in the Montanas, gunnin' for a rip who's wanted in Texas. The boys over at Fort Laramie mentioned you, and we thought, 'Heck, why not make a side trip?'"

Chancellor snorted. "Not our best decision. Shoulda never let you talk me into this."

"You only needed three words of convincin'. You wanted to come."

"Yah. Probably." Chancellor glanced up at Jake. "You gonna

shoot us? 'Cause if not, I'd like to lift my hind parts outta this creek. It's a mite frigid."

Jake stepped back two paces. "All right. But tell me, how'd you know where to look and then slip past five thousand Shoshone and Bannock to find me?"

As the men stood, Hyde shrugged. "Been doin' this a long time. Findin' things that're lost or hidin'. It's what we do."

"But why come so far out of your way on a lark?"

When the Rangers raised eyebrows at each other, Jake knew he was in for a surprise. He hated surprises.

"He don't know," said Hyde.

"Know what?"

"About the bounty on your head."

"Bounty?"

Chancellor retrieved his soaked hat from the creek and began wringing water from it. "A thousand dollars. Five hundred from the government, matched by some feller... What was his name?"

Hyde scratched his chin. "Asher, or Ashton, or..."

"Ashley," growled Jake. "Lucien Ashley."

Chancellor grinned. "I see you know the man. But more to the point, you're a valuable commodity right about now. Every lawman, detective, bounty hunter, glory hound, desperado, and lowlife west of the Mississippi is comin' for you. And every one of 'em aimin' to bring you in, dead or alive. A thousand dollars is five years' earnings for most of that ilk."

The Ranger's pronouncement struck Jake like a fist. No. Not now. Not when he'd finally found a bubble of peace after nearly a decade of conflict. "I just want to be left alone."

Chancellor's eyes softened. "I understand, son. Been there myself. But you don't have that luxury anymore. Eventually, they'll find ya. They'll keep comin' 'til you're dead or they are. I'm sorry to be the one to tell you."

"Why'd you do it, anyway?" said Hyde. "Kill your captain."

The disastrous incident above the Green River burned through Jake's brain in a flash of anger and resistance. "He ordered the slaughter of Arapaho women and children. I refused, so he tried to kill me. And I don't take kindly to being murdered."

"Don't have to tell us that." Hyde laughed and shook his head. "Women and children, you say?"

"Two hundred, give or take."

Silence fell until the whir of a nearby locust dominated the conversation. Chancellor scratched his gray-grizzled chin and turned to his partner. "Whadda you say, Hyde? Should we leave this man to his lonesome?"

Hyde peered at his revolver in Jake's hand and pursed his lips. "Seems prudent. 'Sides. We gotta fetch that bushwhacker off the Powder River and get him back to Texas before the captain docks our pay. Again."

Without much forethought, Jake dunked the pair of Remingtons in the creek before returning them to the Rangers. "Powder's wet now. You'll need to reload and then catch me again down the creek a ways. There's a thousand Shoshone that direction who'll likely respond to further gunshots. It won't go well if they do, I'm thinkin.'"

"We won't shoot ya," said Chancellor as he holstered his soggy gun. "You have my word as a Ranger. One Texan to another. Come on, Hyde."

As they walked back along the creek to wherever they'd stashed their horses, Hyde looked over a shoulder. "Best of luck, Paynter. If we found you so quick, you can be sure a horde will be comin' after us, and right soon. Keep a revolver on yer hip, for the love of Betsy."

The advice proved superfluous for Jake. He knew a storm was coming, and everyone he cared about would suffer from his proximity. More certainly, he knew his old mentor, Ambrose Blackburn, would track him down sooner or later. Vengeance was a powerful motivator. When fueled by the promise of riches, it became a poisonous crusade.

ACKNOWLEDGMENTS

It takes a team to birth a story, and this one is no different. I owe an immeasurable debt of gratitude to a few folks in particular for helping bring Jake Paynter to the page. Author Ann Aguirre, who opened a door by recommending me for a series pitch on the basis of a single social media photo featuring me wearing a cowboy hat. Editor Christa Désir, who became the story's champion and guided its development in ways both subtle and profound. Dr. Aldora White Eagle, who made sure I told the story with accuracy and respect, and who gave me the gift of true history. Karen Nix, my wife, who was the first to read and the first to believe in the story's power.

So, this is my team: a door opener, a champion, a truth teller, and a true believer. Without them, Jake Paynter never would have existed.

ABOUT THE AUTHOR

When I was eight, my adventurous parents hauled our young family from the west coast to a Wyoming mountain town perched on the border of the Wind River reservation. That magical landscape infused my formative years with a wonder of local lore that was both historical and present, and revealed to me that often the greatest stories have been all but forgotten or were never told. After publishing science fiction and historical romance for ten years, it seemed a matter of destiny that I'd eventually return to the tales of my youth. The Jake Paynter series brings together fact and fiction to explore places, people, and themes precious to me. I've called Austin home since 1998 with my wife and three children. The kids are grown now, but remain in and around the heart of Texas and consider themselves honorary Wyomingites. I've been away from that mountain town for a long time now, but never really left the place.